A Sight to Behold

Miracles on Harley Street, Book 1

Sara Adrien

© Copyright 2024 by Sara Adrien
Text by Sara Adrien
Cover by Kim Killion

Dragonblade Publishing, Inc. is an imprint of Kathryn Le Veque Novels, Inc.
P.O. Box 23
Moreno Valley, CA 92556
ceo@dragonbladepublishing.com

Produced in the United States of America

First Edition August 2024
Print Edition

Reproduction of any kind except where it pertains to short quotes in relation to advertising or promotion is strictly prohibited.

All Rights Reserved.

The characters and events portrayed in this book are fictitious. Any similarity to real persons, living or dead, is purely coincidental and not intended by the author.

ARE YOU SIGNED UP FOR DRAGONBLADE'S BLOG?

You'll get the latest news and information on exclusive giveaways, exclusive excerpts, coming releases, sales, free books, cover reveals and more.

Check out our complete list of authors, too!

No spam, no junk. That's a promise!

Sign Up Here

www.dragonbladepublishing.com

Dearest Reader;

Thank you for your support of a small press. At Dragonblade Publishing, we strive to bring you the highest quality Historical Romance from some of the best authors in the business. Without your support, there is no 'us', so we sincerely hope you adore these stories and find some new favorite authors along the way.

Happy Reading!

CEO, Dragonblade Publishing

Additional Dragonblade books by Author Sara Adrien

Miracles on Harley Street Series
A Sight to Behold (Book 1)

The Lyon's Den Series
Don't Wake a Sleeping Lyon
The Lyon's First Choice
The Lyon's Golden Touch

Dedication

Dedicated to my dad, an actual doctor from the famous London street where miracles really happen because of his breakthrough inventions in medicine. Wow!

And to my mom. You are my rock, my idol, and my inspiration. This book, like every endeavor I undertake, is dedicated to you.

We don't see things the way they are.
We see them the way we are.

—The Talmud

Welcome to Harley Street—a place where young doctors make miracles happen, in medicine and matters of the heart. While these characters are fictional, their healing techniques and medical tools have been meticulously researched to portray the time within a few years of historical accuracy with some artistic license. For more insight into the historical research and medical advancements, refer to the Author's Note located at the end of this book.

Chapter One

London, 1820.

On to another Monday morning at 87 Harley Street, Nick thought as he picked up the patient cards from the kitchen table and set his teacup in the sink. The waiting room had already filled with Monday morning emergencies and the doctors rose from their breakfasts eager to prepare for another week of hard work.

"Dislocated shoulder, possibly broken elbow." Nick held the card out with the patient's name, age, and chief complaint—another pro bono case they'd take on without pay.

"Got it," Andre took the card and scanned it. There wasn't a joint the orthopedist couldn't soothe or a bone he couldn't set. If there was one principle the doctors all agreed on, it was that helping patients didn't require a *quid pro quo* because it wasn't about the money. Helping people was what medicine was all about for them—and yet the supplies and medicines were expensive, and they needed some patients who could afford their fees.

Nicholas Folsham, or just "Nick," had golden hands and a perfect track record of surgeries. That's what most people believed. Probably. He picked his cases and only performed surgeries when he knew he'd succeed.

"Do you have the Earl of Langley's cataract today?" Alfie asked about their most prominent case and for whom he'd mixed various tinctures, emulsions, and teas. He was as talented an apothecary as he was a rake.

"Yes, later this morning." Nick didn't look up from the patient cards. If Nick could fix the cataract on the earl's left eye and restore his vision, he could ensure his continued recommendations among his aristocratic clients and, thus, a steady influx of patients for the practice. It was their privilege to treat patients and heal them, but it was also their livelihood.

Next card. "Grace nine, Dorothy eleven, and Kenneth fourteen—"

"Ah, Lord Carvill's children. I'll take these," Felix said, with his signature sad eyes, despite a smile. He wasn't merely the resident dentist at 87 Harley Street but one of Nick's most trusted friends. "Just a few fillings. Everything's ready upstairs."

Felix headed out to the waiting room to welcome his three young patients. Children didn't even mind him. There was no higher praise for a dentist.

"A rash, some warts, and... oh, please read this yourself, I just ate," Nick said, handing Alfie, the apothecary, the cards for his morning clients. He pushed the bowl of green grapes to the center of the oak table. Even though he'd studied the general ailments of the human body, physiology and pathology were two completely different kettles of fish, the latter of which he'd rather leave for Alfie if it was a matter outside the eye.

"Not again!" Alfie groaned. "There's no way he's already used up all the tincture."

"Please mind her," Nick said with a severe glance in Wendy's direction, his nineteen-year-old sister who he'd trained as a nurse. She was the only female who lived with him and his friends, some of the most highly specialized doctors in England. Nick joined his sister and Alfie as they left the kitchen, and walked toward the front of the building. His treatment room was on the left of the waiting room, and

Alfie's apothecary was on the right.

"Who do you think told His Grace that Alfie has a cure for the inability to complete the marriage act to ensure his wife's pleasure?" Wendy asked with a proud smile that melted away when she saw Nick's eyes growing wide in shock.

"It's more like a cure for the inability to even start." Alfie winked and raised his brows giving Wendy one of his rakish *you-know-I-know-how-pretty-you-are* looks before Nick could punch him—lightly, as between friends. But still.

"She's my little sister!" Nick shook his head. Alfie was far too handsome for an apothecary, but it was probably good for business. After the ladies saw him, they sent their husbands for tinctures. What Alfie charged on the first Monday of the month nearly paid for their rent.

"Not-so-little sister!" Alfie winked again and gave Wendy a look over his shoulder as he disappeared into his pharmacy across from Nick's treatment room. He'd say she blushed if it weren't the light on this particularly dreadful London morning. No, he assured himself, it was impossible that she blushed. *It must be the fog, softening the gas light.*

"You know he's jesting, right?" she said with that smitten smile still pasted on, the kind Nick knew would be trouble someday.

"He'd never lay a hand on you, I know that. But I wish he wouldn't flirt with you."

"He flirts with everyone. Alfie's so handsome, he can get away with it." It bothered Nick that his sister wasn't immune to Alfie's charms. She should be since he'd known the apothecary and all the others for almost a decade. *Well, nine years? No.* He counted again. *Just eight.* When he started to study medicine with them, Miss Gewndolyn Folsham had been but ten years old and she'd still not lived down the nickname she gave herself at age two: "Wendy." She was a darling sister and they had endured a lot together a long time ago.

"What about me?" Nick asked, bending down to pick up Chromius's water bowl and rinse it off in the sink. "Come on, old boy, time to wake up. The room needs to be prepared for surgery."

"You're handsome, but you don't know it." Wendy had begun to care about him during the time between growing up too fast and speaking to uncountable patients about far too much that affected matters of the heart. She was his confidante, and even though he wouldn't admit it to her, he often felt as though she could see the world more clearly than he did. Nick trusted her judgment, however, unwillingly.

"I beg your pardon?" Nick wiped the bowl with an old towel and filled it with fresh water for the dog.

"You don't notice when women notice you, so you can't flirt," Wendy added.

That was astute.

Irritatingly so, in fact. Especially coming from his little sister.

But that was neither here nor there. As usual, there was no time to think about women for Nick. "We have three surgeries today."

Wendy nodded and opened the cabinet to retrieve some clean linens. She was the best nurse and the smartest little sister in the world. Or the other way around. It didn't matter. He loved her dearly. The thing was, she was right about him not knowing how to flirt. And that inability to flirt bothered him immensely.

He needed a distraction to channel his focus for the surgery later this morning. Thus, Nick decided it was time to get something sweet from the corner *patisserie*. He tied Chromius's lead on and listened to the sleepy dog following with the pitter-patter of his little feet on short legs. When he closed the door to the practice, he admired the new sign on their door.

The new door sign, a polished brass one, had all their names etched on it. They'd finally arrived at their own office, triggering a celebration with a bottle of sparkling wine the evening before—right after Felix screwed their new door sign in place. It sparkled as brightly in the morning sun as the sight did in Nick's heart.

> 87 Harley Street
> Nicholas Folsham
> Alfie Collins
> Felix Leafley
> Wendy Folsham
> Andre Fernando

Even though it was small and understated, like all the signs on Harley Street, this little brass sign bore his name and filled Nick with pride. Besides the sign, Nick adored this neighborhood. It was peaceful and quiet in the early morning hours.

But he was adamantly ignoring the undercurrent of anxiety, a constant vigilance that kept his heart racing and his palms sweating because he knew that anything one received, no matter how hard earned, could be lost. As quickly as the sign had been installed, it could be removed.

The medical offices on Harley Street were in constant flux. It was a known fact that patients would seek the best care and cutting-edge treatments from experts with degrees and skills from around the world. Discretion reigned regarding the noble patients' treatments since the Ton rarely acknowledged having undergone improvements, such as vision correction or dental work. But the case was the opposite regarding making or breaking the doctors' reputations. A happy patient singing a doctor's praise at Almack's could bring an influx of new business to a practice on Harley Street or ruin someone with a story of a procedure gone wrong. That fear of jeopardizing it all was almost worse than the fear of not reaching his goal.

Then he faced the street and took a deep breath of crisp morning air. "Time to perform some miracles today," Nick said to Chromius. "But first, we need a proper breakfast." The dog cocked his head to the side, his ears perked up in curiosity.

In these early morning hours, Nick usually prepared for the patients scheduled for the day. Today, he needed to prepare himself and calm his nerves. Steady nerves meant steady hands, the most important part of a successful outcome.

"Number one is the Earl of Langley's cataract," Nick told Chromius as if he needed to lay his day's plans out to his terrier companion and let him know that his signature procedure was first. The Earl of Langley was a demanding and domineering character with old-school manners and a vast network among Europe's wealthiest families. Nick's signature procedure, his cataract surgery, would be the first of the day. The terrier emitted a soft, melodious whine which apparently expressed his understanding, so Nick continued to talk as usual on their walk to the *patisserie*.

"You probably remember that he was a difficult patient when I first operated on the earl's right eye a few years ago."

Chromius gave a quick shake of his fur.

"I know, I know. It's a risk but he helped Felix, Alfie, Andre, and me to get a toe hold in with the well-paying patients of the Ton, Britain's aristocracy." Cocky as the earl was, he'd admitted to his friends that he'd had various procedures done and had thus inadvertently sent Nick some of the best patients—the aristocrats who could pay and wanted none of their ailments to show, at any cost. They paid well for discretion and yet gossiped handsomely. It was the right mix for Nick and the others because they were good at their jobs. Very good. When they made their patients happy, those happy patients sent more. As long as this mill was fed, the young doctors at 87 Harley Street stood to profit handsomely, or at least break even, considering the *pro bono* cases.

Chromius let out a series of high-pitched yips when they turned the corner, and the bakery came into view.

"Yes, we're almost there. But you know that the Earl of Langley is one of our first and best clients in London. Without his support, I couldn't buy you the sausages you like so much."

Nick attributed most of the earl's ailments to a life in splendor. He had already removed the cataract on the earl's right eye, Felix had saved his smile with plenty of gold fillings and porcelain, and Alfie had supplied the concoctions to cure his various other infirmities—and the earl paid handsomely for their discretion and ongoing care. He was the best kind of patient—the needy kind.

The iron handle was cold, and the heavy door with the glass pane screeched as Nick walked into the bakery. It was a little gem in Marylebone, this part of London. He'd gotten to know the owners, a French family from the Loire Valley. The *Patisserie de la Loire* was a small, well-lit shop with just one wire chair at the far end of the glass counter. No matter how early Nick showed up, the display was always stocked with decadent treats: flakey croissants, stuffed mushrooms, braided brioches, and glazed eclairs. The madeleines, however, were never on display. They had to be eaten hot and were made to order. They were the fluffiest golden biscuits, elongated seashells shaped with the sweet aroma of salted butter and powdered vanilla sugar. Felix wouldn't approve of these lovely breakfasts and preferred that Nick eat something non-sugary, like carrots, instead. But he wasn't a horse, so the treats at seven in the morning were just fine, thank you very much.

"*Ah, voilà Monsieur le Docteur*! Come on, come on! I am just powdering another batch. Sit! Please," the owner said with his lovely French singsong of linked consonants and vowels.

Just when Nick turned at the ring of the small bell over the door, a cold gust of wind from outside sent a chill down his back. And then he felt as though he'd been punched in the stomach. A demure being walked in, dressed fashionably in a walking gown of plain cambric muslin, with a simple wrap front and frock back.

Time slowed and Nick's body hardened. He tried to keep his gaze on the pastries, but he couldn't help but steal a glance at her face.

Perfect features would have been an understatement. Rules of harmony could learn from the combination of what he should know were just eyes, a nose, and cheeks. But her lips were so pink that a raspberry in a swirl of cream would envy her. A few stray curls fell from her hood and looked softer than the ermine trim. It was absurd, madness, and probably assault if he tried, but his hand flinched with the need to caress the stray curl and tuck it behind her ear. Nick's mind wandered to a kiss, but he controlled himself by clenching his fist and burying his hands in his pockets.

Nonsense. He needed breakfast before preparing for surgery.

He blinked over his shoulder again. Her pelisse of emerald-colored sarcenet trimmed all around with ermine flew up in an elegant wave as she stepped inside the patisserie. The fabric wrapped around her figure, and he imagined running his hands along the glossy fabric—this had to stop! He wasn't fourteen.

Nick squared his shoulders and dug his fists deep into his pockets. Madeleines would have to be enough. He had to get out of here.

She wore a lined hood low on the forehead, tied with a bow in the same shade of green. Oh, he'd pluck the hood off her head and take a deep breath of her perfume. She smelled like fresh flowers and green leaves, the essence of morning and freshness and—he gulped—virtue.

Nick froze. His mouth had gone dry, his body hard, and his mind blank. Every last hair on the back of his neck pricked up. He'd get the pastries and leave.

Unfortunately, that's not how it played out.

Chapter Two

LADY PHILIPPA MAE Pemberton hated to spend her evenings at balls. Her mood usually soured by noon, dipped further by two o'clock, and if it hadn't curdled by four, then it certainly would by the time the carriage was ready to take her to another dreadful social event. While the rest of society considered weekday mornings mostly lonely and tried to bridge the time between social events with calls for afternoon tea, strolls in the park, or visits to the modiste that turned into a day-long endeavor, Pippa preferred the busy weekdays when she could seek solitude and spend time in her orangery. She could retreat to her private oasis and was only available for Bea then.

Evenings were for balls, dinners, and banquets. In Pippa's world, that meant being laced into a tight corset in which she couldn't breathe freely, having her nails cleaned, buffed, and waxed, and having to sleep with her hair rolled up in small but uncomfortable balls around pieces of paper so it would hold better in an upswept coiffure for the balls. Balls meant she had to wear shoes with slippery leather soles and heels that made her even more uncomfortable and increased the likelihood of stumbling—or worse—falling. Just like last time.

This morning, she'd spend the entire bag of coins and put more on her father's tab, preferably on pastries. A selection of *mille feuilles*, Charlotte cakes, and eclairs would make her feel better. She used the pin money doled out to her from her inheritance and she was thankful for even that small amount. Her late maternal grandfather had left everything to her, but Pippa's inheritance was tied to her marriage. Her father received payment from her trust until then, leaving her with little control over her wealth.

Especially now when, bit by bit, her father was losing his own fortune and his wits. Of late, it seemed he started nearly every sentence with, "Sir Matthews feels that…"

Sir Matthews this, Sir Matthews that. Sir Matthews, the crystal healer who used plain glass and intoxicated father's mind with mystical nonsense. Upon Pippa's urging to look into the quack, her father's secretary had confirmed that no Sir Matthews had been knighted in the last century. However, when her father had discovered the invoices for an investigator the man had been forced to quit because the investigation had made Sir Matthews uncomfortable. Of course, it had, the charlatan.

But she was "just" a woman, and there wasn't much she could do about it. Instead, she'd spend the chilly morning enjoying a treat. Pippa tightened her ermine stole around her neck and stepped into her favorite little café. It always smelled of rich French custard and sweet cream. The people behind the counter had warmer smiles for her than her father had ever had, at least since her mother's death.

When Pippa was about to remove her gloves and decide what to order for breakfast, a man entered the shop and stood near her without addressing her. She caught a whiff of his scent, a blend of aromatic spices, warm woods, and invigorating citrus. She closed her eyes instinctively, and smiled, then leaned toward him, drawn to the alluring fragrance that filled the air around him and enveloped her, leaving her intoxicated and craving for more.

Then she opened her eyes. He'd moved alongside her and now, she saw him.

He had a shock of dark blond hair and sported an outgrown cut with a ruffled flair. A knot formed in Pippa's stomach, and she was jealous of the wind outside that had the immense pleasure of mussing the hair of the owner of this scent. For all Pippa knew, he'd tumbled out of bed with five mistresses and into the bakery, just to cause mischief. Surely a man of his attractiveness, even though she only saw his profile, belonged in a Greek painting of Dionysus, the Olympian god of wine, who had flocks of women seeing to his every whim. Yet, Pippa imagined those mistresses would have all been rather satisfied with those whims when he turned sideways and surveyed the glass display of pastries. A glint in his eyes sent her stomach to her knees as he was absorbed in the pastries and drove his hand through his hair. Perhaps the blond bounty was mussed from that motion, driving his fingers through the golden waves as he contemplated something. Could he be a poet, or an artist with creative ideas that he'd change the world someday? Or maybe he was a great thinker and rubbed his head while contemplating formulas to spin hay into gold, and delicious pastries to devour.

She stepped closer and overheard the chef call him, *"Monsieur le Docteur."*

She forced herself to look at the lavish display of sweets behind the glass instead of the dashing man standing beside her. But she could barely focus her eyes and had to blink. She'd found that her other senses took over whenever she closed her eyes, and she became much more aware of her surroundings. With a deep inhale, a whiff of butter and vanilla uncurled in the back of her nose, and then, once again, his scent invaded her senses. There was something else, too, bottled masculinity with a high note of dimples and a low note of flaxen curls that made her insides leap.

But it was his delicious scent that changed the air in the room, more appealing than even the sweet treats. Pippa broke out in goosebumps. She peered toward the handsome source of this heady fragrance, and then, predictably, disaster struck. She leaned back to be able to see him better, and as she did so, she stepped on something slippery and lost her balance. Pippa scrambled in vain; she couldn't stop the freefall, and she began to fall.

Then... something—*someone*—stopped her from hitting the ground.

>>><<<

"Madeleines pour le *Docteur*!" the owner said as he handed Nick a paper bag printed with the golden swirly initials of the *Patisserie de la Loire*. Even through the paper, the fresh cakes were so hot that Nick almost burned his fingers. And today was not the day to be distracted by blisters. The Earl of Langley was a difficult patient; even the slightest slip of hand could alarm him. And everybody knew that a jittery patient could complicate even a simple surgery.

Gruffly, Nick switched the hot bag from his right to his left hand and waved his free hand through the air as if to cool his near burns. He hoped he didn't look foolish to the angel in ermine beside him. But then he heard a shuffle, a squeak, and the screech of a heeled shoe on the floor, and the angel flew into his side. He instinctively caught her, with his free hand but he was off balance because of the burn and now, the beauty. *Whoosh*! The bag flew from his hand and he landed on the floor, his pride wounded, his backside bruised, and his face tingling not only from embarrassment but from the brush of feather-soft hair against his cheek.

Sprawled on top of him was that demure and slim woman who'd stood beside him but a moment ago. Her ermine collar was awash with whipped cream, and she blinked adorably. Before he realized that his grip around her waist had been firm enough to break her fall, he cherished the feel of her warmth. She was narrowly built, but the curves of her body pressed against his made him harder than he'd been a moment ago when he'd watched her. It occurred to him that although she'd entered the shop like a queen intending to conquer the land, she felt like a damsel in distress in his arms. *Delicious.*

Chromius stood by his side, wagging his tail. He took the opportunity to step onto his thigh to begin licking at her cheek with his little pink tongue.

"Chromius! No! Get down!" He pushed the dog gently away.

"I am so sorry, Doctor." She slid off him and *craaack,* something tore. "Oh dear." She reached for her back. Peering over her shoulder he could see that her pelisse had split along the seam and through the gap he spotted a shiny, thin layer of an ochre-colored fabric.

Nick scrambled to move from beneath her and then got to his feet; he bowed, offering his hand. As he did so, he realized the extent of their accident. They had practically crushed an entire cake between them and were covered in its remnants.

"*Les gâteaux*! The cakes!" The owner came around the counter screaming, his arms in the air in a Gallic gesture of defeat. "They are for a wedding breakfast. Even now, they could be on the way to pick them up." He looked at the wall clock of white porcelain with tiny blue country scenes painted under a shiny glaze. "Two hours! Two hours!" And he disappeared into the back of the shop, leaving Nick and the elegant beauty standing in a puddle of custard and splattered cream.

And a happy terrier, who moved about them in doggy heaven, making quick work of the mess. It wasn't good for him, Nick knew, but he'd already consumed so much of it at this point the damage had been done. Besides, Chromius's work made for easier cleanup later.

Later—that reminded him. He was under the pressure of the clock as well. Nick sighed. Two hours exactly until the earl would lie under his knife. *Again.*

He felt a tugging at his hand. "I'll need that back, please," a lovely young voice said. and he realized his fingers were twined with the angel's—*the young woman's,* he corrected himself—gloved digits. He let go with a quick shake of his wrist.

"I beg your pardon, Miss…"

"Pippa, it's just Pippa. And I think I'm the one who has to beg for your pardon."

"Why's that?"

"There was something on the floor, I think, and I… I am unsure what happened, but I landed on your lap." She blushed, averting her gaze from his, and attempted to straighten her coiffure.

She had lovely, honey-colored flyaways that had fallen out of her pins, though some of her hair was still in a loose bun at the back of her head, as far he could tell. Her freed hair curled about her face. He knew that her attempt to knot those curls back into order would in no way tame her mane, which inspired illicit and inappropriate thoughts. His tongue stuck to the roof of his mouth, and he couldn't help but stare.

She was beautiful in an unconventional way, not much like the young women of the Ton who came to the practice. And she struck him as put together, one who knew her path in life, and herself.

Then she blinked and patted the front of her pelisse as if searching for something. Whatever it was, he vowed, he'd find it, even if it meant crawling under a display case on his hands and knees. Fortunately, what she sought was easy to find and didn't hurt his pride at all. Nick spotted a soft, silk scarf in Chromius's mouth. It was splattered with whipped cream and custard. It took him a moment to retrieve it from the dog and once he did, he tried to shake off some of the cream off. "I believe this is yours… Pippa?"

"Oh! Yes!" She took it gingerly from his hand and frowned at it. But then she did the most adorable thing. She pulled her glove off, finger by finger, and swiped a generous amount of the custard from the silk with one of her freed digits. Nick watched as she proceeded to lick it slowly from her finger with the tip of her tongue and obvious enjoyment.

He could only gape at the sight.

Pippa noticed him watching; she shrugged and crinkled her nose as she smiled at him. "It would have been such a waste of the wedding cake," she said.

Nick could only nod.

Chapter Three

INTRODUCTIONS HAD BEEN made, along with profuse apologies, and Nick had decided that the least he could do was accompany her. A split pelisse dunked in cream and custard on such a striking woman could invite all sorts of mischief, even from the driver of a hack. No, it was best to take her himself. At least it would allow him to enjoy her pretty blue eyes a little longer as he ensured her safety. He was a gentleman, above all.

And she was a vision in spite of the torn coat and custard splatters.

"When you offered to walk me home, I'm afraid you failed to ask how far it was," Pippa said with a crooked smile. She was adorable.

Nick was painfully conscious of the large smear of white whipped cream drying on his coat front, and Chromius's need to stop at every grassy spot—the results of the whipped cream surprise he'd enjoyed.

"It was my mistake entirely, yes. But I promised to take you back." He reached to make sure his hat was on properly; at least he'd look neat, if not clean.

They'd walked all along Bayswater Road and were heading toward Sheffield Terrace. Nick's feet were growing tired. And worse, he realized as he checked his pocket watch, he had to get back to Harley Street soon and would need to hire a hack if he wanted to be on time for the scheduled surgery.

"Where do you live?"

"Cloverdale House, on Abbotsbury Road," she said with the nonchalance of a true lady.

"You are jesting," Nick sputtered, unable to fathom how rich this beauty must be if she lived on one of the greatest private estates in London.

"Not at all, Dr. Folsham. Have you heard of it?"

He'd not only heard about its splendor but read about it in the paper. The large gardens surrounding it were even a park open to the public and frequented by none other than the royal family.

"Heard of it?" *Where should he start?* "It has a rich history, and many people know of it, but nobody knows what exactly the arrangement is of the people who live there. It's part of a large estate." He was in the presence of a grand lady and wanted to know the extent of his honor. "Tell me more, please!"

She quirked a brow. "Very well. Well, it's an early Jacobean country house and passed from the Earl of Nunsford, who'd inherited the house and, in 1773, succeeded his first cousin as fifth Duke of Sussex." Nick's eyes fixed on her lush lips while she talked, though he supposed he should stop watching them as his body was beginning to show its arousal from the sight. He forced himself to focus on her words, instead of the lovely wet gleam of her lips and the tantalizing tip of her tongue. And the memory of how she'd sucked the cream from her thumb.

She continued, unaware of his struggle to remain polite and gentlemanly. "It was even used as a military hospital under Oliver Cromwell, but to be honest, it's so damp that nobody wants to live there in the summer." She shrugged. "The Duke of Sussex is my father; he's the seventh duke. I'm his only daughter."

Nick swallowed hard. She was chatty, and oh so beautiful. And so out of his class... He twisted his fists in his pockets to ensure that he didn't touch her no matter how badly he longed to. He'd known she was a high-born lady the moment he'd seen her in her ermine collar.

And yet, there was something about her that awakened his senses like a walk on dew-covered grass in early spring. He felt more masculine around her, and somehow more himself—if such a thing were possible—than ever before. It was the way she'd looked at him and how she'd tumbled onto his body that had made him realize he'd miss her if he let her go without speaking with her. Yet, despite her friendly and nonchalant conversation, she was so far above him. She was of a class where she should be out of reach, and not so close that he could feel the warm air of her breath when she spoke... His manhood twitched and he reminded himself for what felt like the hundredth time since they'd begun walking: *Listen and stop looking!*

"Perhaps you know my father by the name Randall Pemberton." She cringed and then lowered her gaze. Her words hung heavy between them, for there were several ranks of the peerage between them in the abstract sense and yet only a few inches and some air physically. She kicked a pebble with the toe of her dainty shoe, and it was as if telling Nick that her father was a duke—*that* duke in particular—sounded as if she'd admitted to a crime.

It was, in a way, because no matter what one's social class was in London—or all of England for that matter—everyone knew who Randall Pemberton was. Nick tried not to gape. "The one who *beheaded* his wife?"

Her delicate shoulders hunched forward, as if she was trying to shrink in size, while her eyes sparkled with a mix of shyness and dismay. Of all the stupid things he could have said... *Why did I quote the gossip columns?*

He truly was the pauper and felt like a fool for his inability to carry on a conversation with an aristocratic lady outside his practice. There, it was usually easy to speak with his noble patients, but here, with her, he wanted to impress and yet he stuttered nonsense like a green boy. Nick pressed his fists deeper into his pockets, straining against the fabric of the lining.

At the end of his leash, Chromius stopped, hunched, and strained over a patch of grass. Honestly, if *that* didn't prove to him that he was out of his depth and too far below her to even be casually talking to her, nothing would.

"He didn't. My mother died of a fever, and the papers wrote that she lost her head. It was construed to harm his reputation, and he didn't fight it because he'd caught the same fever. My father survived my mother's death but never overcame the heartbreak. He's on wife number six now. Her name is Carolyn Pemberton. She calls herself a lady."

It looked like Pippa shuddered, but he couldn't quite tell. *She* was a veritable lady, and he would have never thought it possible that she'd smear him with whipped cream, lick it from her fingers, then talk to him leisurely on an extended walk home. He could not peel his eyes off her face. Her features were mesmerizing, and her bright skin looked so touchable. She was taller than most women, the ideal height to look him in the eyes. Ideal, perfect, and beautiful. Nick willed his heart to stop thundering lest she heard the effect she had on him, for how could he hide it? Worse, it wasn't proper for him to be found with her alone, yet he couldn't have left her besmeared to fend for herself and hire a hackney. Outside of his practice, he knew he could not speak so informally with any member of the high ranks of the England. He needed an explanation because he was not turning away. Could he feign an excuse that as a doctor that he'd walk her home as a matter of an emergency? What was the emergency? A large vanilla-scented cream stain?

They'd entered the estate through a garden that resembled a park more than a private yard and continued their walk until they reached a one-story glass house with tall windows.

"This is my orangery," she said as she turned a doorknob and led the way into the building. "Really, it's my mother's orangery. Well, it was hers. I inherited it of sorts."

"Why did you hesitate?" Nick asked.

She squinted as if the inheritance wasn't completed but there was such pain in her gaze that Nick decided not to probe further as she hung her pelisse on a hook on the wall and pulled on an apron, once white but now covered with yellow stains.

Stepping out of the crisp park and into the warm orangery, Nick was immersed in a verdant paradise, an oasis of tranquility. The orangery was radiant with sunlight streaming through the glass panes, casting myriad shadows to dance on the stone-tiled floor. Two elongated raised flower beds stretched out before him, brimming with an exotic array of tropical plants. Their leaves, a vibrant spectrum of emerald, jade, and olive, shimmered as they basked in the sun's warmth. Majestic palms in large clay pots were arranged along the wall and towered above, their fronds forming a natural tapestry against the glass ceiling. Glossy ferns and vibrant bromeliads nestled below, their lush textures contrasting with the rough-hewn stone of the raised beds. It was hot, damp indeed, and Nick wished he could take his coat off, roll his sleeves up, and lay her on a bench.

Stop! She's a lady and taboo.

"There you are, Truffles." She bent down as a little brown bunny hopped onto her arms. Chromius strained at the end of his leash and gave a happy, excited bark. Pippa continued speaking to her rabbit. "Have you eaten too much?" She turned to Nick. "He's getting heavier every day."

Nick shortened the leash as he noticed that the little brown bunny only had three legs. But he moved well and swiftly, albeit he was now nestling into Pippa's arms. A good safe place, no doubt.

"He's named after my favorite chocolates, truffles. Sir Truffles Hoppington."

She was too adorable for words. Nick checked his pocket watch again. He had to leave soon but he didn't want to leave the side of this fascinating beauty who'd taken him home with her without regard for propriety.

"What happened to him?" Nick couldn't help but notice the stump that was Truffle's left front paw. He touched the stump, which looked well healed and was certainly not due to a fresh injury. "He's missing the metatarsal, the little bones of the paw," Nick said.

Pippa's eyes locked with his, and she studied him, looking at him with a slight squint. "I found him in a fox trap in the garden two years ago. He was a baby and squealed."

"Poor bunny. Rabbits only make loud noises like that when they are in grave distress."

Her eyes brimmed with tears. "Yes, so I got him out of the trap and brought him here. There was so much medicine left over from my mother, I used whatever I could find. He seems to have forgotten that he ever lived anywhere else but with me."

Nick could see how comfortable the bunny was in Pippa's arms, nestling against her chest. Smart little creature.

"He's lucky to have you."

"Except that he eats too much here. I cannot let him out, and he's munching all day." She set him down. Truffles appeared to flick an ear at Chromius and give him a scornful look before he hopped away.

Nick didn't know much about rabbits, but this one did look a bit chubby, with a wide, fluffy belly. Soon Truffles was happily nibbling on some tiny leaves. Chromius seemed to realize that he wasn't going to get any closer to him, and panting, laid down like a little Sphinx, head raised, paws outstretched. Watchful.

In this secluded haven, their whispered conversations danced amidst the sunlight that filtered through the leaves, casting playful shadows upon their faces. The air was thick with the intoxicating scent of the tropics—the sweet perfume of blooming orchids, the tangy aroma of citrus fruits ripening on dwarf trees, and the earthy fragrance of damp soil. It was a symphony of scents from a far-off forest like in Felix's stories. Yet, Nick was in London. And the only magical and enchanting effect was the one Pippa had on him.

Every time he addressed her as *Pippa*, a rush of warmth washed over him, a potent reminder of their shared connection. But, at the same time, the name felt too intimate for someone with his station to use for a woman of her status. It wasn't merely her noble heritage that gave him pause, but the delicate beauty and her smile that intimidated and fascinated Nick at the same time. Although a part of him yearned to respect her station and address her as Lady Philippa, to uphold the proper decorum, he could only think about tracing the contours of her face with his fingertips.

To his left, a wall fountain burbled melodically from a plain tap, its soothing cadence the only sound in this serene sanctuary. The water sparkled like diamonds under the soft sunlight, providing a cooling respite for the surrounding plants. This was a place of solitude, a place to contemplate and admire nature's bounty.

In the midst of this serenity, Pippa froze, tilted her head as if listening hard to something, and then darted to a raised garden bed partially hidden behind potted palms a few steps away, where little green plants stretched pairs of two leaves each no more than an inch into the air. "Not the sprouts!" She ordered fiercely and shooed Truffles away. He hopped out from behind the palms, greenery hanging from his whiskered lips. "Bad bunny. *Bad* bunny!"

Nick burst into laughter. She was too sweet as she told the bunny off. It hopped off toward the right of their position, to another low, green bed.

But then, he realized, she didn't follow him there. Instead, she looked in the wrong direction, directing her attention to a different place completely apart from the brown bunny. In fact, she appeared to be speaking what was only a pile of dry soil.

His stomach fell. What was wrong with her? She'd been perfectly delightful, and now she was having a conversation with garden dirt a similar shade of brown. Did she think the soil was alive? Did she think it *was* her bunny?

Nick felt as if he was being punched as he watched her trailing her hands over the sprouts. She slowly but deliberately patted the tiny plants and inhaled when she shut her eyes. She was feeling for something. Nick knew that people derived all sorts of energy from plants, but he'd never seen this, except when he had a patient who…and then he understood. It made perfect sense.

She hadn't seen him at the *patisserie*, he'd been too close. She knew her way around London, because she walked toward the points in the distance, but she couldn't see the rabbit when it was closer than a meter from her. Nor could she see the sprouts in the soil and how many of their budding leaves that the rabbit had gnawed off.

"Hyperopia!" Nick blurted out.

She stopped her perusal of the little plants, straightened her back, and turned to cast him a fierce look. "I beg your pardon?"

PIPPA WAS FLUSHED from the heat, or perhaps the intensity of the doctor's gaze. She wasn't quite certain. Plus, he'd called her something, a name she didn't recognize. Pippa bristled. She'd been called too much already. Her father never defended her, and it gave the gossips of the Ton leeway to mock Pippa without restraint.

"What did you call me?" she asked with as much dignity as she could muster. She'd never brought a stranger into the orangery. And yet, the first time she did, he called her a Greek name and stared at her as if fascinated. Or repulsed, more the like. Her heart tumbled to her stomach; she'd been enjoying this young man and his company. He was kind, he was polite, he was smart…and he was handsome. Beyond that, he was different from the men of the Ton, who always seemed to make her uncomfortable. Until this moment, at any rate.

"You are farsighted. Hyperopia is a refractive error, not a name that I called you. What it means is that you—because of your condition—see nearby objects blurry."

How did he guess her secret? "I see perfectly well," Pippa said and put her hands on her hips. Perhaps not a ladylike posture, but certainly one which exhibited her dismay.

Nick shook his head. He seemed oddly delighted. "No, not when something is close. That's why you didn't see me at the *patissier's* counter. And it's why you are feeling for your saplings and talking to a heap of soil instead of Truffles."

She gasped sharply and took several steps away, her eyes searching for the bunny.

"See, that's a coping mechanism. You step away from things to see them better."

"How would you know?" She realized that exasperation pierced her voice, but she didn't care.

He shrugged. She could see *that* at least but decided that to point that out wouldn't make a difference at this point. "I'm an oculist. It's my job to diagnose—"

"I don't need a diagnosis, Dr. Folsham. Thank you very much. I thought you were a *real* doctor, for the body and such."

"Eyes are part of the body." Again, he shrugged.

She deliberately narrowed her eyes at him. Pippa didn't like it when people spoke about her flaws. She'd had more of that than she cared to admit, and no tolerance left to stomach being mocked.

He didn't seem to notice that she was unhappy with his line of questioning, or reasoning, or accusation, or whatever it was. "Tell me, Pippa, do you get headaches when you read for a long period?" He didn't even wait for her answer. Instead, he continued, "I can see that you make up for the blurry vision with touch. It's perfectly logical to compensate for the deficit of one sense with another."

"Deficit?" She mumbled. She'd never wished to hear these words from a man as handsome as the one before her. "You find me deficient?" Her heart sank, and she could barely say the words. He'd be so kind and gentle. The fact that he didn't know her family was an advantage, she'd hoped, because he didn't realize the many nasty things she'd been called. Although Pippa had never considered mingling outside the Ton, the idea of being outside the circle of people who made her feel smaller than a speck of dust had appealed to her. It was the first thought on her mind when she'd fallen onto the handsome stranger's lap. She had a scarf full of whipped cream but a clean slate with him.

"Don't misunderstand me, please. A vision deficit doesn't mean you are deficient in any way."

His gaze washed over her, and she shivered. Nick—Dr. Folsham—made her feel things she and everyone she knew considered absolutely improper, but he hadn't even touched her. But when he looked at her, a bolt of heat shot up her arms and through her chest until it settled deep under her belly.

"I'm sorry. I have to go; an important surgery is waiting for me."

She nodded, speechless and mesmerized by him.

"But please. Come to my office any time and get fitted for a pair of eyeglasses. You'll see so much clearer." With these words, he handed her a white card, bid her goodbye, and left with his little dog following alongside him with a wagging tail.

Pippa fumed.

How dare he call her deficient!

Although, it would explain everything, wouldn't it?

Realization fell heavily over Pippa like a hammer on an anvil.

She didn't see well.

She needed glasses.

And the handsome doctor offered to help.

He could give her exactly what she needed.

Chapter Four

The next day...

PIPPA SAT AT the breakfast table in her family's dining room with her cousin Bea, her father, and—she swallowed bile at the thought—her stepmother.

"Did you see the Earl of Langley and his pretty young wife at the ball last night?" Wife Six asked as she set her teacup on the saucer with a clank.

"Yes, he seems to be doing rather well for himself these days," Father mumbled from behind the paper.

"Why do you say that?" Pippa asked.

"Oh, just an observation. He smiled and flashed large golden teeth. Expensive stuff," Father mumbled, turning large pages of the *Morning Chronicle* with the telltale riffling of pages.

"I wouldn't want to kiss that mouth." Across the table from Pippa, her cousin Bea grimaced.

"Why?" Pippa asked in a hushed tone to not draw Wife Six into the conversation. It was common at the family's breakfast gatherings to have her father seated at the head of the table opposite his sixth wife, at least ten feet away from her, since breakfast was taken in the dining room under Wife Six's regime. Anything she did was an occasion for pomp and circumstance, even if she was only buttering her toast.

"He's a rake. His reputation is that of a rather wild boar."

"He's married now."

"To Violet, I know. I was at their wedding. A sow and a boar are a perfect match. They can roll around in their muddy personalities."

"Still…" Bea tapped on her soft-boiled egg until the top of the shell cracked. With her perfectly manicured nails, she peeled off the thin white shells and piled the bits up on the side of the egg cup.

"Their wedding was lovely. I thought Violet was a gorgeous bride." Pippa felt the need to say something nice after they'd spoken so much of the truth. Didn't everyone deserve the benefit of the doubt? Violet had been a rather mean girl and coined the nasty nickname "clumsy goose" that Pippa couldn't rid herself of. If it hadn't been for Violet, Pippa wouldn't be "the clumsy goose." And yet, Pippa thought that there must be some good in all people, even Violet.

Bea shut her eyes and stuffed her mouth with toast and egg. "If you like that sort of thing." She shrugged and chewed heartily. Her opinion of Violet's doom was seemingly a foregone conclusion.

Pippa set her spoon down, her appetite gone. "What's wrong with kissing the Earl of Langley?"

"Oh, Pippa," Bea exhaled and took a big swig of her tea. "Where to begin?"

Pippa leaned back and set her napkin aside. "Anywhere."

"Imagine kissing a man who has kissed so many women before. It's as if you were kissing them all."

"No."

"Yes."

"Tell me more about that. I'm all ears."

"A little less ears would suit you better, dear. Perhaps even help your chances to marry some third son or widower," Wife Six said from five feet away. She had sharp hearing like an owl, and her personality matched that of a ruffled bird of prey. She was ready to descend on a tiny mouse any time, but she'd circle a larger piece of prey for as long as necessary until she could sink her sharp claws into it.

But Pippa decided to ignore her and press Bea for the gossip. Pippa knew that it was a fallacy in Bea's thinking that was all too typical for diamonds of the first water like her cousin; gossip could easily be taken at face value.

"Well," Bea whispered, turning her back to Wife Six. Every time she took Pippa's side, her cousin endeared herself more and more, and that was hard because Bea was already Pippa's favorite person in the world—the ones who were alive, at least. Mother had been... but that was in the past.

"I heard that the Earl of Langley was rather adventurous in his youth. Daring even."

"His youth? I saw him at their wedding; he looked young to me."

"His adventures have aged him." Bea leaned closer to Pippa and held her hand straight up as a wall shielding the sound from reaching Wife Six's ears. "He's been on a Grand Tour for three years."

"After his studies at Oxford, I assume. He must have had a gentleman's education. Did he graduate?"

"He earned honors a term early and then went on the Grand Tour starting in Paris. He's about two and thirty now."

"It's not uncommon for young aristocrats to pay Louis XVIII a visit these days."

"And is it common for them to go to Carnival in Venice three years in a row?"

"Do you think Casanova was the only man there every year?" She whispered to ensure the duke didn't hear her speaking of such scandalous people.

"I also heard that the earl has been to the Austrian court in Vienna, the Prussian court in Berlin, and the Russian court in St. Petersburg."

"Good for him."

"Pippa, aren't you listening? He's been all over!"

"And that's a problem?" Pippa ate her egg; it had gotten hard and cold already while Bea was undeterred in trying to convince Pippa of the many vices of the earl.

"You're not listening to me. He's been to every place in Europe where scandal soared during the exact seasons he visited."

"*Hmpf!*"

"He probably seduced every woman at the royal courts of Europe." Bea waved grandly and then froze, looking over her shoulder to Wife Six, who'd arched one of her thin brows.

"I hear that the Earl of Langley has excellent diplomatic connections," Father mumbled again from behind the paper. "Sometimes a man shares a glass of wine, beer, or whiskey to forge alliances. He's done well for himself."

Of course, a lady would be ruined by as much as standing alone in a room with a man. But an earl could hop through all the beds in the courts of Europe, and he had "good connections." That was the essence of society's rules. Pippa shook her head.

"His life of splendor made him sick," Wife Six said. "The Viscountess Cunningham told me over tea that the earl paid a certain dentist on Harley Street a small fortune for his treatment."

"Harley Street, you say?" Father folded his paper and held it to his side. The butler retrieved it instantly. "Where on Harley Street?"

"I don't remember. Seventy-eight or eighty-seven." Wife Six lingered on the house number and turned her eyes upward. Then she grew silent for an instant and studied Father's reaction. She was oddly attentive.

Pippa felt for the white card with Dr. Folsham's address in her pocket. It burned as if it were aflame. 87 Harley Street exactly.

"Has he been to anyone else there?" Father asked.

"The viscountess told me he recently had eye surgery, but it wasn't clear," Wife Six continued.

"And how does she know that?" Father peeked out from behind the paper.

"I believe her daughter needs some treatment of the delicate nature, and she inquired about recommendations for physicians. That's how the young doctors on Harley Street came up in conversation, and the viscountess had a recommendation from Violet's mother, Lady Durham."

"What does her daughter need? I didn't expect her debut until next season," Bea said, ever aware of whose turn it was to become her competition at Almack's.

"She may not make it, dear. She needs a lot of dental fillings, and if any self-respecting man sees the girl smile with a mouth full of silver, she won't—"

"I think they can use gold these days and white materials," Pippa said.

"How do you know?" Father thundered. "What did you do?"

"Nothing, Father." Pippa withdrew like a snail in its shell. *But I might need spectacles.* She thought quickly so as to escape his wrathful curiosity. "You just said that the Earl of Langley is doing well for himself with all those gold fillings."

"Ah, yes, I suppose I did." Father shook the paper in a show of dominance, or so Pippa imagined. "But beware of those charlatans; they scrape the teeth of the rich, hollow and fill them with rubbish to charge for silver by the gram."

"They don't have to scrape much to hollow out your teeth, darling," Wife Six said from across the table. It was a friction point in the Pemberton household that Father resorted to various methods to alleviate the pain of his many ailments rather than seek out treatment to cure them.

"Symptoms muted, disease saluted," he mumbled. "Add some sparkle to the deficiencies, and everyone will see them!" He'd probably say that about spectacles, too. They were for men or scholars. He was well matched with the wife of the year, having exchanged the rest of wives two through five nearly annually since Pippa's mother had died with a divorce granted by Parliament. Though, to his credit, two of the wives had run off never to be seen again. "I'd rather have hollow teeth than none." And with these words, Father snapped his paper shut, rose from his chair, and left.

"I still don't understand what is wrong with the viscountess's daughter." Bea was seemingly stuck on her competition, always scouting the prettier ladies at the balls.

"She has a sweet tooth, and she's in pain, and her mother said she won't have any offers this season. Last I heard, they made appointments for her to see a dentist every day for a whole week."

"On Harley Street?" Pippa asked.

"Yes, at eighty-seven," Bea answered.

Pippa recalled that she'd seen the address, 87 Harley Street, when she'd accompanied Father to his appointments and now she had the oculist's card.

"And then she will be compromised. If her smile isn't perfectly restored, she has to trap a good man into marriage before the next season." Wife Six left the table with a scheming plan hanging in the air as if it were naught to manipulate people's lives to suit the Ton's whims. If the sole value in life were to impress the Ton, Wife Six would say that the end justified the means, regardless of their immorality. Fairness, integrity, and morality were not usually thoughts she bothered herself with. If any question of that nature arose, when Pippa brought it up, Wife Six waved it away like a nasty mosquito that buzzed around the imported tropical plants in the orangery.

Pippa remained alone at the table with Bea and stared at her half-eaten breakfast.

"Don't waste the egg. Can I have that?" Bea asked, switching her empty eggshell in a cup against Pippa's untouched soft—boiled egg.

"Doesn't it bother you at all?"

"That you had some of this egg already? No."

"I mean with the girl. She's in pain and needs a doctor."

"Seems like she'll get one." Bea licked her lips and reached for the saltshaker.

"And as a punishment for needing medical treatment, she cannot make a debut and has to stoop so low as to trap a man into marriage?" It was worrisome, to say the least. Not that she'd have the chance to debut, but it was saddening to think of how she herself would need to trap a man into marriage. She was defective, after all.

Nick—Doctor Folsham's—words rolled through her mind as if he'd just whispered them in her ear: *A vision deficit doesn't mean you are deficient in any way.* Easy for him to say, though the words were quite nice to hear…

"Won't be the first." Bea scooped out the egg white with bits of the yellow-orange yolk that had hardened and crumbled on the spoon. "Why do you care? They're not *your* teeth. Yours are fine."

But my eyes may not be, Pippa couldn't help but think. The handsome oculist had drawn her attention to her impaired eyesight and the issue hadn't left her mind since he had. Or was it the thoughts of his lop-sided smile and warm eyes that had preoccupied Pippa more?

"It bothers me because it's a double standard. The Earl of Langley's gold fillings are like trophies for his exploits and experience, making him seem much more accomplished." Bea shrugged.

Pippa lost her patience. "It's not fair that he was considered the catch of the season despite his debauchery while a young woman is easily shelved like an old shoe at the slightest hint of a scuff."

"You admitted it! Debauchery!" Bea laughed and reached for her napkin as she finished the egg.

Bea was far too clever, sometimes. "I stand corrected. I have no facts to judge his life on."

"You don't need facts to judge. He married Violet. A man who marries a venomous snake like Violet can only be a snake himself or be poisoned by her venom."

"That's vile, Bea. Don't catch the nasty gossip bug from the Ton only because you mingle with them. I cannot form an opinion without facts. Judgment based on hearsay is gossip."

"That's the best kind!" Bea gave a mischievous wink and left Pippa alone at the table.

It was a double standard to judge men and women differently, and it oughtn't be a standard at all. Making it the norm to treat women differently than men made Pippa bristle, not in the least, because her father and Wife Six showed such complacency. If a lady needed treatment and there was an excellent doctor to offer it, Pippa decided, then she should be able to receive it without losing her prospects for a favorable marriage.

Pippa's head spun with what she'd been taught and what she believed in her heart. Truth and judgment were not congruent regarding how the English aristocracy picked their spouses nor how marriages were judged. As cruel as Violet was, she'd caught an earl in her first season, so she was forever redeemed in society. The earl, in return, had a young wife, and his rakehell past was instantly forgotten. Pippa shook her head; if Violet was a beacon of respectability judged by people like Wife Six, she attributed no value to the Ton. And yet, their rules were what kept her from finding her path in life.

It was unfair.

And she wouldn't stand by and let life and love pass her by for that.

Pippa wanted to go through life with an open heart and open eyes. And if she'd see better with spectacles, she'd take the handsome doctor up on his offer and get some.

Chapter Five

The previous day (and still covered with whipped cream)...

Nick had managed to return to 87 Harley Street and change for the surgery in the nick of time.

"What happened to you? Where have you been? The Earl of Langley is already waiting in the operating room," Wendy said when Nick half-fell down the stairs in his haste.

"Nothing happened to me; I'll be right there." But he felt the impact of the lie as if he'd been punched in the stomach. Something *had* happened to him, and not just the collision with a cream cake. He felt as if something had thrown him out of his orbit and his mind could only circle the beautiful lady from Cloverdale House, an urban castle. She was out of his reach and most certainly wouldn't want to spend her time with a mad oculist who knew more about the human eye than human nature. Why else would he have given her diagnosis instead of paying her a compliment?

Nick rubbed his eyes and as he leaned over his wash bowl to scrub his hands for the surgery, he stared in the looking glass. An idiot stared back at him. A besotted fool.

A lady like Pippa, intelligent and beautiful, who'd brought him to her sanctuary of botany and introduced him to the rabbit she'd rescued deserved to be kissed, not chastised. What had he called her? *Deficient?*

He ought to kick himself for such a stupid thing. If he had better bedside manners, he would have delivered the blow with more grace. Perhaps he could have given her a kiss instead of a diagnosis.

But there was no time to dwell, not now. He had a difficult surgery ready for him, and it was time to shine in the operating room. At least there, he never needed to worry about his clumsy way with women. He was everything but clumsy with the scalpel.

NICK ENTERED HIS little operating area at the far end of his exam room. There was the leather-upholstered surgical table with the headrest that he'd altered. It was a chair he'd gotten from Felix, just when he'd started his practice here in London. Felix had purchased a new dentist chair and given Nick the headrest from his old one. Nick had had it welded onto the bottom of the metal frame and then upholstered it. Now, it was a cushioned and elevated place where his patients could comfortably rest their heads—and hold still. A still patient and a steady hand were more than half of a successful surgery.

Time to get to work.

Wendy had prepared the patient, as usual. The room smelled as it should, of steaming hot water to clean the blade, a gas lamp to cauterize incisions with heated instruments, clove extract, and Alfie's aromatherapy to calm the patient.

"My Lord," Nick said to the long body under a white sheet on the operating table. He never splattered, but it was well known that even a tiny dot of red would send patients into a frenzy, and a clean sheet could easily prevent the outrage. Patients didn't need to see any blood. Especially not their own. And these rules applied particularly to the aristocrats.

"I'm ready, Doctor Folsham," the earl mumbled from under the fabric. Wendy had put a warm compress soaked in Alfie's concoction of herbal calming balms on his forehead. It also signaled that she'd cleaned his face. "I feel rather foolish, here. Covered in a shroud. It's ghoulish to be honest. Why all the fabric?"

"The benefit of covering your hands and body with the clean sheet means a lower risk of infection from the usual dirt or dust on clothes," Nick said. This was why Nick always wore freshly laundered and pressed white cotton for surgeries though he didn't share this with the earl. The lower the risk of spreading dirt, the lower the infection rate. And his rate had been zero so far; he certainly wanted to keep it at that.

"How terribly thoughtful of you but I'm quite clean." The earl's voice came muffled from under the white sheets.

"It's merely a precaution regardless of how clean and elegant you are," Nick said, casting Wendy a look demanding she offer profuse acclaim for their noble patient, if only to get the man to acquiesce.

"And may I be so bold as to say you are so very elegant, my lord. Only the finest materials can do justice to a man of your stature." Wendy spoke as if she'd rehearsed the compliments for the Ton, her wide eyes met with Nick's in understanding. Their patients' vanities ran deep, and it was not new to them how to handle them. Their priority now and always was a calm patient so that the surgery could be smooth.

When the fabric over the earl's face crinkled, Nick knew he'd smiled. Good.

"My lord, this will be essentially the same procedure as last time, just on the other eye."

Nick cast Wendy a glance. She'd set up the lens in a metal bowl of alcohol. The triangular scalpel was ready on a clean towel on the tray to his right. If only his thoughts could focus and his heart could stop longing for a woman out of his reach, Nick knew the surgery would be over quickly.

"You'll feel a slight pinch, and then it's almost over, your lordship."

The patient nodded, and the compress slid askew, but that didn't matter, for Nick removed it and carefully pulled the man's eyelid open. His iris was just as foggy as Nick remembered. Without the lens replacement, the cataract would soon leave him blind. A well-known consequence of excessive alcohol consumption, cataracts were common among those who could afford to drink. And the earl could afford almost anything he wanted. Although merely in his thirties, the earl had led an indulgent lifestyle on every front. He'd shared his love for brandy with Nick before and admitted that his frequent visits to Felix were due to his love of chocolate before bedtime. Even Alfie had sold him an array of ointments, tinctures, and powders to cure his rashes, likely contracted during his exploits before his marriage. But the earl had surprised them when his betrothal had been announced a year ago. Perhaps the man was on a path to better health in lifestyle and love.

"Is HE TRULY only one and thirty?" Felix asked as he took a spoonful of mashed potatoes and slid the bowl over to Nick. It was dinner time, and they'd just finished preparing Nick's operating room for the next treatments. The odor from the kitchen permeated the entire building, and they'd left the window open to the back. The kitchen was tucked away, and even though the adjacent building obstructed the view from the small window, it was shielded from the bustling streets in Marylebone, where the friends had established their new practice.

"He is almost thirty-two, I think, but his bride is nineteen," Alfie said.

"She's supposed to be quite beautiful," Wendy said dreamily. She'd always had a soft spot for anything related to an aristocratic wedding. Dukes, earls, viscounts, and even diplomats qualified as Prince Charmings in her romantic imagination. She adored fairy tales and love stories and could swoon over the idea of a handsome man even though she was a grown woman. Nick hoped her dreams would remain as that, and never become something she attempted to put into reality.

"How do you know?" Nick asked, constantly worried about his little sister's interactions. He could trust Felix, Alfie, and Andre, the other doctors he'd started this practice with, but everyone else was not as good-natured and respectful of women in general, and especially—his sister. Even though Felix was an older friend, Alfie was like a brother to Nick. With his life and soul, he'd protect Wendy—just like Nick.

"He told Alfie when he came back for more of the oatmeal bath and itch oils," Wendy said, her mouth still full of the roasted venison. They usually couldn't afford meat, but a butcher with cavities had bartered four pounds for Felix's treatment. He was so happy that Felix hadn't removed—but rather, treated his teeth—that he brought two sacks of potatoes along with the roast to thank him.

"What does he need itch oil for?" Nick asked, thinking of the various ailments their first patient of the Ton had.

"*Anti* itch," Alfie said with a sideways glance to Wendy. Patient information was sacred; none of them would carry any of the treatments their patients required beyond these walls. But they finally had their own walls to call a practice, which was theirs together. Thus, discussing the diagnoses and treatment plans was on the menu for every dinner.

"Alfie said it's from too much lovemaking," Wendy said, and Nick sputtered, nearly spitting his mashed potatoes over the table.

"How do you even know about that?" Nick's spoon halted mid sip as his sister's words hit him and without meaning to, he let go of the utensil. It clattered into the soup bowl.

"She's a nurse, Nick; what do you think patients tell her?" Alfie snorted and filled his glass with water from the terra cotta jug.

"He's had too much of a lot of things if you ask me," Felix said.

"By the time I'm finished with my treatment, his mouth will have several grams of gold."

"He needed that many fillings?" Nick wondered. "At his age?"

"That's what I'm saying, Nick. He's always had everything he wanted." Felix shook his head in disapproval. "He got every woman he wanted, and if his escapades ended with an itch, he just found an ointment to apply and carried on. You know, he has the most intricately decorated little chocolates by his bedside and eats them like nuts before bedtime. I'm amazed that he never took laudanum for a toothache."

"What did he take?" Alfie asked, always interested in the old wives' cures and alleged poisons patients told him about.

"Nothing." Felix shrugged. "His cavities are wider rather than deep, so the nerves are unaffected. Never minded them until now."

"He just wants to be perfect for his bride. For their lovely castle wedding." Wendy swayed in her chair as if she was dancing at a royal ball. How could women be so naive and forgiving of human flaws when men couldn't?

"I don't know if that's true," Felix said. "He has to grow up and pass on the torch."

"Well, I hear there's a pavilion of pleasure in his townhouse gardens," Alfie said. Andre gave an appreciative nod.

"Not everything is about lovemaking," Nick said, conscious of his innocent little sister at their table.

"He has to produce an heir," Alfie said.

"He can produce an heir just fine with or without teeth," Nick said to Felix, "no offense to your craft."

"My craft is medicine, Nick. Mark my words if you ever need my help."

"I know, I know. Dentistry is medicine. I won't need your services, but thank you," Nick said.

Felix got up and picked his plate up to wash it. They only had five plates, one for each of them. After each use, they'd wash their plates for the next meal, which was hopefully something they could purchase from their earnings rather than barter for, even though this evening's venison and mashed potatoes had been delicious.

"If you ask me, he's getting into shape for the marriage bed, just like the debutantes," Felix said. "I have several mothers who have brought their daughters to me. They expect me to repair the girls to make up for the neglect during their girlhoods."

"That's rather crude, Felix," Wendy said.

"It is, Wendy. But if they know that their daughters have so many holes in their teeth, why don't they care until just before they debut? It's because their mothers care more about society than their children's well-being, I'm telling you. And suddenly, they ask for polished gold to replace the amalgam and beautification so the girls can dazzle some titled nobleman into a proposal."

"But maybe the girls just need a little nudge in the right direction and fall in love so irrevocably that their grooms are mesmerized by their beauty—"

"Wendy, keep dreaming. It's sweet that you think that," Felix said. He spoke with the wisdom of an older man who'd loved and lost, and Nick knew it was because his friend knew what a broken heart felt like.

"A smile can go to the heart like a dagger," Andre finally said. He'd been quietly eating.

"Another hopeless romantic." Alfie laughed.

"I'm Italian. What do you want from me? Passion runs in my blood." Andre blinked at Wendy and then he cast Nick a sardonic brow.

"Stop that right now!" Nick interjected, and Wendy and Andre broke into laughter.

"Well, I think it's wonderful that he is trying to be healthy for his wedding," Nick said. "It's his way of wooing the woman he already married."

"How so?" Wendy asked.

Nick couldn't help but smile dreamily. He'd known the earl for such a long time and accompanied him on a path to betterment. "He's trying to be the best version of himself for his bride. There's no greater compliment he can pay her, don't you think?"

His sister shot him a look, at first confused but then interrogating.

I'm not going to tell you who caught my attention. Nick winked.

Chapter Six

Lord and Lady Canton from Oxfordshire had come for dinner and Pippa recognized them as soon as she entered the dining room as usual at seven o'clock. The candelabras twinkled, but the chandelier had been left unlit in favor of the ambiance for dinner. Pippa never liked to eat in half-darkness, which didn't add much to the atmosphere for her, either. Come to think of it, dim light truly affected her vision. Could the handsome doctor have diagnosed what she'd struggled with for years in just a matter of minutes?

Or was it as evident to everyone as it had been to him, and only she was blind to her own perspective?

She heard the clanking of spoons on plates and a low slurping sound coming from Lord Canton, one of the bald guests. Nobody had waited for her to start eating, which showed Pippa that she didn't matter to them. And yet, this was her home; the house technically belonged to her because her father only held it in trust for her.

And still, she didn't feel welcome.

The audible sounds of Wife Six's lip smacking and messy dining reached her ears. Truly, her etiquette at the table was akin to that of a farmyard pig. Meanwhile, Father sat at the head of the table, the guests on his right and Bea on the left, next to the empty chair reserved for Pippa.

"Oh, Penelope, look at how you've grown!" The kind voice of the elderly Lady Canton came from the left. Pippa squinted in the dim light. The guest sat next to her husband, and from Pippa's vantage point, her dress was such a dark red that it blended in with her husband's black, or possibly blue coat. "Come and give me a kiss, darling. I haven't seen you since your mother died. Poor thing." Pippa followed the voice, but when she had just reached the elderly couple, found Lady Canton's hands. Soft and wrinkled with manicured nails, the older woman patted Pippa's left hand which was sandwiched between hers and tugged her gown. Pippa dutifully curtsied and bowed to receive a grandmotherly kiss from Lady Canton, but instead, her face brushed against a large, smooth, somewhat greasy ball. It was a little hairy, too. *Revolting...*

Oh no!

"What are you doing kissing his lordship's head for?" Her father thundered and banged on the table. Then he mumbled another insult under his breath.

She froze.

"D—darling girl," the old duchess stuttered. "What's wrong with her? Is she tetched?" Her head was turned away from her. Pippa only just realized it by the scent of the woman's pomade, and she jerked back.

"She's unwell," Wife Six said and then slurped the soup.

"An embarrassment. A clumsy goose," Father said. "Wine?"

"I beg your pardon, but this is... it's—" But before his lordship could finish his sentence, Pippa had stormed out of the room and began heading up the stairs. Tears of embarrassment and anger rose in her eyes. Her useless, *deficient* eyes.

"Stop!" Bea's voice came from the bottom of the staircase. "Pippa!"

"Leave me alone!" She continued to climb.

"It was an accident!"

"Of course, it was an accident! What would I go about kissing the bald head of disgusting old lords?" Pippa fought not to shriek. She lifted her skirts and began to run up the stairs with Bea on her heels.

Downstairs, an uproar and protest continued to emanate from the dining room. Pippa squeezed her eyes shut. In her embarrassment, she'd forgotten that they could hear. She'd stumbled over Lady Canton, kissed her husband's bald head, and then called him disgusting. Clumsy goose, indeed.

Pippa finally reached her room, heaving for air and dignity. An accident happened once or twice. This, however, was a curse.

Life had played an awful joke on her, testing her resolve to survive even the most meager appearances with human beings that confirmed—every single time—that her father could be right: she was an embarrassment. She should know better now, but the disappointment in herself surprised her anew, every day. Wasn't there a cure for *that*?

Somehow, she forgot her clumsiness when she moved about her typical day. Even in the orangery, she had no trouble finding her way around and caring for her plants. She got flustered only when something was out of place, and that's when she made stupid mistakes.

Like the colossal one of... oh, she wouldn't allow herself to think of it. What a disaster. She grimaced, wiping her mouth with her sleeve.

If she weren't embarrassing herself in front of members of the Ton, she was bumping into handsome doctors and smearing custard and cream all over them.

Her heart skipped a beat and she admitted to herself that she didn't mind the young doctor, nor did she mind besmearing him with whipped cream, though the context of doing so by accident in her favorite pastry shop posed the problem. Would she have the courage to return? And if she did—would she meet him again?

Pippa sternly reminded herself not to get carried away by fanciful dreams. Yet, her imagination paid no heed, painting vivid images of captivating moments. The warm smiles gave way to strolls in the moonlight, intense discussions, stolen kisses beneath the twinkling stars, and even—Pippa's cheeks reddened at the thought—a wedding ceremony. Could she really envision herself saying, "I do" to the charming doctor with a heartwarming smile? Nonsense.

Despite her numerous attempts to suppress these absurd thoughts, Pippa finally surrendered. As ludicrous as they were, at least these fantasies were hers alone, hidden from prying eyes and safe from clumsy accidents. No soul need ever find them out. And though the chances of crossing paths with the handsome doctor again were slim, her heart still clung onto this unlikely possibility.

She could see herself playfully smearing a dollop of whipped cream on the doctor's cheek, the corner of his mouth curving into a surprised smile. The image of herself leaning in to lick it off, her lips trailing warm kisses along his jawline, was scandalous enough to make her heart flutter wildly.

She tried to dismiss the thought, shaking her head as if physically attempting to dislodge the dream from her mind. But the picture only grew more vivid, the doctor's surprised laughter ringing in her ears, the taste of sweet cream and warmer skin on her tongue. It was an image that was both exciting and terrifying, a tantalizing blend of sweet innocence and delicious impropriety.

"Stop it, Pippa," she scolded herself, but her imagination, now unleashed, was relentless. The fantasy was hers alone, hidden away in the deepest corners of her heart. And no matter how scandalous, it was a secret thrill she found herself unwilling to let go.

And why did her mind continually find its way back to him? So what if he was extremely handsome, with an angled jawline that she'd imagined kissing, along with the contour of his neck and chest? She'd fallen in his lap, her hand had brushed over his pecs, and he was hard, solid, strong. Pippa's tummy did that whirlwind thing again; it was most unsettling.

She had to stop the woolgathering and control her fantasies. Nobody would want the clumsy goose. Nobody wanted her.

"You have no idea what it feels like when everybody mocks you and your own father hates you!" Pippa's voice wobbled as she cried and threw herself on her bed. There was that chain around the heart again. It made it hard to fill her lungs when she inhaled, and it was impossible to let go of the hurt when she exhaled.

"He doesn't hate you, Pippa!" Bea shut the door and moved to sit on the side of the bed.

"Of course, he does. It's plain to see!"

"I have no idea what it is you think you see. A father can never hate his own child."

"Mine does. Every time I enter the breakfast room, his mien darkens. I'm a walking and talking disappointment for him, and since we live together, I'm also a constant reminder of the failure I am. When he looks at me, I can tell there's nothing left but a pit of sorrow that I'm still around."

"It can't be that bad."

"It is now. Since Mother—" Pippa winced. She still couldn't speak of her in the past tense. There was such finality to her departure, making her death too real. She'd learned so much from her mother, and she always carried her in her heart. How could she speak of her as if she were gone if she was a constant presence in Pippa's mind?

"Pippa, he's grieving. Or perhaps unwell."

"If he were grieving, he wouldn't be on wife number six now. And he's well enough to poke fun at me."

"I cannot believe that your words have any truth. He must love you; you're his only child, and he is happy to have you here."

"Oh please, Bea! It is not so, and you know it. If I married someone, I'd be out of his sight. He'd be relieved to get me as far away as the moon."

"Have you ever considered the possibility that fathers wish their daughters looked after rather than married off? It's why my parents didn't take me on their diplomatic travels; they want to keep me safe."

"If I were more like you, pretty and popular, he'd have a reason to love me!" Pippa inhaled deeply and exhaled with a sigh. Poor Bea was so pretty; she didn't even know how lucky she was. She wasn't a clumsy goose like Pippa. "Or if I had married a well-connected earl as Violet did with Henry, father would have a reason to be proud of me."

"And what makes you think he's not proud of you now? Perhaps he can't show it. You're the sweetest person I know and probably one of the smartest. You grew a pineapple tree from kitchen scraps!"

"It was a pineapple crown. You're meant to plant them so they can grow into a new plant."

"You know that because you're brilliant, Pippa. It's kitchen scraps for everyone else. You even know it's called a crown. Who knows these things but geniuses?"

"Readers of Ellington's *Illustrated Compendium on Botany*."

"My point exactly. It's not a book for normal people; it's a treatise. I couldn't understand it even if I tried."

She brushed this assertion aside as inconsequential. Bea didn't give herself enough credit. But she, herself, was a different story. "I don't *do* anything smart; I knock over platters of sandwiches and take my leave from coat stands instead of hosts."

"We all make mistakes and embarrass ourselves sometimes. It happens, but it doesn't mean that we become our mistakes. Just don't dwell on it." Bea waved her hand in the air.

Pippa sat up and wiped the tears off her cheeks with her hands. "There's nothing but dwelling left to do. It's been going on for so long. I don't think he remembers how it was to love me. Every disappointment I brought on him washed away the bedrock of what was a river of love when Mother was alive. It's all eroded away now."

"Stone is harder than water."

"Yes, but rivers shape the rocks. They polish and break them and turn boulders to sand."

"Pippa, this is a lovely metaphor and a token of your intelligence when you speak of it, but you're not making any sense. Love doesn't just wash away."

"Shame can wash love away. Disappointment essentially dissolves it. My father doesn't have any love left for me." Pippa took a deep breath, expecting the tears to roll down her cheeks, but none came. She had no tears left to cry over her father. The break between them had gone so deep that a cleft as wide as a chasm had opened, and there was no bridge to make her feel for him again. He'd done that. Society had done that. Her father had valued the opinion of mere strangers over his daughter's heart. And here she was, a guest in her home, unwelcome even though she was part of the family. The lucky daughter of a duke to outsiders was a sad captive in a gilded cage atop an ivory tower, locked away on a high mountain of grief, disillusionment, and heartbreak. So, it was true that not only lovers but also a parent could break the child's heart, resulting in unbearable pain.

"Consider this." Pippa straightened her back and shook her hair, so it spilled over her shoulders and down her back. "Every time he entertains people, and I do something stupid, he's embarrassed. Over time, he anticipates that I will do something like drink from another guest's glass and tuck the tablecloth in my sleeve instead of a handkerchief, clearing the table when I take my leave. Or he sees a room with a large palm as a threat to my reputation because I'll mistakenly greet the plant instead of the hostess with a feather hat."

Bea pinched her lips but wasn't hiding the whistle for her nose when she suppressed the laugh.

"See? I'm the laughingstock of the Ton. In his world, I cannot compete with someone like Violet." Pippa couldn't fathom how Violet could have become the Countess of Langley even though she'd been at her wedding. Why did the nasty girls get so lucky in life?

It wasn't that Pippa envied her; she truly didn't, but it was a riddle, nonetheless. There had to be a return on investment, a reward for a good nature or hard work. What had Violet ever done to earn such acclaim in society? Couldn't the universe punish the lazy and wicked people and reward the good ones whose hearts were pure?

"But she's mean, and she married someone she didn't even love," Bea spoke Pippa's mind.

"She married an earl in her first season. She's a success. She checked off all the criteria in my father's book of female accomplishments. If she were his daughter, he'd be happy."

"He must be happy with you, Pippa."

"Must be, yes. But he can't." Pippa tried to steady her already frayed nerves. "He can't see who I am. He's long stopped bothering to look." It was true—as soon as anything triggered her father's scorn, he turned his back on her and then was outright mean. He joked about her as if he could distance himself from any embarrassment by mocking Pippa. When he'd only done it at balls and social gatherings, Pippa had had the chance to avoid his jibes by withdrawing into their stately home and tending to her orangery.

However, he even joked in front of the butler, the footmen, and the cook these days. "Don't make a cream pie if we're eating in a carpeted room, or else Pippa will smear it all over, and it's more trouble to clean it up than crumbs from a teacake."

Or, "Don't stand next to the horses when she wants to kiss you good bye."

And Pippa had had enough of it.

"The first chance I have, Bea, I'll move out."

"You'd be ruined."

"If he lets me get ruined, and if I never have a husband, he won't have access to my grandfather's fortune. It's how the will is set up. Grandfather skipped Father because he didn't want to give him more than my mother's dowry."

"He's getting a large stipend from managing your fortune."

"The bankers are managing the fortune based on my grandfather's instructions. The money is tied up in a trust until the day I marry for love, or at his death. And when it is released, I'll be in control."

"If your husband signs it over to you."

"Do you think I could love a man who wouldn't?"

Pippa put her hands on her hips. It was preposterous. Of course, she'd marry for love. If ever. And, of course, she'd marry someone who'd leave her fortune to her. Even though her father had spent her dowry, giving up hope that she'd ever find such a man in polite society.

Pippa shrugged. She should look elsewhere and keep her eyes open for love.

Where might one look for love?

And could she see it if she came close?

Chapter Seven

AT THE SAME time across town, at 87 Harley Street, Nick sat alone in his treatment room.

The surgery of the Earl of Langley's left eye had gone well. It was rather uneventful, and Nick would pay him a visit the next day to ensure his recovery was as smooth as the surgery. But none of that made Nick feel any better.

In the quiet of his office, Nick held the letter in his hands, the familiar script of the nurse a stark contrast to the handwriting he remembered from Lancefield Ellington, an old friend and former classmate from the University of Edinburgh. He had received many letters from Lance over the years, each a poignant reminder of their shared past. But this one was different. This was not just a letter; it was an impending presence, a specter from the past about to become a tangible reality. The words danced before his eyes, a waltz of ink and parchment that spoke of a visit. A wave of unease washed over Nick, chilling him despite the warmth of the crackling fireplace.

> *It's been such a long time since we were last together, old friend. Wendy, Alfie, Felix, and Andre will hopefully be there, too. I'm counting the days and will try to be there for your birthday.*

Lance was coming to London.

The guilt that had been simmering in the pit of his stomach since

Lance's departure from Edinburgh boiled over. He hadn't been able to restore his friend's vision. He hadn't even been able to try, but even if he had, Nick was certain it would have been beyond his skills.

It had been a bitter goodbye when Lance's noble parents sent a carriage to take him from university to stow him away in their country estate. Their blind fourth son, Lance, was cast aside, buried alive in the darkness of his lost vision. They'd hired a staff for him, a cook, housemaids, a butler, and a nurse. Nick had been told that the estate was sizable, and that Lance wouldn't lack for anything—except for the life he'd chosen. Lance couldn't complete his studies or do much for himself. Even the letters he sent to Nick were dictated and penned in a female hand, surely the nurse, for there was a flourish to her penmanship that reminded him of his sister's. With every letter, the pain flared up in Nick's conscience, a relentless gnawing reminding him of his failure.

Not just as a doctor, but also as a friend.

He'd told himself he'd make it over to Cornwall to visit Lance after the following holidays. After one more critical patient from the Ton. After one more financial milestone. Eventually, one more excuse after another had kept him from fulfilling this promise.

Years had passed, and now Lance was the courageous one announcing his visit.

Nick's eyes flickered away from the ominous letter, drawn to the soft rustling sound from the doorway. Wendy appeared in the frame, her arms laden with fluffy, freshly pressed towels.

"Hello!" Wendy smiled. His dear little sister always had a smile for him, and it tugged at his heart that she was growing up. He'd failed her, making her work so hard at the practice, yet she was amazing and never complained. Bandaging bloody wounds, washing the surgical instruments, holding the patients' hands—or even their heads to still them—was all part of her work, and she carried herself with unmatched dignity when she did it. And none of the doctors at 87 Harley

Street could manage without her. She commanded the same respect among them as any of the doctors.

Her wheat-colored curls bobbed lightly as she moved, catching the yellow-orange glow of the fireplace. She had their mother's delicate features, her beauty unpretentious yet captivating. But her eyes held Nick's attention, the same vibrant blue as his own, twinkling with an intelligence and understanding that belied her years. "What happened?" she asked when she caught Nick's disgruntled mien. If he didn't know any better, he'd say that Wendy had a unique sense of reading people's emotions. It seemed to be one of her unique talents.

She set the towels neatly on the armchair as she leaned over Nick's shoulder to read the letter he still held in his hands.

"Oh, how lovely, Lance is coming to London!" She clapped both hands together. "I'll make up the patient room for his visit. Oh, there's still so much to prepare for your birthday!"

Her gaze met Nick's, and a knowing glint flashed across her eyes. That look always disarmed him, a silent proclamation that his thoughts and fears were not his alone to bear.

There was no doubt that Wendy had a knack for discerning his moods. He knew then that hiding his inner turmoil was futile. The fear probably etched on his face, the tension in his shoulders, the restlessness in his fingers as they traced the contours of the letter—he might as well have been an open book.

"Why are you not pleased?" she asked, her voice soft yet steady, cutting through the heavy missive in the letter he still held. In that moment, Nick found comfort in Wendy's knowing eyes, a testament to their bond. They were siblings, but above all, they were allies in an often-overwhelming world.

"I haven't seen him since... you know..." Nick was so ashamed of himself that he dared not look at Wendy. She'd been too young but probably remembered.

"For an eye surgeon, one might think you'd be more comfortable around a blind man."

"Not this one."

"Nick," Wendy took a deep breath. "You can't fix them all. How many soldiers have you operated on and helped? How many elderly people have you blessed with vision after they'd nearly lost it?"

"It's not the same, Wendy."

"That's right! It's different every time. And yet, you always help your patients."

"Lance is not my patient; he never was. He's my friend, and I failed him."

"Perhaps that's his problem, Nick. It's too personal for you."

"Wendy, he went blind so young; it's not a cataract. Older people get them. I can't do anything for him."

"Yes, I know. Like Baron Melbourne. He's what, sixty-eight?"

"Exactly."

"And the Dowager Countess Greenborough last week. She sent a message but in her hand." Wendy gave a gentle smile, and her eyes glistened. "She's seventy?"

"I know what you're doing, little sister. It's not working."

"That's what you said when the Marquess of Hastings came a few months ago. And he just wrote another treatise. His vision is better than ever; he said so himself! And he's forty-two."

"W-eee-nnnn-dyyyy…" He drew out her name in a long warning breath.

"Don't Wendy me, Nick! I can't even count how many people you've helped. This month alone, we had Lady Margaret, Viscountess Cunningham, Sir James Framingham, and Lord Yates."

Nick inhaled. It felt good to hear the names of this month's patients. Wendy had an impeccable memory, of course, and even listed the cataract surgeries that he'd performed.

"But you didn't even charge for the butcher's wife and her sister, Nick. I know you didn't. You help far more people—"

"You also well know that they can't afford me."

"And you told them they couldn't afford not to see their daughter's wedding. The butcher and his wife said she's pleased with her new husband, and they saw it happen because of you."

"Glad to hear—"

"Oh, Nick, please! You wanted the mother and aunt to see their little girl grown up at the altar as a bride."

"A mother needs to see that."

Wendy smiled like Socrates, who wanted the student to conclude that which she'd prepared long ago. "Did you consider that Lance might miss you? All of us?"

"No. Because even if he comes, he can't see us."

"When he comes," Wendy said, "he'll come to be with his friends. Whether he sees us or not, he still has our friendship. Doesn't he?"

"Of course, he does." Nick waved the hidden reproach off.

"Then it's time to let him know. Show him."

"Show him?" Nick balled a fist. "What can I show him if he can't see, hm? Take him around London and let him see the cherry blossoms? Take him to the British Museum to admire the art?"

"Oh, Nick." Wendy turned away, picked up the stack of fresh towels, and began to lay them neatly into the cupboard. As she worked, she huffed and puffed indignantly, obviously awaiting Nick's imminent apology. But he had nothing to apologize for, or could he be blamed for an act of omission? He'd stood by, watching his friend go blind. He hadn't done much after the chair of the Faculty of Medicine had examined Lance's eyes and then explained that he had to withdraw from his studies.

"I was there, Wendy. When Professor Martins told Lance that there was nothing he could do. Lance couldn't see, and if I had covered for him, I could have been dismissed as a cheat."

"So, you didn't." She shrugged, her back turned to him while she patted the towels straight into the cupboard. They were her little linen soldiers, obeying her every tug and tap, lying flat in the cabinet until she'd take them out and fold them in whatever way she'd need, as a bib for Felix's patients, a neck roll for Nick's patients, or a bandage for Andre's. Secretly, Wendy must have known that she was in charge of the practice. Nothing would work smoothly without her. Probably not even Nick's life.

"I'll let Lance know that we can buy tickets to the symphony. Maybe the opera... do you think Lady Langley would help me to get good seats?"

"Why not ask her if you can get tickets to the theatre, too?"

Wendy ignored the sarcasm in Nick's voice. "That's a marvelous idea!" Wendy turned to face him with a bright smile, but when their eyes met, her brightness melted away. "Oh, Nick, you weren't serious at all."

"Of course not, Wendy! He can't see where he's going, can he? He'd stumble down the stairs at the opera house and break his neck. Do you want each of us to have to lay a hand on our friend? I don't think Andre expects to reset Lance's bones when he comes here."

"I also don't expect to leave Lance wandering the opera house alone. But if you cannot see that he might enjoy hearing the music at the symphony or that he could sense the excitement and hear the arias at the opera, you're more blind than he is."

"Nonsense," Nick mumbled and pushed the letter aside. He'd think about Lance later; there were some angles to calculate and invoices to send. His sister, his confidante, was the lighthouse guiding him through the fog of guilt and fear—and he didn't want to go there. Wendy left, and Nick remained alone, the letter on the table before him.

His first big failure as an eye surgeon was not even taking a chance to operate on Lance. He hadn't been allowed to; it was too early in his studies then, and the matter had never come up again. As far as Nick was concerned, he had stood by while Lance went blind. It was sad for anyone, but for Nick, it was inexcusable. What sort of an oculist let his friend go blind? Now that Nick was a doctor of considerable repute, lauded for his skills and sought after by patrons far and wide, it hurt even more to think about the failure. The mission of helping Lance grew with the skill Nick hadn't been able to use to help his friend. Yet, he remembered the powerlessness to help Lance as he slipped deeper into darkness each day until the world of medicine they once shared was nothing more than a blurred memory for Lance.

Nick's gaze fell on the framed accolades adorning his study wall, their shiny frames mocking him. The irony wasn't lost on him. He, the celebrated eye surgeon, could restore sight to so many, yet his skill was useless to Lance. The sense of failure was stifling.

His last image of Lance was of a vibrant young man, full of life and promise. Now, Nick wasn't sure what to expect. Would he find the same Lance he knew, or a stranger, a shadow of his former self?

Nick felt deep sorrow for his friend. Worse, Lance had been pushed away by his own family, his disability an inconvenience in their aristocratic world. He was left with a nurse, his only lifeline to the outside world. Nick couldn't help but feel a sense of responsibility. He should have done more and should have tried harder. But the past was a locked door, and guilt was the key that opened it, allowing remorse to flow freely.

He wondered how he would face Lance and look into those sightless eyes and not be consumed by the failure that weighed heavily on him, a darkness more profound than the blindness that had claimed Lance.

Chapter Eight

Soon, it would be dark, and it was time to go back to the house. Pippa's father hadn't allowed her to have gas lights installed in the orangery. It wasn't worth it, he'd said. It was just a place for her alone.

She wasn't worth it to him.

But Wife Six, known to the rest of the Ton as Carolyn, had had an entire room converted to her dressing room with a daybed for her face massages. She thought frown lines came from a lack of care. In Pippa's opinion, this wife was the worst one yet and spread through the house like a disease. Room by room, she put her mark on the place and transformed the carefully selected decor that had been their family for generations into many vulgar arrangements. The bright pink curtains she had installed in the drawing room had orange fringes, and the new upholstered settees clashed in the brightest shade of rust red. It was hideous, especially considering the turquoise wallpaper that was partially faded, a leftover from the previous decor that donned shades of blue and white furniture. Wife Six had no decency, no taste, no scruples. But she had a goal: to get rid of Pippa.

And Pippa tried to stay out of her way.

That's why Pippa much preferred her orangery. It was a little house just outside the larger house. One might call it a doghouse for the unwanted daughter, but to Pippa, it was everything her mother had taught her about life. Every time her orchids had offshoots, she reveled in the beauty of the delicate blossoms; it was as if her mother breathed over her shoulder. Especially when the pineapple bore fruit, and she used the same knife with the wooden handle that her mother had kept hanging on a nail on one of the columns, she tasted the sweet and tangy love. For what else could these moments be called except for love? They were rare and precious and almost extinct these days.

By the time Bea found Pippa—not that it was difficult to guess where she'd hide—Pippa was a picture of agitation and had repotted the phalaenopsis orchids one by one. Her cousin, ever perceptive when it came to matters of the heart, quickly picked up on Pippa's distress.

"There was a man here, wasn't there?" Bea asked, her eyes narrowing as she sniffed. "It smells different. Smells like... musk and sandalwood but you don't grow any here."

Pippa nodded her cheeks uncharacteristically hot. "Yes, and he was absolutely infuriating," she admitted, her voice laced with frustration.

Her cousin's eyebrows lifted in surprise. "I've never seen you ruffled over a man before," she mused. "What happened?"

"He said...he implied that I was *deficient*," Pippa confessed, wringing her hands anxiously in her lap.

"Deficient?" her cousin echoed, her voice sharp with disbelief. "Who was this man?"

"Nick," Pippa clarified, her voice wavering. He'd been on her mind so much; how couldn't Bea know who she meant? "To be more accurate, he suggested I had a *deficiency*."

"And what might that be?" her cousin queried, her tone now soft with concern.

"Farsightedness," Pippa finally managed to utter.

"In the figurative sense," Bea said and put her hands on her hips. "He's right."

"He meant *literally*. As in, I need spectacles," Pippa corrected her.

The revelation appeared to give her cousin pause. She studied

Pippa for a long moment, her gaze thoughtful as she processed this new information. The usually vibrant orangery was filled with a tense silence, the air heavy with unspoken thoughts and questions.

Finally, Bea spoke. "He has a point," she said.

A sense of dismayed betrayal rose in Pippa's heart. "No!"

Bea shrugged. "He does. It might explain why you are so clumsy."

"I'm not—" Well, she couldn't actually deny the truth of it. But she could try. Pippa took a deep breath before announcing, "I'm only clumsy at balls and in closed rooms."

"Yes, because you cannot orient yourself by seeing things far from you. But you have the keenest sense of direction in town; you always know where we need to go. Maybe that's because you can see at a distance."

"Oh!" That made more sense than Pippa cared to admit. Could it be true? Could her clumsiness be attributed to farsightedness? Was Nick correct about it being a condition and not a characteristic? She'd struggled with it for her entire life as a fault; it was hard to see it—so to speak—otherwise. "I suppose…well. He said he's an oculist. A doctor."

"Really?" Bea's voice rose in apparent intrigue. "What did he say you should do about it?"

"Come see him at his office, be fitted for eyeglasses." Pippa wrinkled her nose. She was missing a pair of glasses and a hat of whipped cream with a cherry on top so the Ton and her father's friends could make even more fun of her. "Glasses are not very flattering. I'll never catch a husband that way."

"But wouldn't it be nice to cure your clumsiness altogether? So, what if you wear glasses? They might make you look smart like a professor."

"I'm barely a professor; I'm just a girl." She frowned. "Besides, girls can't be professors. I'd be called a bluestocking!"

"Pish-posh," Bea scoffed. "Mark my words, one day, there will be girl professors for all sorts of things. You could lecture people on botany for hours. It's the perfect solution for you if it's not a man you want and just plants!"

"Except that I don't want a solution right now, not if it means I'll draw even more attention to myself with an ugly pair of spectacles."

"Nonsense. If all you need is eyeglasses, get them. If I were you, I wouldn't waste another minute. Do you know where to find him again?"

Pippa handed her cousin the card; she'd been carrying it with her, tucked in her sleeves, since he'd given it to her. Heavens forbid Wife Six or anyone find it among her things.

Nicholas Folsham
Oculist
87 Harley Street

"Go there first thing tomorrow morning!" Bea said.

Chapter Nine

The next morning...

"DON'T SPEND ALL my money again," Father said when they'd reached the distinctive rows of white houses in Marylebone. "I don't want to overdraw my accounts this month."

"Perhaps you should ask Wife Six to wear a dress more than once?" *It's my money. My birthright.*

"It's her way, Pippa. Don't be too harsh on her. She's under a lot of pressure to keep up with all the ladies at tea every day."

Pippa snuffed. "Certainly. It cannot be easy following the daily gossip mill without wrinkling one's dress."

"*Piiiiippaaaaaa!*"

"Yes, Father?" She put her hands in her lap and lifted her shoulder, inclining her head as if she were an adorable little girl. If he considered her so naive as to think that Wife Six was anything but a glutton and a bloodsucking leech, she wouldn't start a fight.

He frowned. "I have to pay Sir Matthews today, so please, Pippa."

"What are you paying him for?" She wished there was a way to deter him from relying on the charlatan with the crystals and "ancient magical medicine." In her estimation, the only magic at which "Sir" Matthews was adept was parting a foolish man from his money.

"Och," her father blew the air from his lips and looked like a fat and old neighing horse. Pippa didn't recognize him these days. When Mother had been alive, Father had been a gentleman, kind, slim, and well groomed. He'd taken Pippa riding on sunny days, and he jumped over the waves with her when she was a little girl when they summered in Cornwall. But when her mother had died, that part of him did, too. He'd withdrawn into his chambers and left Pippa alone. Initially, she'd come to his door and listened to him cry. He mumbled something in slurred speech.

But as the months passed, he started to have female guests. Within a year after Pippa's mother's death, he'd remarried. But Wife Two grew round with child all too quickly. When Father confronted her, she left with her physician, who was probably the child's father. Then came Wife Three, a merry widow who had little interest in her father and rather wanted to rise in station. They'd slept in separate quarters and then, she'd left. And so came Wife Four, but the marriage was annulled during the honeymoon when she introduced her eleven-year-old son to Father and wanted to declare him his heir. Wife Five was a blur because she'd shown up during the time Pippa had been sent to boarding school. And when she came home after she graduated, Wife Six—the worst one yet—had moved in.

Now, Father said, "You have enough money of your own, Pippa. I need mine."

"Well, I cannot access my money until I marry. Isn't it your responsibility to look after me until then?"

"It's my responsibility for the first eighteen or nineteen years of your life. You're twenty, and I doubt that anyone will have you."

Pippa squinted. It didn't even sting anymore—or not very much at least. Instead, she told herself, she'd grown used to being a nuisance for her father. The issue was that she worried he'd discard her completely one day before she could leave on her own accord. If there were no hope for her to marry, perhaps he'd convince a barrister to convert her inheritance into a trust that he could suck dry with Wife

Six. And she couldn't leave without a husband to take her inheritance with her. Yet, she kept the country house running, in case she needed to escape Town. There was little room for her in Father's life, considering how many women had befallen him like diseases, each one bringing another slur of symptoms that made him sicker and more feeble. Nobody could bring her mother back, so all women were a necessary evil for him. He'd become a sad glob of the man she'd known. Mother would be disgusted at the sight.

The carriage stopped and her father made to leave the carriage. Even though he'd insulted Pippa for the thousandth time, she held her arm out to help him. He'd grown so large that his face turned red when he rose, and blue veins popped up on his temples.

When her father stepped on the last step and set one foot on the cobblestones, he pulled out an envelope filled with banknotes. In the process, he dropped his hat. He strained and made a rather unhealthy deflating noise like an old chair cushion when he bent down to retrieve it.

"How much does he charge?" Pippa asked as she left the cabin after him. He didn't even deem her lady enough to let her go ahead.

"No more than the physicians across the street," father said, placing his hat back upon his head. "They are expensive I've heard. Ruining his business."

"How are the physicians ruining Sir Matthews's business?"

"He's a crystal healer, Pippa. Takes years to master the craft. Lots and lots of supplies and knowledge."

"And the physicians who attended medical school earned their degrees over night?"

"How hard can it be to operate on an eye or fill teeth with gold, hm?"

"How hard is it to place some crystals along a patient's spine and chant something?"

"Have you spied on me?" Father thundered.

"No. You made me wait, and I saw you." She remembered it well. Her father had lain face down on a wooden table covered only with a thin sheet. Various wooden masks hung on the walls and there had been a desk in complete disarray with papers and old newspapers. During the entire session, Sir Matthews, the self-declared healer, had walked around Father placing colored crystals on his back. He'd also engaged Father in conversation and elicited more information about the House of Lords and the Ton than Pippa thought necessary for the treatment of Father's ailments.

Her father harumphed, took his walking stick, and turned to leave.

"Those doctors won't last as long as Sir Matthews is looking after Town."

"What do you mean 'looking after Town'?"

"He's all knowing, Pippa. He even predicted that I'd meet Carolyn."

Pippa blinked. *That* was news to her. "You mean, he saw into the future?"

"Sure did! He knew exactly that the next woman to walk through his door would steal my heart."

Pippa stared. He'd lost his mind. All she'd stolen was his health and his money. *Her* money!

For the past three years, her father had had a standing appointment with the "healer" every morning. Nothing would be easier than to predict who'd walk through the door—and to arrange a match. But what did Sir Matthews have to gain from thrusting Wife Six onto Father?

Something was amiss. She couldn't quite pinpoint it yet, but it was worth investigating.

But first, she needed to investigate with a healer of her own.

Would he see her? Would he remember her?

She reminded herself that she had an invitation, didn't she? He'd said he'd fit her for eyeglasses… and her vision was good enough to wish to see the handsome doctor again. It wasn't often that a young man of his muscular build and with an extensive education paid attention to her, much less treated her with kindness.

Pippa stood outside the carriage and felt for the card in her pocket. 87 Harley Street was just across the street. She could make out the house numbers; it was a neat, professional-looking building, with a gold sign. She could read Nick's name there: Dr. Nicholas Folsham, D.O. Perhaps she *was* farsighted.

In the literal sense.

If she could muster the courage, she'd go in.

Then she heard a bark.

And a little dog—more like a fuzzy blur—came running across the street, his leather lead dragging along the ground behind him.

Chapter Ten

"CHROMIUS! NO!"

Nick quickly looked left and right before he sprinted across the street, trying to catch the lead of his runaway dog.

Nick's heart pounded in his chest as Chromius, his normally well-behaved terrier mutt, bolted towards the hustle of the carriages and clip-clopping of horses along the street. The cobblestone streets of Marylebone, lit by the still-low-hanging sun diffused by the morning fog, pulsated with the energy of London waking up—a dangerous place for a little mutt.

The clattering of carriage wheels and the murmurs of conversation from passersby must have scared him—though it never had before. Perhaps he saw a cat or a squirrel; that would be more in character for the busy little hunter. And fast one, besides. Nick barely looked left and right before sprinting after his four-legged friend. Across the street, a young lady had just alighted from a glossy, deep blue landau, her crinoline skirt rustling like whispers in the gaslit glow. Chromius, evidently smitten for some unknown reason, made a beeline for her. Nick's breath caught in his throat as he watched his wayward dog dart across the carriage-filled street, his usually glossy coat now mottled with flecks of London's cobblestone grime.

Chromius's tail, a little white banner, whipped back and forth in joyous abandon, as he approached the young lady across the street.

Nick stopped hard when a carriage nearly ran over his foot and the split second it took to wait for it pass him by, the young woman's laughter rang out across the street, a melodic harmony that drifted towards Nick like a lilting tune. His heart lurched; he'd heard that laughter before, soft, lovely, imbued with warmth and amusement.

As Chromius jumped around her, her laughter only grew louder, the sound weaving an enchanting spell in the cool London morning.

Still a few feet away, Nick watched. "Chromius!"

But the dog ignored him, and his cries were lost among the bustle of Harley Street.

He watched Pippa as she delicately removed her glove, revealing her slender hand. She extended it towards Chromius. The dog sniffed at her fingers, his tail wagging in delight, and she lovingly patted his head with a touch that Nick knew was as light as a feather.

Even from his vantage point, Nick could see the elegant sophistication with which she carried herself, the refined grace that marked her as a lady. Yet, there was an unmistakable warmth in her gesture, a raw and genuine kindness that shone through as she lavished attention on what could possibly be a stray dog as far she was concerned. Yet, there was no reservation in her affectionate welcome of the creature.

By the time Nick reached the other side of the street, out of breath, the lady was squatting and had picked Chromius up. It was a sight that tugged at his heart, a poignant moment that faded in comparison to the jolt that ran through Nick's veins as soon as he saw her face.

She was just as breathtaking as she was in his memories. And her kindness—he hadn't imagined it. It shone through her, in the way she cuddled his dog, and in the smile on her face.

His heart pounded.

"Pippa!" Nick croaked, taking in the picture of the beauty who was jerking her face back and crinkling her nose adorably while Chromius licked her chin.

She giggled with the sound that Nick imagined his mother had meant when she told him how it sounded when an angel grew its wings in the old fairy tales.

Chromius wouldn't stop trying to lick her face—the smart dog's actions were completely understandable—and yet it was prudent to show a little more restraint, even though she was an exceptional vision of beauty. Nick reached for his dog and set him gently back down, holding tightly to his lead this time.

When Nick straightened his back and Chromius finally sat by his foot, she just stood there, beaming at him.

And the sun rose on the gloomy London fog. Pippa's face was alight with the power of her pearly smile and her cheeks were slightly red. It was cold and her breath dissipated in an elegantly swirling mist that diffused the light. Her blond curls emerged from her large woolen hood like spirals of spun gold sparkling in the light. So beautiful.

Nick's heart almost hurt when he looked at her, and he wanted to fall to his knees before the beautiful woman.

Suddenly, a shadow sucked the light out of the moment as if a giant were blocking the sun. And then it thundered. The heavens opened and without a moment's warning, they stood in the rain.

Chromius yapped, and Pippa huddled into her hood.

"I just sent my driver away." She peeked out from under the gray wool and batted her eyelashes. She was so sweet that Nick could feel the motion in his bones.

"Come with me." He took her hand, prepared to hesitate, but she didn't. She let him grab her hand firmly and she followed him across the street. Chromius's walk had to wait—or it would have, if Chromius hadn't stopped at the opposite curb to take care of his needs.

Nick led her up the stairs and to the door of 87 Harley Street. "This is my office. Well, it's the foyer of my...this is where I work." Nick opened the door for her. She walked past him and left a delicious scent in her wake. He didn't have time to analyze what she smelled like, as his body reacted, and he found himself eager to sit down at his exam table to hide the evidence of his arousal. Now, he bent to undo Chromius's leash. The dog shook the rainwater off and then tick-ticked across the floor toward the kitchen, tail wagging. It was time for breakfast. For him, anyway.

"I'm sorry he jumped you... ahem..." Nick rubbed the back of his neck as words failed him. But then he saw that Pippa was struggling to remove her soaking wet, wool pelisse, and reached to help her. His hands were shaking—not a thing a surgeon like him was used to. But he'd jump her like Chromius if he didn't have so many scruples.

"Is he a fox terrier?"

"He is indeed. Do you know much about dogs?" Nick was pleased that she liked his furry companion so much, although he couldn't quite explain why it was important to him.

"I think most animals have far better traits than humans." She bit her lip and a flush of pink spread quickly over her cheeks. "Present company excluded, of course."

"Of course." Nick broke into a smile. He liked her more and more, including the clumsy truths she let slip. She made his heart light up.

"I must say that I have never been to an oculist's office before, Dr. Folsham." She walked right into Nick's office without waiting for him to invite her; the door was open, but she'd probably seen his name on the door. Curiously, she took a stroll through his exam room as if it were Almack's and she was taking a turn about the room. Instead of a ball gown, she wore a dress that was cut rather plain. Instead of an elegant coiffe, her hair was tied loosely in a sort of braid and tied up with a plain white ribbon. And she wore sensible walking shoes with sturdy soles instead of dancing slippers. And yet, her posture was straight and her gaze so intelligent that he couldn't look away. There was something far more elegant and charming about her than Nick had ever seen in other aristocratic ladies.

"I did invite you here to confirm my diagnosis." *Drat!* A beautiful woman came to his office, and he went into automatic doctor mode.

Stupid.

She met his gaze. "Oh, I hadn't made up my mind yet—"

"But you're already here." *Please, don't go away.* He'd be so angry at himself if he scared her away. He wasn't used to talking to women, unless they were patients. He didn't go to balls. He wasn't invited. He was of the wrong class of person, after all.

"Very well." Her voice was quiet and her words hesitant. Was she feeling insecure, too? About *him*?

At least he had an excuse for her to stay. He wanted nothing more than to spend a little more time with her. If he focused on what he knew best—medicine—perhaps things would fall into place. At the very least, he wouldn't appear to be the bumbling boy that he currently felt like.

He would treat her like any other patient. That would work. He cleared his throat and straightened his shoulders. "Feel free to explore, milady. I shall set up the exam over here." Nick moved to rinse his hands in the wash basin by the wall cabinet. When he looked up, Pippa stood before the window, backlit with the gloomy light from the rainy morning. Yet, even in such a drab gray light, she was aglow.

He turned away to pull out a series of lenses from where they were kept, and when he turned back, she was attempting to peruse the shelf of books behind Nick's writing desk, although with her condition he doubted she was successful in reading any of them. The thought occurred to him that because of his skills, this beautiful vison would *have* beautiful vision. A fanciful thought, but Pippa inspired fancy, he thought.

When she turned to face him, she looked almost rosy with the golden curls cascading down her neck. Her complexion was even and clear, and Nick thought of a poem he'd read once about alabaster skin. What had seemed silly at the time was apt in this moment. Atop her head, the loosely braided bit of her hair had come loose, and a strand of silky blond hair spiraled down, barely touching her collarbone. Nick swallowed hard for it was a gorgeous view of her modestly covered neck. Unbidden, a fantasy of placing a slow and gentle kiss just at the nape of her neck rose in his mind.

He shook his head to dislodge the image. "You may take a seat here, please." He gestured to the chair meant for patients.

"Is anything the matter, Dr. Folsham?" Pippa asked as she took the seat across from him.

"Not at all, milady. Shall we begin?"

"I'm a bit nervous," she said as she surveyed the lenses. "What are these for?"

"I will use the lenses to determine the degree of your farsightedness. But first, I need to determine the general health of your eyes."

"Do you suspect anything wrong besides the lens…what is it called again?"

"I do not, but it is my job to ensure all is well. Shall we proceed?" Nick propped his elbow on the table and turned his palm upward. She instinctively knew what to do—most patients did—and stretched her neck until her chin rested on his fingertips. Nick tensed again and wished he could stop the erection under the table, but he was grateful that the table was made of solid wood and hiding his crotch. And, he supposed, he was grateful—at least, in this instance—for her farsightedness, though that was daring of him.

"Would you please tell me what you are doing?" She blinked. "I'm a little anxious."

"Certainly, milady." That was easy, for he'd worked with plenty of students and nervous patients before and was quite used to talking through the steps of an ophthalmic exam. Though sitting across such a gorgeous woman with such a bone-deep effect on him was a first. "I shall, in succession, glance at the eyebrows and orbital margins,"

"Why?"

"To rule out inflammation or look for excessive lachrymation, which might distort my subjective exam." She frowned and appeared somewhat alarmed, and Nick realized he'd used medical terminology instead of speaking a language more familiar to people who weren't doctors. "That is to say, an excessive secretion of tears due to disease or other systemic issues."

"Oh." She pursed her lips and blinked at him with her wide, round eyes. Her lashes were darker than the sun-kissed curls on her head, the irises bright green with clear strands of blue the shade of lapis lazuli. "I guess that's all right, then."

Nick smiled and moved closer. She kept her beautiful eyes wide open and blinked with a girl's innocence but the allure of a minx. She didn't seem to know how just beautiful she was. Or how she affected him. Even now, Nick shuddered because it was so difficult to control his arousal. Even when tending to his work and her condition, his heart and libido had other ideas. He cleared his throat and drew his brows down low over the bridge of his nose in an attempt to get himself to focus. "Next, I'm watching the movements of your eyes, and the surrounding areas. The eyelids, the borders of the lids, and the state of your lashes—"

She withdrew her head slightly and blinked "My eyelashes, Dr. Folsham, they're quite exactly like my mother's."

"Perfection," he whispered. It was inappropriate. Scandalous to compliment a patient. But he didn't want her as a patient, and he didn't care, for it was the truth. He'd hardly ever seen eyes more beautiful and expressive than hers. "The form and appearance of the eyeballs generally seems healthy, milady. Follow my finger."

Why couldn't he be more like Alfie sometimes and tell a woman that she has beautiful eyes instead of commenting on the clarity of her eyeballs? What would he do next, compliment the symmetry of her sclera?

At least that was safe, and familiar. And pathetic. Better that than to behave and feel inappropriately. A woman like her was not—and never could be—for the likes of him. Even if he was a doctor, and a successful one at that. They were from two different worlds, he reminded himself for what felt like the thousandth time. He had no right to think any other way.

"Please, milady. Follow my finger with your eyes only. Do not move your head." With that, he brought his other hand up and pointed his idle finger up, then down, then to the left and the right. She followed without any trouble. "The size and degree of the prominence of your eye is fine and the directions correspond to the axis."

He continued the visual field test and her eyes looked straight into Nick's.

Her focus was fine. His, however, was split between his throbbing cock and thundering heart and finally, he realized, there was no way to stop either from its normal reaction to a beautiful woman. For some reason, this thought calmed him somewhat. A bit. He moved two fingers in each direction. "Tell me when my fingers disappear." He brought his hand to her side, about an arm's length away.

"Gone!"

He wiggled his fingers to define the visual field. She giggled and quirked a brow.

His heart seemed to swell in his chest until he was full of a giddy, elated feeling. She was so absolutely stunning.

"What does this mean?" she asked.

"Nothing at all. Your eyes are healthy. Your visual field is a perfect 120 degrees."

"But you said they are..." Pippa paused before she whispered, "deficient."

He shook his head. "Not your eyes. I suspect that it is only the lens which requires aid. The color of the white of the eye is bright, and the cornea appears fine." Nick picked up a large lens from his workstation. Holding it between his thumb and index finger, he squinted through it. "You have very beautiful eyes, milady." There! Was that so hard?

Her pupils widened, and her gaze softened when he said it. He should have kicked himself, for it was not part of an eye exam to compliment the patient.

"I assume you have no pain, no itching, excessive tearing, burning, or sensation of a foreign body in your eyes?" She drew her brows close and shook her head. "Floaters?" She frowned. He'd used medical jargon again, instead of something commonly used by nonspecialists. He redefined his meaning for her. "Floaters are dots that move in your visual field."

She shook her head again and blinked. Nick knew that she was now searching her field of vision for floaters, just in case she'd never noticed them before. Everyone did it, once he'd made them aware of the phenomenon, but only now, as Pippa did it, did he find the action something to smile about. He turned in his chair to open the wooden drawer under the top of his desk and retrieved the small blue flask he'd next require. "This is belladonna tincture. I shall place a drop or two in each eye and allow for dilation of your pupils."

She sat back on the stool, her posture ramrod, and her shoulders raised in tension. "Is that necessary? Will it hurt? How long will it affect my eyes?"

"It doesn't hurt, the effect will only last for a few hours, and it's necessary, merely to ensure that there is no opaque appearance behind the pupil. It lets me know that the crystalline body is healthy." He held his palm to her, and she brought her face closer to him. However, he couldn't manage to put a drop without the pipette in her eye, for she blinked incessantly. Why was it that everything she did made him want to kiss her? "The world might seem a bit brighter than usual, as your eyes are letting in more light," he told her. "You're lucky it's cloudy, milady. You came to see me on a good day." She seemed to ruminate about this as he expertly and gently pulled her lower lid down with the tip of his thumb, then placed two drops in with the pipette in his other hand. He quickly repeated the process with her other eye. She pulled her head back and blinked as her eyes teared.

"I'm sorry, Doctor," she mumbled as she reached to rub at her eyes.

He reached out to stop her with a touch at her wrist. "Don't rub." Nick grabbed a cloth from his tray of tools. He dabbed the tears from her cheek, not aware it was what he was going to do until it was too late to stop himself. It was unprofessional, to be sure, something he'd never do with any other patient. But this was Pippa, and everything about her was unique. As his hand cupped her cheek, her gaze met his, and the tip of her pink tongue swept out to wet her lips. She leaned toward him, and Nick started to lean closer to her as well as the impulse to kiss her propelled him forward.

If he hadn't banged his knee against his tool tray, he may have very well pressed his lips to hers, but the clatter and clank of his familiar oculist implements reminded him of where—and *what* he was. And who and what *she* was. He stopped himself from moving closer to her, with reluctance, and then dropped his hand to press the soft cloth into one of her palms. "Dab with this," he told her with a voice hardly above a whisper, because it appeared he couldn't catch his breath. "And don't apologize. Tearing is normal, milady. In about ten or fifteen minutes, your pupils will be dilated, and I can examine them." He sat as far back as he could and finally drew in a full breath.

Pippa stared at him. Her alabaster cheeks were rosy with an adorable flush, one he suspected that he'd put there. Was it possible—could it be possible?—that she desired him as much as he did her? It seemed that could be the case. Nick shivered at the thought.

"What do we do now? Wait?" She tilted her head in a way that spoke of mischief. Perhaps. Curiosity? Inquisitiveness, to be sure.

He swallowed hard. He had a million ideas but didn't dare act on them. Or would he?

Chapter Eleven

To Pippa's surprise, the eye exam was painless. Or was that because Dr. Folsham was so...careful?

She trusted him in a way that she hadn't felt in a long time, certainly since her mother had... The truth was, something deep inside told her that it was safe to put herself in his hands, into his arms, even. Pippa chastised herself for thinking it, but she got goosebumps imagining his broad shoulders and strong arms holding her, keeping her safe.

Yet, his muscular hands and long fingers were gentle. So gentle even that she let him drop the purple solution in, and she wished he touched more than just her lids and forehead.

She gripped her dress tightly under the table, wishing it were his shirt she had the courage to grip like that to pull him close to her. It was an odd idea and not one she'd ever had before. But it was overpowering and enticing besides.

His hair was light brown, like ripe wheat with undertones the color of toasted almonds. The top was a bit too long, falling into youthful curls onto his forehead in such an inviting way that Pippa wanted to comb her fingers through his hair. She'd gulped when he touched her lower lids and put the cold drops of belladonna in them. She knew it was a poison in high doses but trusted that whatever he'd do to her would always feel good. And how good it would feel if his hands lingered on her face again.

Her chest tightened with longing to be close to him.

"Ten minutes you said?"

"Indeed," he answered as he capped the vial and set the pipette aside into a small metal bowl with a clink.

The air hung heavy with unspoken words, as the quiet settled between them like an unwelcome intruder. Pippa wished to know more about the handsome doctor. Their eyes sought refuge in anything but each other's gazes, and the ticking of the clock became painfully audible. Nick cleared his throat and shifted in his seat across from Pippa.

"Have you always wanted to be an oculist?" Pippa asked in an effort to bridge the awkward silence.

"No. I didn't know I'd specialize in the eye until later at university." He hid something, Pippa sensed.

"So, you always wanted to be a doctor?"

"A surgeon, yes." He looked away as if he was trying to turn from something dreadful in his past. For some reason he held back, avoiding sharing with Pippa what or who the reason was that Nick focused his work on the eye.

"You seem to be very good at your work." Pippa wanted to pay him a compliment, and he looked at her again. "Your family must be very proud of you."

Oh no, he cringed. She'd touched on something terrible, but what?

"Teach me how to examine your eyes," Pippa said as she clasped both hands together. Her eyes had stopped tearing by now, but her body throbbed with desire to be close to him.

He batted his eyes at her incredulously. "You. Examine *me?*"

She beamed at him.

He shrugged. "Why not?"

"Really?"

"Sure. I have eyes…"

She clapped excitedly and rose from the stool. "Let me sit there."

He got up, and they switched seats. On his side of the table, was a wooden knob and a drawer. Pippa pulled it open and saw a velvet tray with many lenses in two neat rows. "What do I do with these?"

"The left ones are concave, the right ones convex. You check if any of those complement my lens, and if my vision improves with any of them, you read the number on it. Here, use this one, it might make up for your lens' curvature and give you enough magnification to see into my eyes." He handed her a thick lens. "It would tell you, the refractive index for the eyeglasses I need but I don't because this is also a magnifier."

Pippa tested the heavy lens in her hand and looked through it like a monocle. He burst into a wide smile. Gorgeous. A radiant spectacle illuminating his countenance like a diamond would its setting. Pippa couldn't tear her eyes off him and probably ogled him for a moment too long until he changed his expression to a knowing and much slower pace. His smoldering smile exuded such an irresistible allure and an undercurrent of steamy potential that Pippa felt instantly flushed. "And what's this big one for?" She picked the large sickle-shaped lens that looked like the large piece inside a magnifying glass.

"It's a loupe," he said. He leaned in and reached for Pippa's left hand. "You prop my face up and make me keep still with this hand," he guided her, resting his chin on the flat surface her fingers made. "Then you adjust the light to hit my eye, and then you hold the loupe until you see the optic disc." Nick adjusted the gas lamp on the desk to light up his right eye.

At first, everything looked as if it were underwater and doubled, as if she could just squint just right, it would come into focus. Then she held the lens up to her eye and closed the other. She gasped. The image in the center of the lens was clear, but the rims remained blurry. Still, she could not just see but look *inside him*. Pippa gulped.

"What does it look like?" Pippa whispered, leaning so closely that she could feel the cool air when he inhaled and the heat of his exhalation. He smelled deliciously like buttery vanilla and yet earthy like sandalwood. With the thick and heavy lens in front of her eye, Pippa could see better and even magnified what was small.

"It looks like many paths leading to a bright dot. Like a spider with lots of red legs." He held his eye open, and she leaned in closer. "You may have to tilt the loupe until you see it."

She came even closer until the tip of her nose almost touched his. Then she saw some red lines deep in the back of his eye.

"If you see some blood vessels, follow them to the spot where they grow denser." How did he know? Oh right, he was the doctor. The oh-so-smart and tantalizing oculist who made her heart lurch when she imagined how much training he must have gotten to be able to teach her, the layperson, how to find the nerve of her eye.

"There it is!" Pippa suddenly marveled at the dot at the center of a network of thin red lines. "There's blood circulation."

"It's called vascularity; the vessels nourish the eye." Then he pulled his head back and blinked, brought his right hand up and rubbed his eye. "How did that feel?"

Pippa froze for a moment.

Kiss me. Hold me.

She had the impulse to nestle under him, languid and naked.

She shook it off. Absurd. She'd never seen into a person's eye. If one thought of the eye as the window to the soul, then she'd seen so deeply into him that... "Amazing," she whispered in awe that he'd allowed her to look inside. His eye was tearing a bit. "Did I hurt you?"

"No. How does my eye look?"

"Gorgeous."

A deep, rumbling laughter echoed from his chest, a sound as rich and warm as the color of his eyes. "I meant, is my optic nerve healthy?" He rubbed his eyes again but then looked at her with a sleepy sort of look. His hair was mussed, and Pippa could no longer deny her attraction to him. She wanted to drive her hands through his rich hair, even if it was a bit outgrown and youthfully tousled, complementing the intensity of his smile, adding a layer of warmth and vibrancy. The messier, the better. She wished to be the reason to muss his... oh dear. He'd asked her a question.

"I don't know how to tell."

"Well, the spot where the red lines came together, was it bright and even?"

"Very bright."

"It's the optic disc. From there, nerves transmit the image I see directly through the optic canal, which is an opening in my skull, and then to the brain."

Pippa gasped.

He gave a lop-sided smirk. "It's the same for every human."

"Oh," was all she managed. He was so handsome that her stomach drummed, or was it her heart reaching as deep as her stomach? It was nauseatingly strong and yet so wonderful that she couldn't imagine stopping.

"May I examine your eyes now? It's been more than twelve minutes and your pupils are wide and open." There was something else wide and open. Pippa twitched in her seat.

"Oh yes," Pippa barely exhaled, so mesmerized was she by the handsome doctor in front of her. "Shall I get up and sit—"

"No, don't. This will take a short moment." He reached his palm out again, picked up the loupe, and looked into her eyes.

"Are there many medicines that cause the pupils to grow wide?" Pippa asked while he was close, and she felt his gaze trailing over hers.

"Yes, many medicines and also natural responses."

"Like what?"

He set the loupe aside as if he'd finished. "Shock, fear, extreme happiness." He swallowed and she noticed his Adam's apple bobbing as he leaned back and came into better focus. "Arousal." He held her gaze. And she looked, blinking only a few times. She could have sworn that his pupils were quite large, taking over most of the brown rings of his eyes.

"Am I scaring you?" she asked since his pupils were certainly wide and black. And he hadn't dripped any belladonna in *his* eyes.

"Not at all," he said with a low voice. The message was clear, but he made it even clearer when he leaned back with almost a cocky stare and trailed his eyes over her face, along her neck, and to her chest.

Pippa shivered under his gaze. She should have been alarmed, but it felt delicious. No, she felt delicious, as if she were a delectable pastry that he wanted to eat, and she'd be honored to serve that purpose.

The moment stretched out and Pippa felt the heat rising to her cheeks but then the moment ended.

Then he broke the stare and cleared his throat. "I think you will need eyeglasses." Pippa pursed her lips. "My sister, Wendy, can fit you for a pair of your choice." He got up as if he had somewhere else to be. "It was a pleasure, Lady Pemberton. I'm glad your eyes are so beautiful—ahem, healthy." He shook his head and clutched his hand against his chest as he cleared his throat. Was this voice cracking? "Good day." He left.

Pippa stood agog.

Not because he left but because the throbbing feeling from her heart had settled down low.

And it had grown so strong, she couldn't ignore it.

Chapter Twelve

THE DAY AFTER the earl's surgery, Nick took the carriage to Brunswick House Upon Thames. It was a beautiful estate. Perched majestically on the banks of the river, the Earl of Langley's ancestral home donned an imposing façade whispering tales of aristocratic elegance. The entrance, flanked by towering Corinthian columns, opened into a grand marble hallway. Although it rarely made any sense for an oculist to make house calls, it had gone without saying that Nick would tend to the earl's bandages during his recovery.

But when the earl's butler stood in the doorway, apparently expecting him, Nick felt a pinch of nervousness. "Doctor Folsham, good day," the tall man in livery said without changing his mien.

"Good day, Mr. Sutton. How do you do?"

"I'm afraid it's not about me but my master." The butler led the way into the great hall. Stained glass windows with pointy arched frames adorned the high-walled entrance.

"There you are!" Lady Langley came down the stairs, her sky-blue shawl billowing behind her. "Oh, how good that you are here now."

"Whatever is the matter, my lady?" Nick gripped the doctor's bag he'd brought. Tension built in his body for something was amiss indeed. And he couldn't afford anything but a perfectly smooth recovery for his most influential patient.

The young Lady Langley led the way up the stairs to the earl's private chamber. Already at the top of the stairs, Nick heard the low groaning and moans. The door was open, and he stepped into the enormous bedchamber. To his astonishment, the earl was in bed. Last time, after the same surgery, he was sitting in his armchair by the fire reading the newspaper. This, however, was not good.

A woman in a white bonnet and apron removed a compress from the earl's forehead and wrung it into a small porcelain bowl.

"Thank you, Daisy," Lady Langley said, dismissing the maid.

Nick swallowed. He couldn't say *good morning* or *good day* because it wasn't one. "My lord, I am here." Nick walked around the bed to the side on which the earl lay, his eyes pinched, and his angular features drowned in wrinkles of reddened skin. Lady Langley sat on the edge of the other bed after the maid had shut the door upon her exit.

Nick snapped the clasp of his bag open and took out some clean muslin and some sage oil. Then he rubbed the oil on his hands and wiped them off before touching the earl's reddened forehead.

The earl moaned.

When Nick put a hand on his temple, the man winced. This was not good. His forehead felt hot and the skin under his eyebrow looked stretched and shiny.

"I'm afraid that there is a small infection," Nick said as calmly as he could in spite of the tension he felt pressing against his insides.

"Small?" The earl yelled, pushing the covers off. "I've had a small infection before, Doctor, this is not small."

So much about his streak of a few hundred surgeries and absolutely zero infections.

Nick swallowed. An infection could be benign and pass in a few days. Or it could worsen, and the earl might lose his eye, new lens or not. And if his discomfort became new fodder for gossip among the Ton, he and his friends would soon not have a practice anymore. That was not an option; he had to make this heal.

"What did you do wrong this time?" the earl asked in a vulnerable voice that showed how young he was underneath the worn shell of his body. His voice was boyish, despite his crows' feet and extensive dental work that showed even when he spoke.

Nick cast Lady Langley a look. She was rubbing her palms on her thighs. Her hair was elegantly braided, and her nails were manicured meticulously. She was a beautiful young lady; she'd been called a diamond of the first water and the pick of the season—at least that was Wendy had told Nick when she read *Debrett's*.

"Let's replace this bandage," Nick said and got to work. The earl sat up and Nick could feel his exhale sharply when a spot of the round cotton caught on a flake of scab.

"Darling, Violet. Could you call for some brandy, please?" the earl said in a forced voice.

"Oh, but I couldn't," Nick protested.

"But I could."

"With pleasure," her ladyship said and left the room.

"It's ten o'clock in the morning, are you certain you should drink?"

"I'm not drinking anymore, Dr. Folsham. Haven't since our betrothal was announced. Mr. Sutton puts tea in the decanter every morning."

Nick rinsed the wound and the earl continued to speak. "Mr. Collins gave me a special tea to support... ahem... my virility. There's much pressure on me to produce an heir as soon as possible. But it's been nearly half a year with no signs of... you know."

Nick patted the area dry where he'd placed the stitches. The skin was irritated, but the infection lurked deeper.

"She pays attention, you know? She's not just pretty. When we... you know, she wants candles lit and she knows how to take her pleasure—"

"My lord." Nick tried to stop the flow of information. As an eye surgeon, he didn't need to know all the details of his patient's bedchamber exploits.

"Hear me out, please. So, you know what's at stake."

That chain around his throat grew tighter. He knew what was at stake: the earl's vision and their practice. Alfie, Felix, Andre, and Wendy's future at 87 Harley Street. A bad reputation would cost them their livelihoods and the chance to continue to build the practice they had worked on for so long. Was the earl threatening their existence if his eye didn't heal properly?

"She's not disinclined, Dr. Folsham. But she's not in love. Thus, it makes my work all that much harder."

"It shouldn't feel like work," Nick said without thinking. He shouldn't have said it, he was making matters worse.

"But it is. See, I'm twelve years older than her. In her eyes, I'm a bit of a spare parts storage with the lens replacements in my eyes, the fillings in almost each of my teeth. Do you know that my valet used to be my friend? We'd jest and chat every morning. These days, he works so hard to groom me for the day, I'm afraid the poor man can barely stand after the morning routine."

"You feel as though you are aging?"

"Mm. With as much grace as I can muster, I suppose. How old are you, Dr. Folsham?"

"Twenty-six. Almost twenty-seven."

That made him laugh, followed by a wince because the earl moved his face too much. "You're a spring chicken."

"I'm not a chicken, I'm a surgeon. With plenty of experience—"

"What about experience with women? Do you know what it means to work for the love of a woman?"

That gave Nick pause. He didn't know how to answer, so he did what he knew best and applied the almond oil to the earl's temple, forehead, and eyelid. It was good to apply after surgery to keep the skin moist. Still the beautiful blonde came to mind. Wendy would make her glasses, but she hadn't returned yet and Nick already longed to see her again. Was that work, trying to stifle the feeling that had taken flight in Nick's chest, but he knew he'd have to suppress? Honestly, Nick didn't know what it would take to work for a woman's affection, he'd only ever worked for his career. Could he dare dream of earning Pippa's?

The door opened and his ladyship entered, followed by Mr. Sutton carrying a silver tray with a crystal decanter and two glasses. He set it down on the side table that he'd pulled to the foot of the earl's bed and stopped to survey the small pile of used muslin in the metal bowl that Nick had brought in his medical bag. Then, he left without a word but a grim face like a concerned parent.

"May I pour you some brandy, Dr. Folsham?" Lady Langley offered with the practiced grace of a hostess.

"Just a little," Nick said without making eye contact. He was a bad liar and knew how to avoid his tells. "Lady Langley, may I ask whether you might be able to assist your lordship in applying this ointment every hour?"

The earl's eyes darted to Nick. Nick swallowed hard but remained undeterred.

"It's of utmost importance that the skin around the stitches is kept lubricated. This is merely a moisturizing ointment but I'm afraid that it requires a tender touch to care for this wound. I shall be back tomorrow to check on our patient."

"Dr. Folsham," the earl growled, "this is surely not a task for the Countess of Langley." But his polite verbal opposition didn't impress Nick. He needed the earl to recover and be happily in love, or else all of the treatments would have been in vain. He'd be disgruntled and take his frustration out on him and the others in the practice. Plus, Nick was no novice and was aware that a full patient recovery encompassed the physical and emotional aspects. An earl smitten with his wife and expecting an heir was exactly what would accomplish the goal here.

"It's a job not for the countess, my lord, but it is one for your wife.

Tender care is all your eye needs for a speedy recovery." The earl *hmphed* but Nick feigned ignorance.

As he collected his vials and wrapped the used muslin in a small sack, the earl's good eye bore into him like cannon balls burning to make the lethal hit.

Lady Langley, who'd been watching the exchange agog, suddenly said with a sense of enterprise, "Let me, Doctor." She took the muslin and stuffed it into the bag. "I'll have these laundered and pressed. We have others to use under the bandages." Then she sat down on the side of the bed, just next to the earl, and placed a gentle hand on his cheek to examine the bandage.

The earl jerked his face sideways, blinking with one eye and keeping the recently operated-on one shut. It was a self-protective pose Nick knew all too well. By tomorrow, he would have to relax the muscles and open his eye. It needed the moisture of his tears. Hopefully, the tender touch of his young wife would help him relax.

"Thank you for the brandy, milord." Nick snapped his medical bag shut and picked up one of the small glasses. He downed the amber liquid—tea with lemon—and then hissed as if the alcohol had burned his throat. "I suppose it's never too early in the day for a drop from heaven."

The earl snorted but didn't look at Nick anymore. He was busy submitting to the tender caress of his wife.

Chapter Thirteen

Once she'd returned from her eye examination (but what was so much more) the rest of the rainy day passed uneventfully, and Pippa spent as much time as she could in the orangery deeply in thoughts of the dashing oculist. Even the next morning, she pruned the vines, plucked off yellowed leaves, and pressed some flowers to dry between the pages of Sir Ellington's treatise. But she couldn't focus on any task at hand without thinking of the handsome doctor, and his breath on hers when she'd held the glass lens to his eye. And then there'd been the cocky smile when he'd looked her over from top to bottom. Even though it only existed in her memory now, the intensity of his stare sent a shiver through her every time she thought of it.

Despite the awful loneliness, Pippa had been delighted to come into the orangery this morning. It was just after eight and her father had taken the carriage to his quack, Wife Six was busy with her face massage, and the staff had started their usual busy Monday. Not that the afternoon callers on weekdays were any more pleasant, but the late evening gathering and dances on weekends really did Pippa in.

John Nash, a prominent British architect of the Georgian and Regency eras, had been an acquaintance of Pippa's maternal grandfather. Before he became famous and became one of the royal architects, he left an indelible mark on Silvercrest Manor's landscape. Her mother's favorite design had been commissioned in 1789 and the design and construction of the exquisite orangery had been completed just before Pippa was born. Even though Nash's designs were characterized by grand proportions and a heightened sense of space and light, this orangery had been an experiment to make the building especially airy by setting glass panes into the roof. It was a magnificent continuation of the sky and let Pippa look out at the stars from the comfort of her cherished indoor space. How often had she sunk up against her mother to watch and listen to the rain pattering against the glass while repotting shoots or drying bulbs for the next season.

Even though the orangery inevitably had seasons during which the plants grew or rested for the next growth period, most of the plants it contained defied the hasty rhythm of the outside world. Above all, here, Pippa could shut out the laughter and criticism, the gossip and lies. This was her space and only peace was allowed in here.

How delightful the silence was when Pippa shut the door to her orangery and took in the scent of the plants. The morning mist made the glass panes sparkle in hues of pink and white. As if the plants were exhaling perfume at this hour, the orangery smelled like mulch, fresh leaves, and tropical fruit.

Pippa sighed and watched the raindrops on the glass of the orangery. From her perspective from the inside, each droplet looked like a little circle, aimlessly running down a path until it hit another and formed a larger glob. The pitter-patter of the rain on the glass roof whispered sweet nothings. There was nothing to do for Pippa but hide, waiting for something to hit her and catapult her into motion like the little drops on the other side of the windowpanes.

"Where have you been?" Bea asked when she walked into the orangery and Sir Hoppington jumped into her arms. She cradled him and stroked his fuzzy little back.

"I had an eye exam and was fitted for glasses." Even though that was the truth, it wasn't the friendly nurse with the white apron who'd left an impression with her, but the gorgeous young doctor with hair the color of wheat and eyes the color of roasted chestnuts that occupied her mind.

"I came to feed the bunny," Bea said, but Pippa noticed the same number of apples and carrots as there had been earlier that day. The sifter for the barrel of rainwater Pippa had harvested was full of popping bubbles and showing much movement.

"I see that you checked on the mosquito larvae?" Pippa chuckled.

"Are the round ones the ones that have pupated?" Bea bent over the barrel.

"Yes."

"It's such a dastardly plan, Pippa," Bea said, and leaned on her heels, her hands clasped behind her back. "Only you would think of using insects as weapons to antagonize your enemy. It's quite clever." She giggled. "How long now?"

"They will be able to fly in two or three days now," Pippa said. "All I need to do is hide them in Wife Six's bedroom. The maids are very willing to help, of course."

"Not a minute too soon then." Bea cocked her head to suppress a mischievous smile. "Just in time for her ball."

"Yes." Pippa smiled. She was going to sting Wife Six where it hurt her most, her vanity.

"It's justice considering how many times Wife Six had contributed to your embarrassment," Bea said.

"I'm thinking that putting the bowl under her bed will be the perfect place for them. Hopefully, they'll swarm during the night. In the morning, the maids can shoo them out the windows. Some of them, anyway."

A knock on the glass door sounded then, startling her just as she was feeling for the prickly bulb of the pineapple. She cut herself on one of the sharp palm leaves.

Instinctively, she stuck her finger in her mouth. Then there was another knock and Pippa saw a tall figure behind the glass door. Of course, the raindrops broke the light into tiny rainbows surrounding the gorgeous blond figure behind the glass door.

It was him.

"Let me!" Bea walked to the door and just when her hand touched the handle, she cast Pippa a knowing smile over her shoulder. "He's sweet!" She said it just so that Nick could hear her the moment she opened the door. She gave Nick a once over as she left without making an introduction.

Pippa fumed as Bea left, and lowered her gaze to her plant. *How embarrassing.*

"Ouch!" Pippa cursed under her breath when she examined the cut on her finger.

"You are bleeding." He rushed toward her, setting down his doctor bag and rummaging around. "I have a clean muslin but where are my scissors. Let me see… how much shall I cut?"

"Of what?" Pippa took her finger out of her mouth just for long enough to speak, then stuck it back in.

"The muslin. For the bandage." But he'd stopped rummaging around his bag. Instead, his gaze had affixed to her mouth.

"Take this," Pippa turned and reached for the long knife hooked onto the column behind her.

His eyes grew wide, and he jerked his head back.

"Oh, it's just my mother's machete."

"Your mother's machete. Oh good. I thought it was a sharp weapon."

Pippa stifled a laugh and took her finger out of her mouth. She couldn't see red oozing brightly against her pale skin so the cut must have been small, and the iron taste of blood had subsided. Her finger was fine. "It's for the pineapple—it's ripe. It's not your muslin."

He arched a brow and surveyed the raised bed.

NICK FOUND HER irresistible, yet he couldn't bask in her charm. His career hung in the balance, and a patient's vision was at risk. So, he'd chosen to deliver Pippa's glasses himself.

"I need the machete to cut the pineapple," she said, flipping the rather large knife in her hand as if it were nothing but a ruler. "It's ripe today, I was just about to harvest it."

She pushed the sharp long leaves aside as if they were nothing but blades of grass, careful to touch the flat blades rather than the sharp edges. She moved with such dexterity that Nick was amazed. Most people with a vision deficit like hers would be rather clumsy, but Pippa was so intelligent that she must have sharpened her other senses to make up for the diminished vision.

With her left hand, she grabbed a bulb twice the size of her fist and tilted it. Then, with her right hand, she cut the thick stem off from which it protruded. It was a funny-looking prickly thing, rather fat and shiny, and had a pattern on its surface like a closed-up pinecone.

"Is this a cone from a palm?" Nick asked, intrigued by the fruit of this little spiky plant.

"It's a pineapple."

"Apples don't grow on pines," he said, trying not to sound so ignorant.

"You don't know much about botany, Dr. Folsham, do you?" she said with a smirk, a testament to her intelligence, Nick thought. She was witty and easy to talk to. Come to think of it, he'd never had such a pleasant time speaking to girls besides his sister.

"I'm afraid my studies of human anatomy left me little time for the world of flora."

"There!" She exclaimed when the thick bulb fruit finally broke off. She laid it on the wooden plank on the side and whack! With a clean cut, she removed the green spiky hat from the top.

"It's the perfect fruit, Dr. Folsham. Would you like to try it? I only got one this year, this is it."

It didn't seem right to accept. There could have been others in the house who enjoyed the fruit. After all, he'd never tried it and didn't know what he was missing anyway. "Are you certain you wish to share your only pineapple of the year with me?"

She straightened her back and gave him a quizzical look. "Yes."

It would be rude, then, to reject the offer a second time. "Then it would be my honor." Nick gave a curt bow and his most charming smile.

That determined, she set the widest part of the machete onto the cutting board, then, like a seesaw, pushed it down and with one clean cut, split the pineapple in two.

"I thought the inside would look like an artichoke," he marveled when the bright yellow flesh oozed the rose-and-orange-scented aroma that was quite refreshingly unlike anything else he'd ever smelled before.

"It's not a Cynara and not even a little bit in the genus of thistle-like plants, Dr. Folsham. An artichoke is in the family of *Asteraceae*. They come from the Mediterranean, but pineapples hadn't been brought to Europe until Christopher Columbus discovered them in South America. The pineapple is also called 'ananas' and it's part of the *Bromeliaceae* family."

Nick swallowed. He didn't understand a single word of the Latin she spoke but he was in awe for the intelligent tone that Pippa had assumed, speaking of such complex taxonomy of plants as if it were nothing more than a distinction between a rainy day and a sunny day. It was not unlike how he and his colleagues and sister discussed medicine, he supposed, in discussions peppered with Latin and Greek terminology. After all, botany was just another branch of science—just one he'd never really considered, before this. And to think she'd garnered her knowledge by herself, without a university education, made him admire her even more.

He realized she was waiting for him to speak. He wet his lips with his tongue before saying, "I just thought that it has a rather large stem, like an artichoke and a similar shape."

She raised her eyebrows with interest. "When have you seen artichokes growing?"

"In France. Also, in Italy."

"Fascinating. You have traveled quite far, haven't you?"

Nick shrugged. "Not as far as some of my colleagues."

"Well, let me give a taste of South America then, Dr. Folsham." She made another cut and sliced a wedge of pineapple off. "Try it."

Nick picked the slippery fruit up and brought it to his mouth. It smelled fantastic. Then he opened his mouth to take a bite.

"Stop!" Pippa's hand wrapped around his and pulled the wedge of fragrant fruit away. "You don't eat the skin!"

"Oh," Nick managed to croak as his body hardened as soon as she'd touched his hand. Although the moment was brief and fleeting, he cherished the contact. It had been just like at his office, when he'd examined her eyes. Touching her sent a jolt of power through him, awakening his senses.

"Like this," she said as she lifted the fruit from his fingers and moved it to her mouth. Her pink lips opened, and the tip of her tongue emerged as she bit into the fleshy yellow fruit. Nick swallowed as his mouth suddenly grew dry. Moments later, juice rolled down her wrist as she bit down and slurped at the fruit. His head swam. But then she raised the remaining piece of pineapple back toward his mouth, holding on to the rind. His knees nearly buckled as he saw how her mouth glistened with the sweet-smelling juice of this exotic fruit. He wasn't quite sure how not to stare. Second, he'd usually not bite into a fruit if another person had already taken a bite; Felix would hang him for that.

Yet, he didn't mind in the moment. It was her only pineapple of the year, after all, and he ought to be grateful that she was sharing it with him. Except that wasn't it either.

He gulped.

He wished not for the piece of pineapple on the rind but the drop of its juice on her lips… No. He mustn't even think it. It was wrong. He and she were of two different classes. He needed to—.

And before he could complete the thought, Pippa squeezed the elongated wedge open, holding the edges of the rind together and offering him the yellow flesh. "Here. Try it." Obediently, he opened his mouth to receive the sweet taste of the fibrous pulp. He was surprised at the tang.

He bit the piece off and Pippa let go of the rind. Nick wasn't sure how much time had passed when he noticed that she'd shifted from one leg to the other, picked up the machete and sliced another piece.

"I can't give you more than a third, I promised a piece to my cousin Bea," Pippa said as she laid out another wedge for him.

"I wouldn't dare infringe upon more than you are willing to give."

She gave him a stunned look. "I beg your pardon."

Nick shut his eyes. "My apologies, what it sounds as though I meant is not what that sounded like."

"I wish it were," she mumbled, probably unaware that he'd heard her. But he had.

His heart began to pound even harder. He needed to get away from her as quickly as he could before…*No. Don't even think it.* He cleared his throat and opened his eyes, focusing on a point over her shoulder. "I have something to give you, however." Nick pulled out the leather etui holding her new glasses from his pocket. He opened it and revealed the delicate spectacles. Wendy often made them for him since she'd mastered the craft just as well as he, but not this pair. These were special. "I made these myself and hope they will fit you well."

"I don't expect any glasses to suit me, Dr. Folsham," Pippa said with audible reservation in her voice.

Understandably. She had no idea her world was about to change.

"It's not about that as much as the actual fit. They need to sit just right on the bridge of your nose and behind your ears. The temples of the glasses mustn't press too hard behind your... May I?" He flipped the temples of the glasses open and brought them to her face. She blinked at him shyly and then shut her eyes, trusting him. The exotic scent of the tropical fruit, the shimmering light that had dried the mist on the windows, and the thin, flyaway hairs around her face that Nick brushed behind her ears before he fitted the aluminium-framed round glasses on her added to the allure of the moment.

Seconds stretched into moments of far greater importance than the fleeting fractions of a minute and Nick wished this moment could last forever. If only he could make it so.

Chapter Fourteen

WITH THE HANDSOME doctor's hands adjusting the glasses behind her ear, Pippa forgot all about the rain, the pineapple, and everything else. Goosebumps on her neck were the evidence of the effect Nick's touch had on her skin. She felt his dexterous fingers pushing the itchy, unruly hairs away from her cheeks and then he laid cold pieces of metal on the folds behind her ears. He was close and Pippa could feel his breath brushing against her cheeks, scented with a sweet mix of the pineapple and something else, masculine and tempting. As the warmth of his body curled against her front, notes of citrus and sandalwood and a manly soapy scent enveloped her senses and Pippa thought she could sway on a bed of sensual delight in his presence. His scent pulled her in, and she let out a sigh. With her eyes closed, she was even more attuned to his touch, the gentle but deliberate wiggling of the bridge of the glasses between her eyes.

"What do you think?" he asked, sounding hoarse all of a sudden.

Pippa opened her eyes.

At first, everything was blurred.

She blinked.

Then again.

And suddenly the colors were brighter, the edges of the leaves sharper, the droplets from the drying mist on the windows vivid, with sharp definition of light and shadow. For a moment, it appeared that she stood at the edge of a step, clear above, blurred below, but then the world came alive around her in a way that it hadn't in a long time. She pivoted, taking in the gorgeous hues of emerald green and fuchsia from the orchids. And then, she noticed the phalaenopsis' bent of the branches closer and the dark, waxy leaves further in the back. She bent down to pick a blossom, reveling in the sight of the thin, stingy petals that she hadn't been able to see before. Most of all, she reached for the petals and didn't need to fumble to find them. Everything was where she saw it. Then she noticed her little patch of sprouting Brussels sprouts. Thin white stems with adorable little round leaves, each a set of two, stood tall, as if they had goals to exceed their current height of an inch by sheer willpower.

"Oh no!" Pippa exclaimed when she noticed the bunny wiggling his nose and whiskers as he chewed. "If you eat the sprouts, then you won't have the adult plants to eat later!"

He hopped into the leaves and Pippa chuckled.

"Amazing!" she said, laughing, delighted even though she was barely able to trust her own eyes.

"It was easy, just two prisms," the doctor said.

Pippa straightened and turned to him. What she saw made her freeze.

She'd thought him handsome, a blur of wheat-colored hair and chestnut-brown eyes, a broad-shouldered form with white flashing teeth and pleasantly shaped face with high cheekbones and a firm chin, but…she hadn't seen him quite like *this* before.

Well, to be truthful, the first time in the patisserie, she hadn't seen him at all, and had nearly run him over. The second time, she'd seen him up close in his office. He'd been even harder to see then, mostly a delicious smelling blur with a wonderful deep voice and gentle fingers that had warmed her senses and given her chills all the same.

But now, she could see him—*really* see him—and her stomach flipped about inside her like a hungry butterfly in a fragrant garden.

He was easily the most impressive male specimen she'd ever seen, farsighted or not. Especially now as his handsome features were undeniable, as if emerging from the canvas of a painting. His hair, a captivating shade of dark blond, was styled in a side part with seemingly effortless finesse and the light wave of his hair was even more golden and inviting than before. It caught the light in a way that suggested sunbeams had been woven into each strand, giving it an ethereal quality that Pippa longed to touch.

Meanwhile, his eyes, dark and enigmatic, sparkled in shades of mysterious browns. They shimmered with an intensity that riveted her to the spot, holding her gaze as though whispering untold secrets. She blinked, unable to take her eyes—her *new* eyes, thanks to Nick's skill—off him.

Nick's features brightened as he smiled, and his eyes crinkled slightly at the corners. *How is it possible that he can become even more attractive?* But it was true. He had a smoldering expression that radiated warmth, setting her heart ablaze. The play of his sculpted, firm lips hinted at a man who was charming and approachable, yet now he held himself at a respectable distance.

She didn't like it. He was too far away. Pippa swallowed and stepped closer. His smile brightened, and now she could see the dimples on either side of those lips and the straightness of those perfectly white teeth, gleaming with pristine brilliance. All of him gleamed with pristine brilliance. To see him for the first time was to understand the true meaning of captivation. Like looking into the sun, perhaps. She blinked.

"Are you comfortable?" he asked.

"Too far," she managed, still caught up in the shock of seeing such male perfection in her orangery. Pippa couldn't ignore the feeling of unease as she stared at him from mere inches away. Would she not have asked him to call her Pippa if she'd known how striking he was? The thought lingered in her mind, weaving its tendrils around her thoughts like ivy on a tower from which she feared she'd never escape. She had never been one to seek attention, and the sudden attention from such a striking man left her embarrassed and feeling exposed in a way that she had never experienced before.

Unsure suddenly of what to do with her hands—which wanted to reach to touch him—she reached for a wedge of pineapple.

His attentiveness, his gentle touch to adjust the spectacles—each gesture had felt like a warm embrace, wrapping around her heart, yet she couldn't fathom why he had chosen her out of all the women in London. Was it simply because he saw she needed him and his skills?

Doubt gnawed at the edges of her consciousness, whispering insidious questions that danced like shadows between the foliage. She closed her eyes for comfort for just a second, returning to the familiar world where her other senses were stronger. With one deep inhale of the damp but fragrant air, she allowed some of his scent to make it into her chest, deep down. And when she exhaled, she knew without a doubt that he'd latched on to her heart. And just so, amidst the uncertainty, a tender bud of hope began to unfurl within Pippa's soul. She used all of her courage to cast him a grateful smile. He'd made her see more clearly but, most of all, he'd made her feel more deeply than anyone ever before.

"Too far? Do you need me to…" He brought his hands back to the sides of the lenses and pushed them up. "Better?"

"No." *You are too far away.* Pippa suddenly detested even the air between them.

He frowned. "I cut the lenses myself; they should be just right. And this is as close as they should be to your eyes." He tilted his head as if trying to look through the lenses from her side.

Now, he was even closer. So very close.

Pippa touched the curved metal that pressed against the area just above her ear, as he gathered her hair to inspect the temple piece. The ribbon holding it in place loosened and she could feel it falling off. Her hair began to spill down her back and around her shoulders.

He seemed unaware of it, and remained focused on the glasses, leaning in and examining them without removing them. Pippa felt his delicious breath on her neck. It made all sorts of feelings and tingles to flow through her body in ways she'd never felt before. Pippa moved and her chin touched his cheek.

He stopped.

Then he stepped back, looking at her like a stunned deer. "Milady…"

Pippa lifted the wedge of pineapple to her mouth. She hadn't even realized it was still in her fingers. And she didn't know what else to do in this moment of embarrassment. She'd touched his face with hers. *Oh my!*

She took another bite of pineapple, and, with the tip of her tongue, licked the precious juice from the rind before she dropped the leftover on the wooden board. Nick's gaze followed her movement and the moment stretched. She licked the juice from the corner of her mouth, unable to take her eyes off him. But before she could reach for another wedge of pineapple, he laid his hand on hers. He brushed a stray strand of hair from her shoulder with his other hand. She looked down at his hand as it left her shoulder and then he reached behind her to the back of her head.

When Nick came even closer, her mind raced with questions of what she ought to do because she didn't want to withdraw. She couldn't move. Didn't want to. The closer he was, the more her heart soared.

"Pippa!" Nick whispered with a slight twitch of his brow; his gaze locked with hers. He was begging for permission, but she'd already given in when she licked a droplet of pineapple juice from her lips and focused her gaze on his. And then her breath hitched, as he closed the distance, and his tongue swished gently over her lower lip.

She opened her mouth and gasped, and he pressed his lips onto hers.

A tremor shot through her entire body as he deepened the contact. She melted, her knees unable to support her, and he caught her in his strong arms. She was overwhelmed by the intensity of his touch, the oddly pleasant suction of his mouth, and the fragrant perfection of his scent combined with the precious exotic pineapple aroma that lingered between them. Or was it perhaps just the mingling of their scents in the most amazing of kisses?

Chapter Fifteen

THE NEXT DAY, Nick needed a walk to clear his mind. He'd lost his appetite and didn't want to take Chromius on the usual walk around Marylebone. Nick didn't feel as though he deserved even the fox terrier's affection nor a walk in such a lovely neighborhood.

He'd kissed the daughter of a duke. Nick pinched his eyes shut and stopped walking. His heart dropped to his knees and his feet grew heavy as anchors as he thought of all the ways his transgression could be punished. He was a commoner and had compromised a lady; if anyone of the Ton found out and shared the gossip, the practice would be ruined. Everyone at 87 Harley Street would lose credibility with their patients and business would dwindle while gossip would soar, there was no doubt. And then what would become of Wendy? She'd have no prospects and nobody to look after her besides him. Especially if the word spread that one of the doctors at 87 Harley Street had kissed the daughter of a duke, the Ton would ensure that none of them could ever practice in England again. Felix might return to Vienna and Andre to Florence. For that not to happen, Nick needed a miracle. It would take a flock of cherubs from the Renaissance oil paintings to make Andre forgive Nick for losing control, but Alfie never would. He finally had his apothecary in London and Nick's actions could be the reason he'd lost it all. Nick swallowed the bile rising to his throat; he'd failed them all. For that, he was ashamed.

And yet, he didn't regret the kiss itself. It had been a moment of passion and he shouldn't have let himself steal it from Pippa, but then why did it feel so good? No, "good" wasn't enough of a description. It had been fantastic. If ever there'd been an earth-shattering kiss, *that* was it. When his lips had touched hers, the earth had split open, the clouds had parted, and the heavens had sent a beam of light to the spot in the orangery. She'd sparkled with her beautiful smile and her eyes had held a glimmer of hope that channeled the light not merely through a lens but straight as a beam to his heart. He'd given her spectacles and a new vision, but she'd given him such a bright smile that the light finally returned to his heart, the kind of light he hadn't felt since his parents died, Lance lost his vision, and he'd grown entangled in his responsibilities toward Wendy and the others at the practice. And even though he chastised himself in his mind, his heart longed for another kiss from Pippa.

Chromius pulled at the lead, and Nick resumed a slow walk, absentmindedly following his furry friend, his head hung low.

They walked and walked, until Nick glimpsed the park surrounding the orangery where his fate had been sealed less than a day ago. Or rather, he thought it might be sealed though he wasn't sure exactly how it had been sealed, or what his future held now that he'd crossed the unseen but still so evident line between his class and hers Either way, the aristocratic beauty, the one who was completely off limits, lived nearby.

"Let's go the other way, old boy," Nick told Chromius, but the dog didn't listen.

Nick twirled his hand around the lead some more as Chromius pulled. The little terrier had a way to tense his body until he looked like an arrow. He strained and tugged, coughing as his collar tightened around his neck; suddenly, the lead snapped and Chromius darted off.

"Chromius, no!" Nick shouted as he ran after his dog. "Stop!"

Chromius ignored him and continued running, a piece of the lead dragging on the ground behind him. "Chromius!" Nick wrapped what was left of the leather lead around his hand and ran as fast as he could. Along the path and around the corner, past the bushes. "Chromius! Stop!"

The pebbles of the path creaked, and twigs snapped under his feet. Nick continued to run—until he crashed into a paperboy. "Oomph. I beg your pardon—wait—Chromius!"

As if his furry friend had been stung by a wasp, he continued running off in a straight line, barking at something in the distance. Nick ran as fast as he could, one hand on his hat so it wouldn't blow away in the wind. He didn't mind running, he quite liked it, except not in his wool coat and not while calling after his dog in the park near Pippa's estate where he'd rather remain away, if not that, then at least, unnoticed. But what did they always say? Nick always remembered his Latin from university, not that it would serve for the trouble he'd gotten himself into. *"Recidivus ad locum sceleris,"* he mumbled to himself. *Criminals always return to the scene of their wrongdoing.*

In the eyes of the Ton, Nick wouldn't be more than a petty criminal, transgressing to steal a kiss from a lady of their ranks, and if Chromium didn't stop now, Nick would be caught and tried—or at least judged by everyone in the Ton—for his crime of compromising a duke's daughter. *Oh Pippa, what have you done to me?*

When Nick stopped for a moment, out of breath, he looked up and saw Chromius wagging his tail and jumping up and down near a delicate female figure. Heaving for air, Nick blinked. It was Pippa.

Nick approached them until he was within earshot. His terrier ignored him still. Instead, he expressed joy to see Pippa more openly that Nick would ever dare. By the time he'd reached the two of them, Chromius lay on his back in the grass and Pippa was kneeling and rubbing his belly. He couldn't blame the dog, he'd lie in the grass and let her do anything to him she'd want, too.

"Dr. Folsham!" She looked up and blinked at him, pushing her eyeglasses up the bridge of her sweet little nose. Nick's body tensed at the sight of her in a bright blue dress the color of forget-me-nots with white lace sticking out from her... he shouldn't look, but from his vantage point, Pippa had a breathtaking cleavage. No healthy man of twenty-six would deliberately miss the spectacular view. Fortunately, Chromius chose that moment to roll to his feet and begin sniffing about. Pippa got to her feet, too, and Nick was happy she hadn't caught him staring at her like a green boy. He cleared his throat.

"Lady Pippa, what a delight to see you."

"And you, Dr. Folsham. Even though I saw Chromius first."

"He pulled and broke his lead and I... ahem..." Nick unwrapped the leather strap from his hand. "I've been chasing him. He came here on his own..." Nick didn't admit that his feet had taken him close to the park to begin with; the dog hadn't run to see her on his own. It was Nick's fault they'd been close enough for Chromius to remember he had a friend to visit and snapped the leash to get there.

"You cannot walk him all the way back to Marylebone with a torn lead, Dr. Folsham. Would you like to come back to the orangery with me? I'm sure I have something suitable, a rope or a bit of twine that I'd use to tie up a vine, perhaps—"

"Pippa!" A female voice came from the distance. "*P-iii-paaa!*" A young lady about Pippa's age and wearing a silky green gown walked straight toward them. Nick recognized her as the same woman who'd opened the door to the orangery for him only yesterday. "There you are!" She blinked prettily as she peered at Nick, a flirtatious smile playing on her lips.

If Nick didn't know any better, he'd say that Pippa slumped the moment the other woman reached her side. Although she was about Pippa's age and height, her hair was lighter, and her posture was so straight that it was imposing.

Pippa didn't get up and continued to rub Chromius's ears. Without looking at Nick, she said, "Dr. Folsham, this is Lady Beatrix

Weatherby, my cousin. Bea, this is Dr. Folsham."

When her cousin examined him with such a thorough gaze, Nick wished he could wrap himself in a blanket to prevent her from seeing him. He felt exposed, analyzed, and then it was over. She'd dropped him like a hot bun, as if she'd come to some conclusion that he wasn't permitted to be privy to.

"So, you are the eye doctor," Bea said with her chin raised as her eyes traveled over Chromius and finally sank into Pippa's with a meaningful stare.

Pippa rose but shameless, Chromius stood up on his hind legs and put his head against Pippa's leg, begging her to rub him more. She cast him a warm smile that warmed Nick's heart, then bent sideways letting her hand find the dog's ears again.

"My sincere apologies if Chromius frightened you, Lady Pippa." Nick bowed to her and then to her cousin. "Lady Beatrix, it's a pleasure to have made your acquaintance, but I must be off," Nick said as he clutched his hat to his chest ready to take his leave.

"But the lead, Dr. Folsham. I thought you wanted to come back to the orangery with me," Pippa said. Then she winced as her cousin took a clumsy step—or so it appeared—to stomp on her foot and reached to tug on her arm. Nick knew what she was doing and why, and he couldn't say that he blamed her even though he wished it didn't have to be so. Now, Bea gave him a forced smile that was closer to a grimace.

"Pippa, a word in the orangery?" Bea turned to give Pippa a stern look, one Pippa returned. A secret and wordless conversation had just occurred between the two ladies, but he might as well have been able to hear what was silently being communicated. His visit would be fodder for scandal. No need to remind Nick that he mustn't be found alone with Lady Pippa, the daughter of the Duke of Sussex. He tried to remind himself, but his heart thundered, *Pip-pa, Pip-pa*.

When Pippa shook her head slightly "no," her cousin gasped, but

Pippa remained steadfast.

"I'm sure the doctor has patients to look after, Pippa. He won't wish to join you—" but before she could speak the whole sentence through her clenched teeth, Nick interrupted her.

"I'm afraid I don't have any engagements this afternoon, which is why I thought Chromius would enjoy an extended walk." Nick searched Pippa's eyes for a sign of understanding and hoped she knew how hard this was for him as it was for her. Their hearts yearned for one another, but to allow anything else to happen was foolhardy. It could destroy both of them. "It was a pleasure to see you, Lady Pippa, and nice to make your acquaintance, Lady Beatrix. You know where to find me if you need the spectacles adjusted." Nick spoke to gain time because any second longer in Pippa's presence was worth his weight in gold.

"Wait! But your lead is torn." Her eyes were cast down, but she gave a mischievous smirk at Chromius, intentionally giving her cousin the cold shoulder. She shifted from one leg to the other and then lifted her head to blink at Nick with her mesmerizing eyes, batting her long lashes behind the glass of her spectacles. The world escaped him, and he nearly lost his knees when realization dawned on him. He couldn't leave. Not unless he carried his dog, something he could do. It would save Pippa from unwanted gossip, and it would save his practice as well. But she persevered.

"I have another one, Dr. Folsham. Follow me, please." Pippa gave Chromius a gentle nudge and he followed her. Nick was astonished, for the mutt never walked by his heel as Chromius was doing with Pippa. Even more astonished was Pippa's cousin, for she stood back, agog. Pippa gave her a look over her shoulder, raised her chin as if to say, "he's mine" and then pivoted as if she'd brought home a trophy. Nick's chest burst with pride as he sensed the trophy was him.

Whatever had just occurred between the two ladies, he didn't understand, but it was momentous because Pippa's mood had instantly lifted, and she had a lightness to her stride that made Nick chuckle. Her enthusiasm infectious and captivating, instantly lifted Nick's mood. And she had a plan that he was part of. His heart leapt and they walked over the pebbled path and left it for the grassy area leading to a patch of dense trees. Nick made large strides, but Pippa had lifted her skirts to step over the uneven terrain, Chromius trotting behind.

Whoops!

Her glasses slid off the end her nose.

"Got them!" Nick reached to stop them from falling and he'd touched her in the process. "Oh, I am sorry, it's a habit."

She blinked at him, standing still.

"It's just that, this happens sometimes. You ought to fully push the bridge of the spectacles up your nose." He did it for her and she blinked through the lenses as if she'd just had an epiphany.

"Come with me," she said as she grabbed his hand. She lingered for a moment, hesitating. Did she think he wouldn't come along? Nick interlaced his fingers with hers, willing his chest to stop pounding as if he were a green boy, and let her pull him along.

They reached an old stone wall, and she pulled him out of the park at Cope Castle. He supposed she knew a shortcut.

Nick followed her willingly, with Chromius at their heels.

"Where are we going?" Nick asked when the orangery came into view and behind it, the castle walls. Pippa's home. Nick reminded himself that she was a lady, an aristocrat. She lived in that castle surrounded by a battlement dating back to the Middle Ages, while he lived in a room with an old creaking bed that was probably just as old but not in a good way.

And he was nothing but an oculist. He had to work for his money, hard work for little money, and he could never offer her what she was used to. He mustn't give in to his body and heart's desire.

No. She was precious, he had no place in her life. He had to step aside and let her find a man worthy of her. A duke. Or a prince. Didn't Wendy always say that every girl dreamed of being swept off her feet by a charming prince? No girl wanted a studious oculist, and yet here he was. Intrigued. Aroused. Doomed.

Certainly, he was no prince, but he was unworthy to sweep this gorgeous lady anywhere, so she'd have to do the sweeping—of him, of course. Not that a lady of her station would. But even if she did, or would, he'd have to stop her. For her own good, of course.

She stopped walking under a copse of trees where there was a little pond.

Chromius walked on, and he drank from it.

The wall extended higher here; that and the cover of the trees gave them a sense of isolation with a wall of green on one side and of stone on the other. Even though the bustling London streets were not far off, and Cloverdale House was within view, it was as though they had their own little corner of the world here. Pippa's cousin, London, and seemingly all of the reasons to stay away from each other had been left behind. All that was left was Nick and Pippa, a man and woman with an undeniable attraction.

Pippa pressed her back against the wall. She blinked at Nick and gave him a look just like she had in the orangery.

This was bad. So very bad. But his resolve crumbled as soon as she licked her lips. He was unable to stop himself from reaching for her. And this time, he wouldn't let her wait.

Chapter Sixteen

NOT THIS TIME, Pippa told herself. She wouldn't let Bea outshine her. This wasn't a ball. She wouldn't fall and she wouldn't let another minute pass by without making her intentions known, especially to this man, the one who'd noticed her. Who'd seen her, not as a clumsy goose.

Pippa wanted this one for herself. She'd already tumbled over him in the patisserie, besmeared Nick with whipped cream, and had shared the most tantalizing slice of pineapple with him—better than any seven-course banquet dinner. But beyond that, this time, Pippa had caught the attention of the kindest and most gallant man she'd ever seen—a man who had realized she couldn't see well at all and had brought focus to her world—and she wouldn't let the moment pass by without taking action. He wasn't born into nobility, but his work was noble. Beyond that, Nick was intelligent, not merely educated. Instead of treating her with cold distance, he'd brought her blood to boil with a tender kiss. In the few hours they'd spent together, he'd cured her of her clumsiness with spectacles and awakened her from a sad slumber of loneliness with his kiss. What more was he capable of doing to her?

Pippa decided to find out for herself. Finally, a person gave her, Pippa Pemberton, not Lady Pippa, not the daughter of the Duke of Sussex, a chance. Just her. Coincidence had brought him to her; she'd turn it into fate.

Truth be told, Pippa had recognized Chromius as soon as she'd seen him. The new glasses had some advantages, especially when she could run ahead of her cousin and catch the doctor's runaway dog.

Pippa maintained her stance and leaned against the wall.

"I owe you an apology, Lady Penelope." His speech came stilted, almost with a practiced tone and too distant for Pippa's comfort.

"Pippa. You may call me Pippa. I'm only Lady Penelope for strangers."

"Which is what I should be," he rasped with head low like a man who could barely show his face. "You're far above me, Lady Penelope." He combed one hand through his golden-blond hair and Pippa wished to touch the strands that now stood upright. backlit by the sun. "I mean, Pippa." Frustration seeped into his words, each syllable laced with an unmistakable tinge of exasperation. "I shouldn't call you Pippa, but etiquette demands I acquiesce to your wish I address you so. At the same time, it's against etiquette to be so familiar with you, a lady of the Ton." He looked at her, his conflict showing in his eyes. "Honestly, I don't think I know what to do."

"Oh!" Disappointment conquered the excitement that had given her the courage to pull him into this secluded corner of the gardens. "But you kissed me yesterday."

"I did. But I shouldn't have." His eyes met hers and his expression was devoid of regret. A fire burned within him that nearly made Pippa catch flame, but he seemed to stifle it because of her station. "You are a lady and such a beautiful and intelligent woman." He drew out "beautiful" and "intelligent" before it seemed that his voice failed him, and his eyes fell to her mouth.

Pippa knew she never wanted anything more than she wanted his kiss.

Of course, she also knew that it was forbidden. Like a twisted jest of fate, she wanted him and yet she was the forbidden fruit, an aristocratic daughter with the prospect to inherit more than he could probably imagine and yet it was all of this alleged privilege that stood between them. She'd be sorry for herself if she didn't realize how absurd the situation was, with privilege as an obstacle to happiness. It was the material for a Shakespearean drama.

Neither was the irony of her debacle lost on her. A duke like her father could marry a commoner like Wife Six but Pippa was a woman and needed to marry a titled man… for what exactly? So that the Ton could mock her indefinitely? Or worse, she'd become an old spinster holding out for a titled suitor who'd give her a fraction of the respect and kindness that Nick already had? Well, Father had dwelled on her lack of allure and held her inheritance hostage by not encouraging her to wed. "I disagree."

Nick straightened his back. "I beg your pardon?"

"You very much should have kissed me. I welcomed it. You… ahem…" she cleared her throat, "I did like it very much." She nodded for good measure.

He dropped the leather lead that was still tied around his hand and leaned the same hand against the wall next to Pippa's head. Their eyes locked like flaming arrows shooting at each other, hot blazing fire from Cupid's bow. They must not pursue this attraction for so many reasons.

Pippa couldn't afford to lose her reputation, lest she be the *ruined* clumsy goose.

But *this* felt different. He was so right for her that wishing he were the right one became a reality in her mind.

"You," his voice broke and he cleared his throat again, "you liked it." She nodded. "But it was your first kiss, wasn't it?" She nodded again, holding his gaze with her eyes. "And I'm nothing, just an oculist. You are—" he gave her a once-over worthy of a man in Prinny's entourage—*"everything."* He enunciated every syllable and Pippa had to swallow. Her heart pounded so hard, she nearly felt it in her belly. "Yet I must not have you." Now he just sounded unconvinced.

"Again, I disagree." But before she could get his reaction, a yelp interrupted them as Chromius barked at a squirrel or a bird that rustled in the tree above them and the moment was over.

Nick pushed himself off the wall and put some distance between their bodies as if he sought the exact number of inches required to break the magnetic pull he had on her. Time to change the subject lest Pippa combust from the heat that his closeness spread through her. It didn't take long for her to come up with a new subject to discuss, as Chromius continued to bark.

"How did you get Chromius, Dr. Folsham?"

"I didn't get Chromius as much as he got me," Nick started. He stared at nothing in particular. "It's a long story."

"I'd love to hear it," Pippa said, crossing her arms and pretending to lean leisurely against the wall. In reality, her knees were wobbly from his gaze. Had she just imagined that he was about to kiss her before he pushed himself away?

"We were in our last year at Edinburgh University, and we had to perform a surgery to pass the final licensing exam."

"What does this have to do with Chromius?"

"Well, I needed credit for another cataract surgery and didn't have a patient. Fox terriers are known to suffer both glaucoma and cataracts, so I tried to find one with the issue."

"You specifically looked for a dog who needed an eye surgery to pass your exam?" She didn't know how she felt about that. Experiments on animals were cruel, yet the training a doctor received could often be on an animal rather than a human. And if the animal benefitted from the experiment, then was it wrong?

"It was nearly impossible to find one until I went to a breeder known to drown the runt of the litter. When I got there, Pippa, I have to tell you," he rubbed his thighs with the heels of his palms, "it was such a terrible place. No living creature should ever have the misfortune to be caught in such an environment."

"What happened?"

"Well, it was the day the breeder had caged the litter and sold their mother. Chromius was one of them, limping and holding his paw up."

"What did you do?"

"I paid the man off and took them all with me."

"How many dogs were there?"

"Twenty-eight."

"You bought twenty-eight dogs?"

Nick nodded.

Pippa bit her lower lip. She hadn't misjudged him. He was generous and kind beyond measure. He had a much bigger heart than most aristocrats, even the ones who invested in breeding dogs. They did it for vain reasons, not out of love for the animals.

"Where are they now?"

"I took them with me to university. It was our last week, you know. Most of the other students were married or had jobs in sight. I was able to find homes for them with the students, all future doctors. All of them willing to give a dog a happy, safe home and care."

"What about Chromius?"

"Like I said, he had a limp. He'd been hurt and it didn't take me long to see that he was nearly blind. His cataracts were so bad, his lenses were completely fogged. So, I brought him to the head of the department and requested special leave to conduct my final exam surgery on him."

"You mean, you replaced both of his lenses with glass ones?"

Nick nodded. "As part of the exam, we had to do the calculations of the lenses and it was different for a dog's eye. The head of the faculty of medicine came to personally check my math and watch the surgery."

"How did you get Chromius to hold still?"

"Beer."

"What?" Pippa sputtered a laugh. "You're joking."

They resumed a leisurely pace along the story-high stone wall. Judging from the overgrown grass and weeds, not many people came here. *Good, they were alone.*

Nick shrugged. "You won't believe how still a dog is when you give them beer with some laudanum. He was a bit drunk and fell asleep. By the time I finished, he'd woken up and was thirsty. Besides that, he seemed fine. I took him home for observation. I didn't officially pass the exam until the committee was convinced that the surgery had been a success."

"How could they tell?" Pippa didn't even try to hide the fascination in her voice. Nick was easily the most interesting man she'd ever met, and she knew almost all the members of the Ton who resided in London and a great number of her father's peers.

"Well, a human will tell you a day or two after the surgery if their vision is better. A dog can't tell you, so I had to wait."

"How did you know for sure?"

"His paw had healed by then and he no longer stumbled. It wasn't a matter of his leg after all, it was that he didn't see well."

Pippa pitied the dog. And she couldn't help but draw comparisons to her own situation as "the clumsy goose." "And did you pass?"

"First in the class with special honors. The report I wrote on the dog's refractive index and my calculations were similar to how you'd approach a human with a slight anatomical anomaly." Nick spoke proudly, but his face had reddened. A tall and dashing medical genius who was bashful around her, and shy about accolades; how absolutely delicious.

"What does that mean?"

"It happens quite often, actually, so it's a bit of a misnomer. When a person's curvature of the lens is outside the usual range, it's considered a reason to calculate a way to compensate for it."

"Does it make the surgery more difficult?"

"It's the same procedure, except that the lens must be just right or else the surgery is in vain."

"I see." She didn't really see because she had no idea how a lens could be right and what the connection was between the calculations and the piece of glass. Nor did it matter to her as long as she had his full attention. Speaking with him, even in the secluded back of the gardens, made Pippa happier than she'd ever been at the luxurious balls in the past years. Here, alone with Nick, Pippa felt special.

"I had a patient like that this week. I'm hoping all went well."

"Has it been two days?" That's what he'd said, two days were required to know whether or not the surgery had been successful.

"It has, but there's been some swelling... I shouldn't bore you with this." Nick made motions as if he should leave but she took his hand.

"You're not boring me at all, Dr. Folsham."

"*Nick*. Please call me *Nick*. I don't want to be Dr. Folsham to you."

"Whyever not?"

"Because I don't want you as a patient, Pippa." He did it again, combing his fingers through his hair. And this time, Pippa reached out to brush the strands back. His mien grew serious, but he didn't withdraw.

"As what do you want me?" she asked, stopping to hear his answer.

His demeanor shifted, becoming grave as a look of intensity took over. For a moment, he truly saw her, his eyes delving into the depths of hers with a raw sincerity that took her breath away. Then he got the same expression he'd had at the eye exam and then in the orangery, his eyes black with an appetite Pippa hoped was for her.

A slow exhale escaped him, lightly moving his chest. His Adam's apple bobbed subtly in his throat and a silent internal dialogue seemed to be taking place within him. Pippa decided to end it.

"I wish I had some pineapple but I'm afraid we ate my only one," she confessed.

He swallowed again and came closer, leaning one hand against the wall. Chromius had gone off sniffing for something, probably a squirrel. The world, shouts, and traffic sounds of London fell away, replaced by the symphony of rustling leaves and distant birdsong that filled the air around them.

Pippa held his gaze and tried not to blink.

He murmured, "You don't need fruit to get me to want to kiss you."

"W-what do I need?" She blinked up at him as if he were the sun in the early morning, starting a new day.

He exhaled and hung his head, which brought his face even closer. Pippa could almost feel him now even though they didn't touch. But every bit of her skin was attuned to him, and her heart thundered in her chest in hopeful anticipation of when his lips met hers.

"I'm nothing and you're a lady," he rasped. "I'm not supposed to—"

"Oh, but you are." Pippa pushed her middle off the wall just enough to press the length of her body against his. It was new and strange and absolutely forbidden for a lady of her station to lunge herself at... at... a perfect specimen of manhood, a handsome, chiseled sculpture of a man with a good heart, outstanding dexterity, a respectable profession. Reason lost the debate in her mind, and desire took over. She tilted her head back and offered her mouth.

If Pippa were more brazen or more experienced with men, like Bea, she'd press her lips against his. But she didn't know how. It was done, Pippa knew, but even just speaking of it was fodder for scandal. In this moment, however, she didn't care because she'd only be mocked—or mocked more than ever—by the Ton; being shunned for falling for a commoner wouldn't be better.

But anything with Nick was better than anything the Ton could provide, greater even. Magnificent. Just like his lips on hers. Last time, the sweet nectar of the pineapple had given her a map to follow but now, it was just her heart and the need to taste him.

He was close, his eyes focused on her lips. Less than a blade of grass could fit between them, but he didn't cross the distance.

Pippa licked her lips in anticipation. She wanted him with every fiber of her being. Since she'd first touched him—at the patisserie—and then felt his mouth on hers in the orangery, Pippa knew she was incomplete without him.

She wanted to say something, do something, but she was too scared she'd be the clumsy goose. This was not the moment she wanted to fail. Here, in their solitude, with the dotted shadows of the linden trees adding a dreamy magic to the atmosphere, she cared more about what this man thought of her than the entire English peerage.

She wanted him and hoped that just once in her life, she would get exactly what she wanted.

Chapter Seventeen

UNDERNEATH THE IMPOSING silhouette of the castle wall, Nick found himself entangled in an intoxicating battle with restraint. He was about to lose the struggle not to kiss Pippa.

Her expectant breath was the only sound he cared to hear over the backdrop of rustling leaves and muted city life. His hands journeyed down her arms, a path marked by smooth skin and a shiver of anticipation. She watched his hands trail along her arms and met his touch by pressing against his torso with her middle. He lifted her wrists, pressing them gently against the ancient stones above her head. The gesture elicited an arch from her chest, a silent beckoning. He positioned his body against hers, tentatively bringing his thigh between hers.

She was tall for a woman, slender, with gorgeous long limbs. Perfect for him.

And her response was even more than he'd ever imagined.

She parted her legs and let his thigh come to her hot sex. Even through the layers of fabric shielding them from one another, he felt her throbbing need.

His eyes, in a tempest of desire and doubt, lingered on her face before descending onto her exposed neck. He leaned in. Her breath was a warm contrast against the evening chill as he began a tantalizing exploration. His lips grazed her jawline, each kiss a spark igniting the kindling of their shared passion. He knew he'd risked everything, but it was too late already. If he'd compromised a lady with just a kiss, he'd go as far as she'd welcome him.

The thrill of the forbidden coursed through him, the knowledge that she was a lady and he but a doctor adding a poignant intensity to their stolen moment. Yet, her willing acceptance of his touch, the way her pulse quickened under his lips, spurred him on.

He ventured further, leaving a trail of heated kisses across her décolletage, each filled with the simmering desire threatening to consume him. He paused, savoring the intoxicating scent of her skin, the feel of her heartbeat against his lips.

Time slowed, the anticipation building with every passing second. He lifted his gaze to meet hers, finding the same potent mix of desire and uncertainty reflected in her eyes that he felt deep inside. Yet, in this secluded corner of the park, beyond the watchful eyes at the ancient castle, they were no longer lady and doctor, but two souls caught in the throes of a passion they could no longer deny.

And then, in a moment that was bigger than forever, his lips finally met hers. She opened her mouth to his kiss. It was a gesture of surrender that spoke volumes, bursting with passion and longing that was as inevitable as it was forbidden. It was a silent admission of a desire too powerful to ignore, a flame too bright to be extinguished.

This time, she returned the pressure with her lush pink lips, and Nick responded by slightly opening his mouth for her. For a moment, she hesitated. She was new at this, oh so precious a flower he was not allowed to pick, and yet deep in his heart, Nick knew he'd be worthy of her because no other man would ever cherish her as he did.

With one hand, she pulled his head close, and he kissed the apple of her cheek, then the corner of her mouth, and then she opened up more.

Her other hand cupped his face. Her skin was deliciously soft and smelled of fresh air. His heart pounded in his chest as she pulled him closer, her hand guiding his head to hers. His lips found the soft curve of her cheek, then the tempting corner of her mouth, each kiss a silent plea for more. And when she darted her tongue out, it was as if he had been granted access to a world he never knew existed.

Nick hesitated to reach for her breasts. The sight of her hardened nipples, visible through the thin fabric of her clothing, sent a surge of desire coursing through him. Yet, he could not, would not, cross that line. Not yet.

He grabbed her waist, holding her atop his thigh, and she rubbed her womanly body against him a little.

It was glorious to be the subject of her desire, to serve her in pursuing the friction she needed.

As Nick lost himself in the exquisite contact, a sense of liberation washed over him.

When he gripped her waist, pulling her onto his thigh, she deepened the kiss and pressed her center against him, a subtle admission of how much she wanted him that left him breathless. To be the object of her desire, to cater to her needs, was a privilege he hadn't known he craved.

In that moment, under the leaves glittering in the sunlight and the castle's shadowy silhouette, he realized he could no longer imagine a world without her. She had become the first person who ignited a passion within him so strong that he thought his entire world would shift toward her. From now on, she'd be his first thought in the morning and last in the evening. She'd be his priority. His heart.

This kiss transcended the boundaries of their worlds, a kiss that promised a future filled with shared laughter, whispered secrets, and stolen moments. It was a kiss that would forever be imprinted in his heart as the moment he realized he had found his forever in her.

And with that realization, Nick made a silent vow. A vow to cherish her, to protect her, to love her. She was as essential to him as the air he breathed.

Their kiss, a fusion of longing and forbidden desire, was a symphony that played the most beautiful music he had ever heard. It was a melody he wanted to drown in, over and over again. The sight of her, pressed against him, her chest rising and falling with each shared breath, was a vision he wanted etched into his memory until the end of time.

And then, just as the intensity of their kiss began to wane, she pulled away a little. Her eyes, wide and shimmering under the sunlight, met his. There was a question in them, one he knew he would spend the rest of his life trying to answer.

"Nick," she whispered, her voice barely audible over the rustling leaves. "Do you…?"

But before she could finish, a sudden noise from the park interrupted them. They pulled apart abruptly, their moment of intimacy shattered. Nick turned towards the sound, his heart pounding in his chest.

"P-iiiii-pp-aaaa!"

"Your cousin," Nick whispered as he moved farther away. He turned his head to Chromius and slapped his leg to signal the dog to join him.

"Pippa?" A few twigs cracked. *Her cousin must be close.*

"I have to go," Nick said sadly, fearing it was the last time he'd see her, lest he be seen kissing her by the cousin. If they were caught, his career, his practice—his friends' practice—could be completely ruined. And Wendy…

He cast one last glance at Pippa. She was a little disheveled but her swollen lips betrayed what they'd done and had been doing. Nick gulped. "Are you all right? Can you find your way home safely?"

Pippa nodded and then stepped away from the wall. "Coming, Bea. I'm here!" But as she walked away from Nick and he withdrew into the shadows under the trees, she turned and cast him a smile that was so sweet, he knew he'd fought the battle not to love her and lost. Not because she was a lady, but because he'd fallen, he was at her service, with body, heart, and soul.

Chapter Eighteen

LATER THAT DAY, Bea had apparently decided not to let Pippa out of her sight again. She hadn't mentioned anything in particular, but she knew what she and Nick had done.

"Do I really have to go in?" Pippa crossed her arms in the carriage when they'd stopped in front of the Langley estate.

"Come on, it's a courtesy visit," Bea said as she tucked a few stray curls into her bonnet and exited the cabin when the driver opened the door. "Plus, you promised to join me."

"You promised to keep my secret." Pippa gave her cousin a sharp look.

Bea chuckled. "Who would I tell that you kissed the handsome doctor in the arboretum? It's not as though I could forever blackmail you with this delicious bit of information." *Ah, there it was.* Bea's eyes gleamed with mischief, but Pippa knew she could trust her, no matter how annoying Bea's teasing would be.

"I don't know why I need to extend this brat a courtesy where we've already endured her wedding ceremony and breakfast."

"Because she made her debut with us. After all, she caught an earl and is the Countess of Langley now. Time to congratulate her." On the pavement, Bea pulled her day dress straight. Whyever she felt the need to pluck and pull at herself, Pippa would never understand; there wasn't a fuzz that could look out of place on Bea's perfect features. If she didn't love her cousin so much, Pippa would be green with jealousy. But that emotion was usually reserved for Violet, the newly minted Countess of Langley.

Pippa had the same enthusiasm for tea with Violet at her new home as a cat had to swim. She'd instead do anything else, even dine with her stepmother. Pippa shuddered.

"There, there," Bea said as she pushed Pippa up the Earl of Langley's front steps to the lavishly carved walnut door of his home. It was within walking distance of Pall Mall on a lovely street lined with chestnut trees. The sun twinkled between the trees' crowns as if it didn't mind sharing some of its golden brilliance with the home of such a wench; Pippa marveled that the warmth of the sun's rays hadn't thawed Violet's heart in all of her twenty years of life.

"Fine, I'm here." Pippa straightened her back when Bea knocked.

The butler opened and was friendly enough. His light-gray velvet coat matched the flock wallpaper with its off-white and silvery repeating pattern of a bouquet, probably gardenias, and daisies. Pippa's heart jumped with joy that she could now make out the details of even the tiniest patterns on fabrics, throw pillows, and even embroidered handkerchiefs. No more clumsy goose, thanks to Nick.

"Lady Pemberton and Lady Beatrice Weatherby, the countess will be with you shortly. I will order some tea." The butler left with a polite bow.

Pippa surveyed the room, a good-sized parlor decorated in an old-fashioned style. "Do you think his mother furnished this?"

"I have no other explanation," Bea said with a grimace and pushed her lower lip down as she picked up a tattered throw pillow that was as faded a purple as the settee cushions were worn.

"Ah, Bea and Pippa, good afternoon!" Violet came rushing in through the double doors. "Good to see you."

Pippa's eyes widened at Violet's effusive greeting and the way the normally meticulously coiffed and dressed young woman appeared, her normally artfully arranged hair style lopsided and her dress wrinkled.

"Oh, Pippa! I like your glasses. They suit you. Are they helpful?" Violet normally would have teased Pippa about the spectacles; Pippa was taken aback that Violet didn't. Who was this young woman? She certainly looked like Violet, but her demeanor was so different from what Pippa knew that she frowned. Was Violet playing a practical joke on them again?

But the curiously acting countess gestured to the aged settee as the butler entered with a laden tea tray. "I'm so glad to see you, my dear friends! Sit down, please. Here's the tea!" She smiled broadly.

Pippa pushed the spectacles up on the bridge of her nose, self-conscious, and yet determined to go through life with a clear perspective. She'd expected Violet to be the first to tease her about her new glasses, and yet—she appeared not to notice them. How odd!

Even Bea tipped her head back and raised her brows, watching Violet pour tea into the three cups set on the marble-top coffee table with such concentration, like a thief trying to distract them from her guilty face.

Why did she appear guilty? What was she hiding? Pippa frowned at the tea, trying to see if there was something hiding in its depths.

"You look flushed, dear," Bea said, apparently less concerned with potential pranks and more concerned with Violet's appearance.

Violet remained focused on her gesture of hospitality—which was as odd as the way she was disheveled. "Sugar?" she asked without lifting her gaze from the tray. They responded, and she plopped their requested numbers of cubes into each cup with the silver tongs. Then she picked up the correct saucer and cup and offered it to Pippa. "This one is yours."

Pippa gaped. *Violet,* handing her a cup of tea?

Violet.

She peered into the cup expecting something there—as usual—to surprise her. But there was no frog swimming in the tea, nor did the saucer appear to have a spring that would shoot something out at Pippa. Moreover, the tea was the correct color; it wasn't black with ink, prepared just so to stain her teeth for the next few months. It didn't even have pepper flakes floating on its surface—and she could tell, because she was wearing her new glasses.

It was just a cup of tea, elegantly served to her with her requested two sugar cubes, by Violet, who appeared less elegant than usual. In fact…

"What's the matter with you?" Bea asked, following Violet's movements as she sat and placed her cup and saucer on her lap. Pippa squinted, more out of habit than with a need to focus because her eyes were not fooling her. The back of Violet's dress was *indeed* tucked into her stocking.

"Violet, ahem…" Pippa nodded in the direction of her friend's leg.

Violet followed her gaze with surprise and then reddened. "Oh my!" She pulled the hem of her dress out of the stocking, shaking out the wrinkles before lifting her own cup to sip at her tea. "Ouch! Hot!" With urgency, like a nervous almost-debutante back at their finishing school—which had never been Violet's role—she set the cup and saucer back on the table with a click.

"Have we arrived at an inopportune time?" Bea asked with the finesse of the ever-knowing social butterfly now fluttering about like a clumsy moth. Pippa didn't blame her cousin. She too was bewildered but she could trust her eyes—especially now—Violet was not as she remembered her.

"Last we saw you, you were a bride. How have you fared as the new Countess of Langley?" Of course, her status as Beauty of the Ball meant Bea took the lead in the conversation.

"*Ahem.*" Violet swallowed and surveyed the room as if trying to unsee what had happened here.

"I heard your husband was confined to bed for a few days. Is he unwell?" Pippa had heard the rumors of various surgeries and treatments that the earl had had done before his wedding to Violet. Father had mentioned something about rejuvenating himself and turning back the hands of time to please his young wife. She'd mostly disregarded her father's comments since whenever he spoke, his accounts were laced with nonsense about healing stones, broths of flowers, and putrid powders.

Violet inhaled slowly and closed her eyes for a moment. "He's fine." She spoke with a tremor, but not one caused by tears. Instead, it was as if she tried to suppress a giggle. "Very fine indeed." Her usual porcelain complexion resembled that of a well-cooked lobster.

"Violet Mae Sheffield," Bea said sternly. "What has gotten into you? Are you drinking at three in the afternoon?"

"No." Violet sputtered and then finally burst into those giggles. They didn't stop until she bit her bottom lip. "Much more wicked than that." She beamed but averted her gaze and brushed her collapsing coiffe out of her face. Then she reached to twirl a strand of escaped hair around her finger and looked at the writing desk near the window. "We... I mean, *he*...he's *wonderful*," she started. Then she plopped back in the settee and melted comfortably into the faded cushions with a sigh.

The old Violet, the mean girl Pippa knew so well, had disappeared. No supercilious frowns, no sly remarks came out of this new, disheveled one. She looked blissful. *Tamed.*

What could have changed her? Was it possible that she was...perhaps... "Are you in love?" Pippa spoke before she could stop the words.

Bea's head jerked. "I beg your pardon?" She couldn't hide her shock.

"I'm just wondering—"

"Perhaps I am, Pippa," Violet peered up to the ceiling and tapped her lips with her index finger. "Or I am falling."

"With your husband, I hope," Bea interjected. With all her social graces, one aspect of human nature eluded Bea, for she'd never been loved. Admired, adored, desired, envied—yes—but never loved. And in this moment, Pippa realized that she'd rather be loved by one person than have all the empty admiration of many because all of them together didn't amount to as much as she'd started to feel when she was near Nick. Even at just the thought of his kiss and his hard muscles pressed against her had Pippa fanning herself.

"Is he good to you?" Bea asked.

Pippa kicked her sideways and shook her head.

"What? I'm asking to make sure she's well." Bea shrugged.

"Oh, he's more than good to me," Violet sighed dreamily. Then, her eyes darkened. "He's so good, so *very* good." She practically purred like cat stretching out for a back rub.

"What do you mean?" Bea asked, still with an unbelieving skepticism. Pippa suppressed a smile. "I thought he was in bed recovering from surgery performed soon after your wedding?"

"Oh, he was in bed, yes. He had a little surgery. And then I joined him," Violet said with a sparkle in her eyes that warmed Pippa's heart. Bea, however, looked taken aback as their newly married friend clarified, "I joined him *in bed*."

"After the surgery?" Bea squinted.

"Darling, in bed, yes. The surgery went well; it was a small thing. A lens replacement and the doctor was very, very good. In fact, it was he who gave me the idea."

"To bed your husband?" Pippa jested.

Violet paused for a moment. "In a way, yes."

"What?" Bea and Pippa asked in unison.

"Well, I'll tell you." Violet straightened in the settee and leaned forward as if she would give a juicy account of a scandalous seduction at Almack's. "We hadn't yet… you know…" She drew circles in the air. "And then he was scheduled for the surgery and needed to recover at home. I met the doctor when he came the next day, and Henry needed to have chamomile compresses and lavender ointment. You know, for the inflammation and to soothe the—"

"Inflammation?" Bea asked in disgust.

"Nothing major, I assure you." Violet waved it off as if it had been nothing. "It was gone the next day, but he was so grateful to me for applying the compresses and ointment. And it's been four days since…"

"Since what?"

"Since I've come out of his bedchamber," Violet said with a grin, as if she'd swallowed a whole vanilla birthday cake.

Pippa and Bea remained silent, taking in what Violet said. Bea seemed to hear her words but did not comprehend them. But Pippa had a good idea of what Violet had done for four days.

"I mustn't say anymore. If I tell you what Henry did…and does." Violet blushed again and put both hands on her mouth.

"Do tell," Pippa urged her, ignoring her shell-shocked cousin clutching the empty cup of tea as if it were her last stronghold. "I thought he was a little…how can I put it… Experienced? When I saw him at your wedding, he looked like he was at least a decade your senior." She was certain that some of the old Violet must still have been in there and could be cracked with a provocative remark.

"He's not old, Pippa. Please! He's two and thirty."

"That's twelve years older than you, Violet," Bea said.

"All right, I will admit it. He's a bit more mature than I. But I am learning and catching up now." Violet spoke like a patroness of Almack's and folded her hands primly in her lap.

"Catching up on …?" Pippa nudged her further.

"Experience," Violet said, reddening so much that it looked like her dark hair grew out of a cherry rather than her usually pale head.

"Tell me everything." Pippa leaned in.

"I mustn't say what he's done to me, Pippa. Not to you." Violet shook her head. "It's not appropriate."

"Oh please, Violet. You've never been proper. Don't be now. Do tell!" Pippa begged.

"Tell me then," Bea joined in, slightly flushed herself.

Violet looked over her shoulder and then got up to shut the door. She stood then, with one hand crossed behind her back and the other still on one of the door handles. And then she began to whisper, excitement in her tone, of provocative and incredible things. Acts she and her husband and done.

Pippa's insides warmed as she imagined what Violet told her. Like three schoolgirls all those years ago, they huddled together, the two of them hanging on every word Violet whispered. "…and when he kisses me, not on my mouth, you see… he kisses me and uses his hands somehow to make me scream with pleasure." Violet combed her fingers through her hair as if to hold on to her wits. The rest of her coiffe spilled from its pins, falling over her shoulders like a cape. "He's so big and strong."

"But I've heard the rumors of the bad habits. His physique…" Bea's question hung in the air.

Violet shook her head. "I know. I think it's all true. But he's of good health now, well and strong and big especially…well, let me tell you about it." Minutes passed. Perhaps hours, for it had grown dark outside by the time Violet began to run out of things to share. They had eventually moved away from the doors to sit down once more, finishing the tea and hurriedly sending the maid away when she came to ask if they wanted more.

Finally, Violet flopped back against the settee and smiled up at the ceiling. "In short, my husband makes me feel what I've never known my body could…especially when he puts his face down there, and when he touches my breasts and—"

"Stop!" Bea waved her hands in the air. "I can't hear anymore! It's too scandalous!"

"Listen to me," Violet said as she sat up to grab Bea's hands. "It's not what they taught us at school. Nobody ever told me that I was capable of this, Bea. Or of what he could do. But especially, they never told us—it's not bad at all. It's wonderful!" She clasped her hands together and appeared, somehow, to glow.

Pippa had an inkling of how she felt because she was fairly sure she'd glowed after Nick's kiss. But would she glow after…if…? "Is that why you came in such a state when we arrived?" she asked.

"Oh that… I was dressed already… *ahem*…well, *dressing* when he found me at my vanity table."

"And?"

"And he put me on it to kiss me again."

"On the table? Why?" Bea's voice rose.

"To lay me on it and gain access under my petticoat."

Bea tore her hands away from Violet's grasp and covered her ears. "I don't want to hear it; it's too wicked." She squeezed her eyes shut and lowered her head, clutching her ears shut. "*La, la, la, la… Bobby Shafto's gone to sea, Silver buckles on his knee; He'll come back and marry me, Bonny Bobby Shafto.*"

Pippa looked at her in amazement. How could the Beauty of the Ball recite nursery rhymes instead of listening to the bride's juicy tales of seduction?

Violet turned away from Bea and looked at Pippa. "I'm not mad, you must know."

Pippa gave her what she knew was a warm smile, one that she'd never expected Violet would receive from her as deservingly as she did this afternoon. "I'm happy for you, Violet."

"You are?" Violet appeared stunned. "Really?"

"Why does that surprise you?"

"B-because I was always so cruel to you, Pippa. And I'm so sorry for that. I was an immature wretch."

"And now, you're not?"

"I hope my husband will teach me to grow up." Somehow, when

Violet said that it sounded sinfully wicked.

"I hope so, too, Violet. And I truly am happy for you. By the sound of it, the earl has just the right amount of experience to teach you…"

There was a click, and then a dark, masculine voice pierced the air. "Ladies." The three of them turned to see that the white double doors had opened, and a tall, attractive man in beige breeches and a tightly fitting blue coat with golden lapels stood at the door. The earl!

He was a striking figure; his hair, a soft hue of blond that glittered in the ambient light, was neatly combed back, revealing a forehead that hinted at his wisdom and experience. His eyes, a charming shade of blue, sparkled with mischief and warmth, their light-hearted twinkle softening his otherwise stern features. His smile was rakish yet inviting, a disarming combination that could undoubtedly intrigue any lady in the room. But there was only one lady he focused that smile on, and she was blushing and melting into her seat on the settee.

"My lord." Pippa rose from her seat and curtsied. "We were just about to leave."

Bea dropped her hands from her ears and joined Pippa. Her face was bright red, and she appeared to be looking everywhere in the room but at the earl. In fact, if her eyes hadn't been firmly ensconced in her skull, Pippa was sure they'd be bouncing around the room. "My lord. We've overstayed our welcome."

"Not at all, Bea. I hope you shall both visit us again soon," Violet said with a newfound friendliness and a warmth in her voice that Pippa hadn't ever heard there before. She didn't act coy or haughty at all. Instead, standing next to the earl, Violet had an air of serenity and happiness that Pippa had never seen in her. Not even when she was victorious in the most elaborate of schemes or when she had been the one to find and spread the meanest, most salacious gossip.

Violet was changed. And this dashing man in the blue coat was responsible. He gave his wife a warm look, one kinder than any Pippa suspected Violet had ever received.

Indeed, a moment unfolded between Violet and her husband when their gazes met. His face brightened. He was her elder, and looked like a man who'd lived, suffered, and conquered. But when Violet's eyes locked with his, Pippa couldn't help but notice a boyish gleam in his gaze. At that moment, he wasn't an earl, but a man in love with a woman.

Pippa warmed to him, for she'd seen that look before. Nick had looked at her like that just yesterday. She'd received a boyish sparkle and a dark, hungry look that suddenly made her insides twirl like a fairy on a frozen lake.

The earl and his countess accompanied Pippa and her cousin to the front door, where he paused and gave her an inquisitive look. "Your eyeglasses are quite fetching, Lady Penelope."

"Thank you, my lord. They are rather new." Pippa gave Violet a nervous look, fearing the old Violet would lash out if Pippa received a compliment from her husband. "The nurse who made them for me, Miss Folsham, was very kind, and I feel rather lucky to have them now." Pippa felt the need to explain herself.

"Folsham, you said?" Violet said brightly. "That's the name of your oculist, Henry." She looked at her husband with brilliantly sparkling eyes.

"It is indeed." He wrapped his arm around Violet as if they were speaking about an old friend.

Pippa swallowed hard.

"Are you acquainted with Dr. Nick Folsham, then?" the earl asked.

"Indeed, my lord." Pippa was eager to leave lest she blush and give away just how well acquainted she was.

Chapter Nineteen

LATER THAT EVENING after Nick had kissed the aristocratic beauty in the arboretum, he still couldn't get his racing heart to rest. He tossed and turned in bed but couldn't get the image of her pretty pink and swollen lips out of his mind.

Or the reaction of his own body.

When he did finally fall into a fitful sleep, it wasn't restful. Instead, it was full of Pippa, and they did more than just kiss. He'd awakened, bathed in sweat. He pulled his sleep shirt off and tossed it in the corner of the room. The lights from the street had been unlit; it must have been after five in the morning. Not a sound besides the rustling of his covers was audible. The whole house was silent. He had to get some more sleep. If he didn't get enough rest, he wouldn't be able to concentrate on his work in the morning.

Nick pulled the covers over his ears and pressed his face into his pillow. Not that the pressure from the fluffy feather bunch could force him to sleep, but the image from his dream couldn't be erased.

He groaned.

Every time he closed his eyes, he saw her in his dream, and his mind came up with a new variation of what he'd do to her next. Not that he ever would. Or could.

Well, he had.

But not really.

Definitely not as he had in his dream. He opened his eyes and blinked. If only...but he couldn't. Nick closed his eyes again and there she was. In this image, Pippa had just taken a bite of the pineapple, and the juice had spilled down her lips to her chin. Nick wrapped his hand around the back of her head and pulled her in, licking the sweet nectar off, kissing the juice away until she dropped her head backward and granted him access to her perky little breasts.

Nick pulled the covers tightly on his head to make sure the wicked images from his mind couldn't fly out into the world. He mustn't think it. He mustn't imagine it.

And yet, the idea of nudging her breasts, one and then the other out of one of her little, thin silk dresses and taking them, each in turn, in his mouth made his body hard as a plank of wood. He wasn't comfortable in the big bed, and his erection throbbed with the need to... no. *No!*

Pippa Pemberton, Lady Philippa Pemberton, was a well-born girl who was off limits.

But she was so beautiful.

Her eyes were marbled with hues of blues that Nick had never seen in nature.

Her hair was softer than unspun mulberry silk.

And her lush lips had been so hot when he felt them swell under his kiss.

She'd welcomed his tongue, and he could not help but return to the image in his dream: the moonlit greenhouse and nothing but the sound of their moans as he kissed her breasts. Glistening with the sweat of their exploration and the tingle of her skin on his, Nick returned to the land of his imagination. There, and only there, Nick could allow himself to lay the gorgeous beauty down on his coat, generously spread out on the table to cushion her as he climbed over her. He'd slowly but deliberately take each of her swollen nipples in his mouth, like berries he couldn't resist.

He'd kissed her breasts as he peeled the rest of the clothes off her body. She'd moaned his name and wrapped her long, lithe legs around him, and suddenly—it was such a good dream—Nick was naked atop her. He'd propped himself up on his elbows on the sides of her head and looked into her beautiful eyes as he pushed himself into her. Engulfed in her heat and wetness, deeper and deeper, he sank into her and dropped his mouth back onto hers. He felt her tongue in his mouth, which he opened wide as he started to—

"Nick!" Someone called him. "Nick!"

The dream was over, but Nick was still in a daze. The morning light assaulted his tired eyes, and his head spun with the forbidden passion he'd imagined all night.

"Nick!" Wendy's voice resonated through the hall. She knocked on his door and then burst in. "I've been calling you—"

He jumped out of bed and rubbed his eyes. She was his little sister, of course, but he didn't want to tell her what he'd done lest she worry about their future and the consequences of his transgression.

"What happened here?" Wendy asked as she picked up his sleep shirt from the floor and eyed his covers in disarray. "Did you wrestle a bear in this bed?"

"A bear? No. A demon, yes. I couldn't sleep," he grumbled.

"Well, you have a patient waiting for you downstairs," Wendy said as she tossed his shirt in the wicker basket for the laundress to wash.

At first, Nick's impulse was to dress and hurry to his exam room, but then he realized there shouldn't be anyone on his schedule. "It's Saturday." He walked to his nightstand and picked up his pocket watch. "And…it's ten past seven in the morning!"

"Yes, that's why I came to fetch you. It seems necessary for you to attend to this patient right away." She smiled with an amused gleam in her eyes before she left the room. Sure, it could be funny to her—she didn't toss and turn in frustration all night. He quickly dressed and stormed to the shared dressing room on the first floor, where Alfie was shaving his face over the wash bowl.

"Hey!" Alfie protested when Nick pushed him out of the way brushed his teeth, and stormed downstairs.

A patient had been waiting for him indeed.

He urgently needed to tend to this one.

But it wasn't the emergency Wendy made it out to be.

WHEN NICK WALKED into his office, buttoning the last button of his clean shirt, he was still thinking about the dream he'd had last night. It was unlike him to be so taken by a girl. In all his life, he'd been able to put his work first and focus on the tasks at hand, his studies, his apprenticeships, complicated cases, and calculations. But this week, he couldn't recognize himself. He'd fallen over a girl and smashed a cream cake on her with custard and all. Then he'd walked across Town to bring her home safely, the cream still on his coat. She'd shown up to his office and he'd examined her eyes. And then he'd delivered the glasses she'd needed in person.

Nick shook his head. He'd never hand delivered glasses before; he wasn't in the habit of making house calls for such trivial matters. Especially not the kind in an orangery filled with exotic plants in the middle of London where he'd had a fantastic kiss. And then an even better one the next day outside of said estate, one where he didn't belong.

He didn't belong with the beautiful duke's daughter and yet, nothing could stop him from thinking of Pippa since all of this had happened.

Except that there was one person that could get him to stop thinking about her and speaking to her instead. The sight of his treatment room almost knocked him out of his loosely strapped boots.

"L—Lady Pemberton," Nick stuttered. Hadn't Wendy said a patient... oh, Wendy couldn't possibly know... but why did his little sister send him downstairs so urgently? Could she have deduced what he couldn't even understand himself?

"Dr. Folsham, I bid you a good morning." Pippa stood primly in a beautiful dress, her hands in a muff, and a thin pelisse hanging over her arm. Her reticule was the same color as her bonnet, and she looked refreshed, clean, and... Nick stepped a little closer... she smelled so good.

He gave himself a mental slap in the face and took a deep breath to steady himself. His body was still tense from the night. Hard and tense.

"Is something amiss, Lady Pemberton?" Nick glanced at the door and could have sworn he'd seen Wendy's silhouette rush by. A floorboard creaked.

"Dr. Folsham," Pippa started.

"Nick."

She glanced toward the door. "Nick," she said more quietly, with a smile building on her face. Her cheeks grew adorably rosy. Nick's breeches were too tight to hide her effect on him, and he walked around to his chair to hide behind the wooden backrest.

"You said I should visit you if I have any concerns about my vision."

"What is the matter with your vision?" Erection forgotten, Nick rushed to her, put his index finger under her chin, and nudged her face upward so that he could look into her eyes.

She met his gaze, and her pupils widened. A lot.

She was happy to see him.

And then she licked her lips, and her gaze fell to his mouth.

Nick swallowed. "What's wrong, Pippa?"

"You said that I could—"

"Of course, you can. What's with your eyes? They look very good to me."

"They haven't seen... *ahem*... *I* haven't seen you, and so..." She dropped her gaze, but Nick still had his index finger on her chin. He cupped her cheek gingerly and smiled. Oh no, after such a night, he didn't have the energy to suppress the glee bubbling within him. He didn't even care if Wendy heard any of this. She'd find out sooner or later.

Pippa had clumsily asked to see him.

At seven in the morning on a Saturday.

That couldn't have been a coincidence; she knew he had no patients.

"Are you hungry?"

She licked her lips and nodded, her eyes on his mouth.

A rustle outside. *Wendy*. His curious little sister was too nosy to spend the morning with Pippa here.

"I mean, have you had breakfast yet?" Nick asked, hinting toward the door.

Pippa immediately stepped back and brushed a nonexistent strand of hair behind her ear. "Not yet. Cousin Bea is visiting the Countess of Langley, and I snuck away."

"Without a chaperone?" Nick turned and looked over his shoulder. Wendy was behind the door; he could see her shadow. "Shall I call my sister to join us?" He spoke loudly enough for Wendy to hear, not that she'd miss a word anyhow since she was busying herself with something just beyond the walls to Nick's treatment room. He could hear her.

Pippa shook her head.

All right, she wanted to be alone with him. That suited him better. "Would you care to join me for a pastry, perhaps?" Nick asked, again loudly enough for the rustling outside his door to pause.

"Yes, please," Pippa said, smiling at him. She'd caught on.

⟫⟫⟫⋈⟪⟪⟪

Minutes later, Nick offered Pippa his arm, and she placed her delicate hand on the crook of his elbow. He shuddered with pleasure and pinched his buttocks together, hoping to give the raging erection in his breeches a little more room to breathe. This was agony, pure torture. And yet, he was so glad to have the blonde beauty on his arm that he didn't care.

Pippa stood tall and slender, surprising Nick with her choice of pelisse. As she fastened it, the garment elegantly outlined the curves of her figure. He couldn't help but admire her beauty; she was just the right height for him, tall enough to meet his gaze yet slightly shorter, allowing for effortless moments when he leaned in to kiss her—if he dared.

Nick tensed his arm to ensure she had a good grip.

And she did the most adorable thing and squeezed him back.

"Where are you taking me?" Pippa broke the silence.

"Our French *patisserie* is just around the corner. I have a standing order of madeleines."

"Oh, how wonderful," she said, but her voice drooped.

"Why does this disappoint you?"

"Oh, it doesn't."

"Pippa," Nick halted. "Tell me."

She moved her eyes, shook her head, and finally raised her brows as if she had had a whole conversation with herself. "I can't say."

"I promise to keep your secrets; I'm a doctor."

That made her eyes smile, but it didn't quite reach her mouth. She tried to fight it with little success as her lips grew pointy and curled into a smile. "Well, madeleines for breakfast go by too quickly. I was hoping to spend more time with you."

"I would like that very much," Nick said with the charm he thought he'd entirely lost around this beauty, for up until now he'd behaved like an overcome green boy in her presence.

Arm in arm, they walked part way down the street but when they turned the corner toward the practice, Pippa stopped. He didn't want the time with her to end but didn't dare suggest turning the other direction for a stroll in the park.

"Let's go somewhere else."

"Where?" Nick hoped she wouldn't suggest returning to 87 Harley Street because he didn't want to be there. He wanted to be somewhere far away, just with the beauty who had just let go of his arm. He immediately missed her touch.

"Could you hire a hack?" she asked.

Said and done.

"Where are you taking me?" Nick asked when Pippa handed the driver a small card and a few shillings.

"Only about an hour outside of Town."

"What? Where?" Excitement bubbled within him, but Nick thought he should at least act coy and feign a modicum of concern for propriety.

"To a little house in the country. It's not far." Pippa cringed when she said that.

"You're a bad liar, aren't you?" Nick chuckled.

With an enchanting twitch, her nose crumpled. "I suppose so."

"I like that about you quite a bit." Nick leaned back and folded his hands behind his head. "So, if I'm going to be in this carriage for a while, I'll make myself comfortable."

"Are you not upset that I am abducting you?" Pippa asked cheekily once the carriage rolled down the smooth streets in Marylebone and headed to the city's outskirts.

Nick shrugged.

"You are?" Alarm pierced her voice.

He gave her a lazy smile, stretched his legs, and crossed his feet from the opposite bench, where he was seated. "Do I look worried to you?"

She inclined her head and surveyed him from across the little cabin. His feet nearly touched her thighs, but he was careful not to make contact lest it be unwelcome.

On second thought, she was ogling him quite intensely from the three-feet distance between them. "You look very nice like this."

He was so happy to be alone with her.

"What do you mean?" Nick tried to respond with nonchalance, but his heart made a flip. He wasn't in his usual attire since he'd expected to find an emergency patient in his office. He'd only pulled his woolen coat over the plain white shirt and wore simple beige breeches and brown boots.

"You don't look like a doctor today."

"I'm always a doctor."

"Yes, I know. But you look like a boy." It would have been an insult from anyone else, but not how Pippa said it. Admiration and something else that Nick didn't dare consider desire colored her voice. Not yet.

"I'm a boy. A man, actually. And you are a lady."

"I'm a woman," she corrected him.

He straightened and sat up and squinted at her. "I don't think you are yet."

Alarm made her eyes grow wide.

An uncomfortable pause followed.

"You are a man, though, so you have been with other women before?" Pippa asked shyly, wringing her hands.

"I am. I have."

"I thought so." She turned to look out the window. They'd left London behind and were on a cobblestone road heading past some fields. But Nick didn't care for the green hills outside, nor the air that cleared of London's soot. He hoped for a different kind of clarity.

"Is there something you wish to ask me, Pippa?"

She swallowed. "Yes, indeed."

Chapter Twenty

THE CARRIAGE CLATTERED along the country road and Pippa knew they'd make good time on the way to her country house. Looking at the specimen of manhood stretched out in all his long and lean glory, with his muscular arms crossed behind his head and his hair mussed from what must have been a night without much rest, had Pippa all heated. She rather enjoyed the view from the bench across from his.

Still, Pippa couldn't stop thinking about Violet's account. Most of it was scandalous, even if what she had described occurred with her husband. And yet, Violet had said he was experienced and teaching her to grow up. In Pippa's case, engaging in anything remotely as wicked as what Violet did would ruin her. But she was doing that herself right now, wasn't she? Taking a day's excursion out of Town with a bachelor unchaperoned wasn't being done in consideration of her reputation.

And then again, what mattered to her more?

After years of being laughed at, ridiculed, and shunned at social gatherings, was the alleged fragility of her reputation worth considering? Wasn't it merely an abstract idea implemented to keep girls like her on the shelf and away from romance?

What Violet had spoken about was a passion that Pippa had only ever read about in romance novels. And yet, it was real. She could see it in Violet's change, the flush of her face, the wild sparkle in her eyes. Love and passion must be too wonderful to forego. Pippa wasn't going to squander the chance.

And it was too late now; she had him in the carriage and was on the way to Silvercroft Manor.

"Pippa, if you'd like to ask me something, do so," Nick said.

"Have I disrupted your Saturday plans?"

"That's not what you were going to ask me, was it?" He leaned back, crossed his arms over his chest, and eyed her curiously.

"No." Pippa swallowed. How was it possible that the way he sat and looked at her made her belly twitch and her heart skip a few beats? "What were you going to do today had I not interrupted?"

"My sister and I were supposed to order my birthday cake."

"When is your birthday?" Pippa felt her eyes widen with surprise.

"Tomorrow."

"Your birthday is tomorrow?" Pippa asked in shock.

"Yes, this Sunday."

"I didn't think to ask. I'm so sorry." She turned and knocked on the roof to get the driver's attention, signaling him that he could leave. As the carriage made its way down the path, they watched. "I interfered with your birthday plans. Oh, I'm so sorry."

But Nick hopped over to her bench and took her hand. Then he interlaced his fingers with hers. "There's nowhere I'd rather be on my birthday than with you, wherever you'll take me."

He seemed to speak the truth, for his sincere boyish gaze made him look mischievous and yet vulnerable at once.

Pippa slumped.

No, she melted.

Looking down at his large but soft hands, muscular with a few veins surfacing, what else could she do? His fingers were longer than hers, but the way he spread her fingers and fit his palm against hers was most pleasing. He brought his other hand over and laid it on top.

A SIGHT TO BEHOLD

"Why are you so concerned about my plans?"

"Because of something my nemesis said."

"Your nemesis? You have enemies?"

"Many." She immediately regretted speaking the truth, for he might shy away from a girl with as many enemies as she had.

"I don't believe it."

"Nobody likes me very much. Sometimes, I don't even think my father does. Bea does like me. Most of the time, it's just the two of us."

"Your father doesn't... I cannot imagine—"

"Oh, he hates me. He says I'm his clumsy goose, and he won't ever be rid of me."

Nick's head jerked back. "He calls you that?" Pippa nodded and frowned. She wished she hadn't told him, but speaking with him was easy. "Why?" Nick sounded puzzled.

"Because I'm too tall for most eligible bachelors or too chatty or clumsy. So, he's stuck with me, the clumsy goose. And if he's stuck with me, he can't get my money."

Nick blinked a few times. "I don't understand."

Pooh, she shouldn't have said any of it. She was well known among the Ton for her potential to inherit and still, no eligible bachelor with a title had offered for her. Thus, her father profited handsomely from being the trustee for her grandfather's will, or a part of it at least. Pippa knew no way out and feared that Bea would marry one day, and that she'd be all alone, unable to experience love, or benefit from the fortune her grandfather had left in her name despite the condition of marriage.

"First of all, you're not too tall. You're the exact perfect height for me to kiss you." He gave her a peck on the tip of her nose and then waited. Heat rose to her cheeks.

Nick was different, he didn't care about the Ton's opinion or her reputation. He saw her as a person. He smiled. "And there are a few things men like to do with long slender legs that I mustn't say aloud."

Pippa looked away bashfully but didn't manage not to smile back at his playful grin. *Had he imagined her legs?* "You're not too chatty either. When you speak, you share your feelings and thoughts—all of which I find rather brilliant. You're stunningly beautiful, Pippa. And you're not clumsy, not with glasses now, are you?"

She shook her head, her face burning from his compliments.

"Good. Then your father is wrong." Nick paused and swallowed. She saw his Adam's apple bobbing and he seemed to have lost his humor for a second. "Will he think that I'm abducting his daughter? It may not be so healthy for me to get in the line of fire for a peer of the Realm." Nick looked down at their intertwined hands.

"He wouldn't notice if I were gone a few days."

"Days?" Nick asked, alarmed at first, but then a mischievous smile washed over him before it melted away in the heat of their clandestine and forbidden escape from Town.

"I wanted you for myself," Pippa admitted. "But your sister will notice."

"Wendy notices everything, Pippa. I've never been able to hide much from her." His mien fell and he looked out the window, avoiding Pippa's gaze.

"Do you wish for me to take you back to your sister so you can order the cake?"

"No, no. It's not that." He forced a smile, but Pippa didn't believe the gesture.

"Would she disapprove of me?" Pippa bit her tongue when she'd asked the question. Of course, she would. *Stupid question.* Everybody disapproved of the clumsy goose.

"Wendy is naturally curious. So much that she snuck away when my parents took the carriage to the market one day. My father was a carpenter and was on his way to offer his handiwork for sale." Nick's eyes searched Pippa's as if he expected her to be appalled by a carpenter's son. But she only asked another question.

"Where were you?"

"I had started an apprenticeship after my first term of university. I went to work with the local physician."

"You studied *and* worked?"

He shrugged. "Yes, the books, tuition, instruments… it was too expensive for my parents, and I didn't want to use any of Wendy's dowry. She was only fourteen then."

"It's laudable that you worked so hard to study for such a noble profession."

"If I hadn't chosen such an expensive course of study, my father wouldn't have had to try to sell more than he had in his shop. If—" Nick heaved for air—"I've never told anyone about this Pippa. Let's discuss something else. Where are we going?"

"Please tell me. Don't you trust me?"

Now his eyes met hers. At the lower rim she could see some tears welling up. He wasn't crying but his emotions were evident. "I trust you with my life. If I didn't, I wouldn't be here with you. I wouldn't risk being seen in a compromising position with the daughter of a duke. I could lose my business and so could Felix, Andre, Wendy, and Alfie."

Pippa felt terrible. In all of her selfishness to seize a kiss from the handsome doctor, she'd toyed with his life. He was right. One word from her to accuse him, or any evidence of their liaison, and Nick could lose everything he'd worked for his practice. It was too cruel to think but she knew the peerage committee, her father's friends, and the gossips. If they treated her, one of their own class, as a piece of rubbish, Nick had no chance. "I wouldn't let it happen."

"It's not about me as much as Wendy. You see, my parents had an accident on the way home from the market. Villagers carried them home, but they succumbed to their wounds in Wendy's arms that night before I came home from the apprenticeship."

Pippa clasped both hands against her mouth. "We both know the pain of loss." Pippa's eyes burned with unshed tears over her mother's death and with empathy for Nick. "I'm sorry."

"By the time I returned, Wendy had soaked up their blood with towels and her own clothes. She'd washed them all night. And after the funeral, she never wanted to set foot in that house again. We sold everything and used the money to pay for my studies. Wendy has been with me since then. She's under my care, and as a nurse, her prospects are meager. Not even the dowry I continued to save for her will do."

"Why?"

"Because she knows too much about the human body, it's unsettling for most men and compromises her. She helps all of us, Felix, Andre, and me. Alfie is an apothecary, but she knows how to administer the medicines he makes; she even knows how to make some of them."

"And she's lovely. I saw her." Pippa thought she should reassure Nick for he seemed deeply concerned. "But I understand how it feels to be without prospects."

"You? I cannot imagine."

Pippa didn't like the tone he'd assumed. As if he could even begin to grasp the pressure on a high-born girl. "It's just balls, dresses, and offers, you know. They hate me and still make me go to the balls. Every time a distant cousin asks me to dance, it's his pity I get. Or when it's not that, then one of the titled bachelors lost a wager. Or they bet on whether they can survive me stumbling over them. I'm the clumsy goose of the Ton and all my wealth won't protect me from being shunned."

"But your livelihood doesn't depend on it."

"Of course, it does! I cannot access my inheritance without a husband and because of the size of my inheritance, I cannot trust any suitors to want me for me. No one would take the risk to have to my clumsy stumbling enter into their families." Pippa's voice wobbled with anger. She knew it sounded unfair compared to Nick's sad fate, but at least that was substance to his sorrow. All of her troubles were founded in superficiality and gossip. Society's scorn doomed her to remain alone.

"The day we met, on Monday, were you running away?"

"No, I was spending my father's allowance before he could spend it on the charlatan he visits every day."

"Matthews across the street?"

Pippa winced. "He's terrible."

"Yes." Then Nick raised a brow. "But it hadn't been for him, you wouldn't have fallen into my lap." He wrapped his arm around her. "I suppose I should thank him for bringing you into my life."

Despite everything they'd just shared, and to Pippa's utmost surprise, Nick seemed closer to her.

"It's dangerous for you to be with me," Pippa said with a voice that sounded like a wilted flower she couldn't save from her orangery.

"Yes, but if I'm caught here with you, it's not just me. I could hang and then Wendy would never have a chance in life. Our practice would be shunned, and Felix would have to go back to Vienna. Andre might go back to Florence. But Wendy and Alfie—"

"I didn't realize how much you put at risk by spending time with me." Pippa sucked her lower lip in.

"I'm more than spending time with you, aren't I?"

"It's too much of a risk, I'm afraid. I've been so selfish to steal you away from London."

Nick put a hand on her cheek. "It's a risk of the heart, but one worth taking," he whispered, gazing into her eyes with unwavering certainty as they leaned in for a kiss that sealed their fate. The kiss was different than before, slower, deeper, and igniting a love that would defy all odds. As their lips met, time seemed to stand still, and the world faded into the background, leaving only the warmth of their embrace. In that fleeting moment, they both knew that they had found something rare and beautiful that would endure beyond the test of society's scorn. And before long, the carriage came to a stop.

They'd arrived.

Chapter Twenty-One

WHEN NICK EXITED the carriage, he knew he was in trouble. Not only because he'd given his heart too freely, but he'd taken a duke's daughter out of Town. Terrified of the consequences of his action but thrilled to be alone with Pippa, Nick threw caution to the wind. The damage had been done; he might just as well enjoy himself. If all else failed, he'd take Wendy out of town before he'd get caught and start a new life somewhere else. He'd leave the practice and all he'd worked for a moment alone with Pippa. If he didn't, he'd never forgive himself.

He blinked a few times when Silvercroft Manor appeared before him. He hadn't paid much attention to the countryside when Pippa's breasts bobbed ever so slightly on the bumpy country road, but now that he'd stepped out of the hack, London might as well be a thousand miles away.

The "little country estate" Pippa had adorably mentioned as though it were a lodge in the woods was a chateau; a Tudor-style castle with several smoking chimneys, a red brick, like St. James Palace, and poetic rolling hills of greens surrounding it.

"There's a rose garden in the back; you can't see it from here," Pippa said as she began to walk toward the building.

Nick rushed to her side, trying to keep up. She truly had the most magnificent long legs and walked at a healthy pace. She was perfect.

And still off limits.

Which he'd shattered.

There'd be consequences. Nick gulped. But it didn't matter now.

The wind blew in their faces, and Pippa's hair became rather undone. She didn't seem to care and smiled brightly.

"It's the best season to be here, early in the year, just before everything blooms. It's so full of promise and mystery." She winced when she said it and Nick had a sinking feeling that she had something in store for him.

Nick didn't say anything but thought it was perfect because of her, regardless of the weather.

"Mr. George?" Pippa called when she opened the door, letting Nick into the richly decorated hall. It was like he'd imagined when he saw it from the outside: a thick carpet spanned from the door to the hall. "Mrs. George?" Pippa called again.

No answer.

Heavy wooden double doors lined the corridor. A coffered wooden ceiling held onto wrought iron chandeliers. Even an old lance hung on the wall next to a series of crests.

"Who does this castle belong to?" Nick asked when Pippa hung her pelisse on a hook beside an antique grandfather clock.

"My mother."

"But your mother is—"

"Yes, she died. The estate is held in trust for me but I'm free to run it as I like."

"And your mother was?"

"Florence Philippa Cumberland."

Nick felt as if he'd been punched in the stomach. "Of *the* Cumberlands?"

"Yes, are there others?"

"You mean, you are an heiress of the family that even the Regent borrows from? A third of England belongs to them."

"It doesn't. It would belong to my father, who forfeited his inheritance by remarrying. My great-grandfather, Peter Stewart Cumberland, decreed that none of the family's holdings shall pass to the husband of a female heir if no male heir was born upon her death and the husband remarries."

Nick raised a brow, afraid to ask what that meant.

"I'm next in line. Father lost access to the estate. It's all mine."

He gulped.

"Except that I'm a woman, so I can only look after the holding, but I cannot invest or expand without a husband. I'm the clumsy goose with a big dowry, and nobody wants me."

That's not true. I want you.

Nick pursed his lips and bit his cheek. This was too good to be true. She was a lady and an heiress, wealthier than even the princesses of most European nations. She was stunningly gorgeous. And she'd essentially abducted him as her plaything in her castle. In time for his birthday.

He wasn't prepared for this.

"I-I'm honored that you brought me here, Pippa. But I don't think I should be... are we alone?"

She furrowed her forehead and looked at the grandfather clock. "We might be for the night. I only keep a staff of two here these days. Mr. and Mrs. George. They look after everything while I'm gone, but they live in the village. I didn't tell them exactly when I'd be here, so I see they lit the fires, but I'm afraid there's not much else they can do for us." She shrugged. "No servants tonight."

"I should call the hack back and take you home, Pippa." He turned to the window and pulled the curtains aside. The carriage had long disappeared over the hills.

"Why?"

"You ask me why?" Nick rubbed his eyes with the base of his palms. "Where to begin? Because you're the most beautiful, sweetest, most fascinating, and smartest woman I've ever met. Because you're a lady, an heiress, and I'm a pauper. Because you're an innocent. Because you could be ostracized from the Ton and my practice could be destroyed." *Because I'm not to be trusted alone with you in this gorgeous castle without anyone to disturb us.* "Because I must not fall in love with you," he said without thinking about his words. It was the truth, and he didn't know what else to say. It hurt too much to be so close yet feel insufficient to grab the opportunity.

Pippa put her hands on her hips. "You don't want to, do you? So, you'd rather leave?" Hurt colored her voice. "Even with a fortune, nobody wants to love me."

"What are you talking about, Pippa? Do you not see what I see?"

Her eyes reddened, and Nick noticed the tears welling up. "Pippa, you're a duke's daughter, and I'm nothing. I had to train very hard for a long time to finally establish my little practice. It's my livelihood, and I'm also responsible for my sister. If I touch you the wrong way, Pippa, if your father lets out his scorn among the Ton, it's not just my practice but all of us, Felix, Alfie, Wendy, and Andre. Our practice would be finished."

"I understand. I'm inconvenient." She sniffled and escaped his gaze. "I'm never good enough."

"Nev… what?"

"I'm the clumsy and ugly goose. I couldn't catch myself a husband for all the love in my heart and all the money to my name. I'm just not lovable." Tears stained her cheeks, and Nick wanted nothing more than to kiss them away. To hold her in his arms and soothe her. To confess his feelings and share his heart because it was too much to feel all this alone. He didn't know how to bear it by himself.

"Pippa, you are the most beautiful girl I've ever met. Don't tell my sister, but you're the smartest, too."

Pippa laughed at that and then sniffled again.

"Look at how sweet you are." Nick touched her cheek gently.

"You're the only person I've ever seen who can laugh and cry simultaneously. You have such a big heart. You nurtured a crippled bunny to health. Even when you didn't see well, you grew a bounty of the most beautiful plants with your sense of touch alone. How can you not see what I do?"

"My vision... I don't see."

"Pippa, look not with your eyes but with your heart if you think I can just allow myself to feel what I do."

"Feel what?"

"Love? Perhaps more? I've never been in love, so I am unsure, but the symptoms are clear."

"Symptoms?"

"Yes, I lack appetite except for the pineapple from your hand. I can't sleep because my body is burning for you at night. I can't think straight because every thought circles back to you. I can't even imagine the future I had so carefully planned without you, and you've only just come into my life a few days ago."

"And these symptoms make you sick?"

"It hurts so much, Pippa. I mustn't act on my impulse. That's usually not so bad except that every fiber of my being pushes me to act, yet I know I mustn't...I wouldn't allow it." Nick paused.

"You don't want me?"

"I want you so much, Pippa, you don't know how. But if I let myself have you, I'll ruin you. I'm bad for you, Pippa. And the last thing I'd ever do in the world is to hurt you. I swore the Hippocratic oath: First, do no harm."

Pippa gave him a serious stare. "I'm not your patient, and I'm not a disease. And it seems that being with me could hurt you much more."

"That's not what I said."

She held her hand out to stop him. "Wait! I'm also not like the others, the haughty aristocrats who think that being with a commoner could somehow be a crime. My grandmother was a commoner, did you know that? Believe me, there're some gentlemen and ladies who are not so nice once you get to know them."

Nick stifled a laugh. She was unbelievably well bred, yet her mind was sharper, and her wit had more humor than Socrates combined with Shakespeare's.

"Plus," she continued, "whether you may or may not touch me is my decision alone. My father has long lost his say to control my life. In fact, I have more than enough money to look out for my future, my children, and their children. And heed my words, I know very well that it's improper that I brought you here. What else was I supposed to do to make you seduce me?"

"Ah…" Her patronizing tone was unbelievably alluring, and he wanted nothing more than to simply oblige, kiss her senseless, compromise her thoroughly, and more. But he was so far below her station, he knew that it was a double infringement, seducing a virgin—even though he'd let her believe that she was seducing him—and touching a well-bred lady. He sighed. How could he not though?

"Yes! I want you to! And if a dashing and talented young doctor like you might consider showing me what Violet talked about, I want it. I don't care if the Ton approves or my father and Wife Six, whichever hole in the ground she crawled out of but it wasn't a respectable family, I know that for a fact. So what gives them the right to keep me locked up and miserable when I could be happy with you?"

"Wait! Happy with me?"

She nodded heatedly.

Nick had trouble following her speech because it sounded as though she felt inferior to him. That was absurd. "Who's Violet?"

"What?"

"You said that Violet talked about something I should show you? I don't know any Violets."

"Violet is the Countess of Langley. Her husband had surgery. I visited them yesterday, and he appeared to have recovered. He knows

Nurse Wendy, so I thought you were his doctor."

Nick pinched his lips. It was true, but he mustn't breach his patient's confidentiality. If the earl told Pippa, that was another story. He could neither confirm nor deny that he was his treating doctor, which he was, of course.

"What did Violet say to you?" he finally asked.

"Argh... she boasted about how her new husband kissed her."

So it had worked, the young countess had nursed the earl back to health and their relationship had blossomed. Good.

"You know, not on her mouth but *down there*."

What?

Pippa continued, "She said he sent her spiraling into realms of rainbows and stars where she lost her mind. Apparently, they've had to stay in bed for days so he could show her all his tricks."

Nick choked on the air that didn't reach his lungs, but Pippa hadn't finished.

"Violet has always had a tendency for drama. I can't imagine that the earl can make her feel like that."

"I can." Nick rubbed the back of his neck. "Is that why you wanted to ask me earlier?"

Pippa paused. "Yes," she said suddenly in a mousy voice.

Oh, this was going to be fun. Nick's heart lurched, and he tried to stifle the grin that was bubbling within him.

He cleared his throat. "Let me make sure I understand you correctly. You want me to do something that Violet's husband did to her, because you expect that I know then how to make these rainbows and stars happen if I kiss you..." He didn't dare speak the words.

"Down there," Pippa completed his sentence and dropped her head again. Nick was flabbergasted. He mustn't admit it to keep his patient's confidentiality, but judging from the Earl of Langley's experience, he had a rather thorough picture of what his wife had told Pippa. "Do you know what she was talking about?" Pippa asked tentatively.

"Yes."

"And have you done it before?" Pippa asked with such sweet innocence that Nick didn't know how to react. His breeches were so painfully restricting his erection, and yet he was frozen on the spot. In his dream, he'd... he'd... oh boy.

"Not that, exactly."

She exhaled and slumped. "Oh."

Nick gave up and let the smile come out. He beamed at her. "It would be an honor to give it a try. I know the rest rather well."

Pippa's eyes darted to him and sparkled. "You would try? With me?"

"Well, I did study general anatomy for a while. Physiology... I specialized in the eye later on at university." He raised his brows and gave the most rakish "what can I say" shrug because it was true; he knew what she wanted and was more than willing to try. "There's nothing I wouldn't do for the woman of my dreams."

"There's nothing I wouldn't do for you," she said.

Chapter Twenty-Two

THERE'S NOTHING I wouldn't do for the woman of my dreams.

She'd heard him say it. Loud and clear.

Standing in the corridor between her grandfather's library and the stairs to the servants' section of Silvercrest Manor, Pippa nearly lost her footing. She'd wanted to seduce the statuesque young doctor, touch and kiss him everywhere, and longed to spend more time with him. But one thing had led to another, and now that she was here alone in the manor with him, and he'd told her that he was falling in love with her, it just didn't seem real. So many wonderful things didn't usually happen to her, and she wasn't prepared to receive such a gift of fate. She'd been prepared to fight for it. Alas, she hadn't even expected to come out victorious.

So, what now?

"Come on," Pippa took his hand and dragged him down the hall, down a flight of only a few stairs. He followed her into a large kitchen.

The scent of buttery shortbread danced in the air, capturing his attention and beckoning him closer. It mingled with the fragrance of freshly brewed tea, creating an intoxicating aroma that enticed his senses. The subtle notes of salted butter and vanilla infused the space, weaving a thread of temptation that wrapped around Nick's senses, leaving him entranced. Pippa radiated a magnetic charm. Her graceful movements carried an air of mystery, as if she held secrets yet to be discovered. Nick couldn't help but feel a growing sense of urgency and excitement watching each of her steps and gestures.

Pippa's features were cast in a soft and captivating glow in the flickering light of the crackling fire. Shadows played upon her face, highlighting the delicate contours. Nick's heart quickened as he watched her, captivated by the interplay of light and shadow on her clavicle. A rucked layer of muslin covered her chest, but he couldn't stop staring. There was something about how the strands of hair had fallen loose and touched her skin that reminded him of his dream. They'd been in the greenhouse, not a kitchen. But he'd grabbed her, laid her on the table, and climbed over her, kissing her gorgeous little nipples...

"Do you like milk in your tea?" Pippa interrupted his stream of thoughts.

"No, thank you."

"Sugar?"

"Honey, if you have any."

Pippa turned and rummaged around a high cabinet but couldn't see the second shelf. There was a stool in the corner, and Nick picked it up, carried it to her, and set it at her feet. Every sound in the kitchen had a certain significance, drawing Nick further into the scene unfolding before him. The whispering rustle of Pippa's dress against the rough bricks lining the walls created a sensory tapestry that enveloped Nick.

His eyes lingered on the polished wooden table, its surface gleaming under the warm glow of the fire. A fresh bowl of oranges stood as a vibrant centerpiece, each succulent piece tempting his gaze but none as much as Pippa. The bright color and inviting aroma wafting from the bowl invited Nick into a world of luscious flavors and hidden desires, leaving him yearning for a taste.

Nick felt the rising tension between himself and Pippa, an unspoken connection that drew them closer. The kitchen became a stage for their dance of trust and heightened the suspense.

He didn't speak and watched her across the table as she set the teapot, two saucers, cups, and the terra-cotta jar with a wooden honey wand sticking out from a little brown lid on a tray. She added a small crystal dish with what appeared to be homemade shortbread, for each had a somewhat different shape, albeit all were rectangles with granulated sugar glistening on the top. Then she picked the tray up and headed to the door.

Nick opened it for her and followed her upstairs. The rustling of her dress and the slight clinking of the porcelain on the copper tray distracted him. His eyes followed the gentle side-to-side rocking of her hips, and he couldn't think of anything he wanted more at this moment than to grab her hips and touch her taut little bottom. Nick's mind returned to his dream, back to picturing how she'd wrap her legs around him as he drove relentlessly into her.

When Pippa led him to a beautifully decorated and well-heated room on the manor's second floor, he froze as soon as he stood in the door. To his left was a seating area arranged in front of a crackling fire, an upholstered settee in the same teal damask tones as the wallpaper, the throw pillows, and—Nick swallowed hard—the canopy over the bed to his right.

Nick watched Pippa, her back to him, her form a graceful silhouette against the fireplace's warm glow. She was a few steps ahead, poised to place the tray on the side table between the plush settee and the crackling hearth. A question bubbled up within him, curiosity lending courage to his voice.

"Is this your bedchamber?" He gestured towards the bed, its covers invitingly soft and untouched.

The words hung in the air, lingering like a note played on a piano. Time seemed to slow in that moment as Pippa turned to face him. She pivoted on her heel, a cup perched on a saucer in one hand, the porcelain teapot held aloft in the other. Her eyes widened in surprise, the question catching her off guard. It was then that it happened.

With a startled gasp, her grip on the teapot faltered. Nick watched in stunned silence as the teapot tipped slowly, its contents spilling in a torrent of amber liquid. The tea cascaded through the air, droplets catching the firelight. Before he could react, the hot tea splashed against his chest, soaking his shirt instantly. The expected heat through the fabric took his breath away. His shirt clung to his skin, the material saturated with the spilled tea, a patchwork of dampness spreading across his torso.

The scent of the tea, a blend of aromatic floral notes, filled his nostrils. It was a heady mix, but the shock of the sudden spill overshadowed the fragrance. Nick could only stand there, frozen in surprise, as the last drops of tea dripped from his shirt. He looked down at the small puddle seeping into the carpet below.

"Oh dear!" Pippa's gasp echoed in the room, her hands flying to her mouth as she saw him. The empty teapot clattered onto the tray, its job done. The silence that followed was heavy, broken only by the soft crackle of the fire and the distant ticking of a clock.

Nick looked down at his shirt, the fabric darkened by the tea. He lifted his gaze to meet Pippa's, his eyes reflecting a mix of shock and amusement. Despite the discomfort, he couldn't help but chuckle. After all, it wasn't every day one got doused with tea in a moment of surprise.

"I'M SO SORRY," Pippa exclaimed, trying not to laugh. Spilling the tea without breaking the teapot had been easier than she'd thought, and she'd spent all five minutes gathering the tea set and carrying it upstairs, contemplating how to force Nick to stay.

"It's nothing," he mumbled, ever the gentleman, as he stared down at the puddle of tea around his boots. It wasn't all right because his shirt and breeches were so wet that they dripped into his boots.

Yet, he didn't shake the dripping liquid onto the carpet.

He wasn't like the men she'd met at the balls. Any mishap, no matter how small the resulting stain or rip of their garments, and they'd made a fuss as if she'd all but cut off one of their sleeves entirely. Not Nick. He turned and searched for something with which to dry himself.

Pippa rushed to the armoire on the wall perpendicular to the fireplace, turned the key, and retrieved a pressed cotton towel.

With care and her gaze woefully cast aside, she attempted to pat Nick dry, but it didn't help; his linen shirt was soaked.

He looked down at the puddle at his feet again and unbuttoned the top of his shirt—button for button. Slowly, the wet fabric fell limply off his chiseled torso. A chill ran down Pippa's back as he removed his damp shirt, bunched it into a ball, and dropped it onto the floor. He lifted his right foot, pulled his boot off, then lifted his left and pulled the boot off. After he'd set them aside neatly, he stepped on the shirt and tried to soak up all the liquid. Pippa watched in amazement.

"I'm afraid some of the tea is seeping into the parquet. It might stain," he said, squatting on the floor at Pippa's feet.

He was concerned about the flooring.

The muscular man with bare feet and—Pippa gulped—a naked upper body used his shirt to soak up the tea she'd spilled. Air left her lungs, but she didn't find the strength to inhale more as she took in the sight of him. What had she done?

She'd abducted a doctor from his practice on the day before his birthday. He'd responded gracefully and said he'd like nothing better than to be with her. Pippa's heart beat faster.

Then she'd told him about Violet's wicked accounts with her new husband, and Nick had expressed his willingness to try. Pippa's heart beat even faster.

And when she'd spilled tea on him, instead of yelling at her as every single other man of the Ton had done in the past, Nick had taken his shirt off—the only one he had with him—to soak up the puddle lest it stain her parquet. Pippa's heart lurched, and she gasped for air.

He was beyond perfect.

And, he hadn't said that he didn't want to fall in love with her but that he *mustn't*.

Only a second passed, but Pippa's entire life flashed before her eyes. Her world shifted around her as if she was pivoting on skates on a frozen pond. This was when she knew she'd fallen in love with him. It wasn't a mere fancy or desire to touch his perfect face. Gone were the doubts that she might only have wished to feel what Violet had described. She loved him and wanted to show him. Not that she knew how, but couldn't he teach her as the earl taught Violet?

"Your shirt," Pippa said when Nick rose from his squat with the wet and stained mess in his hands. "I'm so sorry," Pippa said as she took it from him and put it on the copper tray.

In her other hand, she still held the bunched-up cotton towel and patted Nick's chest after hesitating for what couldn't have been longer than a heartbeat. She was drying him.

Interesting.

Her gaze was low, and Nick caught on. She avoided his gaze, lifted the towel fully off his chest, and placed it back on slowly. She pressed it against his bared abdomen and stilled.

"I'm afraid your shirt is ruined, I'm so sorry—"

"Are you?" Nick said the moment she laid her bare hand on his chest, next to the place where her other hand pressed the towel on his skin. He was exposed, well, his upper body was. She also noticed his feet, large but clean. Everything about him looked manly but neat, youthful, and strong.

"Did I burn you?" She trailed her bare hand over this chest, and he followed the motion with his gaze. She'd stopped patting with the towel, mesmerized by the perfect male shape.

"You know you didn't, Pippa." His hand grasped her wrist tenderly, and then he pushed her hand onto his heart. His voice sounded stern, but there was a flash of amusement on his mien.

He was playing along.

Chapter Twenty-Three

A SPILLED POT of tea and a soaked shirt later, Nick found himself barefoot and shirtless in Pippa's beautiful manor in one of the elegant upstairs bedchambers in a half-dry puddle of cooling tea and with her hands on his torso. He gave up trying to feign embarrassment because it was a lie, and he was neither good as lying nor at pretending to be a bashful lover. He knew enough of the human anatomy to know that he was well built. Plus, he had nothing to hide and, quite frankly, didn't want to. So, he laid his left hand over her right, pressing her hand on his heart. She must have felt his heartbeat for she raised he gaze and met his.

With the most beautiful blue eyes, she blinked at him. Then she stilled, only batting her long lashes expectantly.

Nick waited and squared his shoulders. With his body language, he gave her access. And she understood.

Pippa dropped the towel to the floor and trailed her right hand over his chest until it met her left near his abdomen. Her exploration was eager but also revealed her innocence. Nick knew how girls of her social standing were raised, protected, and coddled. Except that in all of her isolation, she'd been deprived of the love she needed to blossom in her pretty little greenhouse. Although Nick couldn't give her any of the riches that her standing required, he could give her the love her heart desired.

If he could allow himself and if she let him.

Time to find out.

Nick inhaled deeply and his chest grew wide. He took Pippa's hands and led them down to… and before he could consider how she'd react, she inserted her index fingers in his waistband. "I want to know," she whispered, looking down at his crotch.

"Pippa, if I go too far, you have to stop me."

"Why should I?"

"Because I won't stop unless you want me to." He placed a tender kiss on her forehead, then her cheek, and then her mouth. Nick shuddered at the thought of stopping because he wanted to go all the way. Stopping would probably kill him on the spot and yet he'd never go further than she wanted him to. "If you allow it, Pippa, I'll show you how you make me feel. Not how Violet and her husband make each other feel. Just you and me. Here and now. Do you want me to?"

"How?" Her voice was pierced with the awe of a young fawn taking in the smell of a lovely fresh clover for the first time. "How can you make me feel?"

Nick swallowed hard. He nodded but feared that by speaking now, his voice would break like that of a green boy. For that's what he felt like. He knew all too well that she was a virgin and inexperienced. She couldn't know what he did about the human body, much less what two bodies could do together. And yet, he felt like the inexperienced one. He was in her lavish house, and he had the impression that she'd brought him here on purpose.

"Did you mean to spill the tea on me?" He jerked his head back but tilted it to the side. Thinking of it, the tea had been lukewarm and looked rather light in color. "You watered it down so you wouldn't burn me, didn't you?"

Pippa pinched her lips and removed her hands from his body. Then she spoke with the poise of a governess trying to explain that cod liver oil would taste good. "I'm just so clumsy."

Nick broke into a smile. She was lying.

"I've rather cured you of clumsiness, haven't I?"

Pippa took a step back and brought her fingers to her eyeglasses, removed them, folded the temple stems in, and set the glasses on a side table with great care. "I'm very, very clumsy." She shook her head, but a telling grin built on her face, and the mischievous glint made Nick laugh. Oh, she was so sweet and innocent but also fiercely smart. She knew exactly what she was doing and that he knew. Well, good, then they were in agreement.

Nick stepped closer and took a wide stance before her, offering his body for exploration—no for anything she'd ever want—and waited.

"Dr. Folsham—" Pippa started but her breath caught as her eyes trailed over his upper body.

"Nick."

She inhaled and spoke with feigned gravitas. "Nick."

"Yes?" His voice was dark.

"As you know, I don't see well without my glasses." Her hands returned to his chest, and she trailed them over his muscles as if she couldn't stop herself. Side to side, from one side of his chest to the other, and then one hand found his waistband again, the other cupped the back of his head. "I need to feel for what I cannot see." And she inserted one hand in his breeches.

Nick gasped. She was brazen and oh, so sweet.

He leaned in but stopped short of her mouth just when she raised her mouth to his. Her hand slid farther, and her delicate fingers wrapped around his shaft.

Nick smiled but didn't touch her lips. Two could play a game of teasing.

⤞⤝

HE WAS A little cocky and sure of himself, but Pippa loved it. She couldn't quite say what his manhood felt like, but it was hard and hot in her hand and gave a twitch that she found most pleasing. She gave a gentle squeeze back and Nick smiled, his face so close to hers but still not touching.

But she wanted him to touch her.
Everywhere.

She wanted more of this teasing and the exploration. Yes, he was a little blurred now that she'd taken her glasses off, but she could easily make out the expression on his face, the boyish smirk and the manly seriousness. He was letting her lead.

Pippa hooked her index finger into his waistband and pulled. She stepped back and tugged. He followed a step, never stopping to kiss her. One more step backward.

"Pippa," Nick whispered. He knew what she was doing. Step-by-step, luring him closer to her bed.

His hands came from the back of her neck to her neck. As if he needed to drink from her, he pulled her close whilst leaning his body onto hers. There was little room left between them and it was still too much.

Pippa tilted her head sideways and gave him access to her neck. As if their minds were one, Nick responded by kissing a trail down her neck, tenderly and slowly. Then he reached the edge of her collar. He kissed the last part of her skin that was exposed and gently touched the edge of the fabric as if it were the barrier he wouldn't cross.

She wouldn't have any of it and raised her hand to pull her sleeve down. Nick broke the kiss and stepped back just enough to tower over her. Her hands were a little shaky, and her finger trembled when she tugged at the fabric and pulled her arm out. The other side came out more easily and the gown slid off.

Nick's Adam's apple jumped as he watched her. His gaze was serious but his eyes black.

When the fabric of her dress fell to the ground, he bent down to pull it down over her hips, letting his hands brush over the skin of her belly and then her side. Before long, she was only in her slippers, garter belt, stockings, and stays. Nick nudged her left foot out of the pool of fabric and Pippa put both hands on his glistening shoulders, watching the muscles flex as he pulled her foot out of her slipper. Then the other side. He quickly hung the dress over the edge of the settee but remained squatting before her.

And when he looked up at her, she saw a sincerity in his gaze that sent her insides into tumult. No one had ever simultaneously looked at her with such tenderness, concentration, and vulnerability. He blinked at her like a servant, waiting for the sentence of a queen. And Pippa understood, he'd spoken the words before, but this was the moment. If she allowed it, he'd fall in love. Oh, and she wanted nothing more than his heart because she knew hers already belonged to him.

Her hands still on his shoulders, she was slightly bent over him. He blinked up at her, his hands now wrapped around her calves. He began to stroke her legs. Even though she thought she'd be shy, it was vulnerability she felt more than anything else. But she knew she'd be safe in his arms.

Nick still looked up at her, begging for permission to continue. His wavy blond hair with tones of gold and amber fell deliciously over his smooth forehead. With his lips pursed, he clenched his teeth and the muscles in his cheeks popped and led Pippa's eyes to his angular jawline. She steadied herself and straightened so that her hands no longer reached for his shoulders, but she could still drive her fingers through his gorgeous hair. The messier it got, the more boyishly mischievous he looked. Pippa's heart beat heavily in her chest but her heart felt so light because it felt like it was meant to happen. He was so right for her, and she welcomed his every touch even more than fresh air entering her lungs after a swim in Brighton.

Nick ran his muscular hands over her lower legs and then caressed upward, going toward the knees. He unhooked the stockings from her garter belt with great dexterity and Pippa remembered that he must have done this before. He'd been with others.

A pinch of jealousy shot through her.

"What's the matter?" he asked, apparently noticing her frown.

"Do I please you?" Afraid to ask for fear that the answer would shatter her, Pippa held her breath. Again, she spoke before she'd thought about the consequences. A question deserved an answer and if she didn't want to hear his response, she shouldn't have asked.

"D-d..." Nick stuttered, which was unlike him. Usually the eloquent doctor, he wasn't like his usual self now. Half undressed, barefoot, squatting before her, he seemed younger, disheveled, and yet intent on what he was doing as if he were an arrow shooting through the air. And Pippa was his target, hit by Cupid's arrow.

He trailed his hands to the outer side of her thighs and then brought them to her behind. He cupped her bottom with a gentle squeeze and groaned.

"Pippa, you are—" He bit his lower lip and looked at her middle, then up at her breasts. "You are the most beautiful woman I've ever seen, Pippa." She heard his words but could barely understand them. After a lifetime in Bea's shadow, and being called *the ugly goose* even when she was at a ball with her father had eroded her self-esteem. "You are so beautiful, Pippa. I..." He bit his lip again and took her hand, opened her palm facing up and placed a slow kiss in it. Then he closed her fingers and turned it over. "Pippa, if you allow me to love you, to make love to you, and to give you my heart, I promise I'll spend my entire life trying to live up to you." He blinked, and a tear escaped the corner of his eye.

A moment of silence hung heavily in the air as Pippa tried to understand. He was asking for permission to love her. The gorgeous man at her feet who'd cured her of clumsiness with a little thing like spectacles. He'd come into her life wrapped in whipped cream and custard and since that moment, he'd vanquished the loneliness from her heart. He'd been a perfect gentleman and Pippa had the wicked ideas to abduct him, yet he knelt before her asking for permission to… to…

"I didn't think you'd want my love—" but before she could finish, he dropped his head on her belly button and deflated. He'd let go of her hands, and she placed them both on his head, into the silky mess of his gold-spun hair shining in the light from the fireplace. "Nick?"

"Hm?" He mumbled and something tickled her.

"Nick, if you want me and my love, I'd like nothing more than to be all yours."

Another tickle.

Oh my, what was he doing there?

Chapter Twenty-Four

NICK KISSED HER navel and carefully grabbed her narrow waist. Her hip bones protruded because she was slender but well-built, her muscles twitching when he placed a row of butterfly kisses on her abdomen.

"Such perfect anatomy," he mumbled, kissing a path down from her navel as he pulled the garter belt off and gave her bottom a squeeze.

She exhaled with a half laugh and cupped his face. He'd loved her hands in his hair, but he looked up when she held his cheeks. "You are so gorgeous, Pippa. I love your wit, your intelligent eyes, the curl of hair that always falls around your ear, and the way you speak. But Pippa, I want to show you how beautiful your body is, absolute human perfection as I have never known it to exist."

She drew her eyes wide.

"With your permission—" He kissed the spot just above her hairline.

"Yes. Anything, anything with you and from you."

Nick brought his hand to her middle and gently pressed against her private area. She was so pleasingly warm. She twitched and folded over as a gasp escaped her.

Nick straightened, one hand still there, and took the back of her head in his hand again. She gave him access to show her what her body could do. It was an honor he didn't underestimate. A pleasure he could only imagine, and he steadied himself to make it as perfect as he could for her.

Nick kissed her willing mouth with all the vigor the moment had promised. Pouring his feelings and the raw emotion into his exploration of her mouth, he didn't realize when she'd walked backward to the bed, and he'd followed. He'd follow her over a cliff, and it would all be worth it for a kiss from her.

She stopped when she touched the bed and Nick pressed a bit more with his hand in her middle. She understood and sat on the bed, leaning back.

Reluctantly, Nick's lips left hers, but she was pink and swollen. She'd asked for this and even though Nick had never quite done what she'd described, there was no time like the moment to try. He brushed the hair out of her face with his free hand and then pushed some more. She slid backward until she lay before him. Again, with his free hand, Nick trailed over her stays but decided to reserve that for later. Her turn first.

He kissed his way down to her navel again. And lower.

Even lower.

She clenched her muscles and crossed her legs. He withdrew from her center.

"Why?" Nick said, holding her waist with both hands now. "Is this what Violet talked about?" he asked, lowering his face.

She nodded.

As if she had to consider the matter for a moment, Pippa paused.

Then she relaxed her legs and Nick spread her thighs.

He quickly oriented himself and found her cleft. Unsure where to start, he worshipped every delicious fold and every little hill and valley of her middle.

She inhaled sharply when he flicked his tongue over the bottom wall of her opening. He did it again along the seam and she let out a moan.

So, he brought a finger there and touched the sleekest spot.

She collapsed backward in the soft bed and let her legs fall wide apart.

Oh good, she liked it.

Nick gently inserted the tip of his left index finger. She was so precious in his hands. Entrusting him with her sexual awakening. And he was absolutely going to make sure she'd wake up to a bright experience.

In no time, his entire index finger slid in, then his middle finger. Her ring muscles on the inside welcomed him with near peristaltic convulsions and she wriggled on the bed.

With the other hand, Nick found the little bean. It was pink and shiny.

Nick leaned in and gave it a lick.

Pippa let out a scream and wriggled more.

Nick continued and Pippa propped herself up on her elbows. "I can't breathe." She sat up and with quick motions shrugged out of her stays.

Nick felt his eyes grow wide from his perch in a most erotic position when her perky breasts popped out, bigger than in his dream and yet looking so fresh and cheeky that he wanted to—*needed* to—taste her nipples.

He left his fingers where they made progress in the slick warmth of her center and came up with his upper body to kiss her breasts.

Oh, they were gloriously cool, soft and yet the nipples were hard, and he couldn't stop his onslaught. His fingers continued and the slender blonde beneath him wriggled, moaned, and then she arched her back so much, Nick wanted to take her breasts in his mouth completely, but he felt her trembling on the inside. In response to his fingers, she tensed around him, and he knew she was close.

Her mouth was wide open, and Nick plunged his tongue in, feeling the sharp edges of her immaculate white teeth. She pressed her middle onto his hand and her breathing grew heavy. She sucked his mouth in, and then she did what he'd dreamed of and didn't even dare think could happen.

Pippa wrapped her long slender legs around Nick and clung onto him as she peaked. He knew she did when she clenched her muscles and shuddered. Nick wrapped his arms around Pippa's thighs and enclosed her with as much skin as he could. Her hand came to his and he stopped what his fingers had done, slowly removing them.

There was too much fabric between them, and he wanted to squeeze out the air between them. She was in his arms and still too far away.

Her mouth was hot on his, deliciously moist and eager. All of their kisses had been spectacular. And yet, this felt different. She was taking possession of him as if she'd shrugged off her timid restraint. She'd brought him to her mother's estate and had an air of the mistress of the manor here. This was her territory and Nick had a feeling she'd brought him there because of this.

Oh, and how he wanted her to. She was an innocent and an aristocrat and so many reasons spoke against this. She had all the allure of a forbidden goddess combined with the power of a siren who'd enchanted him.

She let out a moan and tilted her head back, granting him access to kiss her neck. And he did, for how could a man of blood and flesh resist such a beauty?

She was out of breath and yet yearning for more. Her middle pressed against his, she was inviting him, and Nick felt his restraint ripping like an overstretched rope.

"Will you marry me?"

She held his neck and furrowed her forehead. "Yes."

"Even though I have nothing to offer you?"

"Yes." She frowned. "No. I mean, yes I'll marry you if you'll have me."

"I never wanted anything and anyone as much as I want you, Pippa. But it's not too late now to stop. I cannot offer you much, I work for my money and there are people who even want the practice. If we go too far, if you become pregnant—"

She jerked her head back. "With a baby?"

"Yes. Don't you want children?"

Her eyes narrowed to slits and color left her face. "I only know how to care for plants. I don't even have a mother who can teach me—"

"If you take me, you'd have Wendy as a sister."

"And you think she'd be there? For a baby?"

Could she get her father's permission to wed a commoner? Father would think Nick was only after the money and never grant Pippa permission to marry Nick, not for all the love in her life.

"My entire life, I had riches, luxury, elegant balls, and jewels. I have been to St. James Palace so many times, it's boring, but you can offer me so much more than anyone else ever has."

"And what is that?" He couldn't hide the sadness in his voice. He wished to be more for the gorgeous lady in his arms.

"Your heart. Love. Happiness. I don't want to be so alone anymore. Plants never talk back. Neither does Sir Hoppington."

Nick laughed at that. "Oh Pippa," he beamed at her. "I promise you all that with my whole heart."

"Then please continue. Never worry about money, I have enough for both of us." *I just don't know how to access it.*

And with these words, she reached for his laces and unpacked what he'd longed to let out of his breeches.

Chapter Twenty-Five

SHE WASN'T SURE why and how, but from the moment she laid her hand on his manhood, Pippa was crazed with a deep hunger that was lodged somewhere within her and was screaming to be let out. Nick was propped over her now, leaving enough space between them to give her access. His broad shoulders, chiseled abdomen, and even the muscles on his arm twitched as Pippa explored. He was trying to be still but didn't do a good job at all. She touched him most intimately and he looked down at her hands, inviting her to feel him but he let out a groan that was so guttural and feral, that Pippa froze.

"Oh, I'm sorry. Did that hurt?" She quickly let go of the soft skin that covered was felt like a thick wooden stick inside, or maybe a bone. Were there bones in the male... but she couldn't complete her thought when he lowered his body onto hers and took her mouth in a searing kiss.

"You could never hurt me," he mumbled onto her lips.

She opened and gave him access but then she gasped.

He brought his hot and hard shaft to her center.

"Pippa, if you don't stop me now, I'll take your virginity."

She wrapped her hands around his broad back, and he pushed his center against hers. He dropped down, propping himself up on only one elbow and brought his hands down.

A ripple of pleasure made Pippa twitch, but she didn't dare speak, for his eyes were so intent on hers now, as if something momentous was about to unfold.

He gently parted her lips with his hand and touched the blunt tip of his hardness against the same opening that he'd touched so deliciously earlier.

"I'll ask again, Pippa. Are you certain you want me?" Nick asked.

She nodded.

"I'm about to ruin you for any other man if we carry on." He exerted some pressure and even though she was momentarily surprised, a drop of fluid came out as if she'd licked her lips and moistened them to take in a sweet dessert.

She furrowed her brow. "I only ever want you."

He pressed on a little and his tip was now exactly at the opening.

"What if I get you pregnant?" He looked down to where they were about to join and his voice came hoarse, like a stallion strained from exertion.

"We'd have a family."

He pushed a little more and Pippa felt herself stretching to let him in. He was entering her and as odd as it was, even though she couldn't comprehend it, she wanted him to go deeper.

Nick lifted his gaze to meet hers again. "I love you Pippa. I've never been in love before, and I know I'm not much, but I would wish for nothing more than to have a family with you."

She couldn't suppress a smile and raised her eyebrows. He was not high born but he'd worked for what he was, and he was so much more than any of the mean aristocrats she'd met, men his age who laughed at her. He never laughed at her; he'd cured her. And then he'd fallen in love with her. She wanted him. She wanted this. All of it together and forever. Whatever the future held, she knew she'd never be complete without Nick in her life.

And then the clock ticked.

A gong rang out.

And then another. The short and the long hand were on the twelve.

"It's midnight." She beamed and the clock rang twelve times. "Happy birthday!"

Pippa's heart leaped, and she felt empty, longing for more.

Nick swallowed. His gaze was black like a sleek panther's about to pounce.

Then he pushed and entered her.

She lifted her head and put her chin on his shoulder and closed her eyes.

But instead of going on, Nick kissed her delicately. A small kiss on her cheek, another on her chin. Their faces touched but she could see the love in his eyes. She smiled involuntarily but how could she not when the most handsome man, the one she'd given her heart, looked at her as if she were the most important person in the world?

He adjusted his body and put his forehead on hers. Pippa instinctively wrapped her arms around his back, stroking him upward.

Somehow, he slipped in as they kissed. He was large and thick, and she felt herself stretching but it didn't hurt.

He went slowly for her, she could tell. His breathing like that of a stallion eager to go faster than he did.

He broke the kiss and Pippa felt parched for more.

⟫⟩✕⟨⟪

NICK FELT HER tightness around his tip. It couldn't have been anything else and he tried to stop himself from thrusting into her with abandon. She was so willing and slick, and her perky breasts drove him mad. He cupped her breasts and gently drove a finger over her nipple, which immediately perked up against his touch like a tip of meringue.

But he was ruining a high-born daughter. He clenched his eyes shut, banishing the thought of any risk associated with their union.

She was so beautiful, her silky blond hair cushioning her head when she arched her back and set her head down on the pillow.

He'd made her feel him and it should have been enough.

Without her father's blessing, he mustn't go on.

It wasn't allowed and probably not even smart.

But then she twitched around him, like a small peristaltic nudge to go on.

She grabbed the back of his head as she'd done before and pulled him into a kiss. Her mouth was as open for him as her center.

Nick grabbed her left thigh with his right hand, the perfect muscular thigh of a beautiful woman who probably rode astride in the country, he mused. But then, all coherent thought failed him.

She wrapped both legs around him, those long lithe legs perfectly shaped and the ideal length to hook her feet behind his bottom.

The motion made him slip in deeper and something popped.

Nick tore his eyes open and watched her face for signs of discomfort.

None came.

Not even a wince.

Expectation and sincere love were all over her face. She clutched his bottom and pulled him closer.

The decision had been hers. And Nick complied.

Deeper and deeper, he pushed.

A sensual moan escaped her, the most wonderful little sound he'd ever heard.

So, he slipped slightly out, and she tightened her legs around him.

Then he slipped in to the hilt.

She was perfect for him, just absolutely perfect.

And before long, they'd found a rhythm.

She was a quick learner and met his thrusts when he started to pump. Over and over again.

All night, he made love to her, and it became an erotic blur.

When the fireplace went out, and the embers lost their glow, the night's darkness lifted, and a new day sent a lovely purple light through the window. That was when she nestled into his arms and kissed his chest. Then she closed her eyes and drifted off into sleep.

His sleepy beauty. His love.

Even though his muscles were sore, and his body spent from what must have been hours of passion, he knew he'd only just begun to show her how much he loved her. Filled with the grandeur of the sentiment, he let his head sink into the pillow and fell asleep. Whatever the day would bring, he'd tackle later. For now, he had the love of his life in his arms and his thigh on her hot center. For now, the world couldn't be more perfect.

Chapter Twenty-Six

THE MORNING SUN tickled Pippa's face, and she crinkled her nose as she stretched lazily in bed.

Ouch! She was sore.

Suddenly, the memories of the last night flashed before her inner eye. She'd.... Oh, and how she'd... was it a dream?

She turned and peeked under the fluffy down under the covers. What she saw left her agog. A muscular and very male leg was angled in the bedspread, and she followed it, leading to a large, equally muscular body.

It wasn't a dream.

She'd abducted the doctor and taken advantage of him.

She'd seduced the oculist.

No, she'd made love to Nick. *Her* Nick.

Pippa dove under the covers to examine her prey, for the way she'd feasted on his body couldn't be called anything else. There he was, lying in all his glory, fast asleep. His left leg was angled, but his right stretched out as he lay flat on his stomach, his head turned the other way. His gorgeous blond hair was disheveled, but Pippa was oddly proud of that. She'd done it, she'd mussed his golden strands—Pippa bit her cheek—she'd grabbed his head when she'd climaxed. *Oh dear.* It had been every bit as glorious as Violet had said.

A wave of emotions flooded her: pride to have been with the specimen of perfect manhood who lay naked in her bed but also shame for how brazen she'd been to seduce him.

Then she heard footsteps.

And the door.

Pippa cowered under the covers and pinched her eyes shut. Somebody gasped and Pippa had the sinking feeling that Mrs. George had caught her in a compromising position, enough to warrant scandal.

But she remained quiet and still in the doorframe by the sound of it. Even though she'd been like a grandmother to Pippa, she knew her place as a servant. Pippa was the mistress of the manor. It wasn't Mrs. George's place to speak.

Then Pippa realized that she'd pulled the covers over her head, and Nick had moved, stretching his leg so that his foot peeked out from under the sheets.

Pippa winced. There wasn't any chance Mrs. George didn't see a man's foot sticking out.

"Well, I'll be right along and take this cold tea down to the kitchen, I s'pose. And this—" a fabric swished—"stained shirt needs to be laundered and pressed."

Pippa cowered under the covers.

The door clicked shut.

She exhaled.

"We got caught." Nick lowered his head with the boyish, mischievous smile that had gotten her into this trouble and peeked out from under the covers. If she married him, his life was safe, his sister, and the reputation of his practice. If her father granted her this one wish, to marry Nick—for love… Which he wouldn't, she was sure. And yet, she'd promised Nick. *How could she keep this promise?*

"Oh, you're awake," Pippa said, trying to suppress the heat from rising to her head. But the sight of him took her breath away. Most people would not look so appetizing in the morning, but Nick beamed with freshness and brightness, his mussed golden hair pressed against his forehead by the covers.

"Who was that?"

"Mrs. George."

"I think she saw me."

"I am *sure* she did. Nothing escapes her."

"Should I climb out the window now and disappear?" He looked at peace, but Pippa's heart sank. She'd wanted to take the fears from him, to shoulder the burden of their liaison. They were engaged, and she wanted everything they'd spoken about. Pippa vowed to herself that she wouldn't let her father or anyone from the Ton stop her.

Pippa grabbed his head and frowned. She wouldn't let him go away for anything in the world. Nick laughed and climbed atop her.

"Your hair looks wild." She drove her hands through his gorgeous loose locks.

"You are wild." Amusement colored his voice, and he descended to nibble on her breasts.

Again.

Oh, so deliciously.

"It's your birthday, and after eleven."

"The best birthday I've ever had." Nick kissed a path down her middle.

―――※―――

BEFORE LONG, THE sun was past its zenith, and no shadows were outside.

Nick's stomach rumbled so loudly that Pippa stopped kissing him.

"It's your birthday, and I haven't even offered you breakfast." She paused. "Or luncheon." She drew her eyes open in alarm. "And you only had tea and shortbread yesterday. Oh, I'm the worst hostess the world has ever seen."

Nick laughed out loud, and she saw his big white teeth, perfect rows. A luscious mouth. There was that heat and hunger again. "I've had the feast of a lifetime," he mumbled and gave her nipple a lick.

Pippa twitched in response. Then he kissed the bottom of her breast and laid his palm flat on her belly. "Are you hungry?"

"I can smell food." Pippa crinkled her nose. Thinking of it, she smelled mushrooms and cheese, Mrs. George's signature dish. "Chanterelle pies!"

Nick brought his head to her face and propped himself up just so that his hard manhood laid flat on her stomach. "Are you hungry?"

"Insatiable," Pippa said and wrapped her hand around his shaft. "But I could use a bite to eat."

"They'll know when they see me, Pippa." A rueful expression washed over Nick as he sat in bed and pulled the covers over his erection. His gorgeous naked chest and muscular arms were even more appealing in the brightness of day.

"So what? They'll have to know about our engagement at some point."

He arched his brows and gave her a once-over. Pippa folded half the covers over her chest and climbed out of bed. They draped around her body like an evening gown.

It was a new morning, and it felt like a different life had begun.

She felt reborn.

As if the old clumsy Pippa had vanished, she was now Lady Penelope, mistress of the manor, and no longer alone.

"They work for me, and you are my guest." She pinched her eyes shut. "You'll be the lord of this manor soon."

Nick fell silent for a moment. As if he were making a host of decisions, his mien changed from surprise to something dark and finally, he spoke, "I won't take your riches, Pippa, only your love as far as you'll give freely. But I'll never let you go either, for as long as you want me."

She feigned shock and gave the covers one last tug, leaving him naked on the bed.

He jumped up and wrapped himself against her.

His tall, naked body felt glorious around her, and she dropped the white covers with a giggle.

Lady Penelope had blossomed.

Chapter Twenty-Seven

As if by magic, Pippa's bathroom, bearing apricot-orange decor and marble tiles, had been outfitted with a stool and a tray of shaving supplies. One of the finest soaps wrapped in elegantly folded paper sat in a ceramic dish, a glistening new blade was on the side, and there was even mint toothpowder and a toothbrush in a silk bag. Hanging on the side of the tub was an array of clean towels in various sizes and—Nick had to look twice—his shirt or was it a new one in his size?

So, this was what it felt like to have servants.

He thought about the life he could offer Pippa and the life she was used to. But doubting his decision and worrying about the consequences of his actions hurt. *Not today*. He'd rather cherish the day.

He picked the parcel up because he'd recognized the collar. Someone had cleaned his shirt and pressed it. It looked better than new and smelled fantastic.

The waiting bath was steaming hot, and Nick let out the tension of his muscles. He never had a less restless night, nor had he felt more relaxed.

His life had clicked into place, and he had a path now.

How he'd navigate this path, he wasn't sure. All he'd ever thought of was the practice and looking after his little sister.

But he'd declared his love to Pippa and felt elated.

It had to come out.

And her response was glorious.

He couldn't wait to tell Wendy that he was engaged.

JUST BEFORE THEY'D climbed into the carriage, Mrs. George had whispered something to Pippa, but Nick had heard.

"Your mother and grandfather would be proud to see you seize control over your life. Love is worth fighting for, mark my words." And even Mr. George had smiled when he'd shut the door and signaled the driver they were ready to depart.

"I expected them to threaten a scandal," Nick said when they were finally alone. "They must know that I'm nothing."

"They are the last loyal servants left from my grandfather's time, Nick. They know that a gentleman can earn his station regardless of whether or not he's born with it."

Nick didn't fully understand the compliment, but he appreciated it regardless. Pippa seemed changed since their night together, as if she'd come into her own. He loved it because it meant the woman he loved radiated happiness thanks to him, and she was somehow more at peace with herself than ever before.

※

IN THE EARLY evening, Nick and Pippa's carriage pulled up in front of 87 Harley Street. Pippa fumbled with her hair and tugged at the scarf wrapped around her shoulders.

"You look lovely," Nick said as he kissed her on the tip of her nose. She playfully scrunched her nose, and her glasses slid down. She pushed them back up with her index finger, and Nick's heart lurched. This was his woman, his love. She was smart and beautiful, wealthy beyond measure, wild in bed to suit his taste, and easily the best kisser he'd ever encountered. "You are a dream come true; do you know that?"

When they went inside, a commotion was underway in the back rooms of the house, and Nick gently grabbed Pippa's hand and led her to the kitchen. What he saw left him agog.

Several mismatched chairs were around the kitchen table, set with a white damask tablecloth and a small bouquet in the center, including the ones from the waiting room. A pretty white cake, expertly enveloped in whipped cream with strawberries, was on the table with a few plates and forks next to it. Alfie and Andre and a woman in a ruffled dress were seated around the table in freshly pressed shirts. Felix stood at the stove with the tea kettle in hand, and Wendy approached Nick with an expression as if she'd just been hit with an invisible club. Hooked into her arm was no other than...

"Lance?"

"Happy birthday, Nick!" His friend carefully stepped forward as soon he turned his head toward Nick. "Come here!" Lance reached his arms out, and Nick stepped into a manly hug.

He froze at first, unsure what to do. How could he have forgotten that Lance was coming for his birthday? Nick exhaled and collapsed, but then the unexpected happened. Lance tightened the hug, a brotherly and friendly sign of support. "It's so good to be together again," Lance whispered, then let go.

Oddly, it was Nick stumbling about the room even though he had his near-perfect vision. Lance was *happy* to see him. Despite the fact that Nick never had... he'd never even visited him.

"I should have come to visit you," Nick said in a low voice. Wendy stepped aside and gave him a look like the one their mother had when they'd brought a stray kitten home, that needed care and love but had been neglected. Just like their late mother, Wendy had a heart for outcasts and stray souls.

"You'd always be welcome with us," Lance said, gesturing toward a woman in a frilly dress. She was seated at the table but immediately rose and came to his side. She was young and had dark hair, but Nick immediately noticed her hypopigmentation when she lifted her gaze. She had a few pale patches on her face where the skin had no color. It was an inconsequential condition of the skin that didn't affect the patient's health, Nick remembered from medical school. But in aristocratic circles, it was doom. Any imperfections of the skin made a woman unmarriageable, even a harmless skin coloring imperfections like her vitiligo.

"This is Isabel," Lance said proudly, reaching for her hand. She wore an understated golden wedding band. "My wife."

Lance beamed. Isabel curtsied, seemingly adept at remaining unperturbed by the shocked expressions people had when they saw her. But Nick wasn't shocked. She had pleasant features, and when she came up from her curtsy, she showed bright white teeth and a warm smile. She was lovely.

Then why did Nick feel so bad about meeting her?

From behind him came a voice, startling him out of his stupor. "It is a pleasure to make your acquaintance, Lord Ellington; I've heard of your treatise on cacti and have always wished to obtain a copy." *Pippa*.

Oh dear, Pippa was standing behind him!

"This is Lady Pemberton," Wendy said politely but with wide eyes and menacing raised eyebrows. "She's…"

Nick swallowed hard as Pippa stepped forward and reached her hand out. Lance received it gracefully and gave a kiss on her knuckles. They were in the presence of aristocrats. Three of them.

Here.

In the kitchen at 87 Harley Street.

Nick was at sea with a million thoughts and no clear direction. Then he saw Wendy's look, expectant and stern. Pippa exchanged niceties with the woman whom Lance introduced as his wife.

And then the air came back to Nick's head. Wendy chuckled.

Pippa hooked her arm into the crux of Nick's arm, and he instantly relaxed.

"You have some news to share, too, old friend, hm?" Lance gave a friendly pat on Nick's other arm. "Are congratulations in order?"

Alfie and Andre rose, their chairs screeching lightly.

"I—*ahem*—I..." Words failed Nick. But then Pippa tightened her grip on his arm and nestled against his body. Instinctively, his other hand found hers and laid it atop her delicate fingers. They were cool to the touch. Was she cold?

Nick turned to her, concerned for her well-being. And when his eyes found hers, she beamed at him. Her warm, intelligent eyes were miles ahead of him; she'd understood his feelings before he could see the words. And he knew right away that the world had changed. With Pippa by his side, everything would be different. And he felt whole.

"This is Lady Pippa Pemberton." Nick pulled her closer to him. "My fiancée."

Wendy gasped. Her eyes darted from his to Pippa and back.

Pippa let the scrutiny of the onlookers wash over her and lowered her gaze for a moment. But then she did her usual adorable thing: pushed the bridge of her glasses up, crinkled her nose, and smiled.

And the group burst into loud congratulations. Hugs came from all directions, and even Lance welcomed Pippa into the group.

Later that evening, over a whisky that had been a thank you gift from the Marquis of Chelmsford last year, Nick found himself alone in the kitchen with Lance. Alfie and Felix had gone to bed after the last piece of cake had been eaten, apparently a special order from the *Patisserie de la Loire* on Nick's birthday. Wendy led Pippa and Lady Ellington upstairs to see the guests' room.

Lance, despite his blindness, had found a way to live, to move forward. But Nick was stuck in the past, shackled by guilt and regret. He was more a prisoner of the dark than Lance ever was.

With a determined sigh, Nick realized that it was time to face Lance, not out of obligation, but to seek redemption—not for Lance, but for himself. He realized that the first step to helping Lance was to free himself from his own darkness. Only then could he hope to be the friend Lance needed.

As fear gave way to resolution, Nick felt a glimmer of hope. Perhaps this visit was not a specter from the past, but a chance for healing, a beacon guiding them both out of the darkness and into the light.

Odd, last night, Nick had been a guest, and his life had changed so profoundly. Tonight, he was the host and perhaps his life was going to change again.

"I hope you like her," Lance said with a lost gaze, twirling the amber liquid in his glass. But weren't any of his gazes lost? It seemed that his heart wasn't, but he was missing something else, a profound knowledge that had to do with his wife.

"She's lovely," Nick said.

Lance's eyes darted to his as if he could see into his soul far more deeply than a seeing person might. "She saved my life, Nick. She really did."

"How? Were you sick?"

"Yes and no. I'm blind, I don't need to tell you. To my parents, it's an incurable flaw. I was cast aside and sent off into the country house."

"Yes, where I sent your letters?"

"Right. And they hired a nurse for me."

"Who looked after your correspondence, too?"

"She wasn't a nurse, Nick. It was Isabel." He paused. "Apparently, she has some skin color flaw." He waved as if it were naught. For him, it was.

Nick's chest was constricted with the realization. Lance had never seen her, and yet he loved her. It was plain to see when he spoke about her.

"I finally wanted you to meet her."

"Why didn't you tell me in the letters?" Nick couldn't quite put it all together.

"She penned them for me; how could I? There were no words, Nick. She was already there when my parents locked me up in the country estate."

"Why was she there? How did she factor into your condition?"

"She's the daughter of a duke and couldn't make her debut. When my mother spoke to hers, they thought a service life was a suitable fate for a woman like her."

"Because of the hypopigmentation?"

"Yes."

"They sent her away with you to hide you both from society?"

"Yes."

Nick plopped back in his chair and set the whiskey on the table with a clang. No matter how low his expectations were, the evil in this world never ceased to surprise him. "But you're both healthy. Neither of you has—"

"We both have impediments that society doesn't want to see."

Nick puffed. "Society—" he waved grandly to mock the Ton and their haughty goings on—"has more procedures to renovate their physiques than they care to admit."

"Are you saying they're all false?"

"No, not false. That's not the right word. But people aren't flawless. Nobody is perfect. Every person needs to work on something. Just ask Felix how many debutantes come to him, and lords, dukes, earls, their wives, sisters, sons, and even simple folks come for treatment."

"Nick, I'm blind, Isabel is freckled. It's just a few dental fillings."

For a moment, a series of patients that had come and gone from Felix's treatment room with much more than a few fillings flashed before his inner eye. The most recent of the patients with extensive work done was the Earl of Langley, but he couldn't mention it. He'd never betray a patient's trust, and as much as it stung, Lance wasn't a doctor in their practice. If things had worked out differently, he would have been.

Nick realized what Lance had said.

Isabel is freckled.

He didn't know that it was worse than that. And he might never understand.

Still, this was how Isabel got her chance at love, right?

Nick tasted acid when he realized what had been on his mind. How could he be so superficial to think there was nothing more to her than her beauty? Or that a minor flaw that probably didn't even affect her health would render her unmarriageable. Yet, Lance loved her, and he was of noble heritage.

"You two would be the perfect match if society accepted you as you are," Nick said out loud before he could filter his words. "Pardon me, I didn't mean to insult—"

"Not at all. That's actually why we are here. We want your help for a chance to return to society."

"What could I do about the Ton? I'm at risk of losing the practice because I am engaged to the daughter of a duke." He didn't dare mention—even to Lance—that they were engaged without her father's permission and that he'd only recently taken her virginity and compromised her beyond all redemption. The Ton would not be his friend now, and perhaps never unless they married swiftly. It all hinged on her father. "I have no sway."

"But you have a scalpel."

"What? I'm not killing anyone for you, Lance. I'd never—"

"Operate on me."

"What? That's even worse!"

"Worse than to kill someone? How does that even make sense?"

"Well," Nick stuttered. Why was there no air in the kitchen? "Well—"

"You'd rather kill someone than operate on me? Good to know. Thank you very much." Lance rose, and the chair made such a high-pitched noise that Nick cringed.

"No!" Nick tugged at his collar and realized the top button was already open. Yet, he couldn't breathe.

Lance stood over him. "Then do it, please. Give me a chance to see you again."

That was exactly what Nick had feared. He hadn't been responsible for Lance's loss of vision. He hadn't even been in a position to help cure him all those years ago at university. But if he injured him, he'd be the one to rob him of hope forever.

"We don't even know the cause for your blindness," Nick exhaled in protest, knowing that he was about to be defeated by his sense of guilt. Lance furrowed his brow.

"That's true. I never had a conclusive diagnosis."

"See?" Nick bit his tongue immediately upon saying it. Rarely had there been a pun more clumsily uttered than this.

"I don't see, no."

"And we don't know why," Nick said.

"So, let's find out."

Chapter Twenty-Eight

MEANWHILE, UPSTAIRS, PIPPA had joined Wendy and Lance's wife to make up a bed for two instead of just one since Lance and Isabel were staying at 87 Harley Street.

"I'm afraid this room is rather simple and small, Lady Ellington." Wendy fussed with a doily on a dress.

"Please call me Isabel." She inclined her head gracefully and Pippa smiled when Wendy curtsied a little too deeply and a little too long. "Let me make this a little prettier for you. I'll fetch the flowers from downstairs."

She left.

Pippa stood with her back against the windowsill, unsure what to do. She usually had servants for this sort of work and couldn't offer much help to Isabel.

"Lady Penelope, I have heard much about your family and regret we didn't meet sooner," Isabel spoke to her as if they were at Almack's, the Wednesday balls that were nothing more than an elitist meat market for finding a match that she'd never seen welcoming at all.

"Please call me Pippa. I'm not really welcome in society and am beginning to put less value on seeking to be welcome there anyway."

At that, Isabel opened her eyes wide. "How can you say such a thing?"

"Well, they call me 'the clumsy goose.'"

Isabel drew her brows together, but her eyes remained awash with incredulity.

"It's because of my vision," Pippa explained. "I've been so clumsy until I received these spectacles."

"Did Nick, I mean, Dr. Folsham, make them for you?"

"No, he examined my eyes, and his sister made them."

"So, you are cured?"

"Well, I wasn't really sick at all. Nick explained that it was the curvature of my lens that made me shortsighted. The spectacles correct that."

"Oh, your family must be delighted." Isabel clapped excitedly as if all was well with the world, but Pippa sensed a tinge of reservation.

She realized why. "You must have heard of my mother's passing if you, our families, are acquainted."

Isabel dropped her hands and deflated. "Yes. I'm sorry for your loss."

"Thank you. My father had remarried a few times since then actually. But my poor vision hasn't left a good impression."

"If I could have been cured by something as simple as spectacles, my mother would have—"

"Are you unwell?"

Isabel blinked at Pippa. Then she blushed, and the pale spot on her face grew even more white than the rest. "I'm disfigured."

Pippa gave up feigning ignorance. The pale patch on Isabel's face would only grow larger than life and siphon the air from the room like a hot air balloon trying to escape the confines and unable to lift off. "I see." The irony was palpable. She finally could see, but now...

Isabel inhaled and then folded her hands in her lap. "I was born like everyone else. My birthday was in the winter, so I was kept indoors for my first months of life. When I was first taken outside in the spring, a small line of redness appeared on my cheek. My mother told me that it became more and more demarcated. By the end of my first summer, when I was about ten months old and had learned to walk in the gardens of our townhouse, the white patch was clearly visible. It never faded again and extends to my chin and neck."

Pippa saw that the patch of pale skin extended to her neck but refrained from commenting or dwelling on it, because she knew what it meant to be the odd one out.

"I understand."

"You are the first person to say that whom I believe, Lady Pemb— I mean—Pippa. Call me Isabel." She gave her a warm smile.

"Thank you, Isabel. I believe this may be the beginning of a wonderful friendship." Pippa took her hand and gave it a gentle squeeze. They were still holding hands when Wendy returned with a bouquet in a vase and an embroidered quilt.

"What did I miss?" Wendy set down the flowers and plopped on the bed. Instantly, Pippa felt like a schoolgirl gossiping behind the headmistress's back. Not so different from her relationship with Bea, but somehow warmer. Or maybe that was because of the person Wendy was. Either way, it was a comfortable and happy place to be.

"Well, I'm glad I'm here," Isabel said. "Thank you for the warm welcome."

Wendy squinted and pressed her lips together in a suspicious smile. "Why are you here?"

Isabel sucked her cheeks in but remained silent.

"Is there another reason for them to be here, besides wanting to meet Lance's friends?" Pippa asked.

"I'm afraid there is," Isabel said, seemingly displeased. "He wants to see me."

"But you live together, I'm sure…" Yet Pippa's voice trailed off when Wendy gave her a somber look. "Oh!"

"And I'd rather not be seen," Isabel said, rubbing her hands together in discomfort.

Chapter Twenty-Nine

AT FIVE O'CLOCK the next morning Pippa took the doctors' shared carriage home. It had been lovely talking to Nick's friends throughout the night, but she didn't want Wife Six to catch her sneaking back to Cloverdale House. Thus, she returned to the breakfast table as usual and took her customary seat next to Bea, who gave her an inquisitive stare. Pippa couldn't answer at the moment. She sat there, ignoring Wife Six. As she'd predicted, nobody besides Bea had noticed her absence. All was as usual and Pippa felt for the soft spot on the side of her breakfast roll before she split it open, her glasses safely tucked away. And yet, everything had changed. Her little tolerance for Wife Six had evaporated and Pippa had grown impatient with her father's hypocrisy, indulging himself in a destructive lifestyle while scrutinizing Pippa for the slightest transgression.

Not that seducing Nick and agreeing to marry him was a small transgression.

It was all but and it meant the world.

Now Pippa had to get the world to bend to her will the way Nick managed to make light bend through a lens. And she refused to remain silent.

"How can you pay Sir Matthews so much for laying rocks on your back daily?"

"It's called crystal therapy; he's a healer."

"Why don't you go to a real doctor instead?"

"Ah, where would I find a trustworthy doctor, hm?" Father's question was rhetorical, and Pippa knew it was best not to answer. "I've had enough experience with doctors, Pippa. It has sufficed for a lifetime."

"Well, I don't believe Sir Matthews is doing you any good. On the contrary."

"Who made you the expert on doctors, hm?" He had the same telltale you-are-just-a-girl attitude whenever Pippa offered constructive criticism.

"I had the same experience as you. Do you think I forgot the surgeon who came out of Mother's bedchambers shaking his head in defeat? Or the physician who cut her wrist to let her blood? Or the other physician who gave her so much laudanum that she hallucinated?"

Her father grunted and shrugged, which made his big belly jiggle like lemon custard.

"And I remember the last one, the youngest of them all. He sat with us for two days and a night, checking her breathing and her pulse. He didn't leave her side until her time had come."

"He waited with us for her death, Pippa. That's all." Father's voice had a vulnerability and sincerity that Pippa hadn't heard in a long time.

"He knew it was hopeless, yet he stayed to make her comfortable."

"No, he didn't know what to do and couldn't help her, so she died. Pippa, your mother died because none of those damn doctors could help her." Father was always ready to condemn the doctors, but he refused to take responsibility for letting his own health decline.

"She died because she was ill. She'd fallen ill a long time ago, and it got worse over the years. None of the doctors made her ill." *You, on the contrary, are doing something to make yourself ill. And your newest wife makes me sick.*

"They didn't make her better either."

"That may be. But they didn't kill her."

"The hopelessness did, Pippa. Every time one of them told us that there was nothing like it that they'd ever encountered, she wilted a bit more until it was finally too late to come back."

"How can you blame the doctors? She was already ill when they met her. She didn't catch it from them, nor was it their fault that whatever she had was incurable. Even hope couldn't save her."

"Don't be so naive, my child. A doctor is far from a good Samaritan. They don't take on a patient out of the goodness of their heart and try to make them better. It's their job, and they charge a lot of money for that."

"So what? We have enough money to pay them. There's more than Mother could spend in her lifetime."

"Yes, but that's not the point. They started something, a healing process, and made promises to cure your mother, but they failed. And yet, we had to pay them."

"But you pay for food when you get it, not after you digest it, which fuels your body. How is that different?" Pippa was furious with her father, not merely because his worldview was so skewed, but also because she'd taken so long to confront him. How could she have allowed her life to come to this? She'd been mocked by the blob her father had turned into, duke or not, and it had taken Nick risking his practice and life's work to be with her to awaken her good sense. *Enough!*

"Once a healer lays a hand on a patient, they have trust and responsibility to succeed. It's not a transaction that you pay for."

Unless that doctor happens to be "Sir" Matthews. And what successful treatment has he provided you? Pippa knew better than to put voice to that thought. "But they provide a service, medicines, and they use their supplies. You pay a teacher and a cook, regardless of whether a student learns or whether the food is well digested. Why doesn't a doctor get the benefit of the doubt?"

"Because of their expertise, Pippa. Their training puts them above the patient in understanding the ailments more deeply than the patient. And that understanding sets doctors apart."

Pippa thought about that for a moment. She couldn't picture Nick like that, nor Felix. "The way I see it, a doctor is like a teacher. They sell their expertise. But they don't get paid for studying their subject and all the years of training."

"Ah, and that's where your young age forgives human vices, my girl. I'm no longer prone to that."

Even though she disagreed with her father, he'd finally called her "his girl" again, and Pippa's heart warmed. She continued, "Where's the vice in a young person who goes to university and studies uncountable treatises on human conditions for years and years? Then, that person goes through various apprenticeships and training; some even travel the world to perfect their craft. And when they offer their expertise to help patients, isn't it natural that they'd charge for it? They are just people; they need to live and eat. And who pays for their supplies? For the white linens, the clove oil, the glass lenses, and for sharpening their tools?"

Father squinted. "You know an awful lot about what it takes to run a medical practice."

"No more than about running a school."

"And you got that knowledge from attending school, I know. When have you gone to a medical practice?"

The time had come. Pippa reached for her reticule and opened the ribbon that kept it closed. Then she felt for her leather *etui* and pulled the spectacles out. She put them on.

Father saw and clenched his jaw. "Where did you get those?"

"From the oculist."

"Where, I asked."

"87 Harley Street."

He pursed his lips. "*Argh...* take them off."

"No." Pippa crossed her arms.

"Now!"

"No, Father. I won't. They help me to see better."

"Nonsense. Ladies don't wear glasses. Nobody will marry you with spectacles, Pippa. Off with them! Now!" He leaned forward with an alacrity she didn't expect from him anymore, and he grabbed the glasses from her face.

Then he squashed them in his hand.

"Father! No!" Pippa cried.

"I didn't give you permission to seek out an oculist. They're all quacks. Just like the surgeons, dentists—"

"It would do you good to see a dentist!" Pippa shouted, heat rushing to her head as she grabbed the bent spectacles back from her father. One of the lenses had popped halfway out. She tried to squeeze it back into the metal frame with a shaking hand, but she was so angry that her eyes welled up with tears making it even more impossible to see clearly.

"You're embarrassing us with those, on top of making no effort to wed. How do you expect us to continue to pay for you, the clumsy goose on the shelf?"

Pipa seethed with fury. "I'm so ashamed, Father."

Ashamed of what you've become. Who you are. And your foul, common wife.

"As you should be, my girl. Being caught with spectacles could compromise you. It would show the Ton that you're defective and deficient."

There it was, that word again. But it wasn't a comment about her eyesight, it was a comment about *her*. Pippa sniffled. She realized her tears came from anger, not sadness, and the feeling didn't fade when her father reached out to her, his hand swollen, and his skin stretched and purple. This was not his father's loving hand from her childhood; this was a vexing man who'd been manipulated into an unhealthy, thoughtless marionette.

"It's been so hard to watch you degrade, Child."

"I beg your pardon?"

"You withdrew into your greenhouse or your mother's country estate. Don't think I didn't notice how often you snuck out of dinners and feigned tiredness at balls. You made a fool of yourself as a clumsy goose, and then left society as a whole."

"I'm sorry I embarrassed you, Father," Pippa said with all the grace she could muster, her chin held high even though tears ran down her cheeks and dripped from her chin. "I have never felt more shame."

"For your clumsiness?"

"No, Father. For you."

"M-me?" He thundered. "How dare you!"

"How. Dare. You," Pippa growled, rose from her seat, and left.

Chapter Thirty

SHORTLY AFTER BREAKFAST, Pippa walked into the orangery. Something was amiss.

It was quiet.

The faucet was dripping in the back right corner, but she always turned it off completely, as would Bea. She stopped to take in the situation. The philodendron's leaves were bent and had light yellow cracks. Someone had been there—someone with little regard for breaking leaves of precious tropical plants.

Pippa slowly walked farther into the orangery, carefully listening to the familiar sounds of her favorite place. She closed her eyes to take in the atmosphere as she knew it before she'd received spectacles.

The silence in the orangery was punctuated by the faucet's irregular drip—a sound that echoed ominously. As Pippa held out her hands, palms outward to feel her way along the path between the high beds, the cool, waxy touch of the tropical leaves sent an unfamiliar chill down her spine. She closed her eyes, reaching out farther into the strange silence, her fingertips brushing against a broken twig of the ficus.

With each breath she took, the intoxicating fragrance of the blooming citrus trees almost obscured the disconcerting smell of disturbed earth. It was a scent that didn't belong in her carefully tended environment, and it made her heart quicken. The orangery—

the place she knew like the back of her hand—felt different, foreign.

Suddenly, the soft, hushed sound of breathing caught her attention—a breath that was not hers. It stemmed from the corner where Sir Hoppington usually nestled in his haybed, a space meant for tranquility, not fear. Pippa's heart pounded in her chest as she tried to see through blurry vision, her serene sanctuary now a setting of unexpected suspense.

A rush of shock and then anger coursed through her veins as she raced to the corner, the unsettling crunch of the hay under her feet sounding louder than ever. The breathing was there—steady, yet strained—and it filled the orangery with suspense that cast a dark shadow over its usual luminescence. Pippa felt a knot of unease tighten in her stomach as she neared the haybed.

Stepping farther into the corner, her foot crunched on more hay than usual—hay that she hadn't left there. Pippa was meticulous about her orangery. She always swept the ground, and any dry leaves or dead blossoms were religiously piled into a barrel outside. This untidiness was out of place and out of character for her sanctuary. Someone had disturbed the most peaceful place in Pippa's world. Her heart plummeted to her stomach, an icy sense of dread replacing the knot of unease when she reached the end of the path between the high beds and came to the potted palm tree in the corner where a dark shape hovered. It was a woman. But it wasn't Bea.

"I can see you," Pippa snarled and Wife Six emerged from the shadow of the palm. But before she could think of anything more to say, her breath hitched.

The daybed was a mess, and it was stained with blood. Sir Huffington's blood. All she could make out was a ball of fur.

"What have you done?" Pippa hurried to pick up her little friend. His soft fur was no longer fluffy, but sticky with blood and even though she tried to be gentle, he squealed.

"You caught me early. I was planning on bringing him to your room. His bed is made on your pillow." Wife Six stood next to her, her bloody arms crossed as if the stains of murder were no more than hand cream to her. "Imagine my nap before the face massage." She scratched the dozens of mosquito bites on the face and neck. "Look at me!" Her face appeared swollen, and she bore uncountable red spots everywhere on her skin.

If Pippa hadn't been in such shock, she'd laughed at the sight. Wife Six resembled a pubescent boy in a lady's gown but her hands bore witness to her cruelty.

"What do you want?" Pippa's voice trembled as she gently set her trembling friend back onto the hay.

"Revenge."

"For what?"

"You planted those mosquitos in my bedchamber. Don't think I'm stupid. I know what kind of person you are."

"And what kind is that?" Pippa looked at her bunny, trying to ascertain where he was bleeding. If only she could see!

"The devilish kind. You planned to sneak away for a tryst and wanted to cover it up. You thought I'd be bedridden for days after succumbing to a million stings. But you miscalculated, darling." Her evil stepmother *tsked* and wagged her blood-stained index finger. "I have a potion that soothes the sting, you see." She produced a glass vial with a cork from somewhere in her bodice.

"What is it?"

"My father's special recipe; it's been in our family for generations." Wife Six slid it back in her cleavage. "And you can't have any."

"What is it?"

"Liberty cap, dear. A mushroom."

Pippa gasped as she recognized what Six held in her fingers. "It is toxic. It causes delirium."

"Very good, ever the botanist. But it also soothes various ailments, including itches from mosquito bites. It's also tasteless and odorless and more importantly, your dear father doesn't notice it in his wine, and it keeps him malleable."

Pippa's stomach dropped to her knees. "You're poisoning my *father*? Why?" Pippa had fought with him, but what Wife Six had done was criminal. A crime against a duke would send her straight to the Tower of London.

"Nah, darling. I wouldn't go so far. It's harmless." Wife Six retrieved the bottle and shook it, peering at the bottle with a deranged fondness.

"What do you want from us?" Pippa snarled. It was then she saw the machete that Wife Six held. She'd taken it from its place on the wall. Now she held it out, admiring the edge as if she didn't see the blood on it. Or maybe she did see the blood and that was what she now admired. That was exactly like her, admiring the sharp blade and ignoring the rest. "Isn't it always the same thing we want?"

"Money?" Pippa grimaced. "You'll never get any from us. Not anymore. After this, I can promise you that Father won't and doesn't love you."

Wife Six laughed in a low, curling tone like a witch who had found a way to bottle evil. "You're so easy to manipulate, so stupid. While you look for love, the grownups are out for money."

"You won't get any from me either."

Wife Six nodded. "That's true. I don't expect you to hand it over, but the inheritance will come to me if your father dies. Then it would go to you. Or perhaps the order should be reversed."

Pippa should have been appalled with a woman who waited out her husband's death. It was macabre and evil, but she didn't expect anything else from this woman. "I will discredit everything you stand for, and those friends of yours across the street at 87 Harley Street." She let out a vicious snarl of a laugh. "Don't think that your visits there went unnoticed."

Pippa stepped back.

With a trembling voice, seething with hatred, Wife Six continued, "What you don't know is that Sir Matthew is my father. We'd heard about you, with your fortune. But you're pathetic and clumsy. No man will marry you. So, we came up with this plan. I'd marry your father and my father would do the rest."

So *that* was why Wife Six had provoked Pippa. Now that she considered it, Pippa realized that her father had started to get sicker and grumpier shortly before he'd married Wife Six. It had all been a trap. Wife Six was Mr. Matthews's daughter and they'd planned to defraud her father to get to Pippa's inheritance.

That Pippa hadn't expected either. She took another step back, holding Truffles even closer but he grew limp in her grasp.

The witch stepped closer. "See, as long as you don't marry, your father is your closest relation and the next in line to inherit from your grandfather. But I can solve that problem easily. All I have to do is give him a double dose of the mushroom cap to disorient him, then push him over the railing of the gallery. He plunges to his death on the marble floor below. It will look exactly like an accident. A happy accident. For me, anyway." She squinted and touched the tip of the machete to her index finger, twirling it so it caught the beams of sunlight pouring through the glass panes of the orangery.

Pippa stepped back. There was the potted palm. She reached the base of the pot with her foot. She knew the paths between the flower beds as well as her own shadow, regardless of how blurry everything was. One of the advantages of years with bad eyesight was that her other senses were sharpened.

"I saw you running behind the bushes with a man. A man I recognize, from that group of doctors across from my father's practice."

Pippa inhaled sharply. *Oh no, Nick.* "He has nothing to do with this."

"He has *everything* to do with this. Those handsome young doctors are siphoning away all his clients. They are the reason I had to rid your father of two wives and now a daughter and a niece before I can get some money."

A niece? Bea! But it was her first claim that riveted Pippa's attention. "Rid him of *two* wives?"

"Old friends of mine." She waved grandly. "But they were useless, so I had to step in myself." She'd been targeting her father for so long! Pippa wondered when Sir Matthews had appeared.

She also realized that to ask for specifics about who Six had poisoned and was planning to poison now was to put herself in more danger than she already faced. Better to focus on the crazed woman's father and their conflict with the doctors of Harley Street. "Clients? Or patients?" With her right hand on the rim of the flower bed, Pippa felt for the orchid bed—one more step.

"Patients or clients. As long as they pay, it's a wash. Your father first came to us when your mother was ill, did you know? He didn't even see me, so blind was he with love for his wife and consumed by the fear of losing her. Luckily, it didn't take long. And it was easy to convince him to return to my father to dull the pain of lost love."

"Pah!" Her father had been desperate to overcome his loss. And these vile people had taken advantage of it.

Wife Six laughed coldly. "He responded well to anything that dulled his pain and his mind."

"That's not medicine, it's fraud. Chicanery. Charlatanism."

"It's business, nothing else."

Pippa stepped back, cradling her bunny close to her with one arm. Beneath her palm, his heartbeat grew fainter. She willed herself to focus on the orchid bed and the mulched earth it held, underneath her other palm. *There! Tree bark, cork, and dry moss.* She grabbed a fist full of the new soil. There were splinters in the wood chips. *Good.* "You're a criminal."

"If you want to come up the ranks in society, there's no other way."

"There's always another way!"

"Well." Wife Six tightened the grip of the machete. Her eyes, cold and unwavering, bore into Pippa's, a chilling smile playing on her lips. "Well," she drawled again, her voice echoing ominously in the vast orangery. "This is the path I've chosen. The high road you seem to travel is far too lonely for me." She drew closer, and drew her arm back, ready to strike with the machete.

But before she could follow through, Pippa threw a fist full of dry tree bark at Wife Six. She wailed, holding her forearm over her eyes. Blinded, for the moment anyway.

The once peaceful atmosphere of the orangery was filled with Six's screeching, and it was as if the putrid criminal dirtied the familiar, uplifting aromas of the flowers just with the sound of her voice. The knot of fear tightened in Pippa's stomach. She could taste the metallic tang of anxiety on her tongue, and the scent of orchids around her suddenly seemed pungent and overpowering as her other senses heightened. She heard the drip of the tap in the corner on her right and a bird's call outside. She saw Wife Six wiping away the soil yet the way her fingers tensed around the handle of the machete. She'd wanted to discourage the woman, not enflame her ire. But then, the tiny spark of defiance in Pippa's spirit grew into a fiery conflagration that refused to be extinguished. This was her mother's orangery, and Wife Six was an intruder. This was Pippa's territory. Her life.

Seizing the opportunity, Pippa kicked over the three-foot offshoot of the potted Eastern Cape giant cycad palm between them. It was her mother's favorite and probably at least fifty years old. The large plant toppled with a crash, its leaves rustling and its pot shattering, sending shards of terracotta skittering across the polished marble floor. Without glancing backward, clutching Truffles close to her chest, Pippa turned and bolted. Her heart pounded as she darted through the narrow corridors created by her flower beds.

Her mother's orangery, once a place of tranquility and beauty, had been transformed into a battlefield. But it was this battlefield that had just saved her life.

Behind her, there was a low thump followed by an agonized scream. The sound of Wife Six tripping over the fallen palm and hitting the ground was a sweet symphony to Pippa's ears. She didn't slow down, but the corners of her mouth twitched upwards in a triumphant smile. Fear had met feistiness, and for now, feistiness had won.

But Truffles needed help.

Pippa burst from the orangery, her heart pounding like a wild drum in her chest. The garden lay before her, bathed in the soft glow of the morning sun. It was a place of beauty and respite, but now it was just a path to escape. She ran, her satin slippers skidding on the dew-kissed grass, her silken gown catching on the thorns of roses she usually admired.

Her mind was a whirlwind of thoughts, but there was one beacon of clarity amidst the chaos—Nick. He was not an aristocrat; he didn't have an ancestral estate, or a title passed down through generations. Yet, he had something far more valuable, something the people in her world often lacked—sincerity, kindness, and an unpretentious love for her. He was unique. And he had skills—the kind that could save her pet.

He was special in so many ways. And she didn't want to spend another day without him. Unlike hers, his world was straightforward and uncomplicated, not filled with secrets, deceit, and a thirst for power.

She knew she wouldn't have her father's permission to marry, but she had vowed to save Nick from the risks she'd created for him. She was a daughter of the aristocracy, bound by rules, traditions, and expectations, and she'd defied them. But at that moment, as she ran through the garden and into the park, she realized there was nowhere else she would rather be than with him, even if it meant turning her back on the world she was born into. Nick had treated her with more respect, and love, and caring, than that filthy rich world of hers had over the past years.

Pippa commanded the driver of her father's carriage to take her to 87 Harley Street. Seeing the rabbit and the blood on her dress, he made no protests. Pippa cradled Truffles with both hands; his breathing was shallow, and even without her glasses she could see that his eyes were glazing. Blood from his wound stained her hands red.

But as she rode in the carriage toward the safety and comfort of Nick's presence, a chilling thought gripped her. Now that Wife Six's plans had been revealed and thwarted, would she now move to kill her father?

"I won't let any of this happen, Truffles," Pippa whispered to her little friend.

Mr. Matthews and Wife Six wanted her money, her inheritance, even if it meant poisoning her father and killing her. It was Pippa's fault that they'd even targeted Father. They'd ruin everything Nick and his friends had worked for; they'd take good doctors away from patients who needed them for what? Superficial and hypocritical self-enrichment? And still, it was all because of her. She was worse than a clumsy goose, she'd been blind and naïve, consumed with her own petty problems. No more!

Inadvertently, her family was jeopardizing the livelihood of the man she loved and thus, his life. And his sister's! The realization hit her like a punch to the gut, the sense of doom spreading like poison.

The journey to Nick's place was filled with dread, the looming threat of her family casting a long shadow over her happiness. Indirectly, she was paying for the man threatening Nick's livelihood. It was a moment of reckoning, a moment that would decide the fate of their love. And Pippa was ready to fight for love.

Chapter Thirty-One

WHEN SHE ARRIVED, Nick was hunched over his desk, scribbling something on paper. He looked up as she stormed in, and his eyes widened. He scrambled to his feet, reaching out to her blood-soaked form and the bundle of bloodied fur she cradled in her hands.

"Pippa? What—are you all right? What happened?" He put his hands on her shoulders.

Out of breath, cradling Truffles in her hands, Pippa tried to find the right words, but she couldn't stop crying.

"M-m-mushroom cap," she managed to say.

"What?" He ran his hands over her body, and she knew he was searching for her wounds. But it was Truffles's blood he saw, not hers. "Please talk to me!" he pleaded.

Pippa broke into tears, her shoulders shaking relentlessly. She was safe, finally safe. And yet, what had happened was all too cruel. All those years of caring for her mother's plants. All the care for Sir Hoppington... she heaved a shuddering breath. What kind of a person injured a bunny just for effect? A malicious one, that's who—a person bred out of evil, deceit, and charlatanerie.

"I heard the cries; what's going on?" Alfie came into the room; as soon as he spotted her, his eyes flew open wide.

"I don't know. She came here and is bleeding." Nick examined Pippa and lifted the bunny from her arms.

"It's not my blood," she cried. "It's Truffles! He's been stabbed."

Alfie came closer, bending down to peer at Truffles, limp in Nick's hands. "Is this a rabbit?" Concern and surprise warred in his voice.

Pippa nodded. "Mushroom cap," she gasped. She dropped her face onto Nick's shoulder.

"Who took the mushroom cap?" Alfie came to stand behind Nick to see Pippa's face as she cried onto Nick's shoulder.

"My father."

"It's a dangerous poison, Pippa. We have to help the duke if he took some," Alfie said.

Nick took the bunny and carried him to his operating table. "Alfie, water—"

"Here." Alfie brought clean towels and a metal bowl of water, needles and thread; Nick had set the bunny on the table where he stood, trembling, ears back, eyes big and staring with what Pippa thought might be fear and pain.

She realized that Chromius was underfoot, leaning his shaggy side against her legs, but unlike his usual boisterous self he wasn't jumping on her. It was as if he sensed there was something gravely wrong.

"I'm not sure of the safe amount for a rabbit. I have a good idea for a human patient, but even then there's always a risk." Alfie dripped some laudanum onto a cloth that he waved near Truffles's snout. In a few moments, Pippa's bunny had collapsed. She blinked back tears.

Nick held him on his back as Alfie shaved the area around his wounds.

"It's not deep. I don't see any cuts on his organs. I'm not an animal doctor, but I think a few stitches will work to stop the bleeding."

Pippa held back her tears as she watched them work together to stop the bleeding. "He looks so small." She wiped any escaped wetness from her face. "Is he going to be all right? Is he going to…"

"As long as he doesn't develop any infection, he should be fine," Alfie said.

"I've got some ointment," Nick said. He used a flat, wooden stick to swipe over the stitches, and then wrapped a clean strip of linen around the rabbit to cover them. "He'll probably be a bit stiff, and he'll probably be somewhat groggy, but I think he'll be fine."

He was right; within a few minutes, the bunny woke up and drank water from a clean pipette that Alfie fed him. "I'll get a carrot from the back for him soon, or some carrot-flavored laudanum if he needs more," he joked.

Nick nodded, then turned his focus to Pippa. "Now. You were talking about poison. And your father? Pippa, what is happening?"

She drew a ragged breath. "Wife Six is poisoning my father, I think—one dose at night. And I think Sir Matthews gives him another in the morning when he goes for his...treatments. That's why—" Tears spilled down her cheeks once more.

Nick lifted his gaze to Alfie's. "Matthews from across the street?" He turned back to Pippa.

But as soon as Nick asked the question, he saw that a veil had descended over Pippa's red-rimmed eyes. He'd seen it before. It was the same face that doctors put on when they gave a terminal diagnosis, or when they informed family members of a surgery that had gone wrong, or the death of a baby at birth. It was the same face he'd viewed in his mirror after his best friend had gone blind and there had been nothing he could do.

Pippa leaned against the table to regain her breath. "I have to tell you something."

And with these words, she began. Sentence by sentence, she shattered his heart.

Nick was under no illusion that Alfie didn't know what he felt. Alfie stood by, his eyes flicking to Nick, who struggled to keep his composure. As if giving Nick the space to confront his heartbreak, Alfie methodically began cleaning the operating table and their tools, his motions deliberate and seemingly detached.

And it was Nick's fault for not heeding his friend's warnings. He hadn't kept his hands off the lady. It had been impulsive. Exciting, yes. Wonderful. Stupid, certainly. He'd so thoroughly compromised her that it couldn't be undone. The quack from across the street had a daughter, married to Pippa's father, who wanted to keep Pippa unmarried so that he could control her inheritance. If the stepmother outlived Pippa's father, she'd inherit. Pippa would be penniless. And if word got out that Nick had compromised her, the practice might be left in shambles.

Mr. Matthews had found a way to ruin the practice and Nick had gotten entangled in a trap. If the authorities got involved, too, rumors would spread worse than a nettle rash.

And the price he'd pay was ... everything.

Alfie waited until she finished her account. Nick watched the scene unfold as if he were reading about it in a book, but he couldn't shut it down and set it aside. He'd brought this upon his own life, imposed on an aristocrat's daughter, and tried to meddle. Why couldn't he just let her be? He'd diagnosed her because he knew spectacles would cure her hardship. And then he'd deflowered her, compromised her. Because he'd fallen in love with her, even though he'd known it was not his role to play.

Now, he and his friends could lose everything for one pair of spectacles for a pretty lady. When the gentry and nobility clashed, it was like hot and cold air in the sky; there was thunder, lighting, and bad weather. The question would be how and if their practice could weather the storm.

When she'd finished, she heaved for air, tears running down her cheeks.

But something inside of Nick had changed. He suppressed the urge to touch her. A part of him wanted to wrap himself around her and soothe her tears, but the other part, the rational one who'd worked so hard to get here, wasn't willing to sacrifice everything because of the quack's web of traps.

They set Truffles into a wicker breadbasket, softly cushioned with white muslin folded into a makeshift bunny pillow so he could sleep off the laudanum's effects. Then, they moved into the hall and spoke in hushed voices, Chromius following them.

Alfie cleared his throat and put a hand on Nick's upper arm. It was a signal to rise to action. But he addressed Pippa. "So, am I understanding this correctly? Your father has been using the money you cannot access, but that's part of your inheritance to pay for the quack, and your stepmother plans a slander campaign against the Harley Street doctors. Against *all* of us?"

"I think she sent Wife Four and Wife Five to him, but then sent them away. I'm not sure why. All I do know is that she has been planning this all along," Pippa said softly.

"So, through Wife Six's connections at the Ton, she could spread fabricated stories or allegations about us, damaging our reputation and causing patients to question our credibility." Alfie dropped into one of the chairs placed in the hall for patients, but he put his head between his legs and then rubbed his eyes with the bases of his palms. "It could be the end of us."

Nick's heart hurt as if infected with the ugly truth. He'd brought this lady to 87 Harley Street, and she could wipe their practice out. If the Duke of Sussex weren't her father, Nick could expose him and seek the truth. But having compromised and fallen in love with the duke's daughter, Nick had lost even the little credibility a commoner had who pleaded to the aristocrats. No, if he wanted to save the practice and marry Pippa, he needed more fire power.

"Alfie," Nick croaked. He couldn't look at her anymore. It had been such an exhausting day he didn't have the power to withstand heartbreak tonight. He didn't even know if he had the power to survive losing Pippa.

Yet, she wasn't who he'd hoped. She wasn't the sweet wallflower princess with the pretty greenhouse. She was a minx who'd stolen his heart, who had a weak father who was made to be addicted to hallucinogenic mushroom caps with regular and involuntary doses. If Nick didn't succeed, the life of the woman he loved could be in danger.

His throat constricted at the word. It had started as a flirtation, but it wasn't that anymore.

Not by far.

His hands grew cold, but the fire raged within him.

This was love, and he knew it. Yet Pippa's family, even the stepmother she loathed, stood between them and Nick knew no way out.

Heartbreak seemed so sure as if it had been noted in his appointment book.

Except that he wasn't willing to let go of her either.

There was no way he could sacrifice the practice for a life with her, and yet, he wouldn't let go of the future they'd whispered about in hours of passion. He'd made love to her. Perhaps she was already carrying his child? Their hearts and souls had been inseparable; if anything or anyone ever tried to tear them apart now, he'd perish.

No, he wouldn't allow it.

The quack was an obstacle, and her association with him, even indirectly, was an unexpected complication. But Nick specialized in complications, didn't he? He had a perfect track record of tackling the most unusual cases. He just had to apply what he did in the operating room to his life.

Step 1: Diagnosis.

Done. The quack planned on slandering the practice to destroy everything Nick and his friends had worked for. Plus, Wendy. Oh, Wendy. She was his family, his responsibility.

His chest tightened again. He had to fix it. There was no way he could stand between loving Pippa and his sister's happiness. He wouldn't sacrifice Wendy's happiness and security to pursue a life with

Pippa, unless...

Step 2: Prep for surgery.

"How can we get ahead of their scheme?" Nick paced the room and waved grandly like his professor in Vienna when he spoke about the branches of the optic nerve. It was easy to get to the brain and determine if it was operating well. "Who's in charge of the money?"

"The trustees at the bank manage it. My father only manages the portion related to our house." Pippa narrowed her eyes and spoke as if she were thinking something other than what she said. Her eyes were glued to Nick. He understood. She was hanging on to his every word. One wrong movement, one wrong word, and he'd break her heart.

He was an expert at controlling even the tiniest of motions, though. The portion of the body he operated on was delicate and small, regardless of how big the patient was. He had a steady hand.

All he needed was a steady head.

"How can you stop the money from reaching your father?" Nick asked.

Alfie shot him a poisonous look, but Nick brushed the unspoken reproach off. It wasn't about taking her money, even if this were what everyone would think. It was about setting her free and ensuring that her father's slander would land on deaf ears.

"The only way is if I marry, and my husband is immediately in charge of the funds."

"The funds are your entire inheritance?" Alfie asked.

Pippa nodded. "It's a fortune, actually."

"How big of a fortune?"

"Hmm, about a third," she shrugged and tightened her gaze as if she could quickly add a few numbers.

"A third of what your grandfather left you?"

"Of England."

"I beg your pardon?" Alfie's brows rose so high he looked comical. If the situation weren't so dire, Nick would laugh. Alfie coughed. "You stand to inherit a third of England?"

"Not exactly. The king holds some of the land in trust for the Crown, and I'm not sure how much of the money is backed by gold here these days or is otherwise held abroad."

Alfie's mouth fell open, and he looked rather a fish. Then he closed his mouth, scratched the back of his neck, and blinked at Nick. "Whatever you do, don't let her get away." Alfie turned to Pippa. "And whatever you need from me, medicines, or anything else, let me know. Don't let a third of England fall into the hands of the quack and his evil daughter." He nodded and crossed his arms. "Matthews and his daughter both must be reported to the magistrate."

"And bring a scandal to my family? The clumsy goose's fifth stepmother poisons the Duke of Sussex." She was right, the newspaper would distort it and capitalize on her misfortune. There had to be another way.

Back to step 2. Prepping for surgery.

"We need to dull the effects of the mushroom poison," Nick decided. "Nothing can be done if Pippa's father gets sicker. If I'm going to be his son-in-law, I must protect his health."

Pippa's chest inflated, and she opened her mouth, but no words came out.

For the first time, Nick allowed himself to meet her gaze again.

There was hope and a little of that sparkle that took his breath away.

Very well, he'd fight—his way.

"Is there an antidote for the mushroom cap?" Nick asked Alfie, who still stood broad legged with his hands crossed.

"No."

"B—u—u—u—t..." There was always a "but" in alchemy.

"If she's right and he gets two doses per day, we need to absorb the poison he gets or get rid of it before it takes effect."

"I'm afraid to ask," Nick grimaced.

"Pippa, I'll give you some charcoal."

"To draw?"

"Of course not. To mix into his food. It absorbs the toxins. Can you mix it into his coffee? Chocolate crème—"

"Perhaps hide it in an eclair from the patisserie?" Pippa asked.

"Yes! Perfect!"

"That sounds unpleasant, not perfect." Nick shook his head.

"And we need an emetic," Alfie announced.

Disgusting. Nick preferred the part of medicine he'd focused on. Inducing vomiting was not his forte.

"Now I'm afraid to ask," Pippa said. Oh good, she'd regained some of her energy.

"Well, warm water and oil work, but he won't swallow that willingly."

"Isn't there something else to hide for the same effect?" Nick didn't even want to speak about it. "Ipecac?"

"I'm not getting another shipment of ipecac for months. We don't have that much time."

"What's ipecac?"

"The ipecacuanha plant, or simply ipecac, is a species in the *Rubiaceae* family. It's native to Brazil and has been used for centuries as a source of emetic substances," Alfie explained.

"Oh, it's a small one, about this high." Pippa showed the distance of a foot between her hands. "It has slender stems that are reddish-brown and covered with fine hairs. The flowers are small."

Alfie blinked slowly as if to digest the fact that she not only knew the plant, but apparently knew it very well. Nick smiled. He couldn't help but be proud of her intelligence.

"Why do you know that?" Alfie asked.

"I have one. But its little lavender blooms have dried out for the year."

"She has an ipecac?" Alfie turned to address Nick as if he'd discovered that Pippa rode alligators and tamed tarantulas for fun.

"An orangery," Pippa corrected him.

"So, you can easily dig out a piece of the ipecac's root?" Alfie asked.

"She has a greenhouse," Nick said. "The plants are in flower beds and are quite accessible."

"A greenhouse. With medicinal plants?" Alfie asked, incredulously.

"Most of them."

Alfie squinted, keeping his arms crossed and his gaze skipping from Nick to Pippa and back. "Your beautiful blond lady is in love with you, owns a third of England, and has a greenhouse." He coughed into his fist now, before saying, "Excuse me. She has an *orangery* filled with exotic medicinal plants."

Nick couldn't suppress the smile and pinched his lips. Yes, that was his Pippa.

"Where you found her, I'm going, too!"

The three of them chuckled.

Nick inhaled gravely. All would be well. He had his love and his friends; somehow, they'd weather this storm. They'd even saved Truffles.

So, step 2 was taken care of: Pippa's father would be weaned off the mushroom cap.

That left step 3. The incision.

Chapter Thirty-Two

WHILE PIPPA AND Alfie returned to the orangery to dig out some of the ipecac plant's root and infuse into the chocolate desserts they'd laced with charcoal; Nick had to return to Lance.

Lance had been right all along.

"So, my lenses are both cloudy?"

"It's one of the worst cases I've ever seen." Of course, it was. The man was blind, after all.

"And yet, it looks familiar?" Lance asked, oddly hopeful to have a diagnosis that explained his blindness.

"It's the back of the lens, Lance. That's why you lost your vision so quickly. Where the light has to pass through, I mean where it's bundled—"

"Don't speak to me like I'm a layperson. If I have a posterior sub-capsular cataract, say so. I get it," Lance bellowed. He pressed both hands flat on the table and was tense. "Take them out."

"What?"

"That's what you do, don't you? Take the bad lenses out and give me crystal glass ones. Please!"

"Lance, I... ahem..." Was that why he'd come? To coerce Nick into operating on him? He'd had an inkling that there might be an ulterior motive besides introducing his wife to him and their friends, but he was usually the one to pick the cases for surgery, not vice versa.

"You don't want to operate on me?"

"No."

"Why not? I'll pay. I can pay, Nick!"

"I don't want your money. I never asked for it."

"Then why not operate on me? Take them out!" Lance stood abruptly and cramped his hands into claws over his eyes as if he could tear them out and sprout a better pair. "Please!"

"Why do you want the lenses out so badly? It's not something anyone has ever asked me for. People don't just come to me and say, 'Doctor, slice into my eye and take my lens out, please.'"

"They don't understand. It's physics, Nick. Clarity won't come in if you don't let the light through. It's easy."

"The theory is, yes, but the procedure is not."

"Except that your surgeries always go well."

Nick shrugged. It had been a close call with the Earl of Langley recently, but he'd fully recovered by now. Sometimes, the cases were so complicated that he feared losing touch and breaking the streak of immaculate surgeries. One lousy surgery and he feared he'd lose his footing from the slippery top of this mountain. And with the pressure from the quack and the threat of his slander looming over him, Nick feared he might not perform as well as he should. And it was never more critical than right now.

"You're renowned like a puppet master of the eye, Nick. Don't you know?"

Nick mumbled, "No."

"I have read your papers. Isabel read them to me. The journals write about your papers after they publish them. There are seminars at the University in Vienna with hundreds of men discussing your calculations. How do you not know?"

Nick thought about it. Wendy did bring him correspondence with invitations for lectures sometimes. He never gave it much thought because he had surgeries scheduled.

"Your track record is perfect."

"Because I pick my cases."

"Based on which criteria?"

"Well, the case has to be serious enough to warrant surgery."

Lance waved his hand impatiently to nudge Nick on. "What else?"

"The patient has to be healthy enough to recover from the surgery. I need to know that it can heal."

"Fair enough." Lance squared his shoulders.

"The patient needs to understand that the risk of failure is blindness."

"Check. Already there."

"Lance," Nick exhaled.

"I'm already blind."

"You see a light sometimes."

"Fantastic. I can tell when the world has daytime, and I'm still at night. But I want to wake up, Nick. I am only twenty-seven. My wife... Isabel... I've never seen her, Nick. I want to see her when I kiss her, and she lays in my arms. You should know. How would you feel if you held Pippa, and you couldn't see the expression on her face when you made love to her?"

A flash of an image came before Nick's eye. Pippa was atop him, glistening with sweat from their lovemaking. He brushed some hair from her face, and she gave him one of those dreamy looks. The innocent ones that first made him fall in love with her. Then he closed his eyes. If he couldn't see her, how would he feel?

He'd love her just as much. But seeing her meant the world.

"Life's incomplete without seeing your love, isn't it?" Nick asked.

Lance nodded. His head was turned his way, but when he blinked, an instinct the eye maintained despite being able to see, he looked past Nick. He couldn't see him.

"Felix!" Nick shouted, his mind made up. "Wendy!"

Lance's face brightened.

"Andre."

Now, Lance beamed. The door opened, and Wendy soon appeared; Felix came just that moment and stood behind her. Andre peeked out from his apothecary door and wiped his hands on a clean white towel.

"What is it?" Felix asked.

Wendy gave a wide-eyed look when she saw Lance. "Oh, Nick!" She clasped her hands over her chest.

"He convinced me," Nick said. "But I need all of your help, please." Nick looked at Felix, who clenched his jaws.

"You can't operate on a friend," Felix said warningly.

"Why not? You've done it."

Andre came across the hall and had a serious mien. "What do you mean?"

"I did it once and never again. It almost ended my career," Felix said without looking at Andre, who was now standing in the room with them.

No worries, none of them would betray Felix's secret, yet they'd all learned from the mistake.

"I have some calculations to do. We just took the measurements," Nick said as he walked to his desk and pulled open the drawer of lenses. "Could you all prep him for surgery?"

"Both eyes today?" Wendy asked.

"Both today," Lance said sternly. He had the doctor's tone mastered even though he hadn't graduated from university. Some just had the clinical touch in their voice.

Nick heard footsteps coming from the staircase as Felix told Lance to come with him to rinse his face. Wendy began to lay linens on the operating table.

"Lance?" Isabel said from the bottom of the steps when she saw Lance walking upstairs with his hand on Felix's arm. "Why are you going with Felix?"

"I'm prepping him for surgery," Felix said, but Lance had already entered his office.

Chapter Thirty-Three

PIPPA THOUGHT OF everything she'd left behind. The servants had cleaned up the mess, but the void of Sir Hoppington's absence left the orangery feeling strange. Luckily, he'd found a safe little basket and had recovered well enough in the course of the following day to chase Chromius. If Pippa weren't so tense these days, she'd appreciate the humor of the small three-legged bunny chasing a dog four times its size.

Lance was almost ready for surgery when Pippa and Alfie returned from their mission to obtain ipecac root and pastries. Alfie took the ipecac root to his apothecary across from Nick's treatment room and started to do whatever he needed to prepare it for her father.

But it was the first time she'd harvested the root of a plant and not merely a flower or a fruit like her pineapple. She'd started to harvest from the orangery rather than care for the tropical flowers. It was a shift in how she treated her mother's beloved plants. It was time to forge her own luck.

Pippa stood in the waiting room at 87 Harley Street between Alfie's glass door to the apothecary and Nick's room, where Lance had taken a position on the operating table. She didn't particularly want to go into either of those rooms, nor was she inclined to go back home again. Everything was different.

Wife Six had taken such a strong stance against Pippa that she didn't feel safe at home, nor did she expect her father to be sober enough from the mushroom poison to think rationally and defend her. No, home wasn't an option. Neither were the authorities, lest they spread rumors worse than the truth and ruin not only Pippa's family's name, but also Nick's practice. So many people's lives could be ruined. Even Bea's prospect may suffer because she lived at Cloverdale House. No, reporting Wife Six and her father wasn't an option.

Pippa wanted to distance herself from the mess but couldn't. Silvercrest Manor was too far from Harley Street, and Nick couldn't join her there if he had to care for Lance after the surgery.

Then she heard a deep sigh and some footsteps. Wendy led the way, and Isabel followed her.

"Have they gone in yet?" Wendy asked with an enterprising voice as she opened Nick's door. Pippa peeked in, as did Isabel.

Pippa saw Isabel's face fall like an anchor from a ship, splashing into the ocean and sinking lower than the eye could follow. Lance was on Nick's long table covered in white cloths with only the top of his head exposed, safely resting on the special upholstered headrest.

"Pippa, could you take Isabel for a walk or tea?" Wendy asked over her shoulder.

Pippa's eyes found Nick's. He got up from his desk, where he did his calculations. "We will all work together to make this as smooth as possible."

Understood. Isabel would be in the way. And she would be, too. No problem.

"There's a lovely little bakery just around the corner; let's go," Pippa said, taking Isabel's arm.

"But Lance!" Isabel protested. "I need to speak with him."

Pippa looked up the steps at Nick, who nodded at her from inside the treatment room. She understood he wanted her to take on Isabel.

Within a few minutes, both had picked up their reticules and pelisses—Pippa made sure she had her new glasses with her—and the door shut behind them. "This is a wonderful place; they have the most delicious strawberry cream tarts," Pippa said with as light a tone as she could. But Isabel instead dragged her feet, making a shuffling sound as she walked.

"They also have chocolate eclairs if you prefer a richer desert." Pippa tried to distract Isabel. Even though they'd been excluded from the medical procedure, Pippa realized that keeping Isabel away was rather helpful and it made her feel like she was one of the group, one of the doctors and the nurse on Harley Street. She felt honored, and her heart grew with vigor. She was no longer alone with her plants.

"So, there's also orange cake. It's delicious, but I'd dunk it in tea, and the *pâtissier* won't allow—"

"Lance doesn't eat sweets," Isabel said absent-mindedly, her eyes on the cobblestones on the street.

"Why not?"

"He is afraid that his teeth will get ugly, and he won't see it. I tell him I'd let him know but he is stubborn."

"Oh. That's rather vain yet quite sensible of him. I'm afraid I love sweets. The creamier the better."

"You are very beautiful. And your smile is impeccable. You and Nick make a lovely couple." Isabel's compliment sounded heartfelt even though it had a tinge of sadness. Yet, it had been the first time someone had called Pippa and Nick a couple. It was as if she'd been discovered. Her new life had a direction, even though it led to challenges, and the world appeared brighter than before.

"I'm afraid Lance will not be pleased with me if the surgery goes well." Isabel stopped beside a linden tree and hid her face behind her hands. "I'm such a terrible person."

"Isabel?" Pippa wasn't sure what came over her. How did the surgery and the conversation about sweets relate to the quality of Isabel's character?

"I don't want him to see me!" Isabel cried. Her face had grown blotchy.

Pippa sighed. It made little sense to feign ignorance. She might add insult to the injury—or rather the blemish—if she pretended it wasn't there.

"He won't love me if he sees my face. Nobody ever did."

"And here I was thinking that we'd become friends," Pippa tried to joke, but Isabel began to wail. *Oh dear!*

"He loves me now because he can't see me!"

"I haven't known Lance for more than a few hours, but he doesn't strike me as the superficial kind. He surely loves you for many reasons, Isabel."

"He fell in love with me because I was the only eligible woman of his station. They sent us away together to the country, out of sight and out of mind. But he won't want to take me back home with him or he'll get a mistress if he's coming out of his darkness. He's a wealthy aristocrat with an enormous following for his botany books."

"I know. I've read them all."

"You have?" Isabel blinked at Pippa. "I wrote them and drew the illustrations."

"I suspect you did far more," Pippa said.

Isabel reddened in response. No need to say any more. Women could hardly publish books, particularly treatises, and Isabel struck Pippa as the kind of person who worked and studied out of love for the subject rather than the desire to earn acclaim.

However, Pippa's heart constricted with pity for Isabel. Her friend was probably wrong about her husband's reaction, but what if she weren't and Lance would take a mistress? Men of Lance's station strayed.

Even her father had; he married five times after her mother died. In the Ton, people were as interchangeable as the sheets upon which they tumbled with their mistresses. Her father was no exception. And perhaps Lance was just like the rest of them.

Except…there was someone she knew who could solve the problem, or at least, provide some answers. Pippa inhaled as renewed hope flooded her chest. Perhaps someone else's talents could prove helpful.

"I have an idea." Pippa took Isabel's arm and signaled for a hack. "Come with me. I know somebody who can help."

Chapter Thirty-Four

THE PRACTICE WAS in a flurry of activity, even though Lance was the only patient of the day. While Wendy put some water to boil, Alfie infused towels with essential oils, Andre spoke to the patients who'd been scheduled and had to come back later in the day, and Felix had gone somewhere to do...*something*—Nick couldn't keep track.

Before him, on the operating table, sat his friend.

And he didn't want to slice into his eye.

Especially not both.

"Thank you for doing this, Nick," Lance said, dangling his feet from Nick's special operating chair. He was dressed in plain breeches and a thin white shirt, with only socks on his feet. Nick didn't want him to be uncomfortable in any way; he needed him to stay still.

"This is not easy," Nick said.

"I know. It'll hurt. I cannot imagine that it's pleasant—"

"I also meant for me." But he might lose the practice, his livelihood, so he had to try to operate on Lance before it was too late. For Wendy's sake, he'd take her out of England if he had a chance to flee. But if word got out that he'd compromised Pippa and run away, he'd never work as a doctor again. Nick thought of Wendy and how she followed him to Vienna for his studies. She'd packed up the few belongings from their childhood home that they hadn't sold and done everything to help him. He'd do the same for her and find a way to look after her if the Ton gave them the cut direct.

The conversation with Pippa from their night together came to mind. If they could realize their dreams, they could have a family and Wendy would be a part of it until the day she chose to start a family with a man she loved. And if not, Nick would look after her for as long as he lived.

Acid rose to his throat. He had the same obligation to look after Pippa now. He loved her and wanted to marry her. For all he knew, she might even carry his baby.

One step at a time, Nick thought. He'd operate on Lance even if it were the last surgery he'd ever perform.

Lance shifted. "I wish I had the luxury to consider your feelings because I realize this timing is inconvenient, but I want to see again. I *need* to see again."

"Understood." Nick lowered his head and poured alcohol into the metal bowl in which he'd prepared the two tiny crystal glass lenses for Lance's surgery. "These are calculated within a margin of error of zero point zero, zero eight. Chances are, if they work, you will always need spectacles."

Lance waved his hand dismissively. "And it's not as though you'd have to worry about me in the coming days. You have far greater heartbreak to face."

Nick dropped the cork into the alcohol bottle. "What's that supposed to mean?"

"Nothing. Just carry on." Lance settled in the chair, his head between the cushions of the headrest, and folded his hands over his chest like a corpse. "I'm ready."

"Well, I'm not. And why are you lying there like a dead man?"

Lance sat up again. "Because defeat does that to a person, Nick. There's no margin of error in real life. I'm blind and can either regain my vision or not. I don't care about zero point zero, zero something probability that I will need spectacles. I'd love to have spectacles! It would mean that I could see. But you're not seeing anything even though your vision is perfect!"

"What? Are you doubting my calculation of the refractive index?"

Lance slammed both hands onto his face. "You have no idea."

"Don't touch your face! We're going to have to clean it all over again now." Nick turned away to get more oil-infused cloths. But the need to answer Lance's accusation easily overrode his desire to perform the surgery. "I happen to have every idea! There isn't a single facet about calculating the right lens for cataract surgery that escapes me!"

"But the facets of the Ton escaped you. You made every mistake in the book, Nick."

Nick set the bowl with the alcohol and the lenses aside. A bitter dread rose in his throat, and his arms cooled like he'd walked in the dreadful winter. "You mean…Pippa?"

"Yes, Pippa. I don't need to see to sense what's going on. You love her but you're not sure how to go about getting permission to marry her."

Nick nodded, then dropped his head and swallowed, as his breathing grew so heavy it felt as though his entire body was about to crash through the floorboards. He didn't want to hear what Lance was about to say; it would forever erase the power to smile from Nick's life.

"I love her."

"And you compromised her, didn't you?" Lance placed his hand on Nick's shoulder. "Just a little bit?"

"Quite thoroughly," Nick admitted.

Lance inhaled audibly and took his hand off. "I need to see again, Nick. Come on, let's get started. You need my help."

"What does that have to do with Pippa now?"

"I was afraid I hadn't considered you and your perfect track record by being your hardest case. But I might be the most important case in your career." Lance settled back into the chair and put his arms straight on either side of his body. "Let's begin."

"Wait, what do you mean by my most important case?"

"Nick, you compromised the daughter of a duke. Is she pregnant?" Lance looked at him with a piercing expression despite his pupils being grey and unfocused.

"I... I... *ahem*...."

"I understand. She might be, then?"

"It's only been a day since."

"You have to marry her. Yesterday."

"I want to."

"Except that you can't without her father's permission. I'm sure she knows that."

"What if he won't give his permission because I'm just a..."

"Then either you lose your practice, and she's cut out and cast aside into the country as I have been, or I help you."

"And how would you do that?"

"Leave it to me. Your task is to restore my vision. Your love and both of your futures might depend on it."

Nick sat agog on the stool, and Lance lay still. Wendy, Felix, and Alfie came in to help prepare him and to assist during the surgery. As if in a *déjà vu* of a nightmare, Nick watched the routine preparation of a patient for a surgery he'd done over a thousand times. And yet, his hands felt heavy, his skin burned, and his chest was too tight to take a deep breath.

And when the time came for the first incision, he feared he'd cut far deeper into his own life than into Lance's eye.

Chapter Thirty-Five

MEANWHILE, PIPPA AND Isabel arrived at the seat of the Earl of Langley's estate in Mayfair.

"It's so nice of you to call on us," Violet said as she descended the stairs and spotted Pippa in the hall. She brushed her hair out of her face, and Pippa suppressed a chuckle. She knew now what Violet was likely doing upstairs with her husband. It warmed Pippa's heart because she was happy for Violet. She'd finally found someone who could distract her and help channel her energy.

But then Violet saw Isabel, and she froze.

Pippa looked at Violet and then at Isabel. *Oh dear.* Something was terribly amiss.

"Do you know one another?" Pippa asked, hoping that the mistake hadn't been hers, bringing these two women together.

"Why did you bring me here? You said we'd pay the Countess of Langley a visit," Isabel snarled.

Pippa's heart skipped a beat as she observed the intense gaze shared between Violet and Isabel. The air in the room grew thick with a palpable tension, an invisible barrier of resentment and hostility separating the two women. Their eyes, locked onto each other as if in a deadly duel, their cold stares as sharp and cutting as daggers. For a moment, Pippa saw not two refined ladies before her but two cats, their lithe bodies taut with anticipation, poised and ready to pounce at a moment's notice.

A wave of regret washed over her, a bitter taste of guilt staining the edges of her conscience. It was clear now—a mistake had been made. This meeting, this *reunion* apparently, orchestrated with such good intentions, had become a precarious dance of former enemies in an enclosed space. The realization hit Pippa like a violent gust of wind, knocking the breath out of her and setting her nerves on edge.

The butler withdrew, and three ladies were left in the great hall of the Earl of Langley's elegant house. Pippa had forgotten how this was, for it had been so much easier to spend time with Nick, his sister Wendy, and the other doctors on Harley Street, where societal rules and etiquette didn't play such a significant role.

This was different. She was a duke's daughter, standing in the house of a countess, and she'd brought another duke's daughter along.

"Why is she here?" Violet asked with such a calm tone that the touch of her voice sent a chill down Pippa's spine. This was the Violet Pippa remembered. She thought the Earl of Langley had thawed her, but clearly, the old Violet hadn't melted away completely.

"I'm here, I'm here," came a man's voice from the staircase.

Descending the grand staircase came the gallant earl, commanding the room's attention like a beacon of power and authority. Impeccably dressed in another one of his finely tailored waistcoats, the earl's slender fingers worked meticulously at the buttons, ensuring each was fastened precisely. His cravat, a neat arrangement of crisp white linen, was adjusted with a nonchalant tug as he aimed for perfection without seeming overly concerned about it.

"Lady Pemberton, what a pleasure to see you so early in the morning."

"It's eleven o'clock, my lord," Pippa said as she curtsied.

"Oh, that's true." The earl rubbed the back of his head as his eye trailed over a large wall clock with hands of polished brass that danced to the rhythm of time and echoed the heartbeat of the house. *Tick, tock.*

The earl cast his young wife a smitten look. Then a dreamy gaze washed over his face that made him seem rather rakish and reminded Pippa of the reputation he'd been notorious for until just about a few months ago when Violet tamed him.

Yes, that was the term. She'd tamed him, but it didn't seem he'd been able to do the same to her yet.

"You look completely recovered, my lord." Pippa ventured to break the awkward silence.

"I am well, thank you for asking."

Isabel came up from a deep curtsy as the earl extended his hand to kiss her on the knuckles. "It's a pleasure to make the acquaintance of your guest, Lady Pemberton."

"This is Lady Isabel Ellington," Pippa said, purposefully avoiding Violet's poisonous gaze. "Her husband is currently undergoing surgery, and it is my duty to distract her this morning."

"The same as I had?" the earl asked Pippa, but he didn't wait for a response. "You should know, Lady Pemberton, I saw an excellent oculist and eye surgeon, Dr. Nick Folsham. Without him, I would nearly be blind and unable to see my beautiful wife every morning." The earl was still smooth with the ladies and apparently felt quite like a rooster among his nest of chickens with Violet, Pippa, and Isabel nearby. Or he would have, if Violet hadn't coughed a "shut up" and startled him.

"Am I missing something here?" The earl signaled for everyone to enter the salon, the second door down the hall.

"She's just tense because her husband has gone under the knife today," Violet said with the catty smile Pippa hadn't seen on her since she got married. "Isn't that right, Lady Ellington?"

Isabel sneered, and her eyes grew narrow like slits. "You are incorrect. *Violet.*" Pippa could tell by Isabella's icy tone that she was deliberately ignoring Violet's status as countess. And she could. She outranked her.

"You two know each other?" The earl sat down, and a footman began to pour tea.

"My lord, it appears that I just found out that Violet and the Countess of Langley were the same individual. If I had known, I would have dissuaded Lady Penelope from intruding upon your home." Isabella sank into a chair, every inch of her a duchess in a snit of some kind. Pippa was impressed. If only she'd done that to Six from the beginning, instead of attempting to torment her with stinging insects, perhaps things would be different now.

"What am I missing here?" the earl now asked in a low voice. All niceties aside, it was time to speak frankly.

"Pippa brought Isabel Franklin here. I thought she was in Cornwall for good," Violet said as she spooned three cubes of sugar into her cup.

"Because you wanted to ensure I remained there, didn't you?" Isabel snarled, holding the cup and saucer on her lap like a weapon, probably ready to fling the hot liquid in Violet's face if she dared speak out of turn.

"What does Violet have to do with you moving to Cornwall?" Pippa asked. It seemed that only she and the earl weren't privy to the back story that Isabel and Violet had shared.

"Violet and her mother paid my parents a visit the week before I was supposed to make my debut."

"So, you came out together?" the earl asked. "How is it possible that we have never met?"

"Ask your wife, my lord. She didn't want my visage to taint the splendor of her debut," Isabel said with a wobble in her voice.

"That's not how it was, Isabel. My mother spread that rumor along with others as she always did," Violet protested.

"How convenient to point a finger at your own mother. Shall I do the same?" Isabel fumed.

"Your mother?" Violet jerked her head back. "I never spoke to her.

She asked my mother for advice to spare you the embarrassment of a debut."

Isabel blinked incredulously. "Are you trying to tell me that *my* mother asked *yours* for help to send me away before my debut?"

"It seems so. I didn't expect you not to come to your own opening ball; it came as a surprise to me. But you disappeared from Society, and then I heard a few years later that you'd married."

"You were surprised that a man wanted me, weren't you?" Isabel's hurt pierced her voice.

"No, that's not what I meant. I hadn't heard from you, so the news of your betrothal was surprising. That's all."

Isabel clanked the teacup on the table and rose, addressing the earl as she turned to make her way out. "I apologize, my lord, I have taken up too much of your hospitality already."

Pippa followed Isabel out the door, down the steps, and onto the street. "Wait, Isabel!"

Tears ran down Isabel's cheeks, and she stormed down the street, holding her bonnet tightly over her face just beneath her eyes as if she tried to hide it.

But before the end of the block, Pippa had caught up with her. "I'm sorry, it was a terrible idea! I thought Violet could help you, and I just made it all worse!" Pippa's voice shook with horror. It was all her fault to make Isabel feel so bad.

"Lady Pemberton!" sounded behind them, and they turned to see the earl emerging from his house. He looked back and forth, up and down the sidewalk, and then spotted them. "Lady Pemberton! Please! Wait!"

"Let me go!" Isabel withdrew her hand, and Pippa reached for it again. "I have to go away."

"Don't go to him!" the earl said when he reached them on the sidewalk. "Please don't go to your husband today. Take it from a man who has undergone this surgery. We don't want to be seen by anyone, especially not our wives." Pippa blinked up at the earl, usually the epitome of grace. But right now, he looked like a disheveled man in the wind, furrowing his brows. "Please let him heal and save face."

Isabel stilled, dropped her arm, and pinched her mouth shut. But she didn't keep walking—at least that was good.

"Lady Ellington, I implore you to consider my words. When Violet's father permitted me to court her, she sniffed at me as if I was of no consequence. It seems that she needs no introduction as you attended school together?"

"She told you?"

"Only this much, but I can imagine the rest." He inclined his head as if he knew what it felt like to be a victim of Violet's scorn.

"It is I who must save face, my lord." Isabel sniffled and then lifted her head and nose in the air. "I'm going to return to the country."

"But Lance needs you here!" Pippa protested.

Both Isabel and the earl looked at her as if she'd sprouted horns. "He will not want to see me..." Isabel's voice failed her. Then she grimaced and made a terrible face that broke Pippa's heart. "I'm such a bad and shallow person; I don't deserve Lance."

"Isabel! Why would you say such a thing?"

"Because His Grace said Lance might be embarrassed, but it is I who only think of my vanity. I want to run away from my husband because I'm ashamed that he'll see my face. I should have considered his feelings, and I was too vain even to contemplate it. I'm as ugly on the inside as I am on the outside."

You're not ugly at all, was what Pippa hoped the earl would say but he just stood there with horror on his face. A perfect match for Violet.

"Lady Ellington, you mustn't leave your husband on the day of or after his surgery." The earl spoke matter-of-factly. "If there is anything I know as a man, it is likely that he underwent the procedure precisely because he wished to see you."

"And when he does, he will no longer love me," Isabel wailed.

"No, no. That's just not how love works. Nobody falls out of love like that and especially not for a little blemish. Look at me, I had no chance with Violet. She gave me the same condescending look she gave you today. When I saw that expression on her face, I knew something was amiss and that you'd had the pleasure of being more closely acquainted with my wife."

Pippa couldn't believe her ears. The tall and handsome earl had been on the receiving end of Violet's scorn, and he married her regardless? Loved her? How un-aristocratic of him!

"Yes, what a pleasure!" Isabel's tone was sarcastic with an undercurrent of deep hurt. "If she and her mother hadn't told my parents that I'd bring shame on the ball's debutantes, they wouldn't have sent me away."

"But isn't that how you met Lance?" Pippa asked, trying to help the situation, but there was something bubbling between the earl and Isabel as if they shared a bond from being Violet's victims.

"It is but that's not the point."

"I'm sure Violet didn't mean anything by it, Lady Ellington."

"How can you say that? She's vicious and superficial. Anyone who doesn't fit her image of perfect beauty and immaculate composure is ousted from society." Isabel could barely contain her shrill voice, vexed by Violet's actions from years ago.

"I know, but it's not that simple." The earl was undeterred in his honesty but looked flushed and embarrassed to bare his feelings to two ladies on the sidewalk. "See, I was a glutton when I first returned from St. Petersburg. I had bedded women in almost every court in Europe and shared more than a few whiskeys with the peers of various realms. It took a toll on my health, and it showed." Isabel crossed her arms in front of her chest and quirked a brow, but he continued. "I came back and sought out the dentist first." He opened his mouth wide, and Isabel looked away like a dutiful lady. It was unseemly to stare an earl in the mouth. But Pippa looked and saw all of his back teeth, full of gold. The rest were bright white.

"Did Felix do that?" Pippa asked.

"Yes, he's my dentist. And I'm glad for it. If it weren't for him, I'd be in terrible pain or even worse, toothless. Thanks to him, I am donning gold fillings and inlays, but I can smile at my dear wife and will be able to for many years to come."

"Dear wife," Isabel snuffed.

"Yes, indeed. If she hadn't made it so difficult for me to court her, I wouldn't have been able to gather the strength for these improvements. Who knows where I'd be or with whom?"

"What do you mean?"

"Well, I didn't see well because I developed cataracts at age twenty-nine. A side effect of heavy drinking. My connections are glorious and well-known, but they came at a cost. You learn more about diplomacy over a glass of whisky than in hours of debate."

"So, Nick—"

"Yes, and there's a bit more help from Mister Alfie Collins, but the point is that Violet has an unwavering sense of *niveau*. She made me work to reclaim it, and when I did, she opened her heart to me."

"And her legs," Pippa whispered but the earl heard.

"I heard that. It's true. And I'm proud to say that I bring my wife much pleasure now. Is that implausible?"

"No," Pippa mumbled. However, she didn't particularly want Violet to have much pleasure right now after she'd made Isabel cry like that. And she too had suffered at Violet's hand. The name "clumsy goose," for example, rang out in her mind.

Beside her, Isabel tossed her head. "What does it have to do with me?"

"What I'm trying to tell you—not well, I'm afraid—is that you need to embrace your flaws, Lady Ellington. I won't lie to you and pretend that I cannot see the blemish in your face because I won't insult your intelligence. But I've learned that one mustn't be defeated by the cards we're dealt. Sometimes, we must shuffle them around and still get a flush."

With these words, he extended his arm to Isabel and waited.

She hesitated momentarily but then laid her arm in his and followed him back into the house.

Chapter Thirty-Six

BACK IN THE drawing room, the Earl of Langley settled back in his chair and lifted his cup of tea.

Isabel and Pippa followed suit. But then he grimaced and set the cup back down. "*Faugh.* There's no amount of sugar that can make this taste like the schnapps I had in Vienna, darling. I'd rather drink water." He pushed the cup aside and leaned back in his chair.

Considering his demeanor, Pippa was reminded of her father's demeanor when he'd played "The Queen Comes for Tea" with her when she was six years old. He'd been big and imposing, yet loving, willingly drinking tea when it was clear he'd prefer something else. "My grown-up drink," he'd told her. But he'd at least pretended to drink the tea she'd poured him.

It had been a long time ago now and she wasn't waiting for the queen, nor was her father inclined to have tea with her. But it was a welcome memory, one that reminded her of how much he'd changed, and how much she needed to eliminate Wife Six from their lives as soon as possible.

"He's a peer of the Realm and doesn't like tea. What an earl I caught," Violet said in a self-indulgent singsong. She was fishing for compliments. None came.

No time for dallying.

"Lady Ellington, please stay here with us as our guest. I will personally arrange for my carriage to take you back to your husband in the morning," the earl said, demonstratively ignoring his wife's gasp.

Pippa chuckled. He clearly had learned much about diplomacy and how to quiet Violet. Perhaps there was more to the earl than met the eye.

"I cannot stay without Pippa, my lord," Isabel said.

Violet deflated.

He turned to Pippa. "Is it your wish, Lady Pemberton, to join us as our guest for the rest of the day and the evening?" the earl said.

Pippa remained quiet though the answer leapt to her mind immediately. *Yes, please!* Of course, she'd jump at the chance. It wasn't exactly right for her to stay at 87 Harley Street but also going home was impossible. And if she wanted to be there for Isabel and Lance tomorrow, she didn't have enough time to go to Silvercrest Manor then return to London. "Yes, my lord. I'd be quite pleased to stay with you."

"Very good! Then I will send a note to your father to inform him that—" But Pippa interrupted the earl.

"Please don't tell him where I am, my lord."

The earl arched a brow and inclined his head. "Needn't the Duke of Sussex know where his daughter is if she doesn't come home?"

"He wouldn't miss me if I were gone a week, my lord." Heat rose to Pippa's face when she said it, but it was true. As shameful as her relationship with her father was, she could barely explain why a lady of her social standing was free to come and go without being noticed. Although now, she understood that it was, in more likelihood due to the poisonous potion with which he was being manipulated. Again, she thought about the father she'd known, a duke, willing to play tea party with his little girl. He'd loved her very much once. Now, his mind was being poisoned, not just his body.

"Lady Pemberton, is there something I ought to know?" the earl asked Pippa.

Sitting in a chair kitty-corner to the earl's, Violet looked up at the ceiling and sucked her lower lip in, the very expression she always used when... *Oh no, she told her husband.*

"Let me rephrase then." The earl scanned all three of their faces, or he would have, if each lady wasn't more intent on balancing a cup of tea on the saucer in her lap than returning his regard. "Am I harboring a fugitive?"

"No!" Violet said. "There are no criminals here, darling."

"Ah!" He leaned back, crossed his left ankle over his right knee and put both hands on the armrests. Even though the armchair was lushly upholstered, it looked too small as a throne for a commandeering man like him. It was dawning on Pippa what Violet saw in him, even though her heart ached as she thought of Nick. "So short of committing an actual crime, what atrocity am I keeping secret?"

"Nothing, my lord. I just don't wish to go home." There, Pippa had said it. "I had a disagreement with my father."

"About what?"

"My choice of groom."

"You're engaged?" Violet sputtered.

"Yes." Pippa set the cup on the table and folded her hands primly in her lap. *Eat that, Violet. The most handsome and talented young man declared his love and wants to marry me! The clumsy goose is going to be a swan!*

"To whom?" Violet cried out, her eyes doing an abysmal job of hiding her shock.

"Nick Folsham," Pippa said proudly. She held her head high and her back straight like a regal swan gliding across a still pond, every gesture exuding an unassailable dignity.

"Doctor Nicholas Folsham? The oculist?" the earl asked. Pippa nodded. "The one who's operating on her husband as we speak?" He nodded in Isabel's direction.

Isabel took a scone from the platter next to the tea tray and took a bite. This was old news to her. She was determined to project happiness. She was like…well…a goose on a nest, or a swan now, unafraid of Violet's focus or possible determination to upset her.

The earl leaned back in his chair and tapped his fingers together as if he were contemplating a coup. "Doctor Folsham is a good man," he said thoughtfully. "Very good."

Pippa's heart skipped a beat. Something was in the air, and she wasn't sure what, but it had to do with the rest of her life.

"And yet…" Violet said in a low voice. The change in her tone was immediate and distinct, much like a countess addressing her spouse. Pippa and Isabel might as well have been part of the intricate design on the settee's upholstery, so invisible they became. The earl and Violet occupied their own world, with an intense connection reflecting in their eyes as they gazed at one another. It was as if they were engaged in a silent discourse, communicating volumes without uttering a single word.

"A duke's daughter with an oculist? It's unheard of." Violet spoke as if there was no finality to the statement. Pippa's chest constricted. It was true, she was high born. He was not. She was hated, and it shouldn't matter, but it did. Love was wonderful—except if *she* fell in love. It was absurd, but her union with Nick would be cause for disgrace for many vicious tongues among the Ton. Between the earl, Violet, Isabel and her, there was no denying of the cleft between gentry and nobility. Pippa was trying to forge a bridge where none could be built.

"But I love him so much. Why should the Ton have sway in who I may or may not marry if they don't want me in their midst to begin with?" Pippa sucked in a gulp of air, but the earl and Violet's eyes were locked as if she were not in the room. "Once I'm wed, I'll have access to my inheritance and then I can be free. Nobody ever paid much attention to me besides to mock me. This way, I can break free from society's scorn."

The earl gave a nod. Then Violet unglued her eyes from him,

blinked a few times and addressed Pippa. She no longer spoke like a young woman her age; she was the countess in tone and demeanor. "You're an heiress. Once you're wed, you'll be wealthy. But until then, you'll need your father's approval."

"Yes." Pippa's heart plummeted to the floor. "He'll never give it."

"Yet, you gave Dr. Folsham your word?" the earl asked.

"She gave him her heart," Violet said on Pippa's behalf. "I can see it in her eyes."

"Promises are broken without much consequence, Lady Penelope. But a broken heart shall never be mended." The earl spoke to Pippa, but his focus was on Violet again; Pippa was sure she'd missed some part of the story, but she felt as though she were a fox in the crossfire at a country chase.

She said, "I'm shackled to my father who doesn't even want me. Yet, without his permission, I cannot grant his wish and be free. And he won't let me marry Nick for all the love in the world if he risks losing control of the portion of my wealth that he currently uses to support his lifestyle. It's of no consequence to him how I feel. I'm afraid he won't care if Nick becomes a casualty in the process, so much wealth is at stake."

"What makes you think that he won't allow you to marry Doctor Folsham?"

"Wife Six."

"Ah. And what could sway her?"

"You're not even asking me why?"

"It doesn't matter in diplomacy, Lady Penelope. It's usually just a question of the cost to get the result you desire," the earl said.

"The house."

"Silvercrest Manor or Cloverdale House?"

Pippa nodded. "All of them. Including the gardens. And my orangery. They are in my name and my father is only the executor of the estate until I marry. It will all revert to my husband then."

"So hypothetically speaking, if you relinquished your interest in Cloverdale House, your father and stepmother would own it but doing so would set you free?"

"Perhaps. She's out for pomp and prestige. And money."

"What makes you doubt the potential of such a transaction?" the earl asked.

Pippa swallowed hard. So that's what her life and family had become, transactions. Well, if there was no love left between her and her father, then there was at least money. Lots of that. Except…there was more to the story, and maybe it was time to share it. She drew in a deep breath before she blurted, "I suspect that Wife Six is poisoning my father."

The earl's penetrating gaze seemed to unravel her composure, exposing the raw vulnerability she had long sought to conceal but Pippa needed to tell the earl and his countess what had happened if she was going to request their help. Despite the daunting prospect of baring her soul to the Earl and facing the ever-judging Violet, a quiet strength pulsed within her, a resilience honed through years of enduring whispered slights and withering glances.

"Well, a wife does have a certain sway over a man's mind," the earl said, a quick smile forming on his lips as he looked at Violet. "Of course, she has the power to poison his mind as well as enrich it."

Pippa shook her head. "No. I mean actual poison. Of his body. It has been going on for a while and I only just discovered it for myself."

He raised his eyebrows. "That's a rather grave suspicion to hold, Lady Penelope. What is your basis?" the earl asked.

"She showed me a vial of mushroom cap powder the night she stabbed my pet rabbit."

"She killed your rabbit with a poisonous mushroom?" Violet blurted out.

"No, with a blade. And no, he's not dead. But the point is, she showed me the powder in the same vial as that of the crystal healer that my father frequents." She paused, then turned to Violet, who was sitting with her hand over her mouth and her eyes round and big as saucers. "My bunny is all right. Nick stitched his wounds."

"And what does that have to do with the poison?"

"It was an act of retaliation. She tried to kill my pet to hurt me. She was showing her hand," Pippa said. "And threatening to use my liaison with Nick as a scandal. She'd inform everyone in the Ton and Nick and the others would lose their clientele at 87 Harley Street."

"What did you do?" Violet asked in a voice that was both enterprising and insightful as if she were the master of managing an ill-executed practical joke, which she was. Pippa remembered every nasty prank from boarding school.

"I bred mosquito larvae in the orangery and let them hatch in her room." Pippa pinched her lips. "Just in time before a ball she hosted."

The earl massaged his cheeks as if to stifle a laugh and then sucked his cheeks in. "I see."

"Ooh. Well done," Violet murmured. Pippa decided that—should Violet ask—she'd never share with her exactly how she'd grown the larvae to enact her plan. It certainly was a trick she would have played on someone when they were younger.

Then again, they'd both learned that pulling pranks had consequences. She took a deep breath. "Wife Six said she used her father's mushroom cap. And I've seen this style of vial at the crystal healer. My father goes to see the healer—Sir Matthew—every day."

"The healer is Lady Pemberton's father?" the earl said.

"Yes." It didn't seem right to Pippa that the vile woman held the same title that had once belonged to her mother. "The sixth Lady Pemberton."

"So, she's not of noble blood either?" Violet asked.

Pippa shook her head.

"Is she wealthy?"

Pippa shook her head. "About six months ago, I looked into the accounts, and it seems that the amount she brought with her dowry was almost the same amount my father had paid the crystal healer over the course of two years."

"So, your father paid for the dowry of his non-noble wife who's the daughter of the crystal healer who's poisoning him?" the earl asked.

Pippa squinted. Phrased that way it all sounded rather like a big web of lies. "Well...Yes. She's using Nick to blackmail me into not revealing that she's poisoning my father. As long as she's manipulating my father, he won't agree to my marriage to Nick and the practice is at risk."

"Plus, your heart," Violet added. Pippa nodded.

"And you don't think your father will give his blessing for you to marry Doctor Folsham? Why? He's only twenty-six or so."

"Twenty-seven."

The earl drew circles in the air with his hands. "He's young, healthy, smart, and obviously has earned your love."

Pippa felt the heat rising to her face again. She turned to Isabel who was blinking tears away. Even though Pippa was among aristocrats, none of them had mentioned that Nick was merely a commoner. Instead, they focused on his accomplishments, and his skills. "A good man" the earl had called him, and it was true. Perhaps, because of the enlightened earl, Violet, Lance—a duke!—Isabel, and herself, Pippa had hope that the Ton might let her get away with marrying Nick.

"I'll help you." The earl uncrossed his legs and leaned forward. Violet cleared her throat and he cast her a nod. "If you agree to a certain condition, I will make sure you have your father's blessing, permission, and a special license if you need one."

"Whatever it takes!" Pippa beamed when Isabel took her hand and gave it a squeeze.

"Even if it means that you'll be the center of attention at a ball?"

Violet asked, casting the earl another of those leave-this-to-me, I-know-the-Ton looks.

Could she trust Violet? She'd been one to create all manner of chaos and upset during her youth. She never quite trusted her since. Except now…She looked at her childhood friend, now holding onto one of her husband's hands, studying her with an expression free of guile, and filled with—instead—kindness. "Yes," Pippa whispered and gently squeezed Isabel's hand back for support. She and the rest of them knew it meant defeating any obstacle that stood in the way of love, both for Pippa's prospects to marry Nick as well as for Isabel's return to Lance. Violet had a proven record of getting what she set out to obtain and if she was going to help Pippa, there was no price too high for success.

Chapter Thirty-Seven

THE DAY PASSED quickly, and a ball was arranged for the coming Friday. It was easy to do by using the occasion of Violet's brother's return from the continent and announcing that the House of Langley was hosting a soiree. Over one hundred guests, the *creme de la creme* of the Ton, were invited. The Earl of Langley sent a personal note to Pippa's father and his wife, requesting their presence.

The next morning, after plans were hatched, meals were shared, and hatchets buried, Violet came into the room Pippa and Isabel were using to dress.

"You need to look your best," Violet said, bringing a large white box upholstered with embroidered cotton. "This is from France. It's the finest."

Pippa and Isabel sat on the edge of the bed, and Violet pulled up the stool from the vanity table.

"This is a pomade of shimmer made of crushed pearl. If you pat it on your cheeks just so," Violet rubbed some on the back of her hand, "and then buff it with the powder, it'll last all night." She picked up the pouf and dusted it onto her hand.

Isabel and Pippa gasped. A thin layer of shimmering pink was on Violet's hand as if she'd made her hand blush.

"Isn't this for women of ill repute?" Pippa asked.

"If you don't know it's there, it doesn't affect anyone's reputation."

Violet rubbed some on the apples of her cheeks, and it melted into her skin. She looked glowing, but Pippa wouldn't have known if she didn't know Violet's secret now. "See?" Violet smiled and handed Pippa the box.

"Amazing!" Isabel said.

"There's more in here and something special for you, Isabel." Violet retrieved a silver *cachou* box and unscrewed the lid. "A little beeswax, rose oil, talcum powder, and rice flower with gum arabic." She held it to Isabel's face. "I think it will do."

"What are you doing?" Isabel frowned.

"How do you think I got through the prickly periods during finishing school with a mother like mine? Without these little helpers, my parents would have probably treated me just as…" Violet's voice trailed away.

"As ours treated us?" Isabel gave Pippa a look. Isabel's parents had mistreated her, but Pippa's mother would never have allowed her father to behave as he was now. None of this would have happened if her mother were still alive.

And yet, she wouldn't have met Nick then.

Life was different now, and Pippa felt changed. She'd accepted her mother's absence from her adult life and took the reins. Yes, she still needed some help and receiving it from the unlikely ally of Violet showed how the tides had turned.

Well, this was Pippa's life.

So, she'd make the best of it.

She smelled the little cachou boxes with shades of purple-pink safflower, blood-red carmine, and rose-petal pink alkanet. They smelled waxy and a little like honey combined with fragrant oil and something powdery. There was nothing objectionable at all.

"You're trying to mask my blemish?" Isabel asked.

"No, I'm helping you to highlight your best features." Violet set the beige paste in the box and retrieved another larger box covered in blue velvet. She opened the small hook and revealed a beautiful glass bottle with a waxed cork. "And this perfume, my dear, will highlight the best features, your character *and* confidence."

Isabel took the perfume bottle and opened the cork. She rubbed the moisture form the cork on the back of her hand and a scent of cardamom and saffron mixed with jasmine wafted into Pippa's nose.

"It smells exotic and different," Pippa whispered.

"That is my intention," Violet said with the tone of a woman wiser than her age. "The perfume announces something spectacular and yet, gives an aura of greatness."

"It's a shield of courage?"

"A feminine one, yes. The power of scent can help—" Violet waved grandly as if she could catch the right words in the air—"sway people's opinions." And before Pippa could ask, Violet admitted, "Mr. Collins, the apothecary, made this for me. It's a one of a kind, Isabel. Use it well."

And just so, with some magical little potions of *maquillage* from Paris, Alfie's special perfume, and the skill of years of practice, Violet equipped Pippa and Isabel for the ball.

"Why are you helping us?" Pippa finally asked when the initial fascination of the little cremes, scents, and oils had worn off.

"I'm hoping you'll help me in return," Violet said.

Ah! There was never anything Violet did without some strings attached and those strings were usually a ruse, ready to take anyone out of her way who interfered with the glory she sought at that moment.

Pippa sucked in her lower lip, considering what she could say given that she was Violet's guest this evening and that it was rude to challenge her hostess.

"I see that you're not asking what I want. It's fine. There's no secret that I have had less than elegant methods until now, but my husband is helping me to redirect my talents."

"Hm!" Pippa could imagine the talents had something to do with the notorious pavilion of sin and seduction and the spicy things she'd discovered because of Violet. Well, thanks to her.

"Well, if you must know, Pippa," Violet started with a curt smile, "it's about my brother."

She hadn't asked, but Violet had piqued her interest after all. "What is the matter with Scott?"

"He's been injured on the continent."

"Oh, I'm sorry to hear that. So, he's back now?"

"Yes. But he needs to recover and heal."

Pippa's mind raced to the doctors on Harley Street.

"Several of his companions suffered the same fates. Different injuries, but if they don't get the medical attention they need, they'll all be crippled."

"Understandable. I certainly hope they get the help they need."

"My husband has arranged for some, but we require a place for them."

Pippa had a bad feeling about this.

"We were thinking that you could do a little favor in return for our help with your father."

"And what is that?"

"Well, I have something in mind, but it takes some work."

Pippa observed as Violet's mischievous gleam returned, transformed into a more mature and calculated expression. "We also need Bea's help. I'll send her a note and explain it when she comes for tea."

It was no longer just a play of mischief, but a plotting grin that hinted at a depth of understanding and purpose. Despite Pippa's apprehensions, she couldn't shake the growing realization that Violet's intentions were driven by a genuine desire to help. This insight brought forth conflicting emotions within Pippa, a mix of wariness and a tentative flicker of gratitude toward someone she had long viewed with guarded skepticism. As the weight of Violet's unspoken wish settled upon her, Pippa couldn't deny the unsettling sense that Violet held the strings to a secret that could upend the carefully constructed walls of the Ton's scorn.

Chapter Thirty-Eight

Meanwhile, the morning after the surgery...

"Can I take off the bandages?" Lance asked, sitting up in bed.

"It's only been a few hours," Nick said as he sat on the edge of his bed and laid a hand on Lance's forehead. It was cool. Then he tapped on his temples. *Cool. Good.* No heat meant little chance of infection. "Pippa sent a missive that she and Isabel spent the night at the Langleys'. Don't you want to be ready when Isabel returns?"

"Yes, please!" Lance pleaded like a child, eager to get just one more piece of sweets.

Nick had never been more terrified. He'd usually operated on patients he didn't know and who hadn't gone blind for years yet. Even though there was no sign of damage to any other parts of Lance's eye, one never knew.

Lance reached behind his head and unraveled the bandage that Wendy had so expertly tied in the evening before Lance had gone to bed. He'd been groggy after the laudanum and had slept for a long time. It was also good because sleep was the best way to heal. Besides, Nick had needed time to think about his own troubles.

"Let me," Nick scooted up and removed the bandage slowly, searching the white muslin for signs of bleeding, pus, or other stains. Nothing.

He took heart. "Keep your eyes closed and let me do an exam first."

Lance nodded dutifully.

The skin around his eyes was a bit dry, but that was to be expected from the many washings and disinfection with alcohol. There was no swelling, however.

"We need to rinse your eyes with cold water first. I don't want any irritation from dried tears." Nick reached for Lance's hands and helped him out of bed. His friend followed, eyes closed.

They reached the wash basin, and Nick picked up the fresh washcloth. Wendy truly had thought of everything.

"I can do this," Lance protested when Nick squeezed the cool water out of the fabric and let the water trickle back into the bowl. *Splish splash!* Lance washed his face.

And then there was a commotion.

Women's voices.

"She's back!" Lance called out. "Quick, help me!"

Nick reached for a clean shirt and a pair of simple brown breeches; at the same time, Lance found his own clothes, set on the chair in the corner for him by Wendy the night before. In no time, with his eyes still closed, Lance was dressed. Nick marveled at the speed at which he could do it without looking, but then there was a knock. "Enter!" Nick called, and Isabel came in.

She had a solemn look on her face, and she looked dewy. Nick tried to figure out how she had been changed, but all he knew was—she was radiant.

Behind her, Pippa and Wendy stood, a step back.

"Isabel?" Lance turned in her direction as if his every sense had been tuned to her.

"I'm here," she said timidly. Nick was startled at the humility between a wife and her husband.

He watched, mesmerized, but it was as if he weren't there. In the hall, there was the sound of footsteps approaching.

"Is he up?" Alfie's voice.

Feliz and Andre's mumbled responses that Nick couldn't hear. His heart pounded so vigorously in his chest. He knew what Lance was about to do, and if he didn't see... if it hadn't worked...

"I missed you." Lance said in a raw, boyish voice.

"We visited the Countess of Langley. You'd never believe who it is." Isabel chuckled as she came to stand right in front of Lance. "The Earl of Langley had the same surgery you did, and he told me I should leave you to rest." Isabel gave Nick a sideways glance. "Did it work?" Her voice was small and even her posture reminded him of like a mouse about to withdraw in its hole, scared of the enormity of the situation.

"We just took the bandage off and washed his eyes." Nick was still at Lance's side.

"I didn't want to open my eyes without you. I—" But Lance's voice broke. A tear escaped his face, mingled with the water he'd barely wiped off.

The morning sun filtered dimly through the thick drapes into the room, casting elongated shadows on the polished wooden floor. Lance's slim silhouette starkly contrasted against the golden light's backdrop, and he looked like he'd been illuminated for all to see. The question was whether *he'd* see.

Nick's heart hammered in his chest as he watched the dust particles dance in the sunbeams, each speck a testament to the gravity of the moment about to unfold. His eyes found Pippa's, and she had an air of anticipation as if she waited for a happy end to be revealed between the pages of a book, barely containing her excitement. She clasped her hands together and tucked them under her chin.

Wendy's forehead was tense, a sign of worry and concentration. Felix, Alfie, and Andre kept to the background, but Nick could tell that they were holding breaths when Lance's closed lids twitched. The practice was doomed if this surgery had gone badly, and they were about to find out.

The door to the room was wide open, allowing the simmering anticipation to waft into the hallway, where the rest of the friends from 87 Harley Street had gathered. The murmur of hushed voices and the rustle of silk skirts were like the distant hum of Alfie clearing his throat to announce his presence, barely penetrating the bubble of tension enveloping Nick. His eyes remained firmly fixed on Lance, whose face was a mask of trepidation. This was the moment they had all been waiting for, the culmination of their hopes and fears.

Nick could almost taste the suspense in the air, thick and palpable, like the heavy fog that rolled in from the Thames. With a breath held in check, he gently touched Lance's upper arm. "Try to blink first to lubricate the sclera."

"I know," Lance mumbled.

Nick's hand paused, his fingers trembling slightly at the enormity of what was about to happen. This was not just about restoring sight but about hope, resilience, and the human spirit's steadfast refusal to bow down to adversity. His gaze met Lance's closed eyelids, and with a tap of encouragement on Lance's shoulder, he signaled for his friend to open his eyes. Time slowed, each tick of the clock echoing loudly in the room as they waited with bated breath to see if Lance would embrace the world again as a sighted man.

Lance's hands encased Isabel's smaller ones, their fingers intertwining in a familiar gesture that spoke volumes about their bond. He lowered his head until his forehead touched hers, their breaths mingling in the small space between them. Isabel closed her eyes, surrendering to the moment they had seemingly shared countless times. The familiarity of it all made the room hum with a quiet understanding—this was not just a patient and his caretaker, but a husband and wife.

Then Lance swallowed visibly.

And his eyelids moved.

There was a ripple of silence, and then Lance's eyelids twitched then fluttered open, revealing the deep brown eyes hidden away in the darkness. For a moment, he blinked rapidly, his brows furrowed in confusion as if he were trying to make sense of the world around him. His gaze darted around the room, not settling on anything in particular. Nick felt a pang of dread twist in his stomach. Had the surgery been futile?

Just when despair threatened to engulf the room, Lance's wandering gaze landed on Isabel. His eyes locked onto her, staring at her intensely, leaving everyone in the room breathless. A tear escaped from the corner of his eye, trailing down his cheek. Isabel moved towards him instinctively, her hands resting on his shoulders. Lance mirrored her action, cupping her face tenderly with his hands. There was something profoundly intimate in their shared gaze, a silent conversation that needed no words. It was as if Lance was seeing the love of his life for the first time, which, in truth, he was.

Then, Lance swallowed, a visible movement in his throat that echoed loudly in the silent room. His eyelids fluttered again, this time more slowly, more deliberately. He was taking his time, savoring the moment, letting the reality of his regained sight sink in. And as his eyes opened once more, the room held its collective breath. The journey from darkness into light was not easy, but Lance had taken the first step, and it was a revelation.

Chapter Thirty-Nine

NICK COULDN'T HELP but cast Pippa a smile. And when she caught his pleased look, she gasped and covered her heart with both hands. Tears filled her eyes.

"It worked," Lance whispered. He blinked repeatedly as if he struggled to focus, but that was normal. Then, he trailed his hand along the soft waves of Isabel's hair. He reached out, his hands trembling in awe, and cupped her face. He laid his hand on her cheek, where the pigment blemish was, and he brushed his thumb over it as if it was just another part of Isabel that he admired and loved. Nick wasn't sure if he could see it, or if he cared at all. If Nick hadn't been able to see Pippa for years and could suddenly see her, no matter how blurry, he'd kiss her senseless, and there would be no blemish in the world that could stop him.

"Isabel..." Lance began, his voice choked with emotion. "My love." No time for further conversation. He kissed her with an urgency that needed no additional explanation.

A collective sigh filled the room, a mix of relief and joy. Andre and Felix, standing by the door, exhaled deeply, their faces breaking into relieved smiles. Even when Andre breathed, his accent danced elegantly on his lips and attracted the girls' attention. Understanding the intimacy of the moment, Alfie subtly gestured to Nick, indicating it was time for them to leave the couple alone.

A SIGHT TO BEHOLD

But Nick had already understood.

He stepped away from Lance, whose lips had found Isabel's. She let out a sigh of relief, and Nick's heart swelled with satisfaction as he shut the door behind him, leaving Lance and Isabel alone. As odd as it was, after years of marriage, Lance needed to get to know his wife. He'd seen her for the first time.

Nick had done it. He had given Lance his vision back. It was like a huge weight he didn't know he was carrying—or maybe he did—lifted from him, leaving him light and full of joy. That joy only increased as he stepped out into the hallway, he found Pippa still waiting, her eyes wide with anticipation. "We did it, Pippa," he said softly, his triumphant sounding in his voice. "We did it."

"You did it," she responded. "It was all you, Nick."

Wendy squealed with joy, and Alfie rubbed Nick's back appreciatively. "The best oculist ever."

And in the hall, Felix, Andre, Wendy, and Alfie stopped. They stared at Pippa and Nick, the next couple in the room that needed rescuing. Unbeknownst to Nick, he'd taken Pippa's hand. All eyes were on them. But he didn't care, and he squeezed it gently. Lance had his lovely wife and Nick had Pippa—and he'd do anything to make her his wife. And, Nick humbly admitted to himself, he had much to learn from Lance in how to fight for love.

As if she'd been privy to his thoughts, she formed an *o* with her lips and blinked at him and then looked into the round eyes of the others. The world around them faded away, leaving only the doctors from 87 Harley Street standing together as if they'd been called to organize a *putsch* to bring their Lady Philippa Pemberton into their little family. It was a moment of profound joy, a testament to the power of love, resilience, and the will to succeed.

⫸⫷

"You performed a miracle," Pippa said in awe. She said it to all of them, but then she looked at Nick, and her insides hurt. She knew she needed a miracle, not a medical one, but one for matters of the heart.

"It's the same operation I've done a thousand times," Nick said humbly, but Felix and Alfie huffed.

"You did well; it was a long and difficult surgery."

Wendy squealed with joy. "Oh, can you imagine their happiness? He can finally see his wife!" She twirled around the landing and down the two top stairs, holding the railing like an opera singer performing a grand declaration of love. She was quite the romantic. As usual.

"So, what now?" Andre asked, leaning against the railing.

"Now it's Operation Nick and Pippa," Alfie said. "I have everything ready downstairs."

Pippa searched Nick's eyes. "Are you sure you still want to risk everything just to be with me?"

Nick frowned and gave her a puzzled look. "How could you ever doubt my love?"

A man's feigned moan came from the staircase. "Oh, drat! Another one bites the dust." Andre turned and waved as he walked down the stairs. For someone who had conquered so many hearts, he was surprisingly resistant to romance. "Let me know when and where to show up for the wedding. I can't watch all this tender love, it makes me—"

"It just makes you realize what you're missing," Felix called after him, following down the stairs. Felix had once loved and lost but never given up hope to find her again. He waited for the return of his beloved Maisie but that was another story.

"You do-a too much-a missing!" Andre said playfully to Felix in his Italian-enunciated manner of speaking.

"That's not even a sentence!" Felix called out before his voice became indiscernible. There was a story about the love Felix had lost and the woman he missed, but Pippa didn't know the details. Not yet.

"So, how do we get your father in the same room with Nick?" Alfie asked, the last spectator who remained in the hall with Pippa and Nick.

"And how do we get a few doses of ipecac and charcoal in his system before then?" Nick asked.

She grinned. "The plan's already in motion."

Pippa was overcome with emotion; so much had happened. In less than twenty-four hours, she'd been threatened with her mother's machete, run away from home, taken Isabel to the Langleys, and hatched a plan for her future, but truth be told, she didn't know how to go about any of it. A little voice in the back of her mind told her that none of it might come to fruition. She knew how easily a carefully nurtured plant could not bear fruit in one year. It happened all the time. And if her plans didn't work, she'd be alive but stuck, like a bare little fruitless shrub.

"I need the plans to work," she whispered to Nick, who'd wrapped his arms around her warmly. He just held her in the hall. All the rules of the Ton didn't apply here; matters of the heart took precedence, except that the Ton threatened Nick and the practice. If Pippa's plan didn't work, they would lose their livelihood.

"The Earl of Langley will help me, and I have nothing to lose at the Ton. The Langleys will throw a ball and we are the guests of honor."

"You dread balls," Nick said.

"I can weather a ball if it means being able to marry you. But are you certain you want to risk everything for me by announcing our engagement?" Pippa asked.

Nick disentangled himself from her and tilted his head toward hers. "I'd risk everything for you, Pippa. I already did."

Her heart swelled. "I love you, Nick. So much! But I'm—"

He placed a gentle finger on her lips. "I love you, too." And then his mouth took the place of his finger.

And just so, Pippa's whole body soared with love for him. And need.

She opened her mouth, but it was nothing compared to her heart.

"I don't even know where to go."

"What do you mean?" They spoke into each other's mouths.

"I ran away from home."

"So, you come live with me."

"I cannot live here with you, Nick. And you mustn't lose the respect of your noble patients by keeping me here without my father's consent. I'd be in the way of your success, Nick."

"You're never in the way as long as you are with me."

"Nick, I cannot just move in here. We're not even married."

"So, we get married." He stepped back. "Come with me."

"I cannot elope, Nick. It will only fuel the damage Mr. Matthews and his daughter can do to your practice."

Nick laughed. "I'm not suggesting we elope. It's still my intention to request your father's blessing." He took her hand and led her up a flight of stairs.

When he turned the knob of a humble wooden door, Pippa realized that this was his bedchamber. It was small, with a bed centered against a wall and a window facing the alley. The room was neat, but the bookcase was overstuffed. An armoire in the corner, smaller than Pippa's hat wardrobe, probably held all his clothes.

She stood in the room momentarily, and Nick closed the door. He walked to the armoire, turned the key, and opened the double door with a screech. He retrieved a box from a drawer at the bottom of the little armoire. And from the box, a small velvet pouch.

Then he approached her again.

"Pippa, I'd like to offer you my mother's ring." He untied the little pouch, and Pippa saw that the velvet had rubbed off the sides. "It's the only jewelry she ever had and is probably not worth very much."

Pippa's breath caught in her throat. Nick took out a plain gold ring with a single round diamond on six prongs.

"This is a diamond," Pippa said. "Your family heirloom?"

Nick nodded. "I was always meant to give it to my wife someday. It's old; it belonged to my father's mother and then to my mother."

"I'd be honored to care for it and look after it in custody for your family until we pass it on to our son." Nick's eyes locked with hers. "I've never meant anything more earnestly, Nick. I love you from the bottom of my heart, and if you'll have me, I'd like nothing more than to spend the rest of my life trying to live up to the goodness in your…" But then she choked, and tears rolled down her cheeks.

"Pippa, what's the matter?" Nick brushed the tears off her cheeks with the balls of his thumbs.

"I wish you could have met my mother. She wouldn't have let any of this happen. She would have welcomed you into the family as a person without regard for anybody's station and she would have loved you because you love me exactly as I am."

His eyes softened. "I'm sure you're right, Pippa. I don't care about society, Pippa. I only care about you."

She nodded, unable to speak. "Then I'll go back to scheme with the Langleys later?"

Nick gently took her hand and pushed the ring onto her finger. It fit perfectly. It was old fashioned but classic, with an innate beauty only a natural diamond could possess.

"It's beautiful, Nick. I'll try to honor it." She held her hand out and regarded the ring and the way it fit her finger and shimmered in the light.

Nick watched her with hungry eyes.

After all, she stood in his room, wearing his family's heirloom as an engagement ring. And they'd done more than declare their love already.

Pippa reveled in Nick's intense gaze on her hand and brought it to her bodice. She unhooked the first, second, third, and then all the hooks. Pippa felt a little like a blossom emerging from the sepals when her dress split in the middle and fell off her shoulders.

Her décolletage was exposed, and Nick bent down to kiss her collarbone. Then lower.

"You are so beautiful, Pippa."

She tilted her head back, and Nick's hands came to the back of her head, supporting her. He kissed her neck and returned to her jawline and then her mouth.

Pippa melted into his embrace and gave herself over, for the feeling was so strong that it made no sense to resist. She was his and wanted nothing more than for him to devour her.

She unbuttoned his shirt, and he stepped backward, another step and another until his legs touched the bed.

"I'm afraid my bed is not as comfortable as yours," Nick said when Pippa pulled her fingers over his strong shoulders and peeled off his shirt. She kissed the broad expanse of his chest, and her hand drove along his body.

Nick unbuttoned his breeches and gave her access. She inserted her hands in the waistband and pushed his breeches down along with his underthings while he unwrapped her from the day dress she'd borrowed from Violet along with the sinful undergarments Violet possessed these days.

They let the fabric pool on the floor, and Pippa was in front of him in only her corset, garters, and stockings. Then, she unlaced the corset and dropped it on the floor.

Nick turned her around and pulled her stockings off one by one, replacing the warmth of the sheer fabric with the heat of his kisses. When Pippa was in the nude, Nick lay her on the bed. The linens were cool and crisp, plain white cotton. They'd serve their purpose wonderfully.

Pippa nestled into the sheets, and Nick bent over her, unhooking each garter and rolling it down her thigh, over her knee, and then off her foot. Then the other.

He kissed her belly as he pulled the garter off.

"Are you keeping these on?" Nick nudged the bridge of her glasses.

She beamed at him. "You gave me the gift of sight but the even greater one is looking at you."

Then he climbed into bed and lay on her. The length of his manhood pressed onto Pippa's center.

"I want to feel you," Pippa said hoarsely, driving her hands through his hair. Her hand, with his family heirloom diamond ring, looked grown up. And she felt different. She'd blossomed and was ready to fight for love.

But first, she'd make love.

Chapter Forty

PIPPA HAD SPENT more time than was proper with Nick, but eventually she made it to the Langleys' where she'd tell people she'd stayed as their guest while Bea remained at home administering the daily charcoal to absorb the mushroom poison and then the ipecac an hour before the ball.

"Are you certain he ate the chocolate eclair?" Pippa asked, Bea pacing the hall at the House of Langley. It was Friday evening, seven o'clock. Some of the guests had arrived and Violet was playing hostess. She was in her element. Meanwhile, the Earl of Langley greeted the Archbishop of Canterbury and led him personally to the drawing room, before he returned with a smile.

"Lady Penelope and Lady Beatrice, you both look lovely this evening." He demonstratively kissed the backs of their hands as a gentleman should, each in turn, in order of age, Pippa first. With flair of a host in control, the earl positioned himself in plain sight of the guests who'd started to fill the room. And then Pippa looked up from her hand and saw seven rather sweet faces. They were all there, Nick, Wendy, Felix, Alfie, Andre, and Lance with Isabel.

"They're here!" Pippa watched the footmen take the men's hats and Wendy's pelisse. Isabel had a feather stole wrapped dramatically around her neck. It was her first evening back in society since she and Lance had been cast away into the countryside. This was a turning point for her as much as it would hopefully be for Pippa.

"Oh my," Bea exclaimed. "Who's the tall one with the wavy hair?"

"Alfie Collins, the apothecary." Pippa led Bea to her new friends—her new family, with any luck. "The one who made Isabel's perfume?" Bea blinked bashfully in his direction, batting her eyelashes.

Nick wore a dashing ensemble of a black evening frock and cream breeches. His black boots were polished to a shine, and he looked awfully handsome.

"You dressed for an oral exam, didn't you?" Pippa said cheekily as she pushed her glasses up her nose just when it was her turn to greet the doctors. Nick tugged at his stiff cravat. It was a more complicated knot than he usually wore.

"Lance picked this out," Nick said, running one elegant long and yet muscular finger through the inside of the cravat.

Pippa smiled at Isabel and Lance. They were positively gleaming with pride and if Pippa wasn't completely mistaken, there was a large dose of magnificent energy in Isabel's manner of flouting the feather stole. And Lance was prancing beside her with a hand lower on her back than seemed appropriate.

Nick smiled when Pippa returned his gaze with wide eyes, pinching her lips. "They've been at it since that morning."

"No!"

"Oh yes! The only reason they came out of their room tonight was to make a grand reentrance in society." He looked baffled, like a schoolboy who'd emerged from the dimly lit library only to be blinded by the sun's brightness. Except that the dazzling luxury of the ball couldn't dazzle Pippa anymore. With any luck, this night was her grand exit.

She was ready to leave the embarrassments behind, the gossip, and especially her father's complete lack of understanding.

Bea came to her side, blinking bashfully over her shoulder when Alfie reached out to take her hand, pressing a kiss to the back of it.

"This is my cousin, Lady Beatrice Weatherby."

Pippa made introductions for the rest of the doctors and their nurse and then the Earl of Langley came to lead Wendy into the ballroom. Wendy looked every inch a lady in the gown Pippa and Violet had ordered for her at the modiste's. Adorned with borrowed jewels and her hair elegantly arranged by Violet's maid, she must have felt as though she had stepped straight out of one of the novels she so adored. In this moment, Wendy was obviously in her glory, basking in the enchantment of her transformation.

Felix and Andre were quickly lost in the crowd and Pippa remained in the hall on the side of the foyer. Nick was with her.

"Are you truly willing to give all this up for me?"

She turned to him and looked into his gorgeous blue eyes. His gaze was so intelligent and filled such warmth and goodness, her heart hurt. "If our plans work, I'm not giving anything up. I'll finally step into the role my grandfather had intended for me and all I will take my leave from are the same people who never wanted me to have any—"

"Pippa, he's here." Violet swished to her side and whispered in her ear. "Good evening, Dr. Folsham." Violet reached her hand out and Nick greeted her. "Please join us in the library."

Minutes later, in the elegant library with dark-walnut shelves and leather-bound treatises perfectly in rows from the ground to the ceiling, Nick felt thoroughly out of place.

"What's this all about?" an elderly man with sideswept long great hairs over a bald spot said. He was heavyset and sweating profusely. "Pippa! Take those spectacles off, you're making a fool of yourself."

Her father.

Nick noticed Pippa tensing. She pushed the glasses up over the bridge of her nose, making sure they remained well positioned. A sign of defiance.

"Would you like some wine?" the Earl of Langley asked. "You look unwell," he continued, pouring some water into a glass. There'd been a single one on a silver platter. It was already filled with ipecac and now that the earl swirled the water in it, he was ready to administer Father's second dose. It wouldn't be long now.

The earl handed him the glass and the Duke of Sussex took a large swig. A drop of the liquid rolled down the corner of his mouth and Nick tried not to grimace in disgust. How could a blob of a caricature like that be a peer of the Realm and the father of a daughter like Pippa? It must have been her mother who was the amazing beauty, intelligent, and good natured. No wonder Pippa tried to get away from him. And no wonder her maternal grandfather had written the duke out of his will.

"I'm here!" A white-haired man entered and then shut the door. "My apologies for my tardiness, there was trouble with the carriage." The man was short but slim, beyond middle-aged, but his demeanor was sure and deliberate. His elegant but slightly shabby attire reflected his ecclesiastical status.

"What's the archbishop doing here?" Pippa's father asked. "And who's this?"

The earl nodded at Nick. He recognized this was his cue to speak. "Your Grace, my name is Nicholas Folsham."

"*Doctor* Nicholas Folsham," Pippa added.

Her father grunted like a boar.

"I'd like to request your daughter's hand in marriage," Nick said solemnly. Pippa took his hand and squeezed tightly.

"Denied." Her father downed the rest of the water and set the glass on the table with such a thump that it left an indentation in the elegant, polished mahogany.

The Earl of Langley didn't even flinch. Pippa was still as a flag on a day without wind. Apparently, this was no storm to the aristocrats.

"Who do you think you are, cornering me in a study that's not mine and asking for my daughter?"

"This is the library, and nobody cornered you. It's rather difficult to get your attention these days," the archbishop said. "My lord, what's wrong with you? If Dorothea saw you like this, she'd return from her grave—"

"Don't speak my wife's name!" Pippa's father roared at the archbishop. "How dare you?"

"Lower your voices, gentlemen. We're here for a shared goal and that's Pippa's future," the earl said calmly. Ever the diplomat, Nick thought. He had more to show for those years of fostering international relations than the damage to his youthful body. And he'd earned Nick's respect in more ways than one.

"I'm here because your wife promised mine an opportunity. She went on about it all week." Pippa's father ignored his daughter, and Nick formed a fist. He must not punch his future father-in-law, if it ever got to that, but he wished for nothing more than to sink his hard fist into his soft flesh and knock him out with a single blow.

"I have a document here you ought to see," the earl said as he opened the drawer of his writing desk and took out a stack of papers. Nick blinked. Was that a royal seal?

The earl offered them to the duke, but he grunted again, then burped. The archbishop jerked his head back and fanned himself.

"It's a noble cause and has my full support, as well as that of the regent," the archbishop said.

"What is it?" The duke asked, still ignoring his daughter—or did he just give a disapproving look at Nick holding her hand?

Nick stepped closer to Pippa.

"A brigade of soldiers recently came back from the continent and there were several noble sons among them, including my brother-in-law." The Earl of Langley spoke slowly, and Pippa's father set a sausage-fingered hand on the table, leaving a contour of sweat on the polished wooden surface. "You do remember that I married Violet? You were there."

"Yes," the duke growled. "Scott is back then?"

"Indeed, he is. But he's been injured as has the son of the Czar, a Prince from Romania, and several third and fourth sons of peers."

"*Hmpf!*" Pippa's father truly had the grace of a calving cow.

"I'm letting them rent Cloverdale House for two years," Pippa said. "They need the bedchambers upstairs, servants, and the receiving areas on the lower level. The orangery can provide them with medicinal plants for their recovery, and the access to the gardens will offer them places to reconstitute."

The duke interrupted Pippa, "What's this? You're leasing my house?"

"I'm leasing them *my* house. It's for a good cause and Prinny signed a decree as you can see. The rent will be backed by the Crown."

Her father scratched his face and a rough sound of nails on stubble made Nick's skin curl. "Pippa, you're such a clumsy goose. You can't rent my house to anyone!"

Nick let go of Pippa's hand and balled both hands into fists, but the Earl of Langley stepped in front of him. "That brings us to the second issue we hoped to discuss with you."

"*Hmpf!*"

The earl nodded and closed his mouth. A putrid smell emerged from the direction of the duke. It was almost time. They had to hurry before he'd miss the chance to run to a secluded place.

"Pippa wishes to marry Dr. Folsham, and I happen to think it's a marvelous idea. Give your blessing."

"Never." Her father belched again and then a gurgling sound came from his midsection. Ah, the ipecac was taking effect.

"Why don't you want her to marry for love?"

"I don't care who and what she marries for because I won't allow it."

"Because you'll lose access to her trust and the moneys from managing the estate?"

"I'd lose my home if she rented out the castle. I'm sick, but not stupid."

"You're actually not sick, Father. You've been poisoned." Pippa spoke with such dignity, her chin raised high and her back ramrod straight. Nick was proud of her. Clearly, the nobility had a way of handling problems that was new to him. Although he recognized the process. Pippa had prepared the patient and was coming in for the first incision.

The duke was so nasty and disgusting, Nick cringed. He wanted to take Pippa away from him and shield her forever from such scum, regardless of their title.

"Sir Matthews has been poisoning you with mushroom cap in the morning and Si—I mean—*Carolyn* gave you an extra dose each night."

"Why would they do that and where do you get such ideas from, Pippa? Ridiculous. Poison? You're embarrassing yourself again."

His stomach growled again. He began to sweat and turned an unhealthy green in the worst possible way. "Urp." He patted his hand to his chest. "*Urrrrrp!*"

"No, Father. You're embarrassing *yourself*. We've been giving you charcoal to absorb the effects and help you. You just had a second dose of an emetic to release the poison."

"What? You're poisoning me?"

"No, we're trying to purge the poison *from* you."

"Who's we?"

Nick noticed that Pippa bit her tongue. She had concocted the plan of how to give him the medicines with her cousin Bea's help but it was Nick who'd welcomed Alfie's help in procuring the right doses.

"Me." Nick stepped forward. "I'm a doctor and hate to see patients suffer from charlatanerie. Plus, I wanted you to be alert when I ask for her hand in marriage."

"Denied, boy, I told you. Who's the charlatan now?"

"Mr. Matthews is your father-in-law, did you know that?" Pippa stepped forward. Her voice was rigid.

"Pippa, shut up." Her father bent over and held his massive stomach. With the other hand, he still leaned against the elegant desk. He was too vile to hold to such an exquisite piece of furniture. But he was mostly too vile to be in the company of Pippa, Nick decided.

"She injured my bunny and threatened to kill me with Mother's machete!"

"Oh dear, now you've lost your mind. Where would she find that old thing?"

"In the orangery. The day of the flop with her charity ball, Father. Do you remember? I bred the mosquitos that stung her. About three hundred—or more—larvae. I released them into her bedchamber. She retaliated by trying to kill Truffles."

"You stupid little brat," her father growled, bent lower. He let out an enormous groan and Nick stepped back. It appeared things were coming to a head—for the man's stomach.

The duke panted. "You have… no right to… treat Carolyn with… such disrespect. I thought… they'd gotten those pranks… out of you in finishing school. I had hoped… to be rid… of you if… they give you a little polish and refinement."

He drooled.

So much for polish and refinement, Nick thought.

Pippa ignored it. "Father, I wish to marry Dr. Folsham."

"You should give your blessing," the Earl of Langley said. "With a little luck, you might qualify to stay in your current bedchamber and undergo the rehabilitation program with a real doctor."

"What do you mean?"

"Mr. Matthews and his daughter are going to be prosecuted for their crimes. Surely poisoning a peer of the Realm and threatening his daughter rank higher than some of their petty fraud, but it will add up."

"What?"

"There's trickery, attempted murder, breaking and entering, charlatanerie, embezzlement, collusion—" The earl enumerated the various crimes for which Sir Mathews and Wife Six would likely be tried. Once Pippa had felt safe in the knowledge that he and the rest of the doctors at 87 Harley Street would not be affected by Wife Six's blackmail, and with the Earl of Langley and Lance by her side, she was willing and ready to report to the duo's crimes to the constables.

"You damn bastard!" Pippa's father shouted.

The archbishop turned to him with a pointedly arched brow. "Come on now, save your dignity and acknowledge defeat."

"I won't be defeated by my daughter's disgrace. And if I had had a boy, I wouldn't have to put up with this clumsy goose. Look what she's done to me!" He made a terrible throaty noise and gripped his cravat at the same time. "I never want to see her again!"

"But she's your daughter!" Nick protested. "She's precious, smart, intelligent, and there is such goodness in her, you'll never find it again in the whole world!"

"I never want to find *her* again in the world!" her father blurted out, bending over more deeply and gripping the edge of the table until his knuckles whitened. "All I want is to be rid of her," he groaned.

"You want someone to take her off your hands then?" the earl asked calmly.

"Yes," her father forced the words as if it weren't vomit but all of his evil bubbling under his surface, fighting to come out.

"That's good enough," the archbishop said. He turned to Nick and Pippa and reached his hand out.

His hands were cool, and his touch was gentle. A large seal ring bore a crest that Nick had seen before—the same one he'd seen carved into the staircase at Silver Crest... *oh boy!*

"Dr. Folsham, you have my blessing and permission to marry Lady

Philippa Pemberton." The archbishop gave him a warm smile. Then he turned to the earl. "Is that all?" But Pippa hurried to him and surprised him—and Nick—by kissing his cheek.

"Thank you, Uncle Peter."

"My pleasure. There's nothing better in my line of work than paving the way for true love. And these two," he gestured to Pippa and then Nick, then rubbed his chin, "when they'll kiss, angels will grow wings."

"He just wants her money!" Pippa's father growled.

"That brings me to the third point." The Earl of Langley retrieved a second document from the drawer and put it on the table. The archbishop left with a satisfied smile on his face.

"This is a special license, Dr. Folsham. Consider it a personal token of appreciation for everything you've done for me."

Nick took the scroll and blinked at it.

"And this is a contract you need to sign." The Earl handed him a fountain pen.

"You don't have to," Pippa said quietly. "Not on my behalf."

"I do," Nick said. "On mine." Nick turned to the fifth page where a line was drawn next to his name, printed in bold letters. The preceding four pages listed Pippa's many holdings. His head spun just from looking at the list of her fortune; he couldn't wrap his mind around it, nor did he want to infringe upon her inheritance.

"What's the boy talking about?" Pippa's father asked.

"The 'boy' is the best eye surgeon in the country, did you know that?" The earl lost his cool demeanor.

"Did *he* curse Pippa with the spectacles?" her father mumbled.

"No, he diagnosed me with farsightedness." Pippa wrapped herself around Nick's left arm once he'd signed the last paper and handed it back to the earl. "He cured me of clumsiness and now of the mean, diminutive nickname you used about me."

"If you were a far-sighted, clumsy goose, you wouldn't sign your wealth over to a doctor. He'll spend it all."

"No, Father. He just signed a document that will become effective upon the moment of our marriage, and everything will be in my name—and the names of our future children."

"That's farsighted!" The earl said cockily. "My work is done then."

Pippa's father gulped, belched, and heaved.

"Oh dear," Pippa called out.

But Nick had found the wastepaper basket and dropped it at the feet of his future father-in-law. Then they left him alone in the library.

Chapter Forty-One

IF PIPPA THOUGHT she could make an elegant escape from the ball, she'd been mistaken. Society's scorn awaited her among the splendor of Violet's ball. In fact, immediately upon entering the ballroom on Nick's arm Pippa lifted her eyes to the ceiling, where a grand chandelier hung, its golden branches holding up the drip trays with crystal flutes shielding the gas lamps. Made up of symmetrically arranged branches, each was hung with chains of crystals sending beams in all directions and illuminating the drama playing out below. It would all have been rather spectacularly beautiful if she didn't dread entering the large room filled with so many members of the Ton who knew her as "the clumsy goose." Then again, that had been in the past.

The elaborate dance of rococo flair and its intricate designs reminiscent of the flamboyant and ornate style of the late Baroque period clashed with the atmosphere, thick with tension so intense that it made the chandelier quiver slightly. The room was filled with people who shot sharp glances at each other, their hostility causing the air to throb. Balls such as these were worse than exams at finishing school; they tested a person beyond what had been prepared.

Bea, Lance, Isabel, and Carolyn stood in the middle of the dance floor, positioned directly underneath the largest chandelier overhead and even the ceiling molding converged in a rosette over their heads, as if a thunderstorm brewed directly above them.

But, in fact, a storm was brewing on the other side of the room, as Pippa heard a woman's voice raised in anger and—possibly—desperation. It was a voice she recognized, and the sound of it made her feel as if her skin was crawling. "An investigation?" Carolyn shrieked.

The rosette, which she had admired just moments ago, now seemed to press down on her. The room grew even more still, the silence echoing the frozen scene on the parquet, as if everyone and everything in the room were holding their breath, waiting for the world to break apart under the strain of the tension.

Isabel stood ramrod straight, her hand resting on Lance's arm. A circle had opened around them. The Who's Who of the English aristocracy listened to their every word. Pippa and Nick approached Bea, who stood slightly beside Isabel, eyeing Carolyn with disgust.

"You poisoned the duke!" Bea squinted defiantly and crossed her arms over her bodice. A ripple of gasps and murmurs washed over the crowd of curious bystanders. Pippa's heart thundered in her chest, a wild drum echoing her mounting panic. Her breath hitched as she surged forward, the urgency of the situation spurring her into action. Bea had helped her and now she was in the crossfire of the Ton. As the clumsy goose and an outcast, Pippa knew how embarrassment felt, but she feared that it would shatter her beloved cousin. The world around her blurred into a whirl of colors and shapes, the grandeur of the ballroom reduced to mere background noise as her focus narrowed down to the figure before her. She pulled away from Nick to push through the crowd.

But the throng was tight and—predictably—someone in the crush stepped on the train of her gown. She could feel the pull, a sharp tug at her waist that halted her momentum and sent a jolt of surprise through her.

Looking down, the world tilted. The opulent patterns of the ballroom floor swirled and danced before her eyes, a chaotic ballet that made her head spin. Her glasses slipped down the bridge of her nose, teetering on the edge of disaster.

And then, it happened. The grand chandelier above, a magnificent spectacle of gold and crystal, caught her eye. Its brilliance reflected off her glasses. Just the wrong angle of reflection in the worst possible moment. It was blinding, disorienting.

With her senses overwhelmed and her balance compromised, Pippa was falling. The sensation was disconcerting, a slow-motion descent into chaos. The world spun as she tipped forward, the elegant tapestries and gilded mirrors of the ballroom whirling into a dizzying vortex.

And then she held on to something.

She hung onto the fabric but it didn't stop her tumble. A loud ripping noise pierced through the air.

She braced for the impact, her heart pounding against her ribcage. But as she fell, someone gripped her from behind. A strong hand came to her rescue and although she was already on her knees, she was pulled up.

Someone else steadied her from behind and she straightened herself.

※※※※※

NICK HAD RUSHED in just in time and darted to Pippa. "You almost slipped!" he said, gently wrapping his hand around hers, which came to rest on the crux of his elbow.

"She did slip!" the Earl of Langley said who'd appeared a split second later behind Pippa. "Are you well, Lady Pemberton?" he asked loudly, as if he were on stage. As if not enough people were watching them, Alfie, Felix, and Andre joined them in the center of the ballroom.

Pippa had paled, but now she was reddening. Nick surveyed the scene and all the guests in their finery surrounded their little group. He'd walked into quite a society scandal and felt as lost as a fish in the desert.

"Are you injured?" Andre asked Pippa, the orthopedist at the ready for any potentially broken bones or twisted ankles.

"She tore my gown!" a middle-aged woman in a dark green dress cried.

"Carolyn, I'm sorry, it was an accident," Pippa said, lowering her head when the woman's vicious gaze caught her.

"Did you injure yourself, Lady Pemberton?" The earl ignored the infuriated woman and looked at Pippa.

"I think I'm well, my lord. Thank you, Andre."

"I'm not! She tore my…" But the woman didn't have a chance to finish.

"Aren't you glad your dress caught her fall? It's a kind sacrifice to prevent your stepdaughter from taking a tumble in front of everyone here." The earl gestured into the round of his guests and Nick realized that this was Wife Six.

"Why would I do that? The clumsy goose ripped the velvet of my dress!"

"You didn't try to catch her fall?" Violet said. "She has spectacles, and you are supposed to help when some needs assistance."

"Says who?" Wife Six cried out.

"Says common decency," Isabel said cheekily. "If you're in the position to help, you ought to."

"According to whom?" The evil stepmother quirked one of her thin painted-on brows, and it looked like it was being chased up her visage by the overdone, red-painted lips.

"According to Lady Ellington, my wife, the daughter of Viscount Knox," Lance said, giving her a lethal stare.

"They're back." Violet winked at Isabel. Pippa's heart leapt with joy for Isabel because she knew how terrible she must have felt banished to the country. This return was more glorious than her debut would have ever been, and Pippa saw the twinkle in her eye as she let the crowd take a good look at her, bold, beautiful, blemished, and brazen.

For a moment, Carolyn's gaze darted from one to the other and she remained silent. "Who...how...is that...why?"

"They are my guests." the Earl of Langley spoke slowly and loudly, for everyone to hear. "Dr. Felix Leafley, my dentist, Mr. Alfie Collins, my apothecary, Dr. Andre Fernando, the orthopedist, Miss Wendy Folsham, the best nurse in Town, and the esteemed Dr. Nicholas Folsham, with his fiancée, Lady Penelope, with whom you're well acquainted."

With every word, the witch turned more and more the shade of her green dress.

"And you know us, by reputation at least," Lance said. "Looks like we're back." He gave a lopsided smile and exuded sheer noble prowess. It must have been so long that Lance and Isabel had planned a *putsch* of the Ton.

"And why do you need so many doctors, my lord?" Carolyn's voice was seeped in venom of the extra dangerous kind, a woman about to be scorned by society.

"Doesn't everyone?" The earl shrugged.

"The doctors here are rather amazing and Dr. Nick Folsham here operated on me earlier this week." Lance now turned to the crowd and spoke so grandly it was as if he'd rehearsed it. "I was blind for nearly four years and now, thanks to him, I can see!"

The crowd came to life with appreciative chatter.

"You poisoned my husband," Carolyn retaliated with an accusation that had already become a moot point before she'd uttered it. The room filled with excited chatter.

"No, you poisoned my father! All week, we've been leaching it from his system and being absorbed in his body so that he be sober enough to see you for who you really are!" Pippa brushed a strand out of her face that had fallen from her upswept hair. "He's in the library now releasing the poison you gave him from his stomach," she said.

The crowd gasped and a few sounds of *argh* and *ugh* emerged. "You've been poisoning him for years with mushroom cap from your father's..." Pippa waved at Nick. "What do you call a charlatan's practice if it's not a practice at all?" she asked him.

He was speechless and shook his head. "It's not a practice if he doesn't have a license. And he doesn't even have a license of good standing from the local bishop."

"*You* are the charlatans!" Carolyn pointed dramatically and curled her back as if her finger could shoot the doctors with lightning bolts. "You! And you! And you! And *you* paint people's teeth with gold for a bloody fortune!" She stopped on Felix.

"Paint?" the earl asked.

"I saw you smiling at your little wife. Your teeth are—"

"*Filled* with gold, yes. Not painted. Dr. Felix Leafley, as I said, is my dentist. And if he weren't as good at his job as he is, I wouldn't be able to smile at my dear wife. The Countess of Langley, mind you, deserves the best of me."

"And yet, you are a spare parts warehouse!" Carolyn shouted.

The crowd gasped.

"What did you call me?" The earl stepped forward and towered over her.

"False teeth, false eyes, what else did you need help reconstituting for your young bride, *hm*?" Carolyn made a show of trailing her eyes down from his face to his chest and she stopped in his middle.

"If he's a spare parts warehouse, then so am I, by your definition." Lance joined the earl. Isabel tried to hold him back, but he was unstoppable. "Except that you're mistaken with one important thing, Lady Pemberton, the sixth, is it? You've replaced five other wives and I suspect some of their departures can be traced back to your father's influence. For years, 'Sir' Matthews has used the information he obtained in confidence to blackmail the Ton, hasn't he?"

"What an absurd accusation!"

"Is it?" Lance spoke clearly for the other guests to hear. "Then why do I know that Viscount Grantham seeks him out? Or Lady Sheridan?" Carolyn's eyes grew wide. "Isn't it true that Lady Sheridan's second daughter was poised to marry the viscount's oldest son but then that arrangement was unexpectedly dissolved due to an unknown reason?"

Even Nick was impressed. What kind of dirt had Lance dug up on the information Matthews held?

"What if she was?" Her face grew red, and Nick could hear the shaking of fury in her voice.

"Well then why would he pay your father every month?"

She stepped back.

"It's hush money, that's why!"

She *harumphed*.

"And if he doesn't pay the sum that's equivalent of Lady Sheridan's daughter's dowry on the date of their marriage, your father will tell some awful secret, won't he?"

"How does he know?" Pippa asked Isabel, who stood watching her husband with pride on her face.

"Because I planted some juicy half-truth to test the hypothesis," Isabel told her, never taking her eyes from Lance.

"And I helped spread the rumor in just the right directions." Violet smiled. "The gossip spread like a wildfire in less than a week and left a clear trail that led to you."

"With my help," The earl wobbled his head proudly. "I have some connections, as you know."

"B-but the viscount's son is—" Carolyn didn't finish.

"I'm right here, Lady Pemberton." A young man in evening attire cleared his throat. "And none of your vicious gossip is true, except that I love Sophia Sheridan. And you're not invited to our wedding next month." He stepped back and bowed in the direction of the Earl of Langley.

"See, Lady Pemberton, a real doctor would never spread gossip or sell information from a patient. There's no betrayal of trust possible with the young doctors from 87 Harley Street. They keep absolute confidentiality."

"But I can see the work you've had done!" Carolyn cried out.

The earl fumed. Then he walked away and straight to the edge of the crowds where his guests were. "Look at me!" he called out. He didn't need to speak very loudly—everyone's attention was already fixed on the drama unfolding on the dance floor in front of them. He opened his mouth wide and bared his teeth. "I'm admitting to repairs and the use of various medicines to feel good in my body. It's my prerogative to accept the advances in medicine gracefully, and I'm not ashamed." He smiled widely, baring his gold fillings. "I'd be stupid to hide it if it helped me regain my strength after years of ignoring my health."

The guests gasped and some looked away, while others stared curiously, and most gave the group in the center of the throng evil eyes. But the earl kept his chin high and his posture so strong, he oozed control and masculinity.

"And here!" He held his eyes wide open. "Both lenses were replaced because, lo and behold, I drank myself nearly blind! Who knows the feeling, *hm?*" He nodded at some of the peers in the crowd. At first, they were embarrassed but then they slumped their shoulders and approached the earl. "I wanted to be in the best shape possible for my beautiful wife! Is that so bad? Look at her! She's breathtaking! And intelligent!"

Violet chuckled and took Bea's arm. "I love him. Isn't he wonderful?"

"And yet all the money you spent with the doctors won't give you the one thing that you need," Carolyn snarled.

The earl turned back and returned to her. "What?"

"You need an heir, my lord." Her tone was languid and dangerous like a snake curling itself around its prey ready to squeeze tight to suffocate it. "It's been six months and you ought to have made more progress by now."

The earl inhaled deeply, his fury evident on his face and in his movements.

Wife Six continued, oblivious to the fact that he was only just holding his anger in check. Or maybe she didn't care. "A real man would have fathered a child by now, but you are all but a fool who spent money on these doctors and all you have to show for it are spare parts that will remain long after your body has decayed. But I suppose your doctors haven't been able to cure all of your ailments, *hm*?"

Silence washed over the room.

The earl's heavy breathing resonated with the expectant gazes of the crowd.

And then there was a rustle of silk.

Violet came to his side and took his hands in hers, pulling him to face her. "She's wrong."

His gaze lifted and he met Violet's eyes. "What?"

"It's a bit early to say but..." Violet looked over her shoulder at Wendy. "It's possible."

The earl's eyebrows darted up but then his gaze fell to her stomach. He looked like a young boy who'd received the best surprise on his birthday. "A baby?" His voice was hoarse, and his sincerity was plain for the crowd to see.

He was just a man in love with his wife and he'd done what he thought was best to keep up with her. Surely it was a problem to which more than one of the guests could relate.

Now, Pippa approached Carolyn and inhaled a deep breath. Nick knew that what she was about to say would change their lives.

Chapter Forty-Two

"CAROLYN, YOU'VE BROUGHT shame to our family," Pippa said gravely.

"Says the clumsy goose," Carolyn laughed Pippa off and turned to receive support from the crowd.

But none came.

"Carolyn, you schemed with your father against my family, but with the help of the Countess and Earl of Langley, I was able to prove that both of you have colluded against many others in this room."

Silence.

"As the future wife of a doctor, I must not reveal the identities of your victims, but I hope they will come and find the real doctors. There, they will finally get the help they need."

"You have no proof that—"

But Pippa held her hand up and commanded Carolyn to allow her to finish.

"The proof in medicine rests in the body of the patient. Nothing else matters. Your father profited handsomely from the pain he inflicted."

"My father administered medicine—"

"When a patient doesn't consent to taking a medicine, then it's poison. It injures the body. And may I remind you, Carolyn, for a crime against a peer of the Realm, you might hang!"

The crowd remained silent. Pippa knew she had their support. They may have mocked her but when there was a danger posed that threatened the aristocrats, the Ton operated like a closed front. She was using the attribute that Carolyn had relied on to build her ploy for years against her.

"And when *your* father has to repay the blackmail, I don't suspect he'll have enough mushroom cap powder to influence the guards in the Tower of London to let him out."

"My father is a healer!" Carolyn protested weakly.

"He never made anyone better! That's why he had to make them dependent on his drugs and his stones and his crystals. He needed them to return for more treatments and pay him for more. That's all he cared about. That and getting more information from them to use against them."

"As if the doctors at 87 Harley Street cured…" But Carolyn choked on her words when the Earl of Langley and Lance cast her looks.

"I'm cured," Lance said.

"As am I," the earl added.

"It's not medicine if you make vulnerable people dependent on drugs. More blackmail, more misery, more gossip," Pippa said.

"That's not true."

"Oh, but it is. I've been on the receiving end of your schemes for long enough and I have had enough. Today, my father gave his blessing that I shall marry Dr. Nicholas Folsham and I will make sure that the wedding will be as soon as possible. Not thanks to you, but despite you!"

"And I will help her to arrange the wedding of the year!" Violet called out, her husband's arm wrapped around her.

"As will I!" Bea said.

And then the crowd burst toward them, a wave of aristocrats of all shapes, sizes, and maladies.

"I want to be cured, too," a tall man with a short gray beard came to Nick. Another patted his shoulder and asked for an appointment.

"Which one is the orthopedist?" a lady with an orange feather in her upswept hair asked, and Pippa pointed to Andre.

And a swarm of guests encircled Felix.

The crowd was a mess and so many people were around the doctors.

The crowd moved like a single entity, a wave of velvet and silk crashing towards the epicenter of the commotion.

Felix, Andre, and Alfie, the doctors, found themselves in the eye of the storm. Each guest wanted a piece of them, and their personal space was invaded by prying eyes and curious hands. People asked for appointments or just demanded to be seen now, here, in this very room if not sooner.

Of course, the doctors adeptly reminded them they would want the privacy their offices would provide and that they promised each and every patient—unlike Matthews. Pippa felt her heart expand as she knew the practice would be overrun with noble patients for a long time.

Still, some people tried to get medical advice. Andre was subjected to a different kind of scrutiny. A man had taken hold of his hand and tried to place it on his hunchback.

Alfie was led away by a gaggle of ladies, their faces a mix of concern and excitement. They bombarded him with questions about various ailments, each woman eager to share her symptoms and seek his advice.

Amidst the sea of voices, Pippa found Violet and the earl.

They beamed, and the earl had a protective hand on Violet's stomach. As overjoyed as she was for him, Pippa gave him what she hoped was a pleading look. And then he nodded; he'd understood Pippa. He signaled the orchestra to continue their playing.

The music soared with the one-two-three strains of a waltz.

In a few seconds, the crowd had organized themselves and swayed to the music.

"I don't know how to waltz." Nick found Pippa and gave her a sheepish look. "But I'm willing to try if you guide me."

Pippa had never been happier in her entire life. At this ball, everybody came under scrutiny, not just her. And the most vicious tongues were reminded that they were just human, possibly in need of a doctor, most likely two. People aren't perfect, lesson learned. And Pippa hoped the Ton wouldn't forget that any time soon.

"It looks like the practice will be booked up for months," Nick said.

But Pippa had something else on her mind.

She led Nick out of the ballroom. The floors were adorned with gleaming marble tiles meticulously arranged in a classic herringbone pattern, reflecting the warm glow of the crystal chandeliers suspended from the lofty ceiling. Rich, intricate carpets with ornate patterns graced the center of the hallway, offering a sumptuous and inviting path for guests to traverse. After a week at the Langley estate as a guest, Pippa had come to know the house rather well.

"Pippa!" Father's voice came from a settee in the hall. "I heard everything." He patted his forehead with a handkerchief and slumped, his shoulders drawn together with visible tension.

Pippa held Nick's hand and didn't let go as she moved to see Father.

He had removed his cravat and opened the top buttons of his shirt. He looked pitiful, an old man, a mere lump of what he'd been. And she no longer cared.

She'd detached herself from him in a way she never thought possible. Alive, her father had hurt her more than her mother's death had hurt, and she wasn't sure she could forgive him for that.

"You and Bea saved me from the poison, didn't you?"

Pippa nodded. "With charcoal for a few days and the ipecac today. You needed to purge the poison from your body."

"You wanted my permission to marry?"

"Yes."

"You tricked me a little." The duke wagged a finger in the air.

"I provoked you. That wasn't the hard part. But I didn't want your permission as you are now, I wanted it from how you were, when I was little, and Mama was alive."

The duke dipped his head in his hands and groaned into the handkerchief.

When he looked up, his eyes were bloodshot and welling up with tears. He addressed Nick. "Is there a chance that I can get better, Doctor? I don't want to be like this anymore." He pointed at himself, top to bottom, and shook his hand off as if he had to rid himself of the disgrace that he'd become.

Nick blinked a few times and cast Pippa a look. But she couldn't give him any direction; he'd been addressed in line with his profession.

"That depends as much on the patient as the doctor. I can only promise to welcome you for a complete physical exam at the practice on Monday morning with our general practitioner."

"It will take a while to get better, Father. I won't be there." Pippa spoke with finality. Her voice was steady, and she stood straight. She felt more grown up than ever before.

"I know the house will be yours. Can I not stay? It's been my home for over thirty years," Father asked. He was pitiful. The man who'd made fun of her when she stumbled over a potted plant, who'd easily used the nickname, "clumsy goose," and who'd discarded her like an old shoe. Her! His daughter.

He hadn't mourned her mother and had just occupied the place in their marriage bed with another and then another and another. Pippa's heart had frozen for him and splintered; it was still broken. And the heartbreak a father caused ran deeper than even death's pain of loss.

"I leased the house to Violet. It's going to be a rehabilitation center for wounded sons of the peerage," she reminded him. "With Prinny's approval."

"I'm wounded, Pippa. And I was a son of the peerage once, but I've lost the self-respect of my station." He shook his head. "I could at least show the boys how not to become like me."

Pippa cast Nick a glance and he shrugged. "A doctor never gives up on a patient."

"A daughter never gives up on her father," Pippa decided.

Chapter Forty-Three

MUSIC SOUNDED THROUGH the halls from the string ensemble. The ball was in full swing, but Nick and Pippa remained in the halls, walking hand-in-hand through the Langleys' elegant home.

"So, what do you usually do at these balls, if not dance?" The crowd had dissipated, and Nick wasn't sure what to do or say now. He was out of his depth in this environment. He preferred his practice, his office, and his examination room where he knew exactly what to do and how to act.

From the corner of his eye, he could see a group of ladies approaching Felix and Alfie. New clients.

"I don't want to do what I usually do," Pippa said to the grand ballroom more than to Nick. "Come with me." She took his hand and led him further away from the ballroom.

Nick looked at her fingers intertwined with his. His eyes trailed from her hand to her delicate wrist, up her arm, to the lace edge of her sleeve and to the puffy sleeves of her gown. She was so beautiful, like a princess from a fairy tale. He couldn't believe his luck. Such an intelligent, spirited, and gorgeous woman said she loved him. His heart hurt with the overwhelming sense that he could never give her what she was used to. But before he could continue down this path of thoughts, Pippa stopped.

"This is the south hall." She still held his hand and gestured in the direction of a large double door with the other. "The gardens are over there."

"Very nice," Nick said, at a loss of what exactly he should or could say to such opulence in a mere corridor of the house. Why did Pippa smirk at him? She stopped in front of a set of double doors and Nick pushed them open for her.

It took him a moment to adjust his eyes to the darkness in the garden, but he welcomed the fresh spring air. The scent of a magnolia tree made him turn his head toward a structure that looked like a small marble house with windows.

"That's the pavilion," she said, nearly giddy with excitement as she tilted her head in the direction of a white-painted wooden door that was seamlessly integrated with the molding of the wall.

Nick remained silent. She was clearly up to something, but he had no idea what a gentleman should say when a lady was this excited about a garden pavilion. He tried to smile but he was rather nervous now.

Pippa stood straight and had an air of leadership that hadn't quite surfaced before. He was intimidated; this was her terrain.

"Would you like to go for a walk?" he asked when the doors to the townhouse shut behind him and they were alone in the gardens.

She shook her head. A mischievous gleam washed over her gaze like the day before his birthday when she took him away in her carriage.

"Pippa?" Nick tried to let his voice sound deep, but he was too nervous, and she was so beautiful., He rather felt like a green boy.

"This is *the* pavilion." She walked to the marble structure.

"Very well. It's a pavilion."

"No. It's *the* pavilion." She looked so happy about the pavilion door that was unlocked when she turned the handle down. Nick was at a loss but reveled in her excitement, nonetheless. His sweet Pippa. Had she tried the rum-spiked orgeat punch already? Come to think of it, he'd never seen her drink alcohol. Perhaps it hadn't agreed with her?

A small group of two elegant young women and two gentlemen came along the gravel path and headed to the door to the house. "Is that the clumsy goose?" one of the women asked loudly.

"She's not so clumsy now. And look, she's with the doctor," one of the men said, who had the other of the women on his arm.

"Oh my!" the first woman said. "Who would have thought?"

"Never mind that. Here's the pavilion, the temple of pleasure," the other man said, amused, as he pushed the double doors open. "They were here first." And the group disappeared into the house.

Nick turned back to Pippa. She was beaming and flushed. "What's with this pavilion?" he asked.

"It's the temple of pleasure." Her eyes glinted. "And ruin."

"Ruin?" Realization dawned on Nick, and he didn't like it. He pictured men taking from innocent debutantes what they were not willing to give freely.

"Well, trysts. Seduction." Pippa's eyes gleamed. "*Sin.*" She licked her lips.

"Oh dear."

"Nobody ever took me there." She pulled Nick by his hand.

"Good! I'm glad." Nick rubbed the back of his neck uncomfortably as he followed her. Why were his hands sweating so much?

"Nobody ever wanted to take me there. It wouldn't have occurred to—" she waved grandly and shook her head so that her beautiful golden curls bobbed delightfully—"anyone! Nobody!"

Nick's mien fell somber. "I'm missing some context for why that's bad."

"The pavilion gives *carte blanche* to the most beautiful women at a ball. It's a way for the diamond of the first water to test their suitors. What happens in the pavilion stays in the pavilion." She blushed further and reached for Nick's shaft with her other hand. "Take me there."

"You mean..." Nick said meaningfully.

"Yes, please. Just this once, I want to feel like the belle of the ball."

"You are." And he meant it.

"Show me."

He couldn't help the smirk that grew on his lips. As uncomfortable and out of place he'd felt, now that they were alone again, it felt easy. This was Pippa, his sweet Pippa. Despite the pomp surrounding her, she still wanted him. "Do you know how much I love you?"

She tilted her head sideways with the innocence of a girl but the allure of a vixen, as if she were embarrassed. "I never thought I'd stand here with a man as handsome and accomplished as you."

"Says the lady."

Their eyes met and Nick pulled her closer.

Pippa walked backward and led him through the pavilion door.

With her left hand, she let go of his and locked the door when they were inside a small room.

"Well, this is tight." He looked around. Only a slight line of yellow light came through the windows from the house, but the trees shrouded the pavilion in privacy. There was a shelf of linens. By the sheen and colors, they were tablecloths. Some candlesticks were on another shelf with a silver tea set. "What's this?" He looked up and there was a metal ring suspended from the ceiling on a chain.

"I've never been here, I told you." Pippa stepped on the cushions on the floor.

"It locks from the inside."

She shrugged. Then Pippa put her hand on his chest. "This is where young women are compromised. But I think you already understand that." She lowered her eyes and fluttered her eyelashes. "Compromise me, Nick."

"I think I already did that to you quite thoroughly." Nick couldn't hide the pride in his voice. It had been the best birthday in his life. The best day of his life. "But I would be happy to do it again." He couldn't wait, in fact.

She found the opening between the buttons of his shirt and slid her hand onto his bare chest. Nick let go of her and unbuttoned his vest, then his shirt. He granted her access. He always would.

"I'm all yours, Pippa."

She chuckled with delight. And Nick felt like a prize. It was unbelievable how he could feel so good and yet so small around the aristocrats at the ball. But with Pippa, he felt like a king on the top of a mountain radiating light he caught from her. She was his sun. His light. His love. And there was nothing between them to refract the light that she brought to his heart, a bright beam leading him into their joined future.

Her hands trailed up and down his chest and Nick leaned in. She received his mouth willingly. So warm and lush. So perfect. He was whole.

Chapter Forty-Four

PIPPA COULDN'T CONTAIN her excitement. She was in the pavilion. The Temple of Sin.

Delicious goosebumps sent a shiver over her shoulders.

Me.

In the pavilion.

With the most handsome man ever to walk the Earth.

Her hands explored his muscular chest, and he gave her access. Their mouths found one another with a ravishing passion. The experience wasn't as new as it had been in the country house. And she wasn't shy this time. The thrill of knowing his body took control over her and Pippa reached for his waistband.

He let out a guttural, manly groan, that couldn't have been a better compliment for her. His hands came to her breasts, and she stretched her back to push against his palms. He reached into her cleavage and found his way expertly.

It was scandalous and wonderful, forbidden and perfect.

Nick released her mouth and dipped his head. He kissed a trail down from her chin, along her jaw to the curve her neck and then descended. When his head reached her cleavage, hands on her breasts, she inhaled, readying herself, but when his mouth took her nipple, she gasped. It was an explosive pleasure, rippling through her so much that she arched her back and nearly lost her footing. Nick supported her waist, holding her tightly while he continued the sensual onslaught. Pippa wanted to scream with pleasure, but she didn't dare lest someone hear her. She was in the notorious pavilion after all.

The heady feeling of the gorgeous man kissing her nipples such, in the pavilion... she was engaged to him. It all became so real, so different from what her life had been only a few weeks ago. She could no longer contain her excitement; her heart pounded in her chest, and she wanted to lie down.

So that's what the cushions on the floor were for.

Nick held the small of her back, but she was overcome with the need for him where she'd felt him only days ago. Deep inside of her.

She searched for something to hold on to and rested her right arm on the shelf with the tablecloths.

She pushed her core against Nick in need and he grabbed her behind.

"Are you sure this is the right place?" he asked her, mouth open and glistening with desire. The light that came in from the bottom crack under the door and the windows was enough for Pippa to see that his eyes were black with desire. Her eyes had adjusted to the dark, but she could make out his hair, mussed again so adorably as it had been at her country house that morning.

"Please!" She panted, fumbling for the buttons of his breeches.

But then she didn't need to. He freed his large and hot member for her and laid it in her hand. Oh, and she loved it, gave it a squeeze, and reveled in the groan he let out in response.

Then he dropped to his knees and lifted her petticoat up.

His hands trailed up her legs. Higher along her calves. He moved slowly and with such reverence, that Pippa could barely catch her breath when he came to the hollow of her knees and kissed her thighs.

First, a small kiss on each side. But then he went higher.

His movements were deliberate and slow, but she could feel that he cherished her with every little contact. His hand cradled her womanhood and she twitched with need.

Now that she knew how he could make her feel, nothing else mattered. She wanted him so badly, so deeply, and with all of her heart and body.

"You're ready," he whispered, when his finger slipped between her folds.

Pippa had no words, and an odd sound came out of her as she sought to press her hips against his member.

He rose and stood in front of her, lifting her skirts and bunching them up around her waist. Then he grabbed her thigh from beneath it, and raised it so that she wrapped her leg around him. He was in her space but still too far away.

Pippa didn't know when, but Nick had lowered his breeches. Her left hand was still holding on to the shelf but with her right, she grabbed his taut bottom, then caressed his hips and found the dimple just above where his belly muscles were so amazingly bulky that every groove between his perfectly sculpted body made her lick her lips. Her appetite for him was insatiable.

As if he'd known, his mouth took hers again. She opened up willingly and melted backward.

Oh, so that's what that was for.

He grabbed her behind, lifting her center toward his. Then, her left hand wrapped around his neck, and she drove her fingers into his hair, the golden luxury she loved more than any riches in the world.

He lifted her higher, his other hand at the side of her waist.

Pippa grew restless, eager for his entry.

She fumbled and searched for something to reach, unable to lie down. Oh, why did she have to be in this pavilion. Why weren't there beds?

And then, Nick helped her. He gently took her hand from the back of his neck and lifted it, reaching up over his head. There was the odd ring hanging from a chain in the center of the ceiling. He led the way, bringing her fingers to the ring and pressing her fingers to grab it.

Pippa frowned, unsure what he was doing.

"I think I figured out why this pavilion is so special," he whispered, amusement coloring his voice.

Pippa's heart lurched.

He grabbed her other leg from below her waist, trailed his hand to the hollow of her knee and lifted it up. "Put your weight here." He positioned her foot against the frame of the door. "Hold on tight."

Every surface of this small room was perfect for trysts, providing seclusion, hold, and cushioning. She did as she was told, willingly and eagerly.

One leg still curled around him, the other pressed against the door frame, her weight was firmly supported by his strong hands. And then she felt the blunt tip of his smooth but hard member pressing against her entrance, so wonderfully hard as he pushed. She cherished the moment he slowly exerted pressure until he'd penetrated deep into her.

Her heart beat so vehemently that she thought he must feel it, too.

And then she understood the allure of the pavilion.

Pippa adjusted her grip on the ring suspended from the ceiling and her arm on the shelf.

It was a tight space, a perfect space to hold on and make love upright.

And that's what they did.

Nick slid into her, so deeply, so deliciously, and so fully that she let out a little scream.

"Pippa!" Nick feigned admonishing her, but he smirked. In the dim light she could see that his face was bright with mirth and so close that she could kiss the tip of his nose.

"This is so good!" she moaned.

"Someone could hear us," Nick said with a tone that should have alarmed her, but she could hear that it was all in good fun. "Does this still feel good?" He pushed harder.

"Oh!" Pippa cried in bliss. She bit her lower lip.

"That's my job." Nick brought his delicious, big white teeth to her lip and nibbled at her lower lip, then plunged his tongue into her mouth when she opened up wide. At the same time, he slipped into her.

"This is the perfect angle!" She screamed when he pulled out and slid back in.

"My love," Nick whispered half laughing, half strained.

"It is so perfect, it's just that, the angle—" Pippa's voice was strained and then failed when Nick pumped into her, his muscles rippling in the dim light, and she looked down at her legs spread wide and his sculpted body uniting with hers. A cry emerged. It was her again and she laughed, but then her muscles twitched, and Nick pushed deep. That was the end of her last bit of self-control.

Another cry echoed from her throat when Nick's tongue swished through her mouth while below his thrusts hit a spot so perfectly within her that she convulsed.

Then he withdrew and pushed back to that spot.

Pippa held on tight to the ring, however she was overwhelmed with pleasure. A wave caught her from the inside and rushed through her from the center of that magical spot to the roots of her hair. Nick held her waist tight and pumped.

It was marvelous. Easy. Perfect.

Then he pushed so deep that Pippa convulsed with pleasure. He cried out as he followed her.

When they regained their breath, the room was even darker and they held each other.

"Thank you for opening my eyes to life," Pippa said, her cheek resting on Nick's shoulder.

He moved and took her face in his hands.

"You taught me that there's another perspective on life than the one I had. I was locked up, the clumsy goose. I always felt lonely and ugly, but you showed me that life can be so beautiful. I didn't see it until you made me see."

Nick kissed her gently on the mouth. "You are a sight to behold."

>>><<<

Thank you for reading *"A Sight to Behold,"* I hope you enjoyed the story with Nick and Pippa. The series continues with Pippa's cousin, Bea, and Alfie, the apothecary. Bea has her heart set on a prince, and she needs Alfie, the skilled apothecary, to make a love potion. But as they work together, an unexpected love sparks between them in this tale of forbidden romance. Read on to see how they meet before they star in *The Scent of Seduction* a book where all your favorite characters from Harley Street will be back.

Epilogue

Meanwhile, in the hall outside the ballroom, Pippa's cousin searched for her...

BEA COULDN'T FIND Pippa. Where had she gone? She hadn't found her cousin anywhere in the ballroom, so she ventured into the halls.

Then she heard voices from the pavilion. Was that Pippa? It sounded like her. Somewhat. She moved closer. What was happening in there, she wondered, trying to see the pavilion through the windows.

Focused on those voices, and in the dusky gloom, she didn't notice the man until she bumped into him. "Oh, pardon me." she exclaimed, stepping back.

"Oh hello." The tall and—Bea had to swallow and blink—extremely handsome man said smoothly. He had a resonating voice that softened every word and apparently turned Bea's bones to pudding.

"Why aren't you with the other guests, Mister Collins?" Bea asked. He was the handsome apothecary who'd mixed the ipecac that she'd helped Pippa to administer to her uncle. And now that her mission was over, she wondered how she could go about seeing the apothecary again.

Bea reached her hand out and he took it in his. His movements were oddly smooth. Unsettling her deeply in her stomach. He bent his fingers around hers, gently. His hands were smooth and well groomed, but veins and strength rippled under his skin. The incongruity made Bea frown. She didn't know what to make of him. He was too handsome for a member of the Ton, too muscular. Yet he looked most refined. Hadn't he stood next to Nick in the ballroom?

He gave a polite kiss on the knuckle of her middle finger and then—did she imagine it?—he lingered. As if he'd wished to give a second kiss on the next knuckle, but he'd swallowed it, she saw his Adam's apple bobbing as he straightened.

As he did so, she realized that he towered over her by half a foot.

Perfect to look into his teal eyes.

Bea blushed and glanced over her shoulder. Except, when she blinked toward the pavilion, heat rose to her face. Were Pippa and Nick doing the things that Violet had described?

"I think they have gone to the pavilion," Bea mumbled more to herself than to the dashing apothecary standing but a foot from her. He seemed to have noticed the foggy windows of the pavilion and the flickering light inside from their position looking at it through the hall's windows.

"Which pavilion?" Alfie asked with a quirked brow. Was he testing her?

Returning her focus to the handsome man, Bea realized she'd put both of her hands over her mouth after speaking the word—pavilion—aloud. After all, everyone in the Ton knew what…well, more or less—what happened in there. She didn't exactly, but she knew well enough never to speak of it in front of a man.

Especially one as handsome as Alfie.

"What pavilion are you talking about?" the much too handsome stranger asked her, amusement flickering in his gaze. Her stomach jumped under his perusal. It was most unpleasant. Men shouldn't be so pretty, so tall, so glowering. So manly.

Nick's voice came from the direction of the pavilion and they both turned their heads.

"Where are they?" Alfie looked around the hall.

Bea felt heat rush to her head. "Oh—oh."

"Oh—oh? Oh—oh what?"

"The pavilion is real."

"Which pavilion?"

"That one. The Temple of Sin. And seduction." Bea nodded in direction of the window from which it could be seen, windows even more fogged, and candlelight no longer flickering inside.

"I beg your pardon?" He gave a lopsided smile. Probably thinking her a complete dim wit.

"I think it's over there." She pointed to the white wooden door. "Pippa and Nick are inside." She whispered and leaned toward the window…

ALFIE COULDN'T HIDE his amusement, but he certainly tried to hide his attraction to the gorgeous woman. His black evening attire was too tight, especially the trousers. Except they hadn't been this tight before. He rolled his eyes at himself. Why was he denying his body's response and blaming it on his attire? The truth was it wasn't too tight. No, this girl was too beautiful.

She had a shade of blond hair he'd never seen before. In the dim light of the hall outside the ballroom, it looked as though a hint of copper sparkled in her evenly straight hair, falling loosely into a large curl on the bottom.

Instinctively, he angled his arm and offered it to her.

She dropped her hands from her mouth and laid a dainty hand on his arm. "Haven't you heard of this?" She came closer.

He'd heard of it, all right. The pavilion had mythical status in London!

He could feel her breath. Sweet and fresh.

His mouth suddenly felt dry and empty. Longing to taste her.

Pippa's cousin. Almost Nick's cousin-in-law. Alfie shook his head.

Yet he never wanted anyone as badly as this beautiful woman speaking with such a sparkle in her eyes.

"The pavilion of sin and seduction," she whispered, almost as if to herself.

Alfie coughed. He might desire her with every fiber of his being, but he was Nick's friend, first and foremost. As well as a professional. He was no libertine intent on the seduction of innocents. Better to pretend he didn't hear her and steer the conversation and her thoughts somewhere else. "I beg your pardon?"

She looked back at him, then back at the little white house. "The earl's legendary pavilion." She drew a circle with her hand as if it were self-explanatory. "In the garden?"

Alfie remained silent. No, dear sweet girl. Please don't ask me about it.

"Under the magnolia trees?"

"I'm afraid I have no idea what you are talking about." He was not going to tell her that he knew precisely what to do in this pavilion even though he'd never been inside. Even though sin and seduction sounded exactly like what he was thinking about.

"The Earl of Langley has been known to have a certain pavilion somewhere in this grand garden. Terrible things happen in it." She nibbled on the end of her index finger. "I wonder…is that it?"

It was the nibble on her finger that was his undoing. He couldn't help himself. He had to ask. "How terrible?"

"Sin and seduction. That's why it's called—"

"The pavilion of sin and seduction. I see."

She gave him a pleased smile like a governess whose student finally grasped a complicated concept. Then she drew away, moving further into the garden, into the darkness, where anything—or anyone—could happen to her. He couldn't allow it. Especially since she was ripe for seduction, not that she knew it.

He held out his arm for her to grasp, and they walked a few steps. "And you want to go there?" Alfie asked.

Her eyes grew wide, and she almost dropped her hand from his arm, but he gently squeezed his muscle, inviting her to stay. She was so sweet; he'd take her anywhere she wanted. Except maybe the pavilion. At least, tonight.

A moment passed between them. She must have felt it, for something clicked within Alfie that he knew would change his life forever as she raised her eyes to his…

"Bea!" A voice came from the patio near the house. "Bea! Oh, there you are!"

Alfie saw Lady Langley, the young countess approaching from the direction of the double doors. She stood on the top of the steps leading down to the garden, lit from the back with the yellow glow of the halls. And as his gaze returned to the strawberry-blonde beauty, her hand melted away from his arm and the moment was over.

"Mr. Collins, how nice to see you made the acquaintance of Lady Beatrice," the countess said as she approached.

Alfie's stomach dropped. Bea. She was out of his reach.

"Come, there is someone I want you to meet." And Lady Langley led Bea away.

Alfie dropped his head.

He already missed her.

The series continues right here, where it left off. Find out how Alfie and Bea's love story brings the doctors at 87 Harley Street even closer together in *The Scent of Intuition* because they make miracles happen, in both medicine and matters of the heart.

Author's Note I

In the heart of my story is a medical condition that's still common today and often treated: cataracts. To understand the condition better, one must think of it as a clouding of the natural lens of the eyes. This cloudiness is due to changes in the lens's cell structure or its protein constituents, or sometimes both. Essentially, the lens's consistency alters enough to scatter light instead of focusing it properly, causing vision impairment.

Although medicine in the Regency period was not advanced enough to have an explanation or even distinctions between the various cataracts as we do now, it was well known among specialists such as Dr. Nick Folsham that cataracts were a problem of the lens and exchanging the lens usually cured the patient.

His specialization in cataracts is personal in the story as well as the professional calling and his greatest strength as a treating physician. As fate had it, Nick was close to Lance, who suffered from early onset cataracts in his early twenties and the Earl of Langley in his thirties. We now know that cataracts are often associated with aging, but their onset isn't strictly tied to a person's chronological age. They can occur much earlier in some individuals, classified as presenile cataracts if they appear before the age of 45. However, these classifications aren't rigid; some experts might consider cataracts appearing before 20 years of age as juvenile and those after 60 as age related.

It's crucial to note that the timing of a cataract doesn't necessarily pinpoint its cause. For example, congenital cataracts, present from birth, could be hereditary or result from an adverse event during pregnancy, such as if the mother had rubella during the child's gestation. Cataracts associated with certain systemic or genetic diseases may not appear until later in life. Even age-related cataracts, commonly attributed to cumulative environmental impacts over the years, can have a genetic component, making some individuals more susceptible.

In our narrative, Lance's early-onset cataract was likely caused by a condition called *retinitis pigmentosa*, which worsened in his early twenties. On the other hand, the Earl of Langley developed cataracts later in life, potentially due to a lifestyle marked by indulgence and recklessness, coupled with traumas to the head in fistfights that may have expedited the process.

Understanding these complexities adds depth to our characters' experiences and challenges, bringing them to life in a way that I hope resonates with you, dear reader. Thank you for joining me on this journey.

Author's Note II

Much of the history from the Regency era is available but I like to imagine that my characters' lives happen in those bits that were not written down. While I carefully research everything that comes to mind, from the furniture and its upholstery to the dates, street names, and especially the medical equipment for this series, this is still a work of fiction and I take some artistic license. I bring you, dear readers, these beloved characters who are close friends to me with the goal to provide a sprinkle of romance and a dash of story to you. As such, I hope that you enjoy the story as it stands.

Nonetheless for those of you who are inclined to enjoy the rich history of the era, I have a few fun facts for you. Pippa's home, for instance, is a house that was on the market for almost six million pounds at the time this novel was written. Warwick Avenue is close to Little Venice, historically known as Green Lane and Warwick Road before settling on its current name, which owes its moniker to Jane Warwick of Warwick Hall in Cumbria. This London street has a rich history and is located in the heart of the city, close to one of the first Underground stations designed specifically to use escalators over lifts. The station opened its doors on the 31st of January in 1915 as part of the Bakerloo line's extension from Paddington (the station, not the bear) to Queen's Park.

Furthermore, there's a fascinating fact about Warwick Avenue's development. In 1825, Lord Grosvenor tasked Thomas Cubitt with developing Pimlico. The soil and hardcore used to reclaim the marshy ground were excavated during the construction of the docks at St. Katherine. I have been to this area of London and have seen the picturesque waterways, and the trees on both sides that give it a quaint isolation from the bustling downtown, even though it is so close. Although the first houses—some of which were very large—were erected in the 1840s close to the Warwick Avenue bridge over the Paddington arm of the Grand Junction (now Grand Union) Canal, many houses were there (like Pippa's in my imagination). The neighborhood's beloved architecture mostly survives in renovated but original buildings today.

Other fun facts about the historical setting are, as you may guess, from the field of where medical marvels really happened. The story focuses on an eye surgeon, but each of my books about the doctors on Harley Street features different types of medical specialists even if they didn't exist in those specialties as we understand them today. Because this is a work of fiction, this means there is no reason that they couldn't have existed. While real people's advances in medicine inspire the characters' qualifications, I have exaggerated their training by showing them studying more, working harder, and becoming even better at what they do than history suggests possible, since it was often a question of funding and location that prevented young men from studying or that disallowed women altogether from enrolling in university.

In simple terms, my characters are driven by a desire to heal and create miracles and earn their place in society like Nick Folsham. So let me tell you how his expertise is supported in history:

As understanding of eye anatomy and diseases advanced, so did the approach to cataract surgery. Although "couching" was commonly considered the primary method of cataract treatment until the 18th century. It was a historical method of cataract treatment in which a blunt object, such as a needle or stick, was used to displace the clouded lens within the eye without removing it, ancient texts indicate that as early as 600 BC, an Indian surgeon named Sushruta may have been the first to conduct a form of extracapsular cataract extraction. This technique, known as "extracapsular," preserves the lens capsule.

The inaugural genuine cataract extraction occurred in 1747 in Paris, performed by the French surgeon Jacques Daviel. His procedure proved to be more successful than couching, achieving an overall success rate of 50%.

In researching the historical backdrop for this novel, it became evident that the early 19th century was a pivotal time in the evolution of cataract surgery. The earliest documented use of glass or crystal for lens replacements in cataract surgeries dates back to the late 18th century and early 19th century. The pioneering work of surgeons during this time laid the foundation for the advancements that followed. Notably, it is documented that the first use of a triangular blade for eye surgeries occurred in Vienna during the early 1820s, marking a significant advancement in ophthalmic surgical techniques. This innovation played a crucial role in refining cataract surgeries and paved the way for further developments in the field of ophthalmology.

While the narrative of our novel is fictional, the advancements and breakthroughs in cataract surgery draw upon historical facts and figures. The first documented cataract surgeries using a triangular blade are often credited to the work of visionary surgeons in Vienna, such as George Joseph Beer and his disciple, Johann Nepomuk Fischer. Beer, known for his surgical prowess and teaching at the Vienna General Hospital, laid the groundwork for modern ophthalmology. Fischer later authored the *'Lehrbuch der operativen Augenheilkunde'* (Textbook of Operative Ophthalmology), contributing significantly to eye surgery techniques. These historical references are drawn from "The History of Ophthalmology" by Julius Hirschberg, which provides a comprehensive review of the progression of eye surgery throughout the centuries.

The historical context surrounding the practice of cataract surgery during the 1820s provides a rich and compelling backdrop for the characters and events depicted in this novel. It not only showcases the early advancements in surgical techniques but also sheds light on the social and cultural norms of the time. The medical profession was not as highly regarded during this period as it is now but the good doctors and nurses deserved more credit. It was expensive and difficult to amass the knowledge that the doctors at 87 and 91 Harley Street had, so they deserve to distinguish themselves from charlatans like Mr. Matthews in this book and the ones to follow. Now that doctors, dentists, and surgeons are seen as respected members of society, we are reminded that such meritocracies were not. However, there was still some skepticism surrounding cataract surgeries due to their high failure rate at the time.

Furthermore, the introduction of anesthesia in 1846 is much later than our story.

During the Regency period, laudanum was a critical medicine for patients, acting as a potent painkiller and sedative. Composed of opium dissolved in alcohol, it was one of the few remedies that provided any relief from the chronic pains and discomforts of the era's ailments. Alfie Collins, the apothecary in our narrative, knew the value of this tincture well; he provided laudanum, alongside his herbal concoctions and remedies, to ease the suffering of his patrons. In an age where pain management options were severely limited and the practice of medicine was still in its infancy, the availability of such a medicine through trusted apothecaries like Collins was not mere commerce but a lifeline that allowed society to function despite the ubiquity of disease and injury.

Alfie Collins, the rakishly handsome apothecary with a heart as potent as his medicines, has proven himself in his book with his selfless deeds and profound kindness. His compassionate spirit and deft hands have eased the pains of many, bridging the gap between medicine of intuition and the dawn of scientific inquiry. As he emerges from the shadows of 87 Harley Street in *The Scent of Intuition*, Alfie's own tale of romance and intrigue beckons. Who will be the one to steal the heart of a man whose daily alchemy blends the tender aspects of human care with the hard science of survival? Alfie's tale of love is not just another chapter; it's an adventure of the heart that promises to intertwine the ardor of romance with the fervor of Regency-era medicine—a story you simply cannot miss.

About the Author

Bestselling author Sara Adrien writes hot and heart-melting Regency romance with a Jewish twist. As a law professor-turned-author, she writes about clandestine identities, whims of fate, and sizzling seduction. If you like unique and intelligent characters, deliciously sexy scenes, and the nostalgia of afternoon tea, then you'll adore Sara Adrien's tender tearjerkers.

Sign up for her VIP newsletter to be the first to hear about new releases, audiobooks, sales, giveaways, and bonus content at SaraAdrien.com.

Catch up with Sara Adrien here:
linktr.ee/jewishregencyromance
saraadrien.com
instagram.com/jewishregencyromance
facebook.com/AuthorSaraAdrien
bookbub.com/authors/sara-adrien
goodreads.com/author/show/22249825.Sara_Adrien
youtube.com/channel/UCK9OLp1wN6IaGkXe7OugfHg

Also by Sara Adrien

Books with the doctors on Harley Street:

The Scent of Intuition
(Alfie and Bea's story)

A Touch of Gold
(Felix's story)

The Sound of Seduction
(Wendy's story)

A Touch of Charm
(Andre's story)

Don't Wake a Sleeping Lyon
The Lyon's First Choice
The Lyon's Golden Touch
The Lyon's Legacy
and many more!

Acknowledgements

Thanks to Emily, Cynthia, and everyone at Dragonblade.

My gratitude also extends to Susan, who helped me back up much of the historical medical research for this story and the series as a whole. I referenced several books and journal articles, including:

- Transactions of the Associated Apothecaries and Surgeon—Apothecaries of England and Wales, Volume 1
- The Edinburgh Medical and Surgical Journal: Exhibiting a Concise View of the Latest and Most Important Discoveries in Medicine, Surgery, and Pharmacy, Volume 10
- Edinburgh Medical and Surgical Journal. (1825). United Kingdom: A. and C. Black.
- Stancliffe, F. S. (1964). The Manchester Royal Eye Hospital 1814—1964. United Kingdom: Manchester University Press.
- The Principles and Practice of Ophthalmic Medicine and Surgery › books.google.com › books. Thomas Wharton Jones, Isaac Hays • 1847
- Shiels A, Hejtmancik JF. Genetic Origins of Cataract. Arch Ophthalmol. 2007;125(2):165–173. doi:10.1001/archopht.125.2.165
- Davis G. The Evolution of Cataract Surgery. Mo Med. 2016 Jan—Feb;113(1):58—62. PMID: 27039493; PMCID: PMC6139750.

Made in the USA
Monee, IL
03 March 2025